trad... **SEFT**...ters as Henning Mankell b...IES
Forshaw, *Independent*

'The Varg Veum series stands alongside Connelly, Camilleri and others, who are among the very best modern exponents of the poetic yet tough detective story with strong, classic plots; a social conscience; and perfect pitch in terms of a sense of place' *Euro Crime*

'Hugely popular' *Irish Independent*

'Norway's bestselling crime writer' *Guardian*

'The prolific, award-winning author is plotting to kill someone whose demise will devastate fans of noir-ish Nordic crime fiction worldwide' *Scotsman*

'Intriguing' *Time Out*

'An upmarket Philip Marlowe' Maxim Jakubowski, *Bookseller*

'In the best tradition of sleuthery' *The Times*

'Among the most popular Norwegian crime writers' *Observer*

'Dazzling' *Aftenposten*

'Ice Marlowe' *Thriller* magazine

'Gunnar Staalesen and his hero, Varg Veum, are stars' *L'Express*

'An excellent and unique series' *International Noir Fiction*

00 2931709 X

GUNNAR STAALESEN was born in Bergen, Norway in 1947. He made his debut at the age of twenty-two with *Seasons of Innocence* and in 1977 he published the first book in the Varg Veum series. He is the author of over 20 titles, which have been published in 24 countries and sold over two million copies. Twelve film adaptations of his Varg Veum crime novels have appeared since 2007, starring the popular Norwegian actor Trond Epsen Seim. Staalesen, who has twice won Norway's top crime prize, the Golden Pistol, lives in Bergen with his wife.

Yours Until Death

GUNNAR STAALESEN

Translated from the Norwegian by
Margaret Amassian

ARCADIA BOOKS

Arcadia Books Ltd
139 Highlever Road
London W10 6PH

www.arcadiabooks.co.uk

First published in the United Kingdom by Constable and Company Ltd 1993
This B format edition Arcadia Books 2010
Originally published by Gyldendal Norsk Forlag, Oslo as *Din til Døden*
Copyright Gunnar Staalesen © 1979
English language translation copyright © Margaret Amassian 1993

Gunnar Staalesen has asserted his moral right to be identified as the author of this work in
accordance with the Copyright, Designs and Patents Act, 1988.

All rights reserved. No part of this publication may be reproduced in any form or by any
means without the written permission of the publishers.

A catalogue record for this book is available from the British Library.

ISBN 978-1-906413-70-5

Typeset in Garamond by MacGuru Ltd
Printed and bound CPI Group (UK) Ltd, Croydon CR0 4YY

Arcadia Books supports English PEN *www.englishpen.org* and The Book Trade Charity
http://booktradecharity.wordpress.com

Arcadia Books distributors are as follows:

in the UK and elsewhere in Europe:
Macmillan Distribution Ltd
Brunel Road
Houndmills
Basingstoke
Hants RG21 6XS

in the US and Canada:
Dufour Editions Inc
PO Box 7
Chester Springs
PA 19425

in Australia/New Zealand:
NewSouth Books

SEFTON
LIBRARIES

WITHDRAWN FROM STOCK

00 2931709 X	
Askews & Holts	02-Aug-2016
AF	£8.99
FOR	

1

Maybe it was because he was the youngest client I'd ever had. Maybe it was because he reminded me of another little boy in another part of Bergen. Or maybe it was because I had nothing else to do. Anyway, I listened to him.

It was one of those days at the end of February when the wind shoves the temperature up from minus eight to plus twelve. Twenty-four hours of unexpected rain had washed away the snow which had been lying around for three or four weeks, making a paradise of the hills around the city and a complete hell of its centre. But that was over. A breath of spring lay over the city now, and people hurried through the streets with new energy in their bodies towards destinations they could only guess at.

The office seemed unusually deserted on a day like this. The square room with its big desk and a phone, with the nearly empty filing cabinets, was like a little isolated corner of the universe, a place where they stash forgotten souls. People whose names nobody remembers any more. I'd had one call all day – from an old lady who'd wanted me to find her poodle. I'd said I was allergic to dogs – especially poodles. She'd sniffed and hung up. That's how I am. Don't sell myself cheap.

It was almost three when I heard somebody outside the waiting-room door. I was half asleep in my chair and the sound made me start. I swung my legs to the floor, got up and opened the door between the two rooms.

He stood in the exact middle of the floor, looking around curiously. He could have been about eight or nine. He was dressed in a worn-out blue ski jacket and jeans with patched knees. He wore a grey knitted cap, but when he saw me he yanked it off. His hair was long and straight and almost white. He had big blue eyes and a half-open anxious mouth which threatened to cry any minute.

'Hello,' I said.

He gulped and looked at me.

'If you're going to the dentist, it's the office next door,' I said.

He shook his head. 'I want ...' he began, and nodded towards the door. In mirror-writing on the pebble-glass pane it said V. Veum, Private Investigator. He looked shyly at me. 'Are you really a real detective?'

'Maybe.' I smiled at him. 'Come in. Take a seat.' We went into my office. I sat behind the desk and he settled himself in the other shabby chair. He looked around. I don't know what he'd been expecting, but anyway he looked disappointed. It wasn't the first time. Disappointing people is the only thing I'm really good at.

'I found you in the phone book,' he said. 'Under Detective Bureaus.' He pronounced the last word slowly and carefully, as if he'd invented it.

I looked at him. Thought: Thomas'll be his age in a few years. And he'd also be able to find me in the phone book. If he wanted to.

'And how can I help you?' I said.

'My bike,' he said.

I nodded. 'Your bike.'

I looked out of the window and across Vågen. The cars were bumper to bumper. It was stop-and-go all the way to that far-off land they call Åsane, east of the sun and west of the moon. Which you reach – if you're lucky – just in time to turn around, line up, and drive back into the city early next morning.

I'd had a bike once. But that was before they'd given the city to cars and had baptised it with exhaust. The smog was like a hood over the harbour. Mount Fløien looked like a poisoned rat lying on its belly, trying to suck in a little sea air. 'Your bike's been stolen?'

He nodded.

'But don't you think the police …?' I said.

'Yes, but that would cause trouble.'

'Trouble?'

'Yes. It would.' He nodded. It was as if his whole face were filled with something he wanted to say but couldn't find words for.

Then suddenly he became a pragmatist. 'Do you charge a lot? Are you expensive?'

'I'm the most expensive and the cheapest,' I said.

He looked confused, and I added quickly, 'It depends entirely on what kind of work and who's hiring. On what you want me to do and who you are. Tell me about it. Okay, so your bike's been stolen. And you want to know who did it and where it is?'

'No. I know who's got it.'

'Really? Who?'

'Joker and his gang. They want my mum.'

'Your mother?' I didn't understand.

He looked very serious. 'Listen, what's your name?' I said.

'Roar.'

'What else?'

'Roar Andresen.'

'And how old are you?'

'Eight and a half.'

'And where do you live?'

He named one of the bedroom suburbs southwest of the city, a place I wasn't very familiar with. I'd only seen it from a distance. It had sort of reminded me of a lunar landscape, if they have high-rises on the moon.

'And your mother – does she know where you are?'

'No. She hadn't come home when I left. I found your address in the phone book, and I took the bus all by myself, and I got here without asking anybody.'

'We should try calling your mum so she won't worry about you. Do you have a phone?'

'Yes. But she won't be home yet.'

'But she works somewhere, doesn't she? Maybe we could call her there?'

'No. She's probably on her way home by now. And anyway I'd just as soon she didn't know anything about … this.'

Suddenly he seemed grown up. He seemed so grown up I thought I could ask the question on the tip of my tongue. Kids know so much more these days.

'And your father – where's he?'

His eyes widened. The only reaction. 'He … he doesn't live with us any more. He moved out. Mum says he's got somebody else, even though she's got two kids of her own. Mum says my dad's no good. That I ought to forget him.'

I could see Thomas and Beate, and I had to say something in a hurry. 'Listen. I think I'd better drive you home, and then we'll see if we can't find your bike. You can tell me the rest in the car.'

I put on my overcoat and took a last look around. One more day was about to die without having left any special trace behind it.

'Aren't you going to take your pistol?' he said.

I looked at him. 'My pistol?'

'Yes. Your pistol.'

'I don't have a pistol, Roar.'

'You don't? But I thought …'

'That's only in films. TV. Not in real life.'

'Oh.' Now he looked really disappointed.

We left. The minute I locked the door, the phone rang. For a second I wondered if I should answer it, but it was probably only somebody who wanted me to find his cat, and it would probably stop ringing just as I got to my desk. Anyway, I was allergic to cats. So I let it go.

This was the one week in the month when the lift worked, and on the way down I said, 'This Joker, as you call him – who is he?'

He looked seriously at me and his voice shook. 'He's … I can't.'

I didn't ask any more until we were in the car.

2

It was turning cold again. The frost clawed at the milky sky. The morning's champagne fizz was gone. Not much hope in the eyes of those we passed: dinner, or problems at work. Or waiting at home. Winter played an encore, both in the air and in people's faces.

I'd left my car at a meter up on Tårnplass. It stood there looking innocent, even though it knew that the meter had long since run out.

My little client had been glancing up at me the whole time, just as any eight-year-old glances up at his father when they're in town together. The thing was, I wasn't his father and not much to glance up at. I'm a private investigator in his mid-thirties, no wife, no son, no good friends, no steady partner. I'd have been a credit to the National Association for the Advancement of Singles, but they'd never asked me to join.

Anyway I had a car. It had survived one more winter and was on its way to turning eighteen. But it still ran, even though it had minor problems starting. Especially in choppy weather. We got in and were under way after a few minutes of my hard-handed diplomacy. Roar seemed impressed by my soundless cursing.

I've always been good at that. I almost never curse in front of women and children. Maybe that's why nobody likes me.

Suddenly we got stuck in traffic in the middle of Puddefjord Bridge. It was like being on top of a fading rainbow. To our right, Ask Island lay like a smear between the pale grey sky and the grey-black water. A thin veil of late afternoon light began to shimmer on the mountains.

To our left, at the very end of Viken, lay the skeleton of something which – if God and the shipping market willed it – would some day be a boat. A crane swung threateningly over the skeleton as if it were a prehistoric lizard just about to dine off a fallen dinosaur. It was one of those late winter afternoons with death in the air no matter where you looked.

'Now tell me about your bicycle, and your mother, and about Joker and his gang,' I said. 'Tell me what I can do for you.'

I glanced at him and smiled. He tried to smile back, and I don't know anything more heartbreaking than a little kid who tries to smile but can't make it. This wasn't going to be easy.

'They took Petter's bike last week.' he said. 'He doesn't have a dad either.'

'Oh?'

The traffic was slowly moving now. I automatically tailed the red brake-light ahead of me. He went on. 'Joker and his gang they hang out – they have a hut up in the woods at the back of the high-rises.'

'A hut?'

'They didn't build it. Somebody else did. But then Joker and them came and chased the others away. Nobody'll go there now. Too scared to. But then …'

We were on the main road to Laksevåg. On the right, on the other side of Puddefjord, Nordnes looked like a dog's paw lying in the water. 'And then?' I said.

'We'd heard they'd done it before. That some of them took the big girls – grabbed them and took them up there to the hut and … did things with them. But that was girls, not mothers. But then they stole Petter's bike, and when Petter's mother went up there to get his bike, then … then she didn't come back down.'

'She didn't come back down?'

'No. We waited at least two hours – Petter and Hans and I. And Petter cried and said they'd killed his mother and his father'd gone to sea and hadn't ever come back, and …'

'But didn't you go – couldn't you get hold of a grown-up?'

'Who? What grown-up? Petter doesn't have a father. Hans doesn't. I don't. And the caretaker chases us away and so does Officer Hauge, and that stupid youth leader just tells us we should come and play Parchese.

'And then his mother came down again. From the woods. And she had the bike. But somebody had torn her clothes – and she was dirty, and she was crying. Everybody saw her. And Joker and the others followed her and they laughed. And when they saw us they said – so everybody could hear – they said if she said anything to anybody they'd cut off … that something bad would happen to Petter.'

'But what happened after that?'

'Nothing. Nobody'll do anything to Joker and them. One time when Joker was alone, a girl's father caught him outside the supermarket and shoved him up against the wall and said he'd beat him until he couldn't stand up if he didn't lay off.'

'And?'

'One evening he came home late, and they stood outside the door and waited for him. The whole gang. They beat him up and it was two weeks before he was okay. Afterwards he moved. So there's nobody who has the guts.'

'So I'm supposed to have the guts?' I glanced at him.

He looked hopefully up at me. 'You're a detective.'

I let that sink in for a while. A big strong detective with little little muscles and a big big mouth. We were past the first built-up area and the fifty-kilometre limit, but I didn't especially speed up. I felt less and less that we were in a hurry.

'And now,' I said, 'so now they've got your bike, and now you're afraid … Your mother, have you told her what happened to Petter's mother?'

'No! I was too scared to.'

'And you're sure that it's Joker and his gang who –'

'I'm sure! Because there's a fat little kid they call Tasse, and he found me when I got home from school, and he told me Joker'd borrowed my bike and I could have it back if I went up to the hut. And if I didn't have the guts, I could send my mother, he said. And he laughed.'

I said, 'How many in this gang?'

'Eight or nine. Sometimes ten.'

'Just boys?'

'They have some girls – but not always, not when they …'

'How old are they?'

'Oh, they're old. Sixteen, seventeen. And Joker's a little older. Some people say he's over twenty, but he's probably nineteen.'

Nineteen: a psycho's best age. Too old to be a kid and too young to be an adult. I knew the type. Tough as a boot one minute and crying like a baby the next because you've hurt his feelings. As predictable as a day at the end of February. You never know how he'll react. I had a lot to look forward to.

3

We passed the big shopping centre they'd ironically called a market. Two schools stood on the hill: a big blush-pink secondary school and a primary school which clung like an overfed caterpillar to the crest of the ridge. Behind them, the four high-rises reared toward heaven.

'We live in that one there,' Roar said with the air of an astronomer identifying a star in the Big Dipper.

The entire area lay in the shadow of the Lyderhorn. The mountain looked steep, dark and depressing from here. TV antennas bristled on its summit. They sliced into the clouds' bellies and guts of steel-blue sky leaked out.

I parked the car and we got out.

'We live there,' he said and pointed upwards.

I sighted along the pointing finger. 'Where?' I said.

'On the ninth floor. That window with green and white curtains – that's my room.'

'That one.' A window with green and white curtains on the ninth floor. He sounded like Robinson Crusoe.

'We should say hello to your mother,' I said.

He shook his head. 'Not without my bike,' he said. Firm about that.

'Well.' There was an uneasy feeling in my stomach. Gangs of seventeen- and eighteen-year-olds aren't always your daintiest dancing partners. Especially if they think they're tough and if you haven't used your hands for much more than lifting a bottle of aquavit for the last couple of years. 'Where'll we find this hut?'

'There.' He pointed. 'I'll show you.'

We walked around the next high-rise. On the hillside to the right some low-rises had been slung among the trees as if they'd been dropped from a great height and nobody'd bothered afterwards to see where they'd landed. There was a slope of junipers and pines behind the first building. Joker and the gang's hut would be up that slope.

Roar stood at the corner of the last high-rise while he explained where I was to go.

'Don't you want to come along?' I said.

He shook his head. Downcast.

I smiled at him. 'No. I know how you feel.' We'd had such a gang in the road I grew up in. Even if it hadn't been so sophisticated. But then we didn't live in such tall buildings either. 'Better wait for me here. Is it up that path between those trees over there?'

He nodded twice. His eyes were huge. He looked really worried – not for his sake but for mine. It didn't exactly increase my confidence.

I swung my hips like a sailor. It made me feel a little braver. As if this were nothing to a big strong man who'd been brushing his teeth all by himself for years now.

A woman walked by me. She was in her late thirties. Her face was as spare as the leftovers from a dried-fish dinner. To give herself some individuality, she'd pulled her hair into a ponytail. She looked almost like an Indian even though she was blonde. But that wasn't a knocked-down teepee she was pulling – it was a shopping bag on wheels. She was very pale.

She looked anxiously at me, but she had no reason to be afraid. I tried not to smile at her.

I walked between the trees. I've always liked pines. They're phallic. Plump, round, voluptuous, and they stretch toward heaven. Not like pious spruces with their drooping branches and their sad, undertaker's expressions.

The smell of pines has always meant summer to me. Late summer and you're on the way up and through a mountain valley or a pass, up towards the heathery plateaus and the big open stretches and the arched pure late-summer sky with its dark blue strength, there where a long summer season has stored its vitamins against winter.

But it wasn't late summer now. It was February and there was no reason to think of mountain plateaus or pines, or anything at all.

Suddenly I saw the hut, twenty metres further up the slope. It wasn't a hut you could brag about. Somebody had dabbed green paint over pieces of lath, tar-paper and insulating scraps of sacks. High on the wall facing me was a little window covered with chicken wire. A shiny blue bicycle stood against the wall. I spotted a white face behind the chicken wire.

I came closer and heard voices inside the hut. And then they came tumbling out through one of the side walls and down to the front of the hut. They lined up in front of the bicycle. They were like a wall.

The Welcome Committee was in session.

4

They looked more nervous than tough. Six average, overgrown, teenage boys with the same old pimples, the same old downy chins, the same old fatuous sneers. A tall lanky kid at one end of the line tried rolling a cigarette, but he dropped half the tobacco on the ground, and when he finally got the cigarette in his mouth he just missed jamming it in his eye.

The kid in the middle was different. He was short and fat. Ruddy face, yellow-blond hair. The hangdog look in his eyes told me he was the gang's court jester. All gangs have their fool, and God help anybody in another gang who tries anything with him. Consciously or not, the fool keeps the gang together. They've got to defend him. This must be the one Roar called Tasse.

You could see differences in hair colour, expression and size among the other four. Even so, they were amazingly alike. They all wore jeans. Some wore leather jackets, other ski jackets.

When the last one came out of the hut the picture changed abruptly. The others had rushed out like sheep. This one sauntered – as if he'd happened to pass by accidentally. Something deliberate and stagey about him warned me. Psycho.

I could see how they fawned on him. What thirty seconds earlier had been confirmation candidates who'd have meekly recited the Lord's Prayer for me suddenly became a gang. Tight lips replaced the uneasy smiles. The anxious eyes hardened into pebbles. The tall one's cigarette settled down in the corner of his mouth. Tasse displayed his stomach, rested his plump little hands on his hips.

He didn't introduce himself. Wasn't necessary. He seemed totally uninterested in the proceedings. There was something almost drowsy about him. But the narrow squinting eyes weren't sleepy. They were bright and alert. A predator's.

His dark hair was brushed back from a high white forehead. It gave him a priestly look. His nose was unusually narrow and thin, almost like a knife, and you had the feeling he could use it as a weapon. His mouth was a little like Elvis Presley's. The upper lip curled, but the teeth were too decayed to smile on a record jacket.

He wore tight almost white jeans and a black leather jacket with a lot of shiny zippers. A spare taut body – not especially powerful. But I assumed he'd be very good with a knife. His type is.

I knew how his voice would sound: as tense as a steel wire and as gentle as a used razor blade. As soon as he opened his mouth, a ray of afternoon-yellow sun strayed under the pines and shone right in his face. The paper-pale skin turned as gold as an angel's. The full lips were transformed – pouting, Raphaelite. Just an illusion. Like most things the sun shines on. 'What do you want, old man?' he said.

He didn't have to hustle for his applause. They gave him a standing ovation. Ugly teenagers' ugly laughter shattered the silence of the forest.

'I'm looking for the kindergarten. Heard it was here.' I lacked his charm. No one laughed.

His tongue explored the decaying stubs. 'The old folks' home's down the hill. Maybe we should send for a wheelchair?'

More guffaws. That was the funniest thing they'd ever heard.

'Why? Do you need one?' I said. And added while I still had a little headway, 'I came to pick up my bike.'

'Your bike?' He looked around as if he'd just discovered the others. 'Any of you guys seen a bike?'

The clowns looked around, shook their heads. Tasse looked as if he'd explode with suppressed laughter. Joker said, 'Send your auntie instead, grandad. Or one of the nurses. Then we'll see.'

I thought they were really going to split their guts this time, and then I realised that I was going to make a speech. Whenever I'm scared I have to make a speech. I'm going to stand at death's door and make a speech. I'm going to stand at the Pearly Gates and talk St Peter into a coma before he has a chance to send me to the Complaints Department on the first floor.

I began with the lanky kid. Looked him in the eye with what I hoped would remind him of all his childhood bogeyman experiences. We've all had them. The cigarette began wobbling in the corner of his mouth.

I said, 'Maybe I don't look so dangerous at first. Not when there are seven of you and you're fifteen or twenty years younger. But a lion who's spent years in the zoo doesn't look dangerous either to an idiot who's about to step into its cage.'

I moved to the next. He was nearly my height. He had a sweaty upper lip and a large inflamed pimple by his left nostril. 'The Norwegian Alps looking poetic at sundown don't impress me,' I said. He blushed. I moved on.

This one already had a beautiful grey-black stubble. Thick black eyebrows. Clearly myopic. I waved my hand in front of his eyes and he didn't know where to look.

'Hello. Anybody home? Here I am. No. Here. Go home and

get your glasses, pal. You look like a bug-eyed refugee from outer space.'

Joker was next. I skipped him. He didn't like that. Tasse was on his right.

'Hello, Porky Pig,' I said. 'You look as if you could use a bike.' I waited a minute. 'Exercise, Fatso. You'll find "exercise" in the dictionary. If you can read.'

I took the last two together. 'And who have we here? Abbott and Costello?'

I went back to the centre of the line and checked them over one by one. 'You lot know who I am? I'm Veum. Heard of me? I'm in the phone book under M for Monster. I make the papers. Every time I beat somebody up. So I wouldn't advise climbing into my cage. Or look at it this way. I play for the national team and you squirts are backwoods Little Leaguers. You've only got one thing going for you. I'm not crazy about creaming anything smaller than I am. But I've never been religious about it, so you're welcome to try.' I continued while I had a head start: 'I came to get my bike. Any objections?'

I locked glances with Joker. You handle psychos the way you do bears. The best way to tame them is to look them right in the eye. 'When we real men play poker, we never waste time with the Joker,' I said.

And I walked by him, took the bicycle by the handlebars and swung it around.

Turning your back on a wrought-up psycho is one of the stupidest things you can do, but I had a spellbound public and not many choices. As I passed Joker on my way out of that charmed circle, I turned and held him with my gaze. 'Better bring your boss a clean nappy, boys.'

I kept my head as still as if I had lumbago. Kept my eyes on

Joker's until I was too far away for him to jam a switchblade between my shoulders.

Not a sound behind me. Nobody laughed. Nobody ever laughs when he's a witness to high treason. At any rate, not before the king's left the throne room. I was conceited enough to think my performance would become myth. Some day when somebody recited the gang's history beside a shining blue camp-fire in the future's lonely desert.

On the way down I got on the bike. The Lone Ranger riding into the sunset. Trouble was, the real Lone Ranger was constantly busy rescuing people. And this Lone Ranger was me.

5

Roar was waiting where I'd left him. He gazed at me. Open admiration. I jumped off his bike and we wheeled it between us back to his building.

He said, 'What did you do?'

I said, 'I just went up there and took it.' As if there'd been nothing to it.

She didn't have to introduce herself. I knew. She came fluttering towards us like a terrified bird, her dark hair a cloud around her face. She wore blue corduroy trousers, a light white turtleneck, and a red and blue ski jacket she hadn't had time to fasten.

'Roar!' she called from fifty metres away. 'Where have you been?'

She grabbed her son's shoulders, staring at him. Her hair curled wildly. It was cut very short at the neck. She had one of those thin white necks that make you cry inside and remember the thousands of swans you used to see in Nygård Park when you were a kid. That make you regret deeply and sincerely that you've never found such a neck to cry against, ever loved another's more – if you ever have.

'Mum,' Roar said. 'This is … It was Joker and they – they took my bike and so I went …'

She looked at me. Frost in her eyes. Said in a voice you'd welcome on a beach when it's thirty degrees in the shade, 'Who are you?' And to Roar, 'Has this man done anything to you?'

'Done anything to me?' He looked at her. Baffled.

She shook him. 'Answer me, boy! Answer me!' She turned to me again and burst into tears. 'Who are you? If you've so much as touched him, I'll kill you!'

Her face was blotchy, her little nose shone, and the dark blue eyes sparked like gas flames.

'My name's Veum, Fru,' I said. 'And I haven't –'

Roar interrupted. Now he had tears in his eyes. 'He hasn't, he's helped me – he's the one who got my bike back. He got my bike from Joker's hut so you wouldn't …'

He began crying and she looked at him helplessly. Then she hugged him and murmured something in his ear.

It was almost completely dark now and lights shone in most of the windows. Cars went by. Tired, stooped men left them and walked to their doors and to their lifts. Then it was up to their wives and their dinner tables twenty metres above earth, twenty metres closer to outer space and a new workday closer to eternity. A little drama played itself out on the pavement in front of the building they lived in, but not one looked up, not one noticed that a young woman, a little boy, a not-so-young man and a new bicycle stood there. We could just as well have been alone in an out-of-the-way spot in the Sahara.

The face looking over Roar's shoulder was at least twenty years too young. The mouth had the injured pout of a little girl who's been denied her lollipop, but it was a full, sensuous mouth. It told you she'd get what she wanted when she grew up. Just you wait. The dark blue eyes were calm now. They looked like flowers you didn't pick and then regretted not picking for the rest of your life.

'I'm sorry,' she said. 'I was so frightened. He's never been gone so long before. I … Well…'

'I understand,' I said.

She stood up and held out a hand while she brushed the hair back from her forehead with the other. 'I'm … My name's Wenche Andresen.'

I held her hand a few seconds. 'Veum. Varg Veum.'

She looked surprised, and I realised she'd either misunderstood my first name or thought she'd heard it wrong.

'My father's sense of humour,' I said. 'He named me.'

'Named you?'

'Named me. Varg.'

'Oh. So your name really is Outlaw?' Her sulky mouth widened in a brilliant smile, and her whole face turned beautiful and young and happy. Until she stopped laughing and became ten years older and twenty younger at the same time. A little girl's mouth and middle-aged eyes. I ought to see about getting home.

'But what are you really?' she said. 'How did he get hold of you?'

'I'm a private investigator. A kind of detective. He found me in the phone book.'

'A detective?' She didn't look as if she quite believed me.

'It's true, Mum,' Roar said. 'He's got an office in the city, but he doesn't have a gun.'

She smiled weakly. 'That's nice.' She looked around. 'I don't know – maybe I could give you a cup of coffee?' Nodded toward the high-rise.

I looked at my watch. I ought to be getting home. 'Thanks. Maybe you could,' I said.

So Roar, his mother and I walked past my car and into one of the entrances to that twelve-storey building. We locked his bike in the cellar and got into one of the two lifts. She pressed the '9' button. It was a small lift with steel walls painted grey. Here and there the paint had already begun to peel.

Wenche Andresen looked at me with her big blue eyes. 'If we're lucky, we'll go all the way.'

'What do you mean?' I said.

'There's a bunch of kids constantly messing with the lifts. They all press the buttons on their own floors at the same time, and then there's a short or something. Whatever they do, the lift stops between floors and you stay there until the caretaker starts it up again.'

'I can see this isn't a good place for kids. Aren't there any other sports beside stealing bikes and jamming lifts?'

'They've hired someone to work with them, but I don't think it's been especially successful. He's started a youth club. His name's Våge.'

The lift stopped. We'd made it. Two doors led from the lift out on to a balcony which, except for where it was blocked by the lift, ran the length of the building. All the flats faced the balcony. We passed two doors. There was a hand-painted sign on Wenche Andresen's: Wenche, Roar and Jonas Andresen live here. She silently let us in.

She took off her jacket in the foyer and then took mine. I stood in the middle of the green mat. Confused. The way you always feel in strange hallways. Roar took my hand. 'Come on, I'll show you my room.'

'I'll make coffee,' she said.

Roar led me to his room. The green and white curtains turned out to be white trucks on a green background. A double-decker white bed stood in one corner. Posters of comic strip characters and animals hung on the walls. There was a large poster of a clown in a circus ring, and a small calendar photograph of the Bergen Boys' Drill Corps marching through a narrow street lined with low white houses. Toys were scattered all over the floor.

Wooden railway tracks, small model cars, stuffed animals, war-weary cowboys and Indians.

Sketch pads, drawings and old comics were stacked on a little green table. A child loved this room.

Roar looked at me. Formal now. 'What should I call you? Veum?'

I ruffled his hair. 'Just Varg.'

He nodded and beamed. His new front teeth were too big. 'Want to see what I've drawn?'

So I saw what he'd drawn. Blue suns and yellow trees. Red mountains. Boats with wheels, horses with rabbits on their backs. Crooked little houses with skewed windows and flowers rioting in their gardens.

I walked to the window. People, cars – so small. The five-storey buildings looked like crushed matchboxes from here, and the road between them like a track for toy cars.

Then I looked at the Lyderhorn's steep sides, at that grey-black outline you can easily lose in the evening sky. As if the Lyderhorn were the sky. It was as if that dark mountain were the threatening clouds now lying like a snowdrift over the city – like a warning of Doomsday. Or of death.

6

We drank our coffee in the kitchen. The TV quacked in the living room. Roar was watching a children's programme.

The kitchen was yellow with orange cupboard doors. She'd hung white curtains printed with oranges. A yellow and orange dotted circular cloth sat in the centre of the grey-white plastic table top. There was coffee in a green pot with red dots and a selection of biscuits in a raffia basket. 'It's not much, but ...' She shrugged.

'The coffee was delicious,' I said.

'Drink up. There's more.'

Then she said, 'Was it Joker – as they call him – and his gang who took Roar's bike?'

'It was,' I said. 'I've heard there was another incident here – the mother of one of Roar's friends.'

'That's right. I know about it. I've talked to her. She ...' She bit her lip. 'It's incredible. She ... They took her boy's bicycle, and she went up there to the hut to get it back. They ... They actually took her prisoner as if she were a mere girl and not – not a grown woman.'

'Was she ...?'

She banged the cup down. Hard. 'They couldn't care less. If anything like that had happened when we were kids ... If we'd when we were kids ... I can't even begin to imagine it. But that's how it is.' She looked woodenly at me. 'That's how it is when you're a single woman with children. We're hunted by everything that calls itself male – from runny-nosed boys to ageing Don Juans. It makes me sick.'

'But was she actually …?'

'No. She wasn't actually raped. But it's the same thing. They grabbed her. Went for her. Molested her – if you know what I mean. Joker took her trousers off and forced her … He showed them – so they all got a good look. But they didn't go any further.'

'But why didn't she go to the police?'

'To the police? And what can they do? Were there witnesses? Not one! Only the gang, and they won't say anything. They're as frightened of that Joker as the rest of us. There was a man here who tried to do something. They beat him up so badly I don't think he'll ever recover. If she'd gone to the police … In the first place, she'd never get her post again. There were some other parents who went to Joker's – to his mother – and complained. Their post was always burning up after that. They stuff burning rags in the letter boxes. They finally had to get a box down at the post office. And those of us who are alone with young children you have no idea what they'll do. Even to the little ones. There was one six-year-old girl. She came home with cigarette burns on her whole body – her whole body.'

I could feel myself tensing. I could see them, one after another: the tall lanky one, the anonymous ones, fat Tasse – and then Joker himself. Looking like a priest, but with the eyes of a tiger and the teeth of a decaying corpse.

And I thought about what they could have done to Wenche Andresen if she'd tried to retrieve the bike. 'Would you yourself have gone up there?' I said.

'After what happened?' She shook her head. 'We'd have bought a new bike. Even though we can't afford it. No! I'd never go up there – not alone!'

'Isn't there anybody who could have helped you? Don't you know anyone?'

She looked at me. 'Have you ever lived in a place like this? How many flats are there? Fifty – sixty? Almost two hundred people. I do say hello to some of them who live on this floor. Sometimes to other people in the lift. But it's like an anthill. Do ants say hello?' She shook her head again. 'I don't know a soul. We're as isolated now as we've always been – even when Jonas was living here.'

'Are you divorced?' I said.

She lit a cigarette. 'Separated. Eight months.' She clenched her jaw, glanced restlessly around the yellow room. 'Eight months.'

Then she noticed the package of cigarettes and pushed it across to me.

I said, 'Thanks, but I don't smoke.' I took a biscuit instead. Just to show my good intentions.

'More coffee?'

I nodded, and she stood up. She was slim. Straight back, rather small breasts, a round little rear in the corduroy trousers, a little dimple in the nape of her neck.

'Do you work?' I said.

'I do. I worked part-time before … And I don't get much money from Jonas either. He already owes me a couple of thousand. I think … I think he stalls on purpose. He was the one who walked out, but he tries to blame me. But he was the one who didn't have … who couldn't control himself. He was the one who had to find himself somebody else – that tramp.'

'Where do you work?' I said.

'In an office at the naval base. It saves me going all the way into town. Well, so much for that. The worst is suddenly finding you're alone when you're used to somebody being there.'

She hunched her shoulders and stared into her coffee cup. Her lips trembled and her eyes were very dark. I ought to see about getting home.

'I know how it is,' I said. 'I've been there myself.'

She looked blank. 'Where?'

'I mean I've been … I'm divorced. Five years ago. Its better now. You get used to everything. It's like having cancer. Maybe you get used to that, too.'

'God knows,' she said.

We sat in silence for a while. I stared through the window, into that empty black night. I noticed she was looking closely at me. 'Did your wife leave you?'

'I suppose so. Or else she sent me away. Whatever. Asked me to move out.'

'Because of someone else?'

'I really don't know if she'd already met him by then. I think she had. I wasn't home much. I worked for Children's Welfare. I was away a lot. Out at nights, out hunting for the dear little things. I found quite a few of them, too. Took them home and sat up late talking with their parents. And when I got home, I fell straight into bed. She never talked to me at breakfast. Just looked at me. She had a special way of looking, if you know what I mean.'

'Any children?'

'Mmm. A boy. A little younger than Roar. He starts school in the autumn. Thomas.'

Now it was my turn to hunt for reflection in my cup, to look for a face that wasn't there, to listen for a voice that had become silent a long time ago.

Then Roar came in from the living room. 'Varg? Do you want to watch *Detective Hour*?'

Wenche Andresen opened her mouth. I smiled. 'No thanks. I like real nightmares better,' I said. 'And I ought to be getting home now.'

He looked disappointed, but didn't say anything.

I cleared my throat and stood up. 'Thanks for the coffee. It was nice talking to you,' I said to the woman across the table. 'And it was great meeting you.' I ruffled Roar's hair.

All three of us went into the foyer. I put on my jacket, checked that the car keys were in the pocket, stroked Roar's head once more and held my hand out to his mother.

Her hand lay in mine. 'Thank you for your help,' she said. 'Do we owe you anything?'

'Look at it as a friendly favour,' I said. 'And take care of your bike, Roar. See you.'

'See you,' Roar said.

'Bye. And thanks,' his mother said.

I hurried along the balcony. I was the only one in the lift, and felt as if were riding to Hades.

I left the building and walked to my car. When I'd unlocked it I glanced up. I could see a little boy with his face glued to the window with the green and white curtains. He waved.

I waved back and got into the car. There were some long thin shadows, seven or eight of them, up by the corner of the building. It could have been a gang of teenagers. Or it could have been just the way the light fell.

7

Saturday and Sunday went by as such days do when February is about to change to March. You feel as if you're mushing through knee-high snow. It never really cleared up. The clouds were a tight grey lid on the city. Walking on Mount Fløien was like climbing through dirty waterlogged cotton. I felt as if I were standing up to the roots of my hair in a pair of old sea-boots. No birds sang. And when I got home there weren't any goldfish swimming in the aquavit. I emptied the bottle to make sure. I was right.

I walked around Nordnes on Sunday. Once there'd been little wooden houses leaning against each other. Now there were dreary concrete cubes people lived in. Where there'd once been a playground and a seemingly endless park, an aquarium now housed big fish in too small tanks, and there was a Marine Biological Research Institute in a high-rise best suited for studying flying fish. There was asphalt where you'd once walked with a girl and had scuffed the gravel with the toe of your shoe. No goldfish swam in my second bottle of aquavit. Not one.

I went back to the office on Monday morning. The sopping grey cotton had moved into my head, and the phone reminded me of a petrified toad.

My city still lived outside the windows, but it lived without me. Down at the market, fish sellers with large red hands cut neat slices of grey-white fish for the ladies with their blue coats and brown nylon shopping bags. The florists stood around and looked as miserable as their brown-edged flowers. A lone grocer at the vegetable market peddled carrots from Italy, pak choi from Israel and heads of cabbage from the last century.

Rain and sleet fell in curtains, and the water in Vågen rose up and barked. It was one of those days when people go around with faces like clenched fists and it doesn't take much to make them attack. The afternoon arrived slowly and late. As if it didn't want to show up at all. The phone went on being silent.

I sat and stared at it. I could call …

I could call my mother if she hadn't been dead for the last year and a half.

Or I could call a girl I knew in the Census Bureau if she hadn't been so sarcastic the last time. I'd said, 'This is Veum.' She'd said, 'Veum who? The one with the phone?' I'd spent several days getting the point. And hadn't called back.

Or I could call Paul Finckel, journalist. We could have a beer, eat dinner. But then he'd tell me about all the girls he'd had lately, and nothing's worse than hearing about all the girls other people have had – especially if you don't believe a word they're saying. He was divorced too. I often think everybody's been divorced. One way or another.

Finally I dialled a number at random. A man's voice answered. 'Jebsen speaking.'

I said, 'Um. Is Fru Andresen there?'

'Who?'

'Fru Andresen.'

'Wrong number.'

'Sorry.'

'Right,' he said and hung up.

I sat and listened to the dialling tone. A dialling tone's a funny thing. If you listen long enough it begins to sound as if someone's calling you. Or a lot of people. A chorus. If you listen long enough, the lady from the phone company comes on the line and asks you to hang up.

So I hung up, and left the office before it died in my arms.

Monday's a strange day. The weekend's depression hasn't let go of you and the new week hasn't begun. Maybe we could get along without most of the week. In my racket.

8

I ate dinner in the cafeteria on the second floor. Had a kind of meat stew. It tasted as if the street sweepers had forgotten it. But it was my own fault. I'd eaten there before.

When I got home I brewed up a big batch of herb tea to clear the system of all the weekend's fishing in the aquavit and settled down with a biography of Humphrey Bogart I'd already read. The photographs had that grainy grey tone which told you they'd been taken years before in a never-never land that's long since gone. You don't find the likes of Bogie any more. If he showed up in Bergen today, we'd laugh him right out of his trenchcoat. With his mournful eyes and whistling loose-denture voice, there's no place in our world for people like Bogie except in a curio cabinet.

Suddenly my phone rang. It was five-thirty and my phone was ringing. I picked it up. 'You've got the wrong number. This is Veum,' I said.

'Veum! You've got to help me. Come right away. They've got Roar.' Her voice was shrill.

'Take it easy,' I said. 'Relax. Who's got him?'

'Joker. The gang.' She began to cry. 'When I got home he wasn't here, but I found a note in the letter box. It said they had him. That I knew where I could find him and they'd kill him if I called the police.'

'Did you call them?'

'No! Didn't you hear ...?'

'Shouldn't you anyway? Even though it's ... You can't fall for it. They're bluffing. They're just kids. Don't you see? They're just trying to scare you.'

'They have scared me, Veum. I won't call the police. That's why I ... There's nobody else who can help me. Can't you? Of course I'll pay – if it's that ...'

'It's not that. Of course I'll come if you –'

'Oh yes. Yes! Thank you. But get here. Come as soon as you can. Now. Will you?'

'I'm already on my way. Just calm down. It'll be okay. I promise.'

I hung up, took a last gulp of tea, let Bogie rest in peace in his paperback grave and left the flat.

Down in the alley the afternoon light was beginning to fade. Behind blue ruffled curtains a family was eating dinner. A blonde, red-cheeked mother set steaming dishes on the table while a man with a soup-bowl haircut, a pale moustache and a wrinkled forehead sat and stared anxiously at his two children as if they were reflections of himself in a cracked mirror.

Through an open window on the second floor of another house a hoarse voice sang that it had lived its life by the side of the road. But the rolled 'r's were the only thing it had in common with good old Edvard Persson's style of singing. It was one of your normal late afternoons in the alley, and Veum was on his way. Volunteer Veum. Comes whenever you call, except during office hours.

The Mini coughed. Didn't like having its siesta interrupted, and it died twice in the middle of town. When I told it I'd leave it flat and buy myself a Volkswagen the next time that happened, it hummed like a well-fed bee until we parked in front of the high-rise.

I walked into the building. The lift was waiting. It was empty. Went all the way up. Good for it. I walked to Wenche Andresen's door and rang the bell.

Her face was red, her eyes swollen. She pulled me into the foyer and closed the door. Then she sagged against my chest and started crying. Her whole body shook. I didn't know where to put my hands. Nobody's sobbed against my chest for a long time. All too long, as a matter of fact. I put my hands gently on her shoulder blades, my fingertips against her back. I moved my palms carefully, didn't say anything. It's best to let them cry themselves out.

She slowly stopped crying. Then she suddenly stiffened in my arms. I let go. She stared at the buttons on my shirt and I gave her my handkerchief. She dried her eyes, wiped her nose. Then she shifted her gaze to my face. 'I'm sorry,' she whispered. 'I didn't mean …' Her mouth was swollen. It looked as if she'd spent a long sweet night making love.

My voice – if that was my voice – scratched like an old seventy-eight record. 'Have you got the message?'

She nodded and handed me a crumpled piece of paper. I managed not to touch her hand.

The writing was childish. *We've got Roar. You know where to find him. Call the cops and we'll kill him.* No signature.

'When did you get home?' I said.

'Four-thirty.'

'But you didn't call me until five-thirty. When did you get the message?'

'He wasn't here when I got home. So I went out and looked for him. Asked some of his playmates. But they hadn't seen him. I went on looking for a while longer, then I came back at five and the message was there in the letter box. I was terrified. I don't remember. I came straight up here. Beside myself. I didn't know what to do. Who to ask for help. Then I thought of you. We had such a nice talk the other day. I thought maybe you could … But I didn't mean … I mean, well, I'll …' She looked me in the eye. 'I will pay you what you're used to getting.'

'We'll talk about that later,' I said. 'We'd better find Roar first. You still don't want me to call the police?'

She shook her head.

'Well. You stay here in case he turns up. And I'll see if I can find him.'

'Where are you going?'

'I'll begin with the hut,' I said.

Her eyes widened. They were so big and blue it almost hurt to look into them. 'But it could be dangerous,' she said. 'You could be …'

'I can be dangerous myself. Now and then,' I said. I tried to look as if I could be. And then I left.

9

When it gets dark on this side of the Lyderhorn, it's darker than any other place I know. It's as if that sheer mountainside makes the darkness twice as black. As if the mountain is night itself.

I stopped a good way from the hut. Stood and listened. Nothing. Not a sound. I looked at each tree, but it was hard to make out anything in that heavy starless darkness.

The woods could be teeming with life, but they could also be dead. A petrified forest.

I walked up to the hut and stood by the wall just under the little window. It was too high to see through. I listened. Still nothing. But I had a definite, nasty feeling that I wasn't alone. I checked out the trees. Was that a swelling on one of the trunks? Was that a broken branch or a head sticking out? Was that somebody breathing in the darkness?

I inched along the wall. Peered around the corner. There wasn't a door, just a piece of sacking in the opening. Impossible to see whether anybody was inside. I cautiously pulled the sacking to one side with my left hand and stared in. It was darker in the hut than it was out here and far quieter. Or did something move – there on the floor?

Since nobody came storming through the doorway, there was only one way to find out. I stooped and ducked quickly through the opening, and then swung left with my back against the wall. Nothing happened. Nobody jumped me in the darkness. No fists. No knives.

I waited and caught my breath. Let my eyes get used to the dark.

It was a small square room. Some sacking and old newspapers lay on the ground. Some empty plastic bags. An empty carton under the window. A stink of beer, sweat, and something which could have been semen.

A bundle lay in one corner, partly against the wall. It was Roar.

They'd tied his legs together and his arms behind his back. Stuffed a dirty handkerchief in his mouth. He stared at me. Tear stains on his cheeks. When he recognised me, fresh tears oozed from his eyes. His clothes and hair were filthy. Other than that, he was in fine shape.

I flipped open my pocket-knife, squatted in front of him and cut the ropes. When I took the handkerchief out of his mouth something between a gasp and sob filled the hut. He tried holding back the tears, but couldn't. I hugged him and tried to muffle his sobs against my jacket. Tried to calm him. But he cried. Shook almost convulsively. His crying changed the silence. I couldn't tell if what I heard now was silence or sounds which shouldn't have been there. I listened so intently my head ached. But I simply could not hear anything except his sobbing.

Maybe we were alone. Maybe they'd gone home to drink Cokes and play Parchese. Maybe the fun and games were over for today.

'We've got to get out of here, Roar,' I said in his ear. 'Your mum's waiting.'

He nodded against my chest. I heard a long sniff.

'Do you know where the others are?'

He shook his head. 'Th-they left a long t-time ago,' he said. Voice still blurry with tears.

I found a clean handkerchief and wiped his cheeks. Then I said cheerfully, 'Let's go home, okay?' I put my arm around his shoulders, pushed the sack aside, and we walked out.

They stood in a semicircle in front of the door. Roar froze. I quickly shoved him behind me and back into the doorway.

I made a fast count. Five. Two less than last time. Joker. The tall skinny one. Tasse. Pimple Face. And a blond I couldn't remember seeing.

Five of them. One of me.

This time Joker didn't let me start a conversation. His voice was tense. 'Get him, you guys!'

He himself just stood there with his arms folded. Sneering. He wasn't about to dirty his hands, not without being a hundred per cent sure of winning. That cut it down to four. I couldn't take Tasse seriously.

I had to concentrate on the other three. Two were already moving. I parried the tall one's blow with my left arm and shoved the blond with my right shoulder. Kicked the tall one's leg. Not hard enough. Pimple Face managed to land a hard blow to my chest, and I staggered back. Crashed against the wall of the hut.

I should have taken Tasse seriously. He doubled up and charged, his head down. Butted me in the stomach and knocked the wind out of me. Suddenly the forest wasn't black. It was white, blindingly white. Then it was dark again. Tasse was still within reach. So I planted my knee in his face while I tried to sweep away those dancing red-gold specks from the heaving, hard-edged darkness.

I heard Roar whistle and got it on both sides. A fist connected with my mouth. Upper lip went numb. A boot hit the inside of my thigh. High enough to do some damage, too low to cripple me.

I clenched my teeth. Tried to separate the shadows from the darkness. Saw the outlines of a face on my left and planted my left elbow, and then my right fist. Bingo! I heard somebody lurch backwards and a long string of curses.

Then somebody tried for a clinch, but I wasn't in the mood to be hugged, so I kneed him in the groin. When he bent over, I laced my hands together and rabbit-punched him. He fell to the ground and stayed there. Then somebody else hit me in the back of the head.

The stars exploded. I was just about to pass out, but I took a deep breath, turned and struck out blindly. Connected with a broad chest. Heard a yelp. A fist rammed my chin. I swung again. Lower. This time I hit him in the stomach. My fist sank into the flab. I shoved him aside with my left arm. Then I swung around again, my back to the wall.

Tasse was in the distance, holding a handkerchief to his nose. Tears streamed from his eyes but he didn't make a sound. The tall one propped up a tree with one arm. One hand covered an eye while the other glared at me. The blond was on the ground. I could see he was breathing, but he showed no signs of getting up. Pimple Face danced a peculiar solo through the trees to the left. He mumbled, and held one shoulder as if he needed it to hang on to. Finally he sank to the ground. Sat there and stared upwards, searching for invisible stars.

Joker stared at me. His eyes seemed colourless. But the sneer was still there and he had a switchblade in his right hand. Still, he didn't really look as if he wanted to dance.

I looked for Roar. He was still in the doorway. Worry and joy in his face. 'Come on, Roar. Let's go,' I said. But I didn't hug him this time. I wanted both hands free.

Then I turned to Joker. 'Remember me? Veum's the name.

Let me tell you something. If I ever hear that you've bothered this family again ...' I turned Roar into this family with a wave of my hand. 'If I hear one word, I'll be back. And next time I won't fool around with your flabby little handmaidens. I'll come for you. And I'll fold you up like a pocket-knife. And I'll pound you up against every tree in this forest so long and so hard you won't be able to call your mummy afterwards. Got it?'

He bared his teeth, jerked his knife at me, but kept his distance.

'And if you think a little switchblade scares me, think again. They called me Sword Swallower when I was at sea. So you're welcome to all the knives in your mummy's kitchen drawer. Be my guest. I'll take you regardless, and you'll be sorry you ever got out of bed that day.'

I'd never sounded tougher. But I was tough. There were four proofs of it standing and sitting and lying around. Joker must have thought they were convincing because he still showed no signs of wanting to dance.

I left him there in the woods with his knife in his hand and that sneer on his face. Maybe he was one of those who cut their way out of their mother and spit in the midwife's face. Some people are like that. Some get that way. Joker was like that, and that was enough for me. I didn't need to know any more. Silently I took Roar home to his mother.

10

I didn't realise how weak I was until we were in the lift. I had to brace myself against the wall, and I was sweating from head to foot. It seemed as if we'd never arrive. It was as if the lift had escaped from its shaft and was on its way to outer space, as if Roar and I were the last two humans who'd been launched towards the future, the last survivors of a dead civilisation. Then the lift stopped and we got out.

She'd seen us from the window and was waiting by the lift door. She stared at my face and then she knelt and hugged Roar. He put his arms around her neck and began crying again. Her eyes were wet, too, her face soft and blurry.

After a while I coughed, and she looked at me. 'You're bleeding,' she said. She stood up with Roar in her arms. 'Come on, let's go in,' she said. She carried Roar along the balcony and into the flat. I followed. Unsteadily.

I peeked warily in the mirror in the entrance hall. The way a person looks into a room he hasn't been invited into. Saw a man whom I'd once known. He was pale with dishevelled hair and dirty streaks on his face. It bled when he tried to smile so he stopped.

She was still busy with Roar, but she came and stood beside me and looked in the mirror at my bruises. 'What happened?' she said.

'I was a little outnumbered,' I said, 'but I'd say most of them are in worse shape than I am.' I smiled.

'Don't do that,' she said. 'It tears your lip. Come out here.'

She took my arm and led me to the bathroom. It was like walking into the sun. I was dazzled by the chalk-white light.

It was a small room, shiny and white, and the light in the ceiling was unusually strong. You couldn't hide the smallest blemish in here. Her skin must be very beautiful if she had the courage to stand this light.

She filled the white porcelain basin and tilted my face upward. Then she washed it with a blue cloth as carefully as you would bathe a newborn baby. I could feel the pain easing and the weakness running off me like water.

'Does it help?' she said.

I squinted at her through swollen eyelids and nodded. Her eyes were even bluer in this strong light. It was as if she attracted it to her. Her face seemed to fill the whole room. I could see the tiny fine veins in her nostrils, the blonde almost transparent down on her upper lip, the narrow newly etched lines in her forehead and around her eyes. And her eyes were blue, so blue you almost expected birds to fly out of them.

Roar stood in the doorway and watched. He'd recovered now. His voice was eager. 'You should have seen Varg going for them, Mum! He beat them up so they could hardly walk afterwards. And that Joker, he looked like – he looked like he'd wet himself. Varg really fixed them.'

I squinted at him. His eyes shone. 'Right, Varg?' he said.

'Well …,' I said.

'Come on,' she said. 'I'll make you something to eat.'

That evening she invited me into the living room.

It was a pleasant room. Nothing unusual, just one of those rooms you immediately feel at home in. The furniture was old and good, the chairs comfortable, and you could eat off the table without having to lower your head between your knees. There were some bright watercolours of alpine landscapes on the walls, as well as a lot of samplers and embroideries she'd done herself. The books in the bookcase had worn spines: mysteries, books on child care and embroidery, a novel by Faulkner, a best-seller about an old woman somewhere out in the sticks, volume three of a famous statesman's memoirs and a football handbook. Something there for every taste, as we say whenever there isn't.

There were four or five photograph albums on one of the bookshelves and a framed picture next to them. It was a family photograph and I recognised Wenche Andresen with slightly longer hair and Roar with a baby's round face and stare. The third person must have been Roar's father. A pale young man (that could have been because of the sunlight). Blond hair and dark-framed glasses. A nice smile. He and Wenche Andresen were sitting on a wall somewhere and she had Roar on her lap. It was summer. They looked very very happy.

The bookcase's upper shelves were full of little knick-knacks: pottery figures, painted shells, cheap souvenirs and expensive porcelain animals. There wasn't a place left to squeeze in a matchstick.

A TV stood in one corner of the room, talking to itself. A cartoon character went grimacing back and forth. Luckily it wasn't funny enough to make me laugh because I'd stopped bleeding.

I sat in a comfortable chair while Roar perched on the arm and leaned against my shoulder, and the fuzzy blue pictures flickered away at the other end of the room.

Then it was over and a lady appeared and asked whether that hadn't been a funny film? If we wanted to see it again, all we had to do was tune in at five past nine the next morning. That should be fun, she said with a sweet-sour smile. Then came the English lessons. They'd only aired that series five times before so it was still hot stuff.

'Would you like to see it?' Roar said.

'No thanks. You can turn it off,' I said.

Like all children, he hated doing it. Then he came back and sat on the chair arm. Thinking.

I looked at him. Finally I said, 'What's on your mind?'

He blushed. 'Nothing.'

'Nothing?'

After a while he said, 'I was thinking you're a lot stronger than my dad. He could never have done what …'

Wenche Andresen had come in and he stopped. She'd brought a tray of cocoa and sandwiches: cocoa in yellow cups and sandwiches on a pewter plate. Lamb sausage and egg sandwiches, tomato and cucumber sandwiches, ham and beetroot sandwiches, sardines in tomato sauce, strawberry jam sandwiches. It looked like an invitation to breakfast. Or else as if she were expecting a crowd.

While we ate, Roar told us how the whole thing had started. They'd been waiting for him outside the building. Three of them with Joker directing operations in the distance. They'd tied his arms behind his back, gagged him with a handkerchief and carried him off. He'd tried to kick loose but they'd hit him in the mouth and said they'd break his legs if he didn't stop kicking. So he stopped kicking.

Up at the hut they'd tied him to a tree and circled him, kicking and hitting him. He rolled up his pants. 'See?' His legs were covered with bruises. His mother gasped. I chewed. Then they'd told him what they'd do with his mother.

Wenche Andresen turned pale. 'What did they say?'

He turned pale, too, and looked away.

She reddened. 'Those filthy pigs! Oh – I'll ...'

She stood up with her hands on her throat. I saw her fighting for breath. 'What have you got to say, Veum?' she said finally.

I chewed. I chewed and I chewed and I chewed. I could have chewed for a hundred years but that piece of bread was not going to go down. I stood up, went out and spat it into the toilet. Then I came back to the living room.

She'd sat down again. 'I'll ... Oh!' Her fist smacked the arm of the chair.

'What's the name of the youth club leader?' I said.

'Våge. Gunnar Våge. What about him?'

'I'll talk to him.'

'That won't help. He's a nothing. He's on their side. It's their background, he says. You've got to think of the kind of homes they come from, he says. Great! What kind of homes do they come from? Did we come from such good homes?'

Suddenly I saw another living room. Far off in an alley. A mother who sat by the radio and knitted. A father with a drawn face and conductor's uniform who came home to a large warm kitchen. I saw a living room with big green potted plants where we used to sit in the evenings and listen to the radio.

There was a gong and a voice which said: 'Good evening. My name's Cox.' And then there was a melody which sang itself so deep inside us that we could hum every note twenty years later. There was a verse we made up to that tune. We'd remember it to our dying day: 'Cox is my name/ and Peacock's a pain/ and Pip has fled/ and Margot's dead/ Cox is in love with gorgeous Helene/ and next year they'll wed ...'

'Did we, Veum?' She looked at me with tear-filled eyes.

'Did we what?'

'Come from good homes?'

'Some of us, maybe. Not all of us. There's so much that counts. So much is involved.'

'And we bring children into this world, this hell. A world of cheats and liars and – terrorists. What else is there besides misery? Will it ever work out, or will it always be impossible to be just to be – a little bit happy?'

And she looked at me as if I'd seen the Philosopher's Stone. But I hadn't and I didn't know where it was. My name was Veum and my father had named me Varg. Outlaw. He could just as well have named me Cox. It would have made the same difference.

I looked around the room. At the dead TV, at the bookshelves, at all the knick-knacks, at the picture of the happy family, at the watercolours and embroideries on the walls, at the table with its sandwiches and cocoa, at Roar who sat and listened. And at his mother who cried and cried.

I stood up and went to the window. Looked out. Tried to find a little comfort out there. It was dark. It had begun to rain. The lights below winked at me like tear-blinded eyes and I could hear the uneven constant whisper of the traffic on the main road. And there was whispering over the Lyderhorn as if it too had its own wretched secrets to hide, its own dark knowledge of life and happiness. Of everything. It wasn't so strange that the sagas said the witches rested on that very mountaintop on Midsummer's Eve on their way to the Sabbath on Mount Brocken in Germany.

11

Roar had gone to bed. She found a bottle of red wine. One of those inexpensive wines with fashionable labels which change from year to year. This year's would have come from Israel.

'A glass before you go?' she said.

'I could do with one,' I said. 'Even though I'm driving. Maybe it'll persuade me I'm a better chauffeur.'

She found some glasses and poured. They were small and round. Stemless. They looked like little soap bubbles filled with blood. She raised hers in a silent toast and we drank.

It tasted of autumn. Of September with rowan berries and rose hips crushed on the pavement, of old newspapers lying in gutters and fluttering in the first winds of the season, of people walking fast so they'd get home faster. Her lips were moist.

'We were so happy, Veum,' she said suddenly. 'Jonas and I. The first years. That's what I remember – those first years. That's when people discover each other. Right? When you walk around in a haze of love and don't see anything else but ... the other. Oh, God, I was crazy about him!'

She reached for a bowl of peanuts with her long clean white fingers. The TV was on again but neither of us looked at it. The sound had been turned down and a lantern-jawed man talked silently to the living room.

'It must have been 1967. He was in his last year at Business School and I worked in an office. He had a one-room flat in Møhlenpris – up in the attic. We used to lie on the sofa in the evenings and look out of those two windows. Up at the stars.

Or on summer evenings when the clouds raced by, and the windows were open and the smell of flowers and the sound of birds in Nygård Park filled the room. There was only the one room. A sofa, a table, two chairs and a little table with a hot-plate in the corner. The toilet was on the other side of the hall. Before we went we used to listen to see if anyone was coming. And then we'd sneak out. Barefooted.

'When I think about how shabby it was – so small and cramped – but those years we lived there were the happiest. And then Roar came along and there wasn't enough room. We moved into a flat higher up on Nygårdshøyden. Two rooms and a kitchen. We got married. After I got pregnant, I mean. Not because we had to, but because we wanted to. It was just sort of the two of us. There was simply no room for anybody else. The world's happiest couple. And then ...'

She shrugged sadly. She was holding her glass as if it were warm and her fingers were icy.

'Of course, we were younger. You're always younger – then. Seems to me that it's the same for most people, that it changes gradually but not a lot. Jonas finished school and got a job with an ad agency. A small one. Only five of them and there was a lot of work. He'd come home around six with his shoulders hunched up to his ears. A lot of stress.

'But it was still good. Roar was little. I had to think about him. Right? A little child? I stopped working and stayed home. We agreed. We wanted it that way as long as he was little. And then ...'

She looked at me searchingly. 'And then, it sort of just died.'

'It's like that with dinosaurs and marriages,' I said. 'They become extinct.'

She looked puzzled. 'What does?'

'Marriages,' I said. 'A lot of them die for no good reason.'

'I can't tell you exactly when it happened,' she said. 'I can't take out an old calendar and find a month, an exact date, point to it and say: that's the day it ended. It was more like getting sick. Or maybe – like getting well again.'

She refilled her glass. 'You're sick for a long time, right? I was sick once when I was a little girl. Stayed in bed for months. I was bored. Spoiled and looked after. The centre of everything. It was almost painful to be well again, know what I mean? Everything turned so ordinary all of a sudden.

'That's how it was with us. As if I woke suddenly one morning and heard how he slept beside me. And I smelled his sweat and the stale beer and I wondered: What's happened to us? He'd begun to drink quite a bit. He'd come home from work late. Had had to go out for a beer, he said. Then it was dinners with customers, and seminars at weekends and conferences in Oslo. He'd moved to a larger ad agency with customers over the whole country.

'I slept alone more and more. But there was one morning when I thought to myself – before, before when I woke up with you, Jonas, there was a spark and then a fire that burned inside me all day until we slept together. But now? Now I'm cold, I thought to myself, and when you wake up and lean over and kiss me as usual, you look at me and you grunt as if you were saying: you again? Am I stuck with you for ever? Am I talking too much?' she said suddenly.

I drank some wine so I wouldn't have to answer right away. 'Oh, no,' I said.

Just come to Veum, good old Veum, no life story's too dreary to lay on him. No matter how ordinary it is. Just talk. Willing Veum will listen. It's his job.

'It's a long time since I've talked to anyone. I mean – so openly. But we should talk about you, too. Tell me about you, Veum.'

'Can't you call me Varg?' I said.

She nodded. 'Okay.' She poured herself another glass. 'Okay, Varg. Tell me about your wife …'

'Beate?' I shrugged. 'There's not much to tell about Beate. Not any more. We were married for several years. Five to be exact. We had a little boy and then we divorced. She married again. A lecturer at the university. They live out in Ytre Sand-viken. In a few years they'll have a front-row seat overlooking the new four-lane motorway. They've got something to look forward to. Beate, she …'

It was four years ago now and thinking about her didn't hurt so much any more. As a matter of fact, the pain had begun again just before I started talking about her.

'I don't know exactly when I knew he was playing around with somebody else,' Wenche Andresen said. 'But I caught on. Finally. And it had already been going on for years. Her name is Solveig.' She said it with a long drawn-out hissing 's' sound which made you think of a snake. Maybe the serpent in Eden.

'Sometimes I ask myself if maybe I … if it wasn't my fault. If the marriage died first and then he looked for somebody else. Or was it the other way around? But why did he have to? You men!'

She glared at me. I was on trial now. But it didn't bother me much. I was used to it.

'You can't ever control yourselves. If somebody eggs you on you've got to go for it. You can't seem to stop yourselves.'

'The same goes for women,' I said. 'I mean, some women.'

'But you're the worst! There are more unfaithful husbands

and more disappointed wives in this world than the other way around.'

I shrugged. 'Well … who worked out those statistics? UNESCO?'

She banged her glass on the table and pointed at me. 'And another thing is, you always stick up for each other. Jonas was like that. Whenever we heard about this sort of thing he always said we shouldn't judge, there are always two sides to it. Two sides! But I never would have believed, I never dreamed I'd ever be in the same boat.'

Her eyes dimmed again and she said one word almost to herself: 'Disappointed …'

She filled her glass and looked at me. Puzzled. 'Don't you drink?'

'I do. But I'm driving.'

'Obviously I could have chosen somebody else,' she said. There was a pause. Thoughtful. 'I could have married somebody else.' Another pause. 'There were certainly others.'

On the TV, a dark-haired man was silently holding and shaking a blonde, leering at her. A door opened and another man came in. He looked confused. Then he let out a yell that never made it out of the set.

'But after I met Jonas … there weren't any others. That's how love is. Blind and deaf and with no sense of smell. Love never looks ten years ahead. It sees as far as the end of its nose – if it sees that far.'

'What's love? The woman in the dark glasses sitting over there at the corner table?' I said.

She looked uncertainly at me. 'What?'

She stood up. A little unsteadily. 'And we were so happy those first years. I'll show you …'

She went to the bookcase and got out a photograph album, came back and sat on the arm of my chair. It bothered me having her that close. She opened the album and laid it in my lap. Leaned down over me and pointed at the dark pages. 'See?'

It was summer. Wenche Andresen and her husband stood on one of those colourless beaches by a green, sun-dazzled sea. A chalk-white, freshly painted hotel in the background. Their bodies were young and brown, and their teeth were strong and white. They were smiling like kids at a funfair.

'Tenerife,' she said. 'Summer of 1970. That's when Roar was conceived. And look at this one. September. We were in the mountains. Jonas had a week off and I'd just been to the doctor. We were so happy.'

I looked. It could have been the same photograph except for the clothes and setting. They were on a mountain. There was a low grey stone hut in the background to their right. The grass was the colours of autumn and the sky a vivid blue. Her hair blew in the wind. They were wearing heavy sweaters. And they smiled and smiled. Her hair was longer and a little lighter then. His was longish and thick. He had sunglasses on in both snapshots. He was good-looking. Broad-shouldered. In good shape.

She turned the pages and more pictures flickered by. Jonas and Wenche at a party. His arm around her and a big smile for the photographer. Hair growing low on his forehead. The two of them dancing, looking at me and laughing. Then Wenche alone, lovingly photographed on Mount Fløien. Jonas alone on Constitution Day. Standing in front of a flag-decked wooden house somewhere in the mountains: his same joyous smile but a little more forehead showing.

She turned to baby pictures. Roar as an infant in a baby's

bath. In his crib. In a chair. Too young to focus yet. In a garden with blossoming fruit trees and a blue mountain across shining water. Must have been Hardangerfjord. Roar was reaching toward an older grey-haired woman and a younger man with dark hair combed straight back.

Family photographs. The same garden. White furniture and people posed as for a class picture. Children of different ages and Wenche Andresen with Roar in her arms.

'That was at home,' she said.

The door bell rang. She looked at me and at the clock. 'Shall I?' I said.

'No. I'd better …'

I stayed in the living room with the album in my lap. Listened. I could hear her talking softly even through the closed door.

I flipped through the album again, to a time before Jonas Andresen, to a time when she wore pigtails and her face was girlish and round.

In one snapshot she was staring lovingly up at a young man whose blond curly hair stuck straight up. It must have been warm. His shirt was open at the neck. He had a nice face, an open smile – and the body under the shirt hinted that he'd be considerably heavier one day. In another picture she was walking on a gravel road somewhere, hand in hand with a thin, dark-haired boy a head taller than she. He wore a dark suit, white shirt and a tie and she was wearing a flowered dress with a full skirt. She was looking at the camera. Talking and laughing.

Maybe Wenche Andresen should have chosen one of these two instead of Jonas. Maybe they'd also deserved to have been more to her than just a couple of snapshots in an old album, a couple of squares of forgotten life.

I heard the outside door close and saw she was out in the kitchen. Then she came in and said, 'It wasn't anything.'

She sat back down on the arm of the chair, rested her hip against my shoulder and upper arm. I closed the album and put it on the table. Emptied my glass.

'I'd better be thinking about getting home,' I said.

I looked up at her. She looked at me with those huge dewy eyes. 'I have more wine.'

'I don't think it's …' I said.

She sighed.

'You look sad,' I said. 'Don't. It's going to work out. I'll talk to the youth club leader in the morning. Drop by and see you later if that's okay.'

She nodded.

'Just to be sure everything's all right,' I said.

She smiled but it was sad.

I stood up. She still sat on the armrest. I reached down and gently stroked her hair. 'Wenche Andresen is dressed in mourning,' I said, mostly to myself.

She looked up at me. Her lips were trembling.

So I bent and kissed her. Carefully. As I'd kiss a child. Then our lips opened. Searching. Tender.

She melted against me. I could feel her warmth, her fingers on my back and around my neck. I closed my eyes and slept. A thirty-second Sleeping-Beauty trance. And then the picture of Roar bound and gagged up in the hut broke into the dream. I squeezed my eyes together and opened them. Hers were closed. I gently freed myself and went out into the entrance hall.

The spell was broken. Now she wouldn't look at me. She stood like a shy teenager, almost hiding behind the door jamb.

I got my jacket and went to the door.

'See you, Wenche,' I said and nearly didn't recognise my own voice.

She nodded and finally looked up. Her eyes had turned almost violet. Because of wonder or worry? Or for another reason? They didn't look as if birds might fly out of them now. They looked as if they led to dark tunnels, to smoke-filled cellar rooms, to rooms with garishly painted walls, to opium dens. To villages deep in the jungle.

I smiled stiffly, shut the door on those eyes, and walked along the balcony. Took the lift down. Got in my car. Drove. Didn't come to until I was back in the city.

12

I woke the next morning with heartburn, a stiff neck and eyes full of sand. Sleet and rain pawed at the window. The light was straining itself through a sieve, and across the alley the clouds were about even with the roof-tops.

I got out of bed and lay on the floor. Three sets each of twenty neck exercises and then thirty push-ups which left me lying flat and gasping. That took care of the neck.

Then I went to the kitchen and mixed the apostate Boy Scout's morning toddy: a glass of ice-cold milk and two Titralacs. That took care of the stomach.

I poured lukewarm salt-water into an eye-glass and bathed my eyes. It didn't fix them permanently but it did get rid of some of the sand. I was now ready for a shower, breakfast and a new struggle for survival.

I checked the office to make sure that it was still there. After a little trouble, I was able to get in touch with Gunnar Våge, the youth club leader. Told him I was coming but not why. Then I was in the car and on my way.

The roads were wet and slippery and there was frost on the grass. I could see a long open wound of new unwelcome snow on the Lyderhorn. Suddenly it was winter again.

The youth club was located in the first of the four high-rises. I walked through the main entrance. Two signs hung on the wall to the right. One of them, made of yellow metal and shaped like an arrow, said *Air-Raid Shelter*. It pointed towards a cellar door which was wedged ajar. The other was hand-painted in fresh teenage-type colours. It said *Y-Club. Youth Leader.* A red arrow on it pointed in the same direction.

I followed the arrows down the cellar stairs. It was one of those grey cement stairways which look as if they lead you straight to the catacombs. The right-hand wall was marked with a stream of red arrows. You didn't need much imagination to find your way. Then I walked past a row of storage rooms, all of them fitted with unusually solid padlocks, stopped in front of an iron door with the same triple greeting: *Air-Raid Shelter. Y-Club. Youth Leader.*

It was a large low-ceilinged concrete room, simply furnished with a long table, some benches, stools, rickety slat-back chairs. The walls were decorated with posters of pop stars, football players and a couple in a sunset. There was also a picture of Per Kleppe, the Minister of Finance. I didn't quite understand what he was doing there but it looked as if he'd been used as a dart board. There were as many holes in him as there were in his budget.

A worn brown-painted piano stood in one corner. And on one wall a sign in dayglo colours said: *Stop Smoking and Start Jogging!* Some kind of poetry! A wooden door stood ajar at the other end of the room. Light oozed through the crack. I knocked.

'Come in.'

I accepted the challenge.

It was a small office with pine-panelled walls and a yellow-brown desk which looked as if it had been bought at a flea market. A large calendar displaying all the months of the year hung on the wall. Some dates were marked with circles, others with squares. There was also a poster of a white mountaintop framed by the needles of a red-brown pine branch. A little bookcase held loose-leaf notebooks, magazines, mimeographed circulars and worn comics. An old black Remington with keys the size of bar stools stood on the desk, but you couldn't tell whether it worked or was just part of the decoration.

The man behind the desk had an animal's big brown eyes. He wasn't much past thirty, but he was bald except for a fringe of thin curly blond hair hanging down over his ears and neck. It looked funny.

He looked as sad as his eyes. Dark stubble edged his face with a band of mourning. He was wearing a brown polo-neck and grey corduroy trousers. When he stood up I saw he was quite heavyset. He stretched out a pale hand. 'Veum? Is that right?'

I nodded.

'Gunnar Våge. Have a seat.' He waved me to one of those slat-backed chairs. He himself settled into a large office chair with arms as broad as jumping skis.

There was the kind of note-taking silence which sometimes happens when two people meet for the first time.

I studied him more closely. Pale oily eyebrows with a little red pimple in between. Dark half-moons under his eyes. A little tic flicking in the corner of his right eye. One earlobe was longer than the other, and he'd clearly had problems shaving around his nose. He'd left some whiskers and a cut was slowly healing.

'Finished playing Sherlock Holmes?' he said. 'Find anything interesting?'

'You use a straight razor but your hand shakes when you try shaving around your nose. Fear of castration. A domineering mother. Anxiety at being alone. Isn't that how you people solve all your problems?' I said.

He smiled sourly. 'Not all of them. How do you people solve yours? With your right fists?'

'Depends on the problems you mean. You know a guy they call Joker?'

He nodded slowly and his mouth looked resigned. 'It's about Joker.' He didn't say 'again', but then he didn't have to. The word hung in the air.

'Problems with him before?' I said.

He didn't answer right away. He stroked a thumb slowly along the desk, opened a drawer, looked in it, closed it. Then he looked at me long and searchingly.

'I believe I'm one of the few people who've made some kind of contact with – Johan,' he said. 'I believe he respects me in a way. In some way. I ... When I first came here he had to test me. Obviously. The previous leader was sent to the funny farm. He's out now and I hear he's better, but just mention Joker to him and he cries like a baby. So I knew what I was getting into before I came. Maybe I don't look so tough – I mean, not to a detective ...'

He paused for effect, to see if he'd hooked me, but I let the line silently float by. I don't bite all that easily.

'But I can be very tough,' he said. 'It doesn't involve muscles or anything like that. Has to do with your attitude. If you can make kids see you understand and respect them and want them to be okay and to decide for themselves as much as possible, then maybe they respect you.

'Get them involved, direct them – where you want them to go – show them the friendship they almost never get and never will accept at home, be their pal without looking down at them – but set limits. Most of them need limits.

'Anyway, a kid like Johan needs them. When he shows up

here and waves his knives I take them away from him. It's as simple as that. Then he can come back and ask for them. A day or two later.

'I remember the first time. We had a get-together down here one evening. Cokes. Buns some of the girls had baked. There was dancing. Singing. One boy read a poem he'd written. And then Joker showed up. He'd been drinking. Didn't like the look of one of the boys. He pulled his knife. There was a lot of screaming. I turned off the loudspeaker and there was dead silence.

'I went over to Johan. He'd shoved the other kid up against the wall. Put my hand on his shoulder. Swung him around. Looked him in the eye and said: Give me the knife. He stood there looking furious. I said: Give me the knife. I need it for the buns. Unless you want them without jam.

'Somebody began laughing and I could see him getting madder. They weren't laughing at him, naturally. They didn't dare and he knew it. Then he started laughing. And so I got the knife and I sliced two hundred buns with a switchblade.'

His hand wandered over his skull as if it were searching for new growth. 'The next day, just about now ... Well, he'd already asked me that same evening if he could have his knife back. Stop by tomorrow, I said. So he did. He stood in that doorway there. Tall and dark and as unsure of himself as a three-year-old. What about the knife? he said. I got it out and asked him to sit down. Put it on the desk between us. Then I asked him some questions, tried to start him talking. Not much happened that first time. Or the second. But gradually... For a while he was almost a steady customer.

'That first time he felt he had to act tough. On his way out, he folded the knife, stuck his thumbs in his pockets, gave me a hard look and said: Don't ever take my knife away from me again, mister. And then he left. But later, it was as if he had to pull his knife just so I could take it away from him. Then he could come back the next day. He obviously needed to talk. All macho teenagers are lonely little boys. And he's had a tough time.'

'Could be,' I said. 'But so do the people who get in his way. It's tough on them, too.'

'Anything special in mind?'

'Well. A person hears – and sees – certain things.'

'Listen, Veum. I don't know why you're here and I don't know who asked you to come. But if you're here to clean things up like some kind of hero in a western, you're talking to the wrong person. Private detectives can't ever be social workers.'

'I graduated from Social Work School myself. Stavanger. 1969. I worked in child care. Five years. Not that that necessarily means anything.'

'But you don't work in child care now. You make money out of other people's problems. I suppose social work didn't pay well enough.'

'If you think it's the money, you're welcome to read my bank book. Any time. It's as wide open as an old whore and as loaded as a temperance preacher. Don't forget to take your magnifier. The size of the deposits'll make you dizzy. I gave social work five years of my life and I mean gave. And I mean five years. It was before the Workers Protection Act and … okay, I had three weeks' holiday but the rest of the time I couldn't tell the difference between Sundays and the rest of the week. My wife couldn't either. When I had a wife.

'And after social work had used me for five years, chewed up my energies, my marriage and all that shit – then it spat me out because I made one little mistake. So it's not the money, Våge. This is just another way of doing the same job. It's just that this way you're your own boss and you can't ever afford a holiday.'

'Anything more I can do for you?' Gunnar Våge said.

'I hear Joker – Johan if you insist – has a gang terrorising this neighbourhood. I hear single women, mothers, are forced up to that hut in the woods. I hear they have some pretty nasty experiences. I hear people who try to stop it get beaten to a pulp. I hear …'

He raised his hands as if he were defending himself. 'Hold it. Hold it. Hold it, Veum.' He swallowed. 'If you were a real detective, you'd stick to facts, not believe what you hear. Not depend on rumours. In the first place, the man you say was beaten to a pulp – well, that was some time ago now. A neurotic. A troublemaker. He jumped Johan outside the supermarket and beat him up.

'Well, if you beat up kids you've got to expect them to hit back. They jumped him one evening and he did get a few bruises. That's right. But three of the kids had to go to Casualty and he was released before they were. He moved out just after that. True. But he was evicted. Because of drinking and raising hell and because he knocked down the caretaker when he tried to cool things down. There was a warrant out for him but I never did hear what happened after that. And as for these other things …'

'Yes? Well?' I said.

His voice was full of denial. 'To tell you the truth, I don't believe them, Veum. Not unless I see them with my own eyes. People ought to know … Do you know what they say? They say that Våge, they say, he's on the side of those kids. They circulated a petition a few months ago. Wanted to shut down

the club. But not many signed. Most of the parents understand we need a youth club, a place for the kids to go to. If
we didn't have the club, we wouldn't have just one gang. We'd
have twenty and they'd be a lot worse than Johan's.'

'That's very likely,' I said. 'But we're talking about this one
gang. And angels they're not. Or if they are, they're certainly
not wearing kid gloves.' I pointed to my face which was still
marked by yesterday's to-do. 'I wasn't pretty before, and I'm
not any prettier because of the beauty treatment Joker and his
gang gave me up at the hut yesterday.'

'Maybe you were asking for it?'

'I was doing somebody a favour. I freed a stolen little boy.'

That shook him. 'What are you talking about?'

'We call it kidnapping in my part of the city. A little boy
named Roar. The other day they took his bike. Yesterday they
took him.'

'They didn't mean any harm.'

'Of course they didn't. He certainly didn't look as if they
did, with his hands tied behind his back, a filthy handkerchief
stuffed in his mouth and tear stains on his cheeks. He looked
just like a toy they'd been playing with and then got tired of.'

Gunnar Våge stood up and walked around the desk. 'Listen,
Veum. I'm a realist. I don't think these kids are angels. I don't
try understanding them to death. But I do try to understand
them and I know something about their backgrounds. Which
aren't pretty. Not always. And you can understand why some
of them are bitter. Angry at everything around them. Take
Johan for example ...'

He sat on the edge of the desk and folded his hands. He
reminded me of a minister just about to tell his favourite confirmation candidate that he too had jerked off when he was

young, but that it was something you grew out of when you were over ninety.

'He never had a father.' He thought that one over.

Began again. 'Or maybe he had a thousand fathers, if you see what I mean. I don't think his mother ever knew who got her pregnant. There were too many of them. And there still are too many of them. And there have been too many of them all Johan's life. People around here call her a whore. I've talked to her a bit about Johan. She's a bright woman when she's sober. Which isn't often. And she's the way she is because of her background. An orphanage, raped by one of the employees at thirteen, sent to a girls' home at fifteen. Got friendly with the Germans in the last years of the war and was branded for it afterwards.

'So Johan's had his problems. And he's not stupid. Not at all. He's smart. Lightning-fast on the uptake. With such a mother and such a brain there's only one way he could have gone. Or maybe two ways. He could have been an artist or a psycho. And so he's a psycho.'

'He could still be a private investigator,' I said.

He looked icily at me. 'I know your type, Veum. Seen too many of them. You're so afraid of life you build a wall of wise-cracks around you. You've got a smart answer for all the human tragedies and you'd sell your mother for a good joke.'

'My mother's dead and I don't know any good jokes.'

'Right. Ha ha ha. You're the living example of what I'm talking about. I think you'd better go, Veum. I don't think I really like you.'

I stayed put. 'Where can I find Johan's mother?'

He jumped off the desk. Came over to me. Stood with his legs wide apart. 'I really don't think you should get involved in that, Veum. I think you can ruin more than you realise. You're the right type. I try to do a decent job here, give the kids something. Help them. You could call me a sort of gardener and I'd just as soon you didn't start stomping around in my flower beds …'

'Not even to weed them?'

'Piss off, Veum. If there's one thing I do not like, it's talking about myself. I won't say I'm an idealist or anything like that, but I do try to do something with my life. I was once an electrical engineer, as a matter of fact. Had a well-paid job in industry. The private sector. High salary. I could have had a house, a wife, the whole ball of wax – if I hadn't looked around one day and asked myself: what the hell are you doing with your life, Gunnar? Look around you. You work for one of the worst polluters on the Bergen peninsula. You wander around in these air-conditioned offices and you plan new projects, new pollution. You work out how to cram free waterfalls into new tunnels. You plan new housing developments in open parklands. And in the city where you live people need help. Real live people. Kids.

'It wasn't a political conversion. At least not directly. I didn't become a revolutionary in the sense that I thought every revolution has to begin at the beginning – with each generation. Our generation, yours and mine, has already had it. We're a bunch of anxiety-ridden clowns who never had our parents' revolution or our grandparents' Jesus to believe in. We're a generation of cynical atheists, Veum. And you, you shit, are the prototype. Just as I was a few years back.'

He held his breath before he continued. For someone who didn't like talking about himself he did a pretty good monologue.

'So I got out of the rat race,' he said. 'I did what you did – went to Social Work School and began to do something. Well. Look at us. At least I go on doing what I was trained for, but you ...?' His mouth was contemptuous.

'I do it, too. In my own way. In another way,' I said.

He studied me. 'Do tell! Outside the establishment, right? Typical post-war individualist. A lone wolf. Outside all establishment, all the rules. You're playing hippy too late, Veum. Ten years too late.'

I stood up. 'Sorry, Våge. Got to go, but it's been great sitting here listening to you. My wife would love you. My ex-wife, I mean.'

'Right,' he said. 'Self-pity strikes again. The telling symptom. That and alcoholism. Or maybe you're so with it you do hash instead.'

'Aquavit,' I said. 'Just for the record.'

'And so you sit by yourself these dark winter evenings and whine because you're lonely, right?' He came even closer. I could smell coffee on his breath. 'But some of us have chosen loneliness, Veum. Some of us have chosen to live alone. Because maybe it's just as valuable. Because maybe it gives you a better chance to give yourself to what you believe in. Don't think I couldn't have got married. Many times, in fact.'

'Many times?' I said and tried to sound as if I envied him. Wasn't so hard to do.

'But no. I said no. When it got right down to that point in my life – that turning point – I told myself: if you've come this far alone, you can go the rest of the way by yourself.' He looked around his office. 'This is home.' He nodded towards the emptiness behind me. 'And the ones out there – they're my kids. What more can I ask for if I can help them?'

'A spoonful of love morning, noon and night?' I said.

'Love isn't something a person takes or is given. Like cod liver oil. Love's something you give – if you've got somebody to give it to.'

'Right,' I said. And that was that. I was out of jokes, out of all the things a post-war individualist ought to say. There was only one thing I could tell myself and that was to leave.

I didn't say goodbye. I think he knew I had a lump in my throat and couldn't trust my voice.

I was blind with tears but I found my way out. Slowly. Past a stream of red arrows.

13

I stood in the road for a while. Now what should I do? Was there anything more I could do about any of this? I looked down at my watch. Looked up at the high-rise where Wenche Andresen lived, at the ninth-floor balcony, at Roar's window, at the kitchen window and at her front door. A light was on in the kitchen.

I walked up to Wenche's building, went in, and over to the lift.

While I waited, a woman came and stood by me. I said hello cautiously – and she looked at me as if I'd made an obscene gesture. Perhaps people out here didn't say hello while they waited for lifts. Perhaps they never said hello. It was a different world out here and I'd better not forget it. Then she got hold of her fear and smiled: a quick broad smile.

She looked good. She had been beautiful. Ten years ago. But she was over fifty and those first five decades had left plough furrows on her face. Somebody had sowed and somebody had reaped, but God only knew who'd made a profit out of the crop.

Her hair had been black but now it was striped with grey. Decorative. If you like zebras. Brown eyes but bloodshot, and her mouth was bitter – as if she'd just drunk one too many Camparis.

She wasn't very tall. I couldn't tell whether she was thin or plump. She was wearing a billowy dark brown fur coat. It too had seen better days but it could still warm a frozen soul in a frozen body. Lovely legs. She must have replaced them some-where along the way. They belonged to a thirty-year-old.

When the lift arrived, I held the door for her. She didn't smile. She'd already used up her quota.

The lift was long and narrow. Like a coffin. It looked as if it had been designed to haul pianos and beds and sofas up twelve storeys. She walked all the way in and I stood by the door.

'Which floor do you want?' I said.

'Seven.' Hers was a whisky voice. Too many drinks and not enough sleep. There were bags under her eyes.

The lift stopped between the fourth and fifth floors. The light in the ceiling blinked twice and then settled down. Just like the lift.

The woman took a deep breath. 'Oh dear God. Not again!' She looked at me as if it were my fault. 'It's stuck.'

'That's what I thought,' I said.

I could see ten or fifteen centimetres of the fifth-floor door. The rest was concrete wall.

Being stuck in a lift is a totally special experience reserved for people who live in so-called civilised countries. In countries where they build houses higher than five storeys. The world stops when you're stuck in a lift. It doesn't matter much if you're fifty or fifteen. You feel old. Very old.

There could be a war going on out there. The Russians or the Americans or the Chinese could have landed. There could be a power failure or an earthquake or a hurricane. People could be running around naked in the streets, carving hunks out of each other. Or a thousand tons of unicorns could be chasing virgins. None of it has anything to do with you. You are stuck.

Claustrophobia isn't one of my phobias but just the same I

could feel my forehead and back getting a little sweaty. Nobody likes being stuck in a lift. You get stuck? You want to get out. As simple as that.

And we were stuck.

The woman I was stuck with didn't look as if she were enjoying it either. Her face had sort of expanded: eyes, nostrils, mouth. And she was breathing heavily. Her knees seemed to wobble. She braced herself against the wall with a limp white hand and held the other to her forehead.

'Maybe we should introduce ourselves. My name's Veum,' I said.

She looked as if she didn't believe it. 'I … We're stuck. Stuck!' Her voice sounded hysterical.

'I've heard that when claustrophobes get into situations like this they sometimes strip. Don't. I'm too young. I couldn't take it,' I said.

She took a step back. 'What in the world are you babbling about? Get us out of here. Out. I've got to get out.'

She'd turned around so her back was against the wall. She began hammering the other one with her useless little fists. 'Help,' she yelled. 'Help.'

I pushed the button marked Alarm and heard a bell ring somewhere. I hoped it wasn't one of those so-called 'comfort bells', the kind they install to reassure people who get stuck but which can't be heard more than a few metres away. I hoped that this bell was ringing somewhere else – in the caretaker's heaven, wherever he usually hung out – and that he was at home.

The woman in the old fur coat had sagged to the floor. She was sobbing. I squatted beside her. 'I've rung the caretaker. It can't be very much longer.'

'How long can we last? How long will the oxygen hold out?'

'Oxygen?' I looked around. 'Long enough. I once heard about a Swedish cleaning woman. She got stuck for forty days in a goods lift in a factory. For the entire general holiday. But she survived. Of course, all she had was soapy drinking water.'

'Forty days! But my God, man ... Dear God! I didn't think we'd ...'

'No, no, no. I only meant there's no problem with the air supply.'

I looked cautiously around. It was already a little close in here. Warm. But one thing was certain: the air wasn't a problem. I sweated a little more.

I looked up. There was no trapdoor in the ceiling like there used to be in the old days. The kind you could climb through and feel as if you were sitting in the bottom of a volcanic crater. They were always such a comfort.

To my surprise I realised I was sweating even more now. You should never take a lift, I told myself. Lifts are for the old and for babies. Not for big strong ...

An old rat started crawling around in my belly. I looked from wall to wall to wall of the lift. It seemed smaller now: narrower. More cramped.

Suddenly I knew my fists wanted to beat on the walls, break them down, that my voice wanted to yell: Help! Help! I even felt faint.

I coughed loudly to reassure myself. 'It won't be long before we're out. Not long now, Fru.'

She'd collapsed. Sat staring at the floor. Knees drawn up. She'd lost her suburban modesty. She wore black panties under the brown tights and I saw she was plumper higher up than her legs had hinted at.

Then I looked away. I'm a decent fellow. Never take advantage of helpless women. Or maybe I'm afraid of sex? I could certainly stand there and think about it for a while, analyse myself. I'd been pretty good at it once. That was just before I'd requested treatment.

I listened to the sounds of the building around us. Concrete transmits sounds in the strangest ways. I heard rushing in the pipes and something which reminded me of coded signals being tapped from one jail cell to another. Maybe the whole building was full of lifts with people stuck in them two by two. And nobody could get out and nobody would come and help us. Maybe this was hell.

I looked at her again. Spend eternity – with her? I was really sweating now. I couldn't think of one relaxing thing. I tried. I thought of summer. A white sun-dappled beach, an open blue-green sea, high blue sky. Lots of air. Air. But all the other people on the beach spoke Danish.

I thought about beer, golden beer in full glasses topped with white fresh foam. About red-and-white checked tablecloths, an open veranda, a woman. It was Beate. So that wasn't relaxing either. Then I thought about Wenche Andresen.

'Hello!'

'Hello. Hello.' My voice worked the third time. 'Hello!'

Someone was beating on the door to the fifth floor.

'Somebody there? Are you stuck?' It was a rough, caretaker's voice.

'We're here and we're stuck,' I said. 'Can you get us out?'

Something was happening. I stopped sweating and the woman raised her head and began listening.

'Of course I can. It's those damned kids again. One of the fuses has blown. Just wait. It'll be five or ten minutes.'

'Thanks,' I whispered to the heavy footsteps as they moved away.

Then fifteen minutes went by. The woman and I had nothing to discuss. Just one common interest: getting out. I looked at my watch. Could she be at home?

The woman had already stood up, tidied her hair, and was fanning her face with a little ecru handkerchief. Her eyes were red-rimmed but it didn't make much difference. She looked almost the same as she had when she got in the lift – maybe a couple of years older. I bet I did, too. That's one of the things about getting stuck in a lift. You age so quickly. And sometimes you collapse.

Before she left me, she suddenly shook my hand. 'Solfrid Brede,' she said in that same husky voice.

'Nice meeting you,' I said.

Then she was gone and I rode up two more floors. Hello and goodbye, Solfrid Brede. Maybe we'll meet again in another lift, somewhere else in hell. You never know, Solfrid Brede, you never know …

I opened the door and stepped out. Wenche Andresen was standing there waiting. She wasn't alone. A man was with her.

14

He was tall. Strong. Athletic. Probably in his late forties or early fifties. His face was lean and tough. Dark, deep-set eyes, a little hidden by bushy grey-black eyebrows. What I could see of his hair had the same grizzled tone and that, together with his slightly wary stance, reminded me of a wolf. He was wearing the uniform of a naval commander and he looked as if he expected me to snap to attention the minute I saw him.

Wenche Andresen looked a little embarrassed. 'Va ... Veum?' she said, glancing back and forth between the wolf and me.

'I wanted to find out how Roar is,' I said.

'He's fine,' she said. 'But I'm just on my way to work. This is my boss, Commander ...' She mumbled something.

He repeated it, pronouncing each letter as if he were talking to a moronic sailor. 'Richard Ljosne,' he said, and shook my hand with his strong muscular fingers.

'Veum,' I said.

Then there was silence. Wenche Andresen was still looking embarrassed. There were dark circles under her eyes and she was very pale.

'I wasn't feeling good so I called and said I'd be in a little later today and so Richard – so Ljosne – said he could come and pick me up because ...'

'We have some very important papers to get out today,' he said. 'And Wenche's the only one who knows the format. Otherwise we'd have to get a substitute and it would take hours to explain it to her.'

His voice was deep and musical. A voice I could have fallen for if I'd been ten years younger and a woman. But I wasn't. Wenche Andresen was still embarrassed.

I looked at her mouth. Thought about the previous evening, about how it had felt getting acquainted with her mouth, learning about the contours of her lips against mine.

I looked at Richard Ljosne's mouth. A large, wide mouth with narrow red lips and sharp yellow-white teeth. The stubble on his face was blue-grey. The hair curled high on his throat and around his neck. His eyebrows met.

'Well, don't let me keep you,' I said. 'I just wanted to find out how things were – as I said.' Then I added, 'Listen. Where does Joker live?'

Wenche Andresen looked toward the high-rise further down the hill. 'Over there. With his mother.'

'Well. Thanks.' I held the lift door for them. As I was about to close it she said, 'But aren't you coming, Veum?'

'No thanks,' I said. 'I'll walk.'

Then I let go of the door and it dosed slowly behind them.

I kept thinking about her mouth and I wasn't sure that was a good idea. Not today. Not now.

I walked along the balcony in the opposite direction from her flat to the south end of the building. From there I could see Wenche Andresen and Richard Ljosne strolling towards a big black car which could have been a Mercedes. That's the way it looked from the ninth floor anyway.

That's how they go out of my life, I thought. They just get into a car and drive away.

But I had an uneasy feeling it wasn't going to be like that, that I'd see both of them again and that it wouldn't be especially pleasant. For any of us.

I walked slowly down the stairs and wondered what to do next.

15

I could do one of two things: go back to the office or do something constructive. Or something which looked as if it were. The office wasn't going to disappear and the only thing that could happen to the phone was that somebody would come and take it away because I hadn't paid the bill. No matter what, I was better off not going to the office.

Wenche Andresen had said that Joker lived with his mother in the high-rise across from hers. Gunnar Våge had told me that Joker's real name was Johan Pedersen.

I could see if he was home. I could recommend a course in Norwegian floral painting to fill his spare time. Or maybe an evening seminar in the history of the picaresque novel. Today's educational system offers so many choices. If you don't know something, you can learn about it and it doesn't cost much. A little effort maybe, but that's all. If you take a ten-hour course at the Free School or the Workers' Information Association you can learn how to make the traditional regional costume they wear in Hardanger or how to handle a pocket calculator. Or you can learn how to paint almost as well as Edvard Munch or how to speak Spanish. Handy for your next trip to the Canary Islands when you want to talk to Swedes. Or you can learn how to take perfect back-lit photographs of your mother-in-law and screaming kids. So Joker had a lot to look forward to if only he were willing. Or at home.

I found the name on a letter box inside the lift room. H.

Pedersen, 4th Floor, it said, but I didn't take the lift. I walked up. I was glad they didn't live on the tenth floor. If this kept up I could cut out my weekly jogging.

Hildur and Johan Pedersen, mother and son, lived nearest the lift. The name was on the door. I looked in the kitchen window but didn't see anything except white curtains which had needed washing a long time ago.

I rang the bell.

A couple of years passed but I can be very patient. I rang again.

A couple more years went by before I heard a voice from far inside the flat. It sounded like the stomach rumblings of a man who's standing at the very end of the bus. No way you could understand the words. It was either a deep female or a high male voice. I bet on the first and waited.

The woman who opened the door and looked suspiciously at me had a face only a son could love. At first glance anyway. The next time I was short of nightmares I'd try remembering it.

It was a face which had seen too many nights and too few days. It was a face which had been through life's darkest corridors and had never got as far as the daylight. A face you could like if you saw it on the far side of a dark room you were leaving.

Hildur Pedersen's hair wasn't grey or brown or black or red. It was uneven tufts of all those colours, and it hadn't seen brush or comb for a couple of months. It stuck out in all directions like the mane of an ancient lion in a dilapidated circus. It was the right frame for her face.

Maybe Hildur Pedersen had been really pretty twenty years and several kilos ago. I've never been good at guessing people's weights but I'd have bet she was in the one-twenty kilo class and about thirty of them were in her face.

Her eyes had sunk between folds of fat and her nose had to be at least twenty centimetres long for its tip to stick out at all. She had a mouth somewhere but it wasn't easy to find it among all those chins. But one of them was painted red.

Her whole head, and it was a big one, rested on a collar of fat and the body under it was huge. She was an avalanche of a woman and I wouldn't have wanted to be in her path if my life had depended on it.

She opened her mouth and I caught the unmistakable smell of cheap booze. 'What do you want?'

A harsh but highly educated voice. As if she'd been born and raised in silver-spoon Kalfare but had never found her way home again.

'A little chat. About old times. About nothing much.'

'Who are you?'

'My name's Veum and I'm a sort of private investigator.'

'Sort of? Either you are or you aren't.'

'Yes. Well. But it's always embarrassing to come right out and say it. If you see what I mean.'

'I certainly do. And if I went around looking like you, I'd really be embarrassed.'

'You would?' I had a lot of snappy answers ready but I didn't want to be thrown out before I got in. And I sort of liked the lady. She sounded as if she'd be fun to play ping-pong with for half an hour or so.

'Aren't you going to ask me in to admire the view?' I said.

'Take your vodka neat?'

'I'd sooner aquavit.'

'I've only got vodka. No mixers. No coffee or tea. No milk. But there's water if you get thirsty. Or there's vodka. Tastes like hell but it works wonders. For a while.'

As she talked she began to ooze back into the flat as if she were being pulled by a powerful invisible force. But she left the door open. I took it as an invitation, followed her in and closed the door behind me.

The flat was almost identical to Wenche Andresen's – except for the contents. The furniture was worn out. The chairs and sofas had held up too many kilos, the tables had been through too many drinking contests. You could see the floor through the rugs. Somebody had performed euthanasia on the plants in the window if they hadn't died by themselves, and the newspapers under the coffee table were six months old. The team which had won then was now in the bottom of the second division. Where we all end up sooner or later.

Hildur Pedersen gathered up a half-full bottle of vodka and two dirty glasses, and sat down in the middle of a sofa which sagged like a hammock. She waved a huge hand at an exhausted armchair the colour of old pigeon shit.

For one brief moment I saw a glass-clear azure spring sky (the way the skies always are over our childhood's sun-gilded streets) and a flock of pigeons flying. Over the low red roofs down towards Vågen and across Vågen toward Skoltegrunn's quay and the America-bound ships. And lagging behind all the other birds, in meaningless helpless somersaults, a tumbler pigeon came rolling and spinning in the air.

How many times I've felt like that – like a tumbler pigeon, always lagging a little behind the others. Too dizzy to be able to get an overall view of existence. With that blue sky below me and the red roofs above, I went swerving through life from one temporary landing to another, just like the tumbler pigeon. And now I was in a fossilised living room with a dinosaur of a woman.

Hildur Pedersen poured neat vodka into the glasses and pushed one towards me. The coffee table between us was yellow-brown, covered with the pale rings of many a glass and bottle, small scars from years of cigarette ash and a varnish of dust.

'Skål, Fatso,' she said and emptied the glass.

'Skål, Slim,' I said and took a cautious sip as I thought of the car in the car park and about getting home today. Preferably not hanging from a tow-truck.

'Spit it out. What do you want? Who's sent you to old Hildur?'

'Nobody's sent me. But what I want is – Johan.'

'Johan?' She said it as if it were the name of a distant relative. 'What about him?'

'I ran into him recently. Accidentally, you could say. Or maybe he ran into me. Or to put it another way, some of his mates ran into me. He stayed in the background.'

'What are you raving about?'

'Always had problems with him?'

'Problems? With Johan? What the hell do you think? Have you ever heard of anybody not having problems with their kids? Johan's been a problem from the time he was a month old – and I mean for the eight months before he was born. But that's how it is with most of them.'

'His father.'

'That fool!'

'You never married?'

'I wouldn't have married him if he imported vodka. Anyway, he was already married. A sailor, a happy sailor on shore leave in the big city. A real *stril*, a bumpkin from somewhere up in Sogn. Met him at the Starlight Ballroom and asked him home to my one-room flat in the Old Quarter. Top floor, with a view right into the house next door. The fool was so drunk I had to stuff him inside me. It wasn't what you'd call fun. But it was somebody to sleep with. Didn't have to wake up alone. But I've got to tell you I was bloody furious when I found out Johan was on the way!' She glowered at me as if I were guilty.

'I looked up his address and wrote him a letter. Asked for money. He called the next time he was in town. He was so nervous that he almost dropped the phone with every other word. He said of course he'd pay. He'd give me as much as I needed. He'd be glad to pay for the kid's food, clothes. Education. And there'd be no limit to it … as long as I didn't send any more letters. He'd had problems explaining to Madame who'd sent the first one. But that was his problem, right? A man shouldn't have a free ride with kids.'

'And then what happened?'

'Then what happened? What do you think? He's sent money every damned month. I had to promise not to name him as the father, but I've got a kind of insurance policy running around here somewhere, if you get what I mean. Said he was going to send me money, and he did.' She looked wonderingly down at the vodka bottle as if it delivered the money.

'And Johan?'

'Johan grew up. Not with the best of mothers, but at least he had a mother. He never went short. He got what he needed clothes, food, drink – until he was old enough to take care of himself. When he finished secondary school I said to him, now you're damn well finished with school, Johan. Get yourself a job and earn the butter for your bread. And if it's not butter, at least go for margarine.'

'What kind of job was it?'

'No idea. Ask him. I haven't had any … These last few years we've … I reckon I'm done with him. He lives here but he might as well be renting. We don't talk. He calls me a fat old whore. Won't answer me. And I know why.' She squinted drunkenly at me and poured more vodka into her glass.

'Are you a High and Dry or something? A member of AA? Mother's baby boy? Drink up and keep me company, damn it!'

'Sorry. But I'm driving. Have to keep my head above water.'

'So you're old enough to have a licence?'

'Got it the day before yesterday. Eighteenth birthday. I look over thirty-five in the photograph. The truth is I feel over sixty.'

'Your tongue's in the right place anyway.'

'It is. Right between my eyes. Why does Johan call you an … old whore?'

'Why do you think?'

I acted as if I were thinking, but she answered first. 'Because I won't tell him who his father is.'

'Why does he want to know? I mean, any special reason?'

'Ask him. If that fool had been my father, I'd have been better off not knowing. But you know how kids are.'

'I can remember.'

'They're always wanting to know things that aren't good for them. What's going to become of them, who their fathers are. Things like that. The fools.'

'But you haven't told him?'

'No. Not in – how many years is it – eighteen, nineteen? I've told him the same thing I told them at the Women's Clinic. No idea. There'd been so many. And that was that.

'But it wasn't like that then. There was a lull in my life then. I'd just been … very disappointed. And so here came another disappointment – in the middle of my life. Nine months of disappointment that never went away. I tell him, I don't know, Johan. It could have been anybody. Can't you tell me the name of one of them? he says. I say, I don't remember. There were so many of them. Not all of them introduced themselves. Not many left calling cards and the repeaters came for the booze. Is it so strange he calls me a …?'

Her gaze disappeared into the glass and when she suddenly looked up her eyes were wet. 'It's a hell of a life, isn't it? Veum?'

I nodded. 'Every other day,' I said.

'Every other day? You're damn lucky.'

I drank. Just for something to do. She found a well-used handkerchief and swabbed the upper part of her face as if she were digging ditches in June.

'Have you seen him since – the father?'

She drank from the bottle now and wouldn't look at me. 'No. Why should I? As long as he sends the money. He got this flat for me – for Johan's sake. Paid the down payment and everything. Otherwise I'd never have been able to afford it. And I would never go on welfare.'

'What's his name?'

Now she was looking at me again. 'None of your bloody business. Why are you asking about this ancient history? Nothing better to do? Go home and play with your electric trains or something.'

'You know Johan terrorises this neighbourhood, don't you? Mention him, people shiver. Did you know they call him Joker?'

Her eyes were like furled umbrellas. 'Who? Johan? That little twerp? I could mash him between my thumb and forefinger. If they're afraid of him, they're afraid of the evening breeze.'

'It's not just him. He's got a fair-sized gang and they think they're tough. Sometimes.' Without meaning to, I felt my face.

'He does have some mates who come here now and then. They sit in his room. Drink beer and smoke and play some bloody awful cassettes. But I never pay any attention to them. As long as there aren't any girls.' She suddenly looked pious. 'I won't stand for that kind of thing. Not in my house.'

I looked around her house. A picture hung crookedly over her head. A kind of painting of a kind of boat somewhere on a kind of lake. The proportions were all wrong. The fir trees on the far side of the water were taller than the ones on this side, and the boat was so big it took up almost the whole lake.

It reminded me of her. A boat too big for her little pond. A big woman whose life was all too confining. A life that hadn't had room in it for more than some wham-bam disappointments, a money order every month and some ghostly old memories.

Faces without names, faces that hadn't left anything behind but empty whisky bottles and had disappeared when the party was over.

I looked at her face. She was holed up in there somewhere. A long way back. The young girl of twenty or thirty years ago. The child who'd skipped up and down an alley, who'd bounced a ball against green-painted wooden walls along with other little girls but who later had kissed and hugged many too many and never the right ones.

But she was still holed up in there if the booze hadn't washed her away, hadn't washed her up on a faraway beach where you'd never find her. Hildur Pedersen from Bergen.

For some reason I thought of 1946. 1946. That was sort of the beginning for all of us. The war was over but the city was still paralysed. It wasn't until the fifties that it rose out of the ashes, set square high-rises on its crooked spine and let the past fall into ruins.

The America-bound boats gave up sailing and they built Flesland Airport. The Laksevåg ferry was shut down and they built a bridge over Puddefjord. They dug holes through the mountains and built housing developments where there'd been farms and forests and marshlands.

But that hadn't begun in 1946. It was still like the thirties then. Those who were already grown up during the war spat on their fists and started again. The old died away like the old houses they'd lived in. And there was no end to the possibilities for us who were still young.

Hildur Pedersen had been in full bloom in 1946. A beautiful young woman. Maybe a little overdeveloped but not excessively so. A beautiful young woman with full breasts and hips, swinging gaily down and along the alley with milk bottles in a brown net bag and a smile for everybody.

Joker hadn't been born yet, and Varg Veum ... He was a four-year-old with a mother who hadn't got cancer yet and a father who still was a conductor on the trolley to Minde.

But that trolley was also shut down and the father turned to dust like so many before him. But he was my father and I can still see him when I close my eyes. Small and sinewy, with the marks of the village still on him, the village he'd left when he was two and had come by boat to the city. When I close my eyes, I can still see the fierce harsh smile he always saved for those good rare times when he and I were alone and my mother hadn't yet got cancer.

When Johan Pedersen closes his eyes he can't see anything. He hasn't got a joker in his pack, no father who suddenly pops up between the jack and queen with his conductor's bag over his shoulder and his cap a little askew. Nobody who ever said, 'Hello! Anybody at home?'

1946. Four digits that contain a long-dead past, streets that are gone, houses that have fallen down, houses that have been demolished, people long since dead and dug up again, ships that have stopped sailing and trolleys that have been scrapped. 1946 – and the beginning of all of this.

'Where were you in 1946?' I said to Hildur Pedersen.

'In 1946? Why do you want to know? Are you nuts? Who the hell remembers where he was in 1946? I can't remember where the hell I was the day before yesterday. You ask too many questions, Veum. Can't you just shut up for a while?'

I nodded. I could shut up for a while.

Just the same, I didn't want to leave. I wanted to sit there and drink straight vodka with Hildur Pedersen. Silently. Until my legs melted and I'd have to drag myself by the arms to the door, out along the balcony and down all those steps to the car.

I didn't want to leave. But I finally did. When Hildur Pedersen began to nod, I quietly stood up, took the glass out of her big fist and set it carefully by the bottle – in the middle of the table. Screwed the cap on tight. There were still a few drops left, something to wake up to. If and when she woke.

Then I went slowly out of her life. For a while.

I ran into Gunnar Våge again. Outside the building. He grabbed my shoulder. 'Now where have you been, Veum?'

'What's it to you?'

'I told you to keep away from – Johan. Leave them alone, Veum. Him and his mother. Don't make things worse. You don't know what you're getting into out here. You can ruin more than you –'

'What can I get into out here? What can I ruin that isn't already ruined?'

'You don't understand anything. You're as cold as, as …'

'As?'

'Keep out of this, Veum. Stay the hell away.'

I stared into that distorted face. 'And where were you in 1946, Våge?'

Then I walked past him, got in the car and drove off without looking back. They didn't like me out there. For some reason or other they did not like me.

16

I let myself into the office. Turned on the light. Even though the sun was high over Løustakken somewhere behind that grey cloud cover, it was dreary out. Like the lights in a cinema before the show begins. Maybe the sun was about to go out. Maybe we'd wake up tomorrow in eternal darkness, in an eternal starry night, and there'd be a journey to ice and death and everlasting plains of frost.

The office was like a gallery in a museum. One nobody visited but where I was the guard for some reason. I sat behind the desk and opened the third drawer. The office bottle, round and lukewarm, was in there on the far left. I took it out and read the entire label as if for the first time. Water of life. The blood of the lonely. The comfort of tired wolves.

I unscrewed the cap and stuck the bottle in my mouth. The clear strong aquavit rinsed away the insipid aftertaste of Hildur Pedersen's vodka.

I wondered what I should do. Whether I had anything to do. Thought about the people I'd met these last several days. Roar. Wenche Andresen. Joker and his gang. Gunnar Våge and Hildur Pedersen. Wenche Andresen again – and the man in the naval uniform. Richard Ljosne. And Roar …

I thought of Thomas. Maybe I should call him, find out how he was, ask him if he ever happened to think of his father. I could call and ask if he wanted to come down to the office and keep me company. I could read to him. As I once had – the one evening I'd had off. The first chapter of *Winnie the Pooh*. His mother had had to read the rest. And all the other books. I'd begun to think of her as 'his mother' now. That at least was a step forward. Not Beate any more but 'the mother'.

But then I realised that he probably wasn't home yet and that he was too old for *Winnie the Pooh*. He was seven, and the last time I'd called he hadn't had time to talk. He was on his way to a football game with 'Lasse', his new father.

I lifted the receiver and listened to the dialling tone, listened to the ghosts of long-dead conversations, to the skeletons of women's soft voices, to the heavy tramp of men's. All of them gone now. All of them dead.

When I hung up, the phone rang.

I let it ring five times before I picked up the receiver. It was a great sound and I could certainly wait another half-minute before I talked to one of my creditors.

After the fifth ring I said in my business voice, 'Veum speaking.'

'Oh, Varg, I was afraid you wouldn't be in. This is Wenche. Wenche Andresen.'

It was Wenche. Wenche Andresen. Her clear voice sounded like distant bells over the line, and the phone's black jaw gaped wider as it began smiling. The corners of its mouth turned up a little anyway. I smiled back. 'Oh, hello.' I could hear the hopeful tone in my voice. 'How are you?'

'Better. Not too bad. I'm calling from the office. I just wanted to … Thanks for the other evening, by the way. It was – nice. I haven't had such a nice time – for quite a while.'

'I haven't either.' If she'd enjoyed herself with me, it didn't say much for her social life, but I couldn't tell her that.

'I wondered in fact if you could do me a favour. I mean, I insist on paying.'

'It's no big deal. What is it you want me ... Is there something I can –'

'As an investigator you do all kinds of jobs, don't you?'

'There are all kinds and all kinds.' Some things I didn't do and there were a lot of things nobody asked me to.

'I just wondered if you could look up Jonas for me. My husband. The man I was married to.'

It sounded like the kind of assignment I didn't take. 'What am I supposed to do with him?' Steer him into a back street and beat him up? Hit him over the head with an empty bottle? Tie him backwards on an old horse and chase him out of town? If I could find an old horse?

'Just talk to him. I can't cope with it. I'll just start complaining and making a scene and I can't stand any more scenes. I don't want to see him again, Varg. Do you know what I mean?'

'Well ...'

'It's the money, you know.'

'What money?'

'Not the monthly payments. He's almost always on time. He has been late a couple of times and I've had to get an advance at the office or borrow. And when Jonas does send me money, I've had to pay back what I borrowed and then there isn't any more. And Roar wears out his clothes. They all do at his age and if his bike had been stolen, too ... They're always wanting something, right?'

'Seems so. That's what it says in the papers. In the ads.'

'But it's not about the payments. It's the insurance money.'

'What insurance money?'

'We had a joint life-insurance policy. And when we separated we agreed to cash it in. It's not a lot, but … Jonas was going to take care of it and then we'd split the proceeds. But I haven't seen any of it yet and I really need the money.'

'Maybe I could lend you some,' I lied.

'I know that, Varg.' She knew more about it than I did. 'Thank you. But I'm tired of borrowing. I won't borrow again – from friends, acquaintances or anybody.'

I wondered for a second whether I fitted into the category of friends or acquaintances or anybody. 'I suppose I could do it. Talk to him.'

'Oh, could you, Varg? Thank you so much. I'll pay. How much do you charge?'

How much do I charge? Oh, I'm a cheap whore, my love. I don't charge much. A kiss on the cheek and maybe one on the mouth, a sidelong look from under that fringe of hair, a forefinger run along my mouth where the stubble becomes lips and the other way around. I don't charge much. 'Don't worry about it,' I said. 'I can do it in my lunch hour.'

'But I don't want you to lose anything because of this.'

No? No! 'We'll talk about that some other time.' Over a glass of wine by candlelight, darling, in the light of the glass-clear moon, under the stars' silver rain, on a sailing ship to China. Some other time, my love.

'Well. Do you know where Jonas works? Did I tell you?'

'Wasn't it some ad agency?'

'Yes. It's called Pallas and they have offices out in Dreggen, in the same building as the State Liquor Shop.'

'I know where it is. They know me there. We're on a first-name basis.'

'I …' she began. I was afraid she was going to back out so I quickly changed the subject.

'It's settled,' I said. 'I'll talk to him and we'll see how it goes. I'll give you a report.' I jumped at that idea. 'Maybe I could drop by tonight?'

She was silent. 'Couldn't you phone instead? As a matter of fact, I can't tonight.'

No? The moon turned muddy, the stars' silver rain to tinsel and the sailing ship to China had already run aground. 'That's okay,' I said. 'You'll hear from me. Take care.'

After I hung up I remembered I hadn't sent my best to Roar. But I didn't call back. I'd remember it the next time.

The office bottle still stood on the desk. But it didn't tempt me any longer. In fact, it looked disgusting with its gaudy torn label. I screwed the cap on tight and slung it roughly back in the drawer.

I looked around me. There was a heavy unpleasant feeling in my stomach. 'Of all the dusty damn holes …' I said aloud. Just to be sure I heard it.

Then I got myself together and left without turning off the light. Maybe it would make things cosier when I came back. As if someone were at home.

If I ever came back. You never know. A fast car – and a pedestrian crossing in Dreggen. You're never safe. Especially on a pedestrian crossing. That's where you're really a sitting duck.

17

I walked through the fish market and along Bryggen's quayside. It was too early in the season for tourists. The nameless live fish swam in their tanks. The fish sellers swung their big red fists to keep warm and the housewives went suspiciously from stall to stall as if they didn't believe the fish lying there were real.

Out on Bryggen a red truck snapped up one cargo pallet after another and spat them through the open green doors of a marine warehouse. Reminded me of a rat building up a hoard.

The usual drunk stood on a corner and held up a wall, with a bottle in his inside pocket and a bilious look at the passers-by. He was inevitable. In a certain way, he was also a tourist attraction, a part of the atmosphere, necessary in the city's pattern. Except it was always the tourist season as far as he was concerned.

The Pallas Advertising Agency was in the new red-brick building by the new Bryggen Museum. Almost everything you needed to survive lay within a few square metres: a liquor shop, a museum for the cultured, a church for the pious, a dentist's office, a park with benches – and an ad agency.

You could spend your whole life out here. There was a bank around the corner and a hotel. A post office. An old cemetery and a bingo hall. They'd catered for all life's needs. You could post a letter, send money orders, play bingo. The new Dreggen was a miniature Bergen, a pocket-sized Norway with all the conveniences built in.

The first thing you notice when you enter an ad agency is that you see only young employees. You rarely see anybody over forty because they've become obsolete, or are drained of ideas, or can't keep up any longer. Maybe an older grey-haired boss sits in one of the inner offices but that's because he just happens to be a major stockholder and nobody dares ask him to leave. But that's the only reason he's there and he isn't much use to himself or anybody else.

In Reception sits a young woman who's always pretty. If she's not, it means she's too clever to be the receptionist, and she smiles at you. That is, she'll smile at you if you're under forty and you look as if you're there on business and haven't come to borrow money. But it's seldom a real smile. It's mechanical. Beautiful maybe – but mechanical. And it doesn't last long. It's gone before you've turned completely away.

All ad agencies try to look as if theirs is a 'young, dynamic milieu' and there are always people in trendy clothes rushing from one office to another. They wear the latest fashion in glasses and they always have a wisecrack for one of the girls who are plugged into earphones and play electric typewriters.

The men wear coloured shirts and wide striped ties; those at the creative end of things have long hair and beards and they wear jeans so you'll know they've been to the Arts and Crafts Institute even though they still haven't made their final artistic breakthrough. But its coming. Or not. When they've designed ads and brochures for five or six years, they cut their hair, shave and make their breakthrough by buying this year's car and a house in Natland Terrace.

The Pallas Advertising Agency's young dynamic milieu was in vivid red, green and brown. Green floor, red walls and brown ceiling. You entered a long narrow hall with long narrow people in it. The walls were hung with old beer posters from the days when it was legal to advertise beer.

The woman in Reception wore a black Afro, a kind of greenish white tunic and large gold-rimmed glasses with grey-tinted lenses. But there were no grey tints in her smile.

'My name's Veum,' I said. 'I'd like to talk to Jonas Andresen. Is he in?'

She looked at a lighted board and nodded. 'Do you have an appointment?' Behind the grey shadows her eyes were as blue as the sky behind today's clouds.

'Do I need one?'

The smile became a little strained. 'Are you a client?'

'In a way.'

Now the smile flashed off. 'I'll see,' she said coldly. She dialled a number and spoke softly into the receiver so I wouldn't hear what she called me. She looked up. 'Andresen wants to know what it's about.'

'Say it's personal and say it's important.'

She said that, listened a few seconds and hung up. 'He'll be out in a minute.'

She forgot I was there and turned back to whatever she'd been doing with a dictaphone or a typewriter. Answered the phone several times a minute with the same gracious voice. 'Pallas. May I help you?'

I stood and waited. Nobody asked me to sit down which was lucky. The chairs looked as if you couldn't get out of them.

Farther down the hall a young man in light brown trousers and striped shirt was slowly showing out an older grey-haired gentleman in a tailor-made suit, in just the way you show important clients out of an ad agency when you're finished with them.

A young woman came through a door. She had a large green folder under one arm. She walked straight towards me. A little thing with small breasts, wide hips and a pretty face. Clear brown eyes and a well-shaped chin.

But the first thing you noticed was her hair. It shone. It was brown but more than just brown. It had a glint of red and it wasn't the colour you buy for twenty kroner a pint and pour on your hair when you wash it. It was the kind of red that you find in the secret quiet corners and the trees in the forest inside you. But at the same time, it wasn't an obvious red. You'd never say she was a redhead. Her hair was brown. That red glint was simply there, like the soul somewhere in her body, like the woodwind in her symphony orchestra.

She was dressed according to the agency's colour scheme: a dark red blouse and a green corduroy skirt. She smiled at me as she walked by. The laugh lines told me she wasn't so young. Around thirty. But it was an unusually warm and beautiful smile. It came from the same place as that red glint in her hair and that had to be a good place. I'd have liked to spend my holidays and the rest of my life there.

That did it. One smile as she passed and I was so dizzy I didn't know where to look.

I said to myself: you haven't been in love in a long time, Varg. All too long. And I thought of Wenche Andresen and tried to hear her voice. But for some reason I couldn't. Or imagine her face.

That little thing delivered the big green folder to Reception, said something and walked back through the hall. Her hair floated. Freshly washed. Loose. And it floated with her down that too-short hallway. Then she went in through the same door she'd come out of. And she was gone.

That's how people come into your life. And that's how they go out of it. Here and gone in a couple of minutes.

A man came towards me out of another door. His walk wasn't totally dynamic. Maybe it was too late in the day or maybe he'd worked there too long.

He was well dressed. A grey-green suit nipped in at the waist. A waistcoat. Turn-ups on the trousers. He had dark blond hair and new glasses. An attractive little Wild West moustache. The kind that droops sadly at the corners of the mouth, but I recognised him from his pictures. Jonas Andresen.

So he wasn't telling me anything new when he said, 'I'm Andresen. Do you want to talk to me?'

We shook hands. 'I do. My name's Veum.' I lowered my voice. 'I'm here on your wife's behalf. I'm a kind of lawyer.'

He lowered his voice. 'Step into my office.'

He turned and I followed him down the hall.

It was a small office with a view of the Maria Church's twin towers and Mount Fløien. I could look straight up and see the roof of the house I lived in. It was enough to bring tears to your eyes.

Jonas Andresen's big black desk was covered with neat stacks of papers, publications and sketches for ads. The 'In' basket was considerably fuller than the 'Out'. Alongside the baskets sat a hollowed-out plastic skull, sawn off above the ears, and it held pens and pencils in the firm's colours: red and green. A single dark red rose, long since brown at the edges, stood in a plastic vase. The green ashtray was full. If it had been emptied that morning, he was a heavy smoker.

There were posters on the walls and four enlarged pictures of a younger Roar, and there was a bulletin board covered with newspaper ads, pages torn from weeklies, photographs, calling cards, memos for future assignments and other assorted junk.

Jonas Andresen sat behind his desk and waved me to a comfortable chair opposite him. He offered me a cigarette and when I refused lit his own. It was a long white cigarette. His hand shook.

He looked questioning. 'Well?'

'Your wife asked me … It's about some money you've promised her – from a life-insurance policy. She has problems. Economic ones.'

His eyes were clear and blue through the colourless lenses. Large aviator glasses with light brown rims. He exhaled through tightly pressed lips.

'Let's get a couple of things straight first. You said you were a kind of lawyer. Are you my wife's lawyer or aren't you?'

'No, I'm not.'

He leaned forward in his chair. 'Are you her *friend*?'

'I can assure you …' I said.

He raised his hands and talked, the cigarette bobbing in his mouth. 'Take it easy. I don't see anything wrong with that. On the contrary. I'd be very happy if Wenche'd found herself – a friend. Someone new.'

'Well, I'm not it. Not that way. As a matter of fact, I'm a private investigator.'

His face tightened.

'Your son Roar contacted me. He wanted me to recover his stolen bike.'

'Roar? He hired a private investigator to find his bike? That boy!' He laughed. Resigned.

'The next day I had to find Roar.'

He wasn't laughing now. 'What do you mean?'

I told him briefly about Joker and the gang, and about how

I'd found Roar bound and gagged. But I didn't tell him how I'd had to fight my way out of the woods with Roar in tow. And I didn't tell him I'd kissed his former wife.

He turned steadily paler and his voice was depressed when he finally said, 'Terrible. Those bastards. I ought ...'

'Relax,' I said. 'I already have. But that's how I met your wife. And then she hired me to talk to you. About this money. She didn't feel she could do it herself.' Jonas Andresen took a deep drag. 'I'd rather not discuss it here. Could we meet somewhere – say, in half an hour?'

I looked at my watch as if I had a busy schedule.

'Is it a problem?' he said.

'No. I can manage. Where?' Generous me.

'Bryggestuen?'

'Bryggestuen is fine. Maybe we could have dinner there. I will anyway.'

He shrugged. 'Let's say in half an hour.' Then he stood up and gave me to understand he had other things to do in the next thirty minutes besides sit and shrug his shoulders. He'd smoke at least three cigarettes and the slow death which waits for us the day we're born would creep up on him half an hour sooner.

He showed me to the door. The woman with the Afro tried a cautious smile as if she weren't sure I wouldn't be a client some day. And as I wasn't yet forty, she had a little smile for me regardless.

'Meet me next Tuesday behind the library,' I said, winked at her, and left.

18

Bryggestuen is one of the few places left in Bergen which still have a simple, real connection with the past. Per Schwab's large murals with their marine motifs, the houses that don't exist any more and the ships that have been scrapped long ago, take you to a timeless world.

The people who come here to Bryggestuen are neither loud graduate students nor the half-drunk young you find in most of the other restaurants where they'll let you drink a beer without your being a taxpayer. Ordinary solid working people come here: people who work in the market, seamen, office people. Mostly men. It's not one of the places you go to to pick up a girl. It's a place you go to for a quiet drink or to eat good, reasonably priced food.

I settled myself in one of the back booths. Ordered a beer and a whale steak. Contentedly ate and drank.

The booths were arranged in three parallel rows. I sat in the one next to the wall. In the booth across from me, a large man in a grey coat, with a belly that hid his belt buckle, fished for his past in his glass of ale. I don't know if he caught anything. In the booth against the far wall a young couple sat with intertwined fingers, and they looked as if they'd never part again. But they probably would after a couple of years of marriage. Or something.

The noise of Bryggen's traffic was muffled by the lead-glass windows. The whale steak tasted as it should. It was a good half-hour. The best in a long time.

I was halfway through my second beer when Jonas Andresen came in and looked around. I lifted a finger. He nodded and came over. He should have been a waiter.

He had a light coat over his arm and a black briefcase in his hand. He laid both beside him on the seat. When the waiter came, he ordered a pint of export. When the waiter served him, he immediately ordered another. 'Just to get myself together after a day's work,' he said.

We drank in silence, I with my light beer and he with his strong export. We drank the way old friends do who meet every day after work and who don't need to talk to one another in order to be together.

But a beer and an export later we had to talk. He'd already begun slurring his 's's. 'Don't know how much Wenche's told you,' he said. 'Or what she's told you.'

He suddenly looked bashful. Then he said, 'We are on a first name basis, aren't we?'

'We certainly can be,' I said and shook the hand he held out. 'Jonas,' he said.

'Varg,' I said.

'What?'

'That's right, Varg,' I said. 'Outlaw.'

'Oh. I get it,' he said and laughed cautiously as if I'd told a joke. Then he picked up where he'd left off. 'I take it that she ... I mean, she probably hasn't painted an especially pretty picture of me? She can be quite ... strong with her descriptions of people. Their characteristics.' It was a tricky word but he made it. He wasn't in advertising for nothing. 'You married?' He shot a sideways glance at my right hand.

'No. I was.'

'Congratulations. Then we're in the same boat.'

'That we are.'

'Did you ever play around when you were married? Was that why …?'

'No. But I had a job.'

'I understand,' he said.

He'd got me started. 'I mean – there are a lot of different kinds of playing around. With some men it's other women, with some it's the bottle. With some it's their jobs. Don't ask me which is the worst, but in my work I get the impression that most women think the worst is when their husbands go for other women.'

'Right. And they never ask why. Or they rarely do, anyway. And the circumstances don't matter either. An unfaithful man or woman, for that matter – is always the sinner. Always the guilty one. If the marriage fails apart it's always the fault of the one who's had an affair. Or a lot of affairs. Because nobody ever asks why it happened.'

'Right. And that's why I never take those cases.'

He looked confused. 'Which cases?'

'Those cases. I never shadow married people to find out where they are when they're not where they're supposed to be – and who they're with. Because there's no way in hell of knowing the reason why they're there.'

'Right. But listen, Veum. Don't think I'm sitting here – saying this to lay the blame on Wenche. Because I'm not doing that.'

No. He wasn't doing that. What he was doing was ordering another pint of export. I'd already stopped trying to keep up with him. Sipped my third beer.

There was foam on his moustache and it fluttered gently as he went on. 'That's what she's doing. Blaming it all on me. She can't see any of her mistakes. Okay with me. Let her, if it makes her feel any better. But the truth is – the truth is it wasn't a marriage. Never should have been a marriage. But we're always too young to see it. Right, er … Varg?'

'The question is, are we ever old enough to see it?'

'No way. I mean right. But we were … we were too different from the beginning. I don't know if she's told you anything about herself. She doesn't come from Bergen even though she sounds like it. She comes from darkest Hardanger. One of those little ribbons of land which sneak in somewhere under the mountain wall. One of those places where chance has slung together a farm with two cows. Her background's strict, pious. When she started school, she moved in with an older sister in Øystese. That was a step forward. They're okay – both the sister and her husband. But you can't get away from it. The child-hood environment. Jesus on the wall and only one book in the bookcase. Right? And a year's subscription to piety's official magazine *For Rich and For Poor*.

'I'm a city boy. I was fourteen the first time I got drunk, and I had my first girl when I was fifteen. Stole cars and went joy-riding on Fanafjeu and Hjellestad. But I landed butter-side up. Finally I went to the Business Institute. That was pretty wild. Beer parties around the clock, and chubby little students from eastern Norway who got loaded and danced half-naked on the tables. Later it was advertising with all that action. Confer-ences and seminars and lunches in the city with clients.

'She liked to sit at home with her embroidery. Read maybe. Play records and watch TV. She liked to cook and do the laundry. Wasn't interested in life out there. She only drank to be polite, and I had to teach her to smoke. While I was used to going out for a beer with the boys, flirting a little, coming home a little late. And not exactly steady on my feet. But what the hell difference do these differences make anyway? If people really love each other?'

He looked at me. Depressed. 'Well. Maybe we didn't really. Or maybe *I* ...'

'How did you meet?' I said.

'How do people meet each other? She knew somebody who knew somebody ... The old story. There's always a girlfriend of the girlfriend of the guy you're sharing a flat with, right? And some of these girlfriends – or one of them – some time or other has got to come from Hardanger, right?'

'And?'

'Well. That's how it was. She really turned me on. She was so different from all the others. She was reserved. Shy. Didn't say much. When I'd ask her something, she'd look down and twist her fingers around in her lap. She really got to me. Really turned me on. I had to have her. Had to ...' He shrugged and emptied his glass. 'She liked me, too. Didn't take her long.'

He ordered another glass. 'Suddenly it was a new life. After years of running around like a chicken with its head cut off from one end of the country to the other, after years of hopping in and out of different beds – suddenly it was beautiful. Peaceful. Strolls on Mount Fløien on soft velvet nights. Sunday morning walks on the quays. Trips to the cinema as if we were kids. Sitting and holding hands somewhere far in the back. Wenche, Wenche, Wenche ...'

He'd almost forgotten me now and the fifth glass pulled his head even closer to the red-and-white checked tablecloth.

The man at the next table had left. All he left behind him was a wet circle on the cloth. The young couple beyond him had got as far as each other's elbows, but they still had a way to go before they completely ate each other up.

Jonas Andresen said, 'And then I had her. And it was as sweet as a rose just opening. Or like when a trout jumps out of the stream, hangs in the air – and lands in your arms. And then she got pregnant. And then we got married. And then we had Roar.

'Suddenly there were three of us, right? And so we sat there in a fiat on Nygårdshøyden. The start of a nuclear family and nowhere to go. After six months I was already in love with somebody else. It began to break up. Pretty quickly. I mean, if I could fall in love with somebody else after only six months of marriage it tells you the lie of the land.'

'What land?' After three beers my brain was beginning to tire. I ordered another to help it think.

'Never-Never Land. And I was Peter Pan and Wendy had already disappeared. She got so old, Varg. I don't mean her looks. Jesus! She still looks sixteen. At least she did a couple of months ago. But she got so – settled. The only things she cared about were me and Roar. And that damn endless sewing. We had walls full of little embroideries. Sofas full of cushions. Tables and chests covered with darling little runners. Doilies. She even made a hand-embroidered cover for the toilet chain. And ...'

I tried to remember Wenche Andresen's flat. 'Aren't you overdoing it?'

'Well. That's how it felt. As if I were in danger of drowning in all those little embroidered thingies.'

A woman came in and sat down at the empty table. She was in her late fifties. A little smile lurked around her wrinkled mouth. It was like the wolf waiting in the woods for Little Red Riding Hood. But Little Red Riding Hood had joined Women's Lib and flew around and burned books in bonfires in the city. So she was busy. And if she had shown up it wouldn't have been good for the wolf because Riding Hood had taken a course in judo and knew how to handle men with hairy arms and legs.

The woman ordered a beer and a hamburger and began eating up her own obvious loneliness bit by bit until it was gone.

Jonas Andresen talked on without noticing anything as the foam in his moustache dried to nothing. 'Those first dirty little affairs were like the little lies people whisper behind your back except in this case they weren't lies. A willing colleague. A waitress you once picked up in a restaurant on a trip to Oslo. A friend's wife. A recently divorced opera singer. Short cannibalistic affairs which seldom lasted longer than a few nights.

'I was in love twice. Really in love, but I slept with only one of them. As if that means anything. As if sex wraps the whole thing up. As if screwing confirms or denies anything except maybe your own pride – or lack of it. But then …'

He stopped focusing and started looking dreamy. I quickly ordered him another export. The waiter was doubtful, but he served us anyway.

'Something to eat, Jonas?' I said.

He looked at me. 'Eat?' It was a word he'd never heard before.

I tried to steer him back on to the track. 'But then … but then you …' I said.

'Yes, then. Then I met Solveig.'

A new pause. His face softened and his gaze was warm. He tried to sit up straight. Not so easy after five and a half exports. 'And that was it. That. Was. It.'

I didn't say anything. I knew it'd take time. That maybe we'd go through five or six more pints before we reached the end of the road. But his expression told me that I'd hear it all. I'd hear the whole 'Ballad of Jonas and Solveig'. If I were patient.

'Solveig,' he repeated. The image was no longer that of a slithering snake. It was an image of the morning sun itself that rose over the landscape. The sun that broke through the faded brown murals and sent its slanting rays across the red-brown booth, the torn tablecloth and the half-empty beer glasses.

Just as it would send them across a wet green morning landscape. It was a sunrise somewhere between the sea and the mountains, with the sea like a moving mirror in the foreground and the mountains like high bluish promises for the future in the background.

It was the sun that rises over the rich and the poor. Over advertising types and private investigators. It was the sun that fills us and consumes us and spits us out. Turns us into ashes after life's volcanic eruption – after love's sudden destroying fire.

'She began at the agency three or four years ago. At first she was just around. She'd come straight from the Arts and Crafts Institute. Started in layout: lettering, setting up ads. That kind of thing. A nice girl. Friendly. Open. The kind you like being with and having as a colleague. Until suddenly you pinch yourself and realise you're head over heels in love with her. Until you realise the next day you love her – more than you've ever loved anyone. And you can't tell her because you're married. And she's married. And you have one child and she's got two. And you realise the train's left too early and you got off at the wrong station and it's too late now. Much too late. Right?'

Yes. Right. I'd felt that way myself once in a while. Except my train had left a long time ago and I'd never got off at a station. I'd been thrown off somewhere. Head first as the train rounded a curve.

His hand searched the air as if he were looking for her. Or maybe he was trying to draw her, sketch her so I could see her. 'You would ... She's the type you feel everybody's got to be in love with. The first – the first thing you notice is her hair. It's not brown. I mean it is, but it's red. Except that it isn't – if you know what I mean.'

I knew what he meant. I'd seen her.

'It shines, as if the colour's coming ...'

'From the inside? Right?'

'Right! From the inside. And all her warmth too – it comes from the inside. Because the next thing you realise is that she's so damned nice. All the time. She's always in a good mood. Easygoing. Friendly. Even though you disagree about things. Argue about them. And we were so lucky – I was so lucky – that we worked together a lot.'

'What is your job exactly?'

'Consultant. That's what we call it now. Once it would have been called head of marketing. When each man was his own boss and had his own office. I'm involved with contracts and agreements, organising campaigns and the financial end of it. Things like that. She was in the graphic side of the business. The side that puts the ideas on paper. And she was – is – good. She's got a simple approach but a real feel for the right expression. She can express an idea either visually or verbally so it makes sense. Gives depth to the whole thing. If you see what I mean.'

I didn't see exactly what he meant. But I could imagine. Because I'd seen her.

'So I went around for months, gnawing on this secret of

mine, this love, until suddenly one day I … We were working late. I'd been to dinner with a client and we'd split a bottle of wine and so I was a little – the way wine makes you sometimes. As if you could float. Right?'

'Right.'

'And I suddenly felt we were so close there at her drawing board. So I said. Very carefully. You know, Solveig, I think I've fallen in love with you. Well, maybe just a little bit, I said – just to keep her from taking it the wrong way.

'And she looked at me. Searching. The way some women do when you say things like that. As if they've got to read the lies or the truth in our faces. And then she said: are you? And her voice was so soft. So soft. And later when I had to leave, I wanted to give her a little hug and she came to me. And I kissed her throat and smelled her hair. And in a split second our lips met and she didn't turn her face away, but I left the room in a daze and never even shut the door behind me.'

He tilted his head and looked wonderingly down into his empty glass. 'And then – then, as a matter of fact, a whole year went by and nothing else happened. It's the truth, Varg. I tried to get over it. I thought – you're in love with her but she doesn't care about you. Why should she? She's happily married and has two kids and anyway you're – married. And you have a child.

'And I had no idea then. In my wildest dreams I couldn't imagine that a woman like S-S-Solveig could feel anything at all for me. But she did.

'Then there was one autumn. A long slow wavering towards a certain point. It was clearer and clearer to me she was for keeps. In my head. I was obsessed by her. She was all I could see. My work began to suffer. I knew that. I couldn't concentrate. Routine saved me. I started making mistakes. Once we nearly lost a client because of it. But it didn't seem to matter – as long as she was there all the time and we were together. Just as long as we could go on working together.

'And in all those months we never once talked about what had happened. What I'd said. We became better and better friends. I don't think I've ever been such good friends with anybody. Man or woman.'

I filled his glass from mine and he looked gratefully at me from the other side of the Atlantic. 'But then one day ...'

'One day?'

'Then one day. It was late. We'd worked overtime. Had to finish a project. It was just the two of us, alone in the office. When we wrapped it up, we sat and talked. I mean, she sat. I was standing on the other side of the drawing board. We each had our cup of coffee. I don't remember what we were talking about. The only thing I remember is that I thought: Now Jonas. You've got to tell her now. The time's come.

'But I couldn't. Couldn't get it together. Couldn't express all those feelings inside me because – just seeing her sitting there. And then she lit a cigarette. And then she said: I don't smoke very often. It makes me feel – wild. And I said: wild.

'And I reached over and stroked her cheek. And she blushed and then she reached over and stroked my cheek. With the back of her hand. And I sort of fell apart, Varg. Melted.

'I leaned across the drawing board and took her face in my hands. I could feel her cheeks against the palms of my hands. I laid my face against hers, against her hair, her wonderful soft hair. I kissed her ear, her cheek, the corner of her mouth and I could feel those soft lips trembling ... And I sighed, Varg. I sighed like an old woman.

'Solveig, I said, you're a good person, you are. Solveig. She looked at me with those big bright eyes of hers. Said: do you think so, Jonas?

'I said: if you can believe this, I don't think I've ever … It's been years since I've felt about a person the way I feel about you, Solveig.

'I kissed her. Her ear, her cheek. But not her mouth. Not really. She turned her face away. I said: you like me a little bit, don't you? I like you a lot, Jonas, she said.

'I kissed her some more. I'm glad you're here, Jonas, she said, but it can't go any further. Not today.

'I stroked the hair away from her forehead, her eyes. I said: what I feel isn't physical. Not that way. It's romantic. Like being young again. Sixteen. Seventeen. I want to be good with you. Kiss your mouth. And I looked at her mouth, at her soft beautiful lips, narrow but open. At that mournful yearning lower lip. If you know what I mean.'

I knew what he meant. My lower lip looks like that too. Just before I cry.

He went on. 'She smiled. Shyly, I think. And she said: I've also … I say so many stupid things. I'm impulsive. Much too impulsive and I'm an emotional person. I need to be tender too. With others …

'She was holding both my hands with hers, Varg. And she was looking totally at me. And it was as if her face filled the whole room, as if the only thing in the whole universe was that beautiful face framed by that hair. The thin little nose, the dark blue eyes. Almost black. That trembling mouth. The soft round cheeks, that chin … Solveig. Solveig.

'And I knew it then and I know it now that I love her, and that I'll always love her no matter what. And I'll never stop loving her …'

He searched the room as if he were looking for someone else he could love. Share his tender feelings with. Sit and talk with for hours. But the only other person he found was an investigator. Not one of the most expensive but not the cheapest either. A listener.

'Then we heard somebody out in the hall,' he said. 'We broke away from each other, fumbled blindly for our coffee cups, lifted them to our mouths and sat a decent distance apart. And the door opened and someone came in ...'

I waited for the rest of it. 'Who came in?'

'Her husband.'

19

It had begun to get dark outside and the waiter had given up trying to stop us. He brought us two fresh glasses and I was one hundred per cent certain this day would end just one way: two quick aquavits and then down with the window-blind. I'd already had problems finding my way to the men's room and back.

'Did I tell you about her husband a little while ago?' Jonas said.

'I can't remember,' I said. I had the feeling he had, just before I'd started forgetting.

'Reidar Manger,' he said. 'But he's not from Manger. He's from somewhere down south. Kristiansand, I think. He's a postdoctoral fellow – God, the jargon they use, Varg! – he's a postdoctoral fellow in American literature. One of those pasty-pale guys who sit up late and write doctoral dissertations about Hemingway but who'd pass out cold if they saw a live trout. But he's okay. I've always liked him. Except "always" is an exaggeration because I haven't met him that many times and "like" is a complicated word. If you ...'

'Right. I know what you mean,' I said.

'Right. Right.' He was talking much more slowly now and his head hung a little lower. But otherwise he could have been completely sober. I'd stopped noticing the other customers. We were the only ones there now. The two of us and a woman named Solveig.

'You said her husband showed up.'

'Right. Right. Nice guy, Reidar Manger. We spent a couple of hours one evening talking about *The Sun Also Rises*. I'd only read the first half. He'd read the whole thing a hundred times. So we came out even. But we never agreed.'

'Agreed about what?'

'About the last half. The part I hadn't read.'

'I know what you mean. I've read it myself. But he showed up – that day.'

'He didn't say anything. He didn't do anything. I don't know if he could tell anything had happened. If he'd wanted to act like Hemingway he could have tried knocking me through the window, but it would have cost him a couple of cracked knuckles.

'He'd stopped by to pick her up on his way home to his books, and we sat and broke the ice over coffee. Oh, yes. We poured a cup for him. But it was hard to keep things going. I didn't dare look at her. And if I'd looked at him he might have thought I fancied him. You know how these specialists in American literature are. They see homosexuality in everything. They've read *The Great Gatsby* and all the critical studies. You know. And *Huck Finn* and all the rest of it.

'So. After a while we went our separate ways. They went out to Skuteviken and I drove that long way out there to – my family. When I got home I was beat. Had to lie down. I was exhausted. Beat up. Legs shaky. She told me later she'd felt the same way and had had to go for a long walk on Fjellveien. By herself.

'The next day, just as we were about to go home, she handed me an envelope. And then she left. I still remember almost word for word what she wrote.

'*My dear good friend. Where feelings are concerned – I've never been especially good at expressing myself in words so I really do admire you because you can say all these beautiful things to me. I haven't been able to stop thinking about you for a single second since yesterday. As you said yourself – it's just the way it happens. For me, too. I truly hope we can meet in other circumstances and whenever we can. Take care.* And then the signature: *a hug and a kiss from a good friend.* And a PS. *Please tear this up into a thousand pieces.*

'I could tear it into a thousand pieces and I could jump on it and I could burn it to ashes. But I'll never forget the words of the most beautiful letter I ever got.'

He shook his head for emphasis. 'Never. And that's how it got serious. How we got to be more than just good friends.'

We drank. Then I said, 'And then what happened, Jonas?'

'Then what happened? Everything happened. We began meeting after work as often as we could. Went somewhere for a cup of coffee. Sat. Talked. Played with one another's fingers. Just talked.

'We did meet one evening. I had the car and we drove – it felt like a long drive – up to Fana Church. Parked. And walked along the road. We kissed for the first time. I mean, we really kissed.

'And it was like kissing a little girl and a grown woman at the same time. A little girl who openly and freely kisses you on the mouth without really knowing what she's doing to you. And a grown woman who knows exactly what she's doing.

'A few weeks later she invited me home. Her husband was at a seminar in Oslo and I got there after the kids had gone to bed. They have a little wooden house which they've completely modernised on the inside. And we … we sat and talked and drank tea and listened to music – it felt like hours – and we kissed like teenagers who've just discovered another human being. And we really hadn't thought – we never planned to – we didn't mean to … but it got the best of us and we … well, we made love. We made love.

'We began on the living-room floor and went on to the bedroom. Believe me, Varg, I've never been with anybody that way before. I never would have believed she'd be that warm, that passionate. And when she arched under me like a white bridge and let all her joy and pain out into the room around us … I can't find the words for things like that.'

No. There aren't words. I knew what he meant. And some people never find the things like that. Not ever.

'It's simply gone on,' he said. 'We've got closer and closer. We haven't been able really to be together very often – not that way, I mean. Maybe once a month. Sometimes every other month. Sometimes not even that often. But afterwards, we've lived off those times for weeks. Whenever we're together, there isn't anybody else. It's just the two of us.'

'Did you keep it a secret?'

'You'd be amazed how long. As far as I know, it still is. Unless – but I don't know if – I don't think Wenche's said anything to him. At least he hasn't given Solveig any reason to think he knows. But I couldn't hold out in the long run.

'Wenche. I could pretend, play-act in a way as long as there really wasn't anybody else. But after I met Solveig and it got serious – it was impossible. I ended up feeling as if I were cheating when I was with Wenche. Being untrue to Solveig. Know what I mean?

'I wasn't a husband or a father any longer and finally, finally I just gave up. Told Wenche I was moving out. And when she asked if there were somebody else I said yes, and when she asked who, I said … Well. It was stupid. But I told her.

'And then I moved out. Followed by curses. Weeping and wailing and gnashing of teeth. The whole scene. It was a beautiful exit. The whole building must have heard it. She stood out on the balcony and screamed at me as I stumbled down to the car, sat behind the wheel and drove off. After that we only met at the lawyer's. And at the settlement.'

'And Roar?'

'I've hardly seen Roar. We haven't come to a custody agreement yet. I've wanted to postpone that. I can't stand any more confrontations.'

So he couldn't either. 'No,' I said. 'That's why I'm here. To save you and Wenche from any more confrontations. It was the money …'

'Solveig,' he said. 'She hasn't wanted. We're still together. But she hasn't wanted to go all the way yet. Move out. It's okay. She's got two kids. I've got just the one. The relationship between Reidar and her isn't the greatest but they manage to get through most days in one piece, and she does have two kids to think of.

'And even though she denies it, I'm not sure her feelings for me are as strong as mine for her. Anyway, I've given her time. I can wait. I've waited for her since I was a kid, and I can wait longer. You always have a dream girl, right? And when you finally do meet her, really meet your dream – right away you feel as if you have all the time in the world. You have your life before you and you can afford to wait - if she'll just finally come to you.'

'In the last street of the last city of all? Yes. I know what you …' I'd seen her.

'So now you know the dirty little story of my adultery, Varg. Two people who met too late – three kids and two marriages too late. Two people who loved each other outside the pages of the programme and after the show was over. The others? They'll only see the surface. They'll pin it on the usual sex thing.

'But it wasn't that. It's been my big love. If the big love exists anywhere outside those novels they write for teenage girls. Later on it did become erotic, yes. And I've never had it so good with another woman. That way. But it was erotic. It wasn't just sex. It wasn't. I never told her that we screwed or fucked because we never did. We made love instead. We made love …'

He looked at me as if I were going to object. But I wasn't about to. I had seen her. And she'd smiled at me.

'I don't know why I'm telling you all this.' He looked reproachfully from his glass to mine. 'I've never talked about it with anybody else. Before now. Nobody else besides Wenche. And I tossed her Solveig's name. Like bait. To give her something to snap at before she threw me out.'

He looked sadly at nothing. 'It's been a little iffy recently. Along with the practical problems. It's one thing supporting your son and your – Wenche. Another thing entirely getting on your own feet again. Adulterous husbands don't qualify for support. You have to find a flat and that's not cheap today. And you've got to put something in the flat. Something to sleep on, to eat off, to hang your clothes on – or in.

'So say hello to Wenche for me and tell her I'm sorry. Sorry about everything. From the moment I stumbled into her life. Tell her that I'm sorry I haven't done anything about the insurance yet. But I will. Tell her – tell her she'll get the money tomorrow or the day after. Tell her I'll come out and personally deliver all of it to her. For her long and faithful service in the

Betrayed Bedfellows Brigade, etc., etc., etc. Just say hello from Jonas and tell her Jonas is sorry. Okay, Varg?'

I was tired and I was drunk. 'I'll deliver the message,' I said. 'I'll tell her I've come straight from the whale and Jonas is sorry. I'll tell her that.'

I was too tired and too drunk to say any more.

We paid for our last two pints and sat for a while. Mainly because we couldn't stand up.

When we finally did, we sort of joined ourselves together on the way out. Like Siamese twins. The doorman held the door for us and we lurched out on to the pavement.

We stood there, swinging and swaying like two young lovers who can't stand to say goodbye. 'Where are you going?' I said.

'Prestestien,' he said. 'But I need a taxi.'

'Well,' I said, 'you've got a choice between the statue of Holberg and the fortress.'

'I'll try the fortress,' he said. 'At least it's in the right direction.'

'Well. Have a good crossing.'

'You too. Which way are you going?'

'To the heights,' I said.

He looked at the sky. The grey cloud cover had peeled away and you could see stars between the shreds. 'Up there?' he said.

'Not that high up,' I said.

Then he thumped me on the shoulder.

'Remember the Alamo, Reidar,' he said.

I didn't have time to react to his suddenly calling me Reidar. He'd already gone. He went weaving along Bryggen. An advertising executive in a suit with a briefcase in his hand and a coat over his arm, a man with a tattered reputation and a vulnerable love somewhere inside him. One of the many who'd landed on the wrong planet in the wrong century. One of the many …

I turned and headed the other way. I could see that lonely light in my office window across Vågen. Two floors above the cafeteria on the second. But I couldn't cross the market to turn it out. It could shine until tomorrow. Like a beacon in the night. A secret message to all shipwrecked souls.

I walked towards the heights instead. Up towards the fire station at Skansen and the endless high plateaus. Up towards two quick aquavits and the window-blind. Nothing else was waiting for me. I didn't need anything else.

Not today. Not tomorrow. But some day. Some day.

20

When you wake from a dream you feel as if you've been slung on to the floor. I opened my eyes. I was awake. I was naked under the quilt and I was very much aware of my nakedness. I'd been dreaming of a woman. Of a woman whose hair wasn't red and it wasn't brown. But floated like music around her face. And she was smiling. Her smile hung in the air after she was gone. It was like the cat's smile in *Alice in Wonderland*. One of those smiles that drill right into you and never die away until you're lying in your grave. One of those smiles that spring up as beautiful flowers from the earth you're lying under. When it's spring again. And when you're dead.

When you're dead and the mountains all around the city stand there as they always have, and the sky bends down over houses that have been demolished and houses that have been built.

And there'll be Mondays when you're dead. And people will walk and drive to their jobs. And they'll stand around in shops and they'll sit in offices, and they'll take buses and trolleys. When you're dead and it's spring and all your women are dead. Except one.

She'd smiled at me and had told me her name. Wenche Andresen, she had said. And her face had become fuzzy. Blurred. And a little boy had called to me from a long way off. A clear little boy's voice. And he'd run towards me with a football under one arm. He was wearing trousers which were about to be too small for him. It was Thomas. No. It was Roar. And I'd tried to hang on to her smile, to the half-moon that had come loose from one of the drawing-pins and had fallen part of the way down, and I'd tried to pull myself up by it and – I woke up.

I rolled out of bed and on to the floor. Reached up and fished the alarm clock from the bedside table. Peered at it. Past twelve. I'd forgotten to set the alarm. What if somebody had rung the office? Somebody who wanted me to walk the poodle. Or find a runaway washing machine. Or the snows of yesteryear.

My mouth tasted of withered grass. It was that one aquavit too many.

The six – or was it seven? – pints of beer lay in my stomach like lead weights. There'd be trouble with the spark plugs today. I wished I hadn't been slung sideways out of my dream.

I tiptoed to the bathroom and turned on the shower. Soaped myself slowly from head to toe. And I stood with my eyes closed. I stood there until the hot water was gone. After two minutes under the cold I was conscious enough to turn off the tap.

I towelled myself warm again. Then did a fast combination of relaxing yoga exercises and battery-charging neck and stomach exercises on the living-room floor. Then I went to the kitchen.

I needed tea. A lot of very weak tea with a lot of sugar in it. I needed thin-sliced wheat bread topped with big juicy slices of cucumber and tomato. And a lot more tea. With a lot more sugar in it.

By one-thirty I was able to get in the car.

I drove down to the office and turned off the light. Then I

sat and stared at the walls which had tuned grey-green in the mouldy daylight.

It was March. Spring would come soon. All our winters would melt away and spring would clear a path inside us like a smiling willing woman – a woman whose hair was neither …

I thought about Jonas Andresen and what he'd told me. I thought about Wenche and what she'd told me. And I decided that no one marriage is like another – especially not to those involved. Nobody sees things the same way.

Wenche and Jonas Andresen had told me about two entirely different marriages; they'd told two entirely different stories of adultery.

It had been a game neither had won. And for some reason or other they'd dragged me in. As a referee. Or a linesman. Or God knows what.

I looked at my watch. Almost three. How long would she be in her office at the naval base? Until four? I could call her. Or I could drive out there and report in person. But what could I report? Tell her I'd drunk so many pints with her former husband that I'd lost count? Maybe I ought to put them on the bill. If I had a bill to put them on.

At least I could drive there. There were more than enough fun and games to amuse even the choosiest private investigator. I could stroll in the woods. Go a few rounds with Joker and his gang. Acquire a few bruises. I could argue with Gunnar Våge. Get stuck in the lift with Solfrid Brede. Drink vodka with Hildur Pedersen. Play Parchese with Roar.

I could kiss Wenche Andresen.

I touched my mouth. Her kiss was still there. Like a memory of being young. It had been a long time since anybody had kissed me at all. I haven't got a kissable mouth. Not as far as strangers are concerned anyway. And only a few people ever get to be more than strangers. And they aren't about to kiss me.

I thought of Beate. Tried to remember how it had felt when she'd kissed me. But it was too long ago. Too many dark moonless nights ago.

So there were a lot of possibilities. I locked up the office. Didn't turn on the light. Walked down. Started the car.

This day was about to die, just as all our days die inside us one by one. Until we wake up one morning from a dream and discover that we haven't woken up but have gone on dreaming. And all days become one day and all nights melt together.

And your bottles of aquavit sit there getting dusty until somebody comes along and drinks them for you. And a doctor or a letter-addressing company or someone who peddles one-room flats takes over your office.

But then you don't have to worry any more. No more utility bills. No more heartbreaks.

21

I parked and sat in the car. Nearby a thin young man leaned against a high curving street light. Thumbs in the pockets of his faded jeans, black leather jacket half open, cigarette dangling limply from one corner of his mouth and an expression like the onset of a plague on his face. Joker.

His eyes had followed me as I'd parked and now they clung to my face like leeches. I got out. Looked around sort of accidentally. The Lyderhorn was in its usual place and so were the four high-rises. Nothing had moved or collapsed.

Automatically I looked up at Wenche Andresen's flat. Light shone through the windows. Then I glanced at Joker. Our eyes met. He shifted the cigarette to the other side of his mouth.

I looked around me. Looked back up at Wenche Andresen's fiat. There was somebody walking along the balcony in front of the flat. It might be …

'Come for another whipping, Hopalong?' His voice was reedy.

I looked him up and down and walked over to him. 'Maybe you'd like to be my horsey,' I said.

When I got closer I could see the sweat on his downy upper lip. His gaze wavered.

'I don't see your mates, the trusty ladies-in-waiting,' I said. 'Have they had it? Want to go one-on-one? Is that it? Without steel? The song says it's steel in the arms and steel in the legs. Not in the fists. Sure as hell not in a switchblade. It'll really hurt when I stamp on your fingers. Some of them could get smashed. Then you wouldn't be able to play with your moustache for a couple of months.'

His voice was even reedier. 'I don't want to fight you, mister. Not right now. But I'm warning you. Don't step on my toes –'

'I said *fingers*.'

'Because it gets dark out here in the evenings, and –'

'Who said I planned to spend my evenings out here?' I looked up again without meaning to. Now the door had opened. There was somebody standing there, but from this distance …

'Looking for your whore?' Joker said. 'Don't worry. She's got company. The old man himself. Andresen.'

So it was Jonas Andresen I'd seen.

I got so close to Joker he started shaking. 'Call her that once more, little one, and I'll break you in two and I'll send you by Line Transport in two different packages. To the same address. That way you can bet you'll never meet up with yourself again.'

His eyes narrowed but whether from fear or anger I couldn't tell. 'And don't bother my mother,' he said. 'Because then I'll kill you!' That last came out as a falsetto.

I wanted to smash him. Hard and quick in the stomach so he'd fold up and meet my other fist on the way down. But I didn't. I thought of his mother. Of Wenche Andresen.

I looked up again. Her door was still open. Something was wrong. But what?

Then I saw her. She was running out of the stairwell. Holding something. Then she disappeared into her flat.

I stood there. Staring. Barely aware of Joker beside me. I glanced sideways. He'd followed my gaze and was looking up. 'What's going on?' His voice was suddenly young and weak.

Then Wenche Andresen reappeared in the doorway. She was walking strangely. Uncertainly. She came straight to the balcony railing. Leaned over it. For a second I almost thought she was going to jump, throw herself into space and float down toward us like a huge bird.

But she didn't. I could hear her screaming at this distance. 'Help. Somebody! Help – somebody. Help! Help!'

Then the gaping doorway swallowed her again. I moved. Heard Joker behind me.

He was running in another direction, but I couldn't think about him. The only thing I could think about was a woman named Wenche Andresen. Who wasn't a bird. Who was screaming, 'Help! Somebody!'

That somebody had to be me.

22

I rushed into the lift area. A note on one of the doors said Out of Order. The other lift was on its way down, but I couldn't wait. I ran to the stairway and started up. I stopped half-way to catch my breath. Checked the front of the building.

No bird had taken off yet. Yesterday's acquaintance, Solfrid Brede, was on her way out. She must have been in the lift that worked. She'd got over her panic.

I climbed. Blood pounding behind my eyes. I began seeing dancing black specks. My breath sounded like one of those autumn gusts that suddenly come sweeping around corners.

Then I was there. I lurched out of the door to the balcony and sort of trotted the last lap. Sick to my stomach.

The flat door was still open. I didn't bother ringing.

I didn't have to go far. Just inside the door was far enough. More than far enough.

Jonas Andresen lay on the floor. Partly on his side, partly curled around the lethal midpoint of his last moment. A bleeding hole in his belly.

Both hands clutched at the torn shirt as if to keep his life from escaping. But it hadn't helped. Life had seeped out of him like air from a leaky balloon. Somebody had holed him with the decisive blow. His eyes now stared at eternal peace. His body had lain down to rest some time ago now. He wouldn't be drinking any more pints of export. He wouldn't be doing anything at all.

And standing over him was Wenche Andresen, her back to the wall, a bloody knife in her hand. There was a silent shriek, a frozen cry of Help! Somebody! Help! on her face. A nightmare outlined clear chalk-white marks on a face that would never be exactly the same again.

I heard his voice inside my head. What was it he'd said last night? When you finally meet her – really meet your own dream girl then you feel you've got all the time in the world, that your whole life's before you and that you can wait …

But Jonas Andresen hadn't had all the time in the world. Hadn't had his whole life before him. And he hadn't been able to wait. He'd met his dream girl and then? Bye bye. Exit. He's gone.

His moustache looked very moth-eaten now. Glasses sat crooked. His shirt was ruined and his suit rumpled. He lay in a lake of blood. And he didn't have a life-jacket and he didn't need water wings. But he looked peaceful. As if he'd just bent down, picked a flower and inhaled its scent.

Jonas had entered his last whale and he'd never come out again.

All the rest of us – the survivors – we stood on the outside. We who'd carry the black banners of his death.

I got myself together. Tried to note details. A broken jam jar absurdly lay beside him. The red jam had already mixed with his blood.

I went to Wenche Andresen and carefully took the knife away from her. By the handle. It was a switchblade. The kind Joker would use.

But Joker hadn't used it because I'd been standing and talking to Joker. Who had used it?

I glanced at Wenche Andresen. Her eyes were huge. Black.

Terrified. 'I-I came up from the cellar with the jar of jam. He-he was lying there. I don't know what I did. I must have … as if it could do any good.'

'You pulled out the knife?'

'Yes. Yes! Was that stupid of me, Varg?'

'No, no. Not at all.' Sure it was stupid but who'd have the heart to tell her that?

'Did you see anyone?' I said.

'No.'

'Did you take the lift?'

'No. The stairs. I don't like … Oh, Varg. Varg! My God! What's happened?'

'Wait a minute. Just hold on.' It wasn't necessary, but just to be sure I bent and felt for a pulse. I wasn't going to be the one who talked while life ebbed from a dying man. But there was no pulse. He'd long since been called to that innermost office at the end of that farthest hall where he'd be judged by the last of his bosses.

'Did he call and say he was coming?' I said.

She shook her head. 'No. I had no idea. I had to go down to the cellar and get a jar of jam and when I came back – there he was. Lying there. Just like he is now. I guess – I must have dropped the jar – and the knife. It …' She looked at her empty hand. The knife was gone. It lay on the chest like a poisonous snake in a museum. But it couldn't bite now.

'But you left the door open when you went for the jam?'

'Out here? Of course not. Are you crazy?'

I shook my head. No, I wasn't crazy.

'He must have let himself in with his own …'

I looked around the floor. There weren't any keys lying there. But he'd probably put them back in his pocket.

I quickly tried to reconstruct it. He'd let himself in. Nobody home. He'd gone back to the door. Opened it. Somebody or other had been standing outside.

Or he hadn't locked the door behind him and somebody had followed him in. Or had somebody already been waiting for him in the flat?

No. That didn't make sense. Nothing did. A body on the floor never did.

A last thought hit me. 'Roar,' I said. 'Where's Roar?'

She shrugged helplessly. 'Out somewhere.'

I went to the outside door and carefully shut it. Checked that it was locked.

Then I stepped over Jonas Andresen, passed Wenche Andresen and made a phone call.

23

After I'd phoned, I came back to Wenche Andresen and led her out on to the balcony. She needed fresh air. I needed fresh air. And I wanted to stop Roar before he got into the flat.

In the pale grey March afternoon we stood on the balcony with its view of the Lyderhorn. The Bukkehorn clawed at the low-lying sky. When you approach from the sea, the mountain lies there like a sleeping demon. From here it looked like a demon's fang, stained dirty brown by old blood.

Wenche Andresen was silent. She stood with her arms clasped around her as if she were cold. Her face had closed up once again. It had closed over a sorrow and a pain no one else could understand, for sorrow and pain are lonely things. Like love.

She was wearing a blue polo-neck and a grey cardigan. Dark blue corduroy trousers and jogging shoes. The hair around her pale face was dishevelled and her mouth had a bitterer crimp to it than it had ever had.

I wondered where she'd be spending the night. I was afraid she'd end up in an oblong room with a tiny barred window, a bunk, a washbasin and a pail. The circumstantial evidence was too strong. No matter what she'd say, I knew what they'd think. The ones on their way. I knew what they'd say. I'd heard them before.

The detectives showed up first, along with two uniformed constables. A few minutes later three or four men from

Forensics. They reminded me of grocers in their long blue-grey aprons.

I breathed more easily when I saw who was in charge. Officer Jakob E. Hamre was one of the best they had. He was one of the ones they always called in to save their faces when there was a royal mess. If it was a complicated matter involving the interests of other countries or the hunting preserves of other government agencies Hamre was sent to the front lines.

He spoke three languages. Not perfectly, but better than most people. And for a policeman he was unusually sensitive. Intelligent. He also had faults but I hadn't discovered them. On the other hand, I didn't deal with him often. They usually sent out the field artillery when it concerned me.

I had no idea what the E. stood for. When you pronounced it it sounded as if you were hesitating over his last name. Jakob-eh-Hamre.

He was in his late thirties but looked younger. He was one of those good-looking young cops they would have used for their recruiting posters, if they'd had them. Be like Jakob E. Hamre and you too can be a cop. Maybe it would have helped.

His dark blond hair was combed from his forehead but a lock fell to one side. He was well dressed. Grey suit, light blue shirt, black and red tie. He wore a light trenchcoat and was bare-headed.

Regular features. A sharp, hooked nose, strong chin and quite a wide mouth.

Jon Andersen was with him. Ninety-five kilos of police officer.

Sweating like a whale as usual. Dirty shirt collar, greasy dandruffy hair and a lovable sneer playing at the outer edges of those ugly teeth. We were old friends. One of the older and better friends I had 'in there'.

Hamre took over. 'Where is he, Veum?' he said. He was businesslike. Neutral. Not unfriendly.

I nodded toward the door. He looked at Wenche Andresen. 'And this is … ?'

'This is his wife,' I said. 'She found him.'

He looked searchingly at her. She looked down.

'Naturally it's been a shock,' I said.

He focused his sharp light blue eyes on me. 'Naturally. We'll go through the whole thing later. I'd like to see him first. I think we'd all better go inside and settle down.'

'Just one thing,' I said. 'Her son – theirs – Roar. He could show up any time now. He can't see his father – like that. Can't a constable wait out here for him? Head him off?'

'Of course.' He told Jon Andersen to pass the word along.

Then we went inside.

Wenche Andresen began sobbing as soon as she saw Jonas's body. Painful dry sobs coming from somewhere deep inside her.

'One of you phone for a female officer,' Hamre said. 'Take Fru Andresen into the living room, and heat some water. She's bound to have tea or something.'

Jon Andersen and one of the constables took care of Wenche while Hamre and I stayed out in the foyer. I heard Andersen phone the station.

Hamre squatted by Jonas and felt for a pulse.

'Too late,' I said. 'It's long gone. I've already checked.'

He nodded, lips pressed together. Then he stood up. Saw the knife on the chest. 'That's it?'

I nodded. 'That's it.'

'Was it on the chest when you arrived?'

I hesitated. Too long. Jakob E. Hamre looked at me

expectantly. He was a walking lie-detector. Too sharp. I'd never beat him at hide-and-seek and that was as certain as the body on the carpet.

'No,' I said. 'It wasn't on the chest.'

'Where then?'

'She ... was holding it.'

He nodded. As if he'd expected it.

'But she said she pulled it out herself,' I said quickly. 'She came up from the cellar with a jar of jam – that broken one there on the floor – and found him like this. She wasn't expecting him. They were separated, but he still had his own keys. So he let himself in and she – she was in the cellar for a while. But during that time I was outside the building and saw him arrive. Saw him at the door. And ...'

He looked at me with something that could be amusement. 'We'll work out the sequence later. But you've got to agree that it looks pretty routine. For the moment. Even so, nothing's settled. There are a lot of loose ends. For example, how do you fit into the picture?'

'It's a complicated story,' I said. 'It involves her son. Her. Her husband ...' I nodded automatically. 'I'll give you the whole thing. There's nothing significant there. I mean, it has nothing to do with this.'

'Well, that's something we'll decide.'

I felt a chill up my spine. I knew this was a very competent investigator. I had to ask myself: did it have anything to do with this? Was the whole thing a large, complicated jigsaw puzzle I hadn't yet begun to figure out? Whose destiny lines led to that unlucky body in that sad little foyer? Wenche and Jonas Andresen's? Solveig Manger's? Joker's? How much should I tell Hamre and how much should I keep to myself?

The Medical Examiner arrived. A little man with rimless glasses, and pursed mouth, a large nose, a minute moustache, and eyes which displayed a routine, relaxed interest in the dead.

The men from Forensics came in, one of them holding the knife. 'Fingerprints?'

Hamre nodded.

'You'll find Wenche Andresen's fingerprints,' I said. 'And you'll find mine. On the handle. I took the knife from her. I don't know if you'll find others.'

Well. Now let's go to the living room,' Hamre said. 'Come on, Veum. Give the folks some elbow-room.'

I took a last look at Jonas Andresen. I could still hear his voice from last night. I could still see his sad eyes as he told me about his marriage. And about a woman called Solveig Manger.

He hadn't changed much. There was only one little difference. He was dead.

I turned my back on him and followed Jakob E. Hamre into the living room.

24

The constable on the sofa by Wenche Andresen looked as if he'd won an award. As if he were guarding something very valuable. His square-cut face was proud and he sat with his huge fists solidly on his knees. He was two sizes too big for this sofa but he was two sizes too big for all sofas. When he stood up he was about two metres tall. I wouldn't have liked playing football with him. On the opposing team anyway.

Jon Andersen sat and stared through the window as if he was searching for the truth itself out there in that dismal grey weather.

Wenche Andresen sat with both hands wrapped around her teacup. She sat hunched, staring into the cup, leaning over it as if it could keep her warm. From now on she'd always feel the cold somewhere inside herself. She looked up when he came in.

Hamre nodded to her. Friendly. 'Any more tea?' he asked Jon Andersen.

'There is,' Andersen said and brought two fresh cups and a half-full pot from the kitchen.

'There's lemon in the cupboard,' Wenche Andresen said weakly. She raised her head as if she were listening for something.

'No thanks, not for me,' Hamre said.

'Lemon's not a bad idea. And a little sugar, if there is any,' I said. It made the tea into something you could fiddle with.

'I'm sorry we have to bother you, Fru, but we need to clear up a couple of things as soon as possible,' Hamre said. 'I'll try to keep it short. Would you like to talk to a lawyer?'

She looked blankly at him. Then she looked at me. I don't think she understood the implications.

'Maybe it's a good idea,' I said.

She shook her head. 'A lawyer? No. Why?'

'No,' Hamre said. 'You never know. But all right. Now tell us about it. Everything.'

She stared into space. Past him. Past all of us. At a half-hour or so ago. Her voice was quiet, almost apathetic. 'There's not a lot to tell. I'd just come home from the office. Was going to make dinner. Hash. The – the – have you turned off the burner?' she suddenly said to Jon Andersen.

He nodded. 'I turned it down to one.'

'Yes. Maybe Roar will be wanting … When he …'

'Yes?' Hamre said carefully.

'Dinner. And then I thought of making a pudding. With some of the strawberry jam I have – in the cellar. So I went down to my food locker.'

'Just a minute. Did you take the lift?'

'No. I walked down.'

'The stairs in this wing?'

'Of course.'

'Meet anybody on the way down?'

She shook her head and swallowed. 'Nobody.' Then she stopped. Her eyes glistened with tears. Her lips trembled weakly. She looked around her.

I found a handkerchief, leaned across the table and gave it to her.

She took it but didn't dry her eyes. She held it against her mouth and slowly inhaled through it as if it contained some kind of tranquillizer.

'Would you like a cigarette, Fru Andresen?' Hamre said and held a package out to her.

She nodded, took a cigarette, and let Hamre light it.

We'd both done her a favour now, and she could continue. The tears in her eyes were like carpets of dew. 'He … Then I came back up. I saw the door was ajar. I ran out to the balcony right away and it … So many things have gone on here lately – I was very frightened. I thought – Roar –and then – then I found him.'

'That's right, Hamre,' I said. 'I was down in the car park. I saw her running.'

'Don't interrupt, Veum,' he said. 'We'll get to you later.' He turned to her. 'And you also walked back up the stairs?'

She nodded.

'Did you meet anyone?'

'No. But …

'Yes?'

'No. I mean, there are two lifts and the stairway in the other wing, so somebody could have …'

'We know. One lift's out of order. But there are other ways of leaving. Obviously.'

'It could even be somebody else in the building,' Jon Andersen said. 'I mean, somebody living dose by.'

Hamre looked at him. Considering. 'Maybe so. Yes. Maybe.' But he didn't look as if he put much stock in it.

Then he turned again to Wenche Andresen. 'Try to remember what happened. When you saw him. I know it's painful, but …'

She was almost matter-of-fact. 'He was on the floor. Bleeding. I hadn't seen him in – for weeks. It was strange seeing him.

Suddenly. Like that. We were separated, you know. He'd left me. And then – I think I ran out, out on to the balcony. In a panic. I think I screamed.'

I nodded.

'And then – I ran inside again. I wanted to stop the bleeding. I didn't know what to do. I pulled out the knife. It was sort of standing there in him. But it only bled more and then … Then he came.'

She looked at me. I looked at Hamre. 'As I told you,' I said. 'She was holding the knife.'

He looked through me with his sharp eyes. Jon Andersen coughed. The constable stared.

'Fru Andresen,' Hamre said. 'You said a lot of things have been going on out here recently. Anything special in mind?'

She nodded vigorously. 'Oh yes. Yes!' She looked at me. 'Can't you tell them, Varg? I just can't cope.'

The three policemen looked at me.

'Of course I can. It explains how I fit into the picture,' I said. And then I told them the whole thing. From the beginning.

I told them about Roar's trip into town to hire me. About how I'd found his bike and had taken him home. About Wenche Andresen's phoning me the next day. About how I'd found Roar bound and gagged in the hut and – with becoming understatement – about the little battle in the woods.

I said that as a former social worker I'd developed a certain interest in Joker's case, and explained that I'd talked to Gunnar Våge and his mother about him.

I told them about how Wenche Andresen had phoned and asked me to talk to her former husband about the insurance money. About how he'd said he'd bring the money to her in the near future. 'It's probably on him now,' I said.

I didn't mention my meeting Wenche Andresen with Richard Ljosne.

And I didn't mention Solveig Manger. That was up to her to do. I'd keep quiet about it. A last salute to Jonas Andresen. It was a secret he'd trusted me with, and I wasn't going to give it away unless I had to.

Hamre and the others listened intently as I talked. Jon Andersen looked disturbed when I described the achievements of Joker and his gang. Hamre's expression didn't change. He wasn't the type who talks to his cards. You couldn't tell what he was or wasn't holding.

When I finished, he said, 'And today. What were you doing here today, Veum?'

'Today? I wanted to tell Wenche Andresen what her – what Jonas had told me. That he was going to bring her the money.'

'So you were on your way here when you saw … As a matter of fact, what did you see?'

'I saw … First I saw Jonas Andresen – or somebody I thought was Jonas Andresen – and it must have been him – on the way to the flat door. Then my attention was sidetracked by something else, and when I looked up again, I could see the door was open. There was somebody in the doorway. And then I realised something was wrong. I saw Wenche Andresen running from the stairway towards the flat. I was already on my way here when she screamed for help.'

'Did you use the lift?'

'No. One was coming down. The other one is out of order. I couldn't just stand there, so I took the stairs. The ones closest to her flat.'

'Slow down. You said the one lift was coming down. Did you see …?'

'As it happens, I did. A woman. Her name's Solfrid Brede. And in fact, I got stuck in the lift with her only yesterday.' I explained briefly.

'Solfrid Brede,' he repeated and wrote her name down in a little orange notebook.

Jon Andersen's cheeks were red. He looked as if he were on fire. 'Listen. Listen!' he said to Hamre. 'The murder weapon. The knife. You saw what kind?'

Hamre nodded. 'Naturally. It's a switchblade.'

'Exactly,' Jon Andersen said. 'And Veum's just said this Joker, that he and his gang … Anyway, that he flits around here with a switchblade.'

Wenche Andresen took a deep breath and her eyes grew even darker.

'There's no way we're not going to talk to this – Johan Pedersen,' Hamre said.

There was a tense, loaded pause. I hated ruining the excitement. But I had to. 'It's just that Joker – Johan Pedersen – has a one hundred per cent watertight alibi for the time of the murder,' I said.

'How?' said Hamre and Andersen together.

Wenche Andresen stared at me. She looked baffled, almost suspicious. Her fingers clutched the handkerchief I'd given her, and the cigarette smouldered between her bloodless lips.

'Because at that exact moment he was in the car park with me,' I said.

25

'Well. That takes care of that,' Jon Andersen said.

'A one hundred per cent watertight alibi,' Hamre repeated. Thoughtfully. Almost absently.

A constable knocked and came in. Nodded quickly to her colleagues. She was in her thirties, good-looking. Blonde hair with a hint of grey. Eyes and lips which hadn't seen make-up for a long time. 'There's a little boy out there with Hansen. Says he lives here.'

'Roar. Roar!' Wenche Andresen suddenly burst into sobs. 'What's going to happen to us? What's going to happen?'

Hamre motioned the constable over to Wenche Andresen. Said to Jon Andersen, 'Go out and tell them to wait. We can't let the boy in here. Not while ...'

He didn't have to finish the sentence.

We sat and waited for Wenche Andresen to get hold of herself. The constable put her arm around Wenche and tried to calm her down.

My neck was stiff and it hurt. I knew it didn't look especially bright for her. Nor for Roar, and I was mixed up in this, too, for reasons I didn't quite understand. I sat there with a heavy feeling. Sad. These people mattered to me. A week ago I'd had no idea they existed. And now they mattered to me. For keeps. Until death us do part.

Roar. He'd come to my office. Reminded me of another little boy. He'd believed in me, and I'd been his hero for a while. Maybe I still was.

Wenche Andresen. She'd been unlucky. Somebody who'd got the crooked end of the stick. A young woman suddenly left alone. Who missed being cared about and – she'd kissed me. Or I had kissed her. And the memory of her lips lay like a breath across my own.

And Jonas Andresen. I'd liked him. He'd unfolded his whole life for me on that red-and-white tablecloth. Unfolded it like a road map. He'd showed me the side roads, the secret paths, and he'd trusted me with the direction he planned to take. But it had been the wrong road. It had led straight to a dead end.

And there were the others. Joker. He'd frightened me and he'd angered me. But somehow I could understand him. Or I thought I could. There was his mother. Hildur Pedersen. I'd liked talking to her through the fog of vodka. There was Gunnar Våge. I hadn't liked talking to him, but he'd told me some things which perhaps had done me some good.

And Solveig Manger. The mysterious Solveig, but still someone I felt I knew from that quick wordless meeting – and from Jonas Andresen's descriptions of her and of a love I could well understand. All too well.

I looked around me. I'd seen all these little embroideries before. The ones he'd told me about, the ones he'd felt hemmed in by. He'd been right. There were a lot of them. Too many, in fact.

Wenche Andresen was calm now, and Jakob E. Hamre was saying in his implacable, always friendly voice, 'Do you have any relatives in the city, Fru Andresen?'

She shook her head.

'Friends, then. Someone who could look after Roar for a while?'

I knew what was coming. I'd been waiting for it. But she

still didn't understand what he was telling her. 'But – can't I … ?' she said.

Hamre was the only one with nerve enough to look at her as he said, 'I'm afraid we'll have to take you to the station for a while, Fru. For the moment. Just as a witness, but I'm sorry to have to say this. The circumstantial evidence is a little too strong. We can't risk your being out as long as the case isn't cleared up. It involves tampering with the evidence. Things like that. You'll be given a fuller explanation later tomorrow morning. Before you're brought before the court. And of course you need to talk to a lawyer. Do you have one?'

She shook her head. 'No. Does this mean I'm under arrest? But you can't believe that –'

'Now, now. We don't believe anything. We don't have the right to believe anything. But we don't have the right to stop thinking either. And frankly, the whole thing looks pretty clear. But we're going to have a full investigation. You can count on that.'

Her eyes searched for mine. I'd helped her before, but I couldn't help her now. Not now anyway.

'But Roar –' Hamre said.

She interrupted him. 'Varg! He really likes you. Since you were here – the first time – you're almost the only thing he's talked about. Can't you drive him to Sissel – to my sister – in Øystese?'

Hamre looked at me. Doubtfully.

I nodded. 'I can. If I'm allowed to. He can spend the night with me, and I can drive him there in the morning. If the police will fill them in on what's happened.'

I looked at Hamre. He nodded. 'We'll do that. Looks as if everything's settled. If it's all right with the boy.' Then he looked at Wenche Andresen. 'Would you like to talk to him?'

'Oh, no. *No!*' she burst out. 'I can't. I can't do that. Not now. I'd just start crying. I – no!' She turned to me. 'You do it. Can't you take him with you before I leave?'

'Yes,' I said.

'And ...'

'Yes?'

'Just – just tell him everything's going to be fine. Say I'll be away for just a little while. Tell him I'll explain everything – when I come back.' Tears veiled her eyes.

'Keep in touch with us, Veum,' Hamre added. 'We're going to need your statement again. More formally.'

'Right,' I said. 'I'll get in touch as soon as I get back.'

I stood up. Went on standing there. I wanted to walk over to Wenche Andresen, put my arms around her, hug her and say, 'It's going to be all right, darling, it's going to be all right.'

But I couldn't. We carefully shook hands. 'We'll talk later on,' I said. 'I'll let you know about Roar.'

She nodded mutely and I left her there. With the four cops and that silent corpse. I left her there – with a completed past and an uncertain future. With the memory of a kiss and the touch of a hand. That was all I'd had to give her. The only comfort I could offer.

Out in the foyer they'd laid the white sheet on the floor alongside Jonas Andresen's body, and I knew from experience the only thing they were waiting for was the go-ahead from Jakob E. Hamre. Then they'd lay Jonas on a stretcher, tie him down and take him to Gade's Funeral Home. They'd better be sure to tie him down tight – so he wouldn't try to escape.

I left the flat and went to Roar.

26

He was out on the balcony. All the way down by the lift room with the other constable. He was big and jowly with a ruddy face. He looked like a nice guy.

Roar looked lost. His face was so pale it was almost translucent and his light hair seemed lustreless and dead. His eyes were huge. Anxious. It was clear that nobody had told him anything. And that was probably the worst of all.

I went over to him. Put a hand on his shoulder, moved my fingers up along his neck and ruffled his hair. 'Want to come home with me, Roar?' I said. My voice sounded like a stranger's. Rough. Choked. I coughed. 'Would you like that?'

He looked at me puzzled. As if he didn't recognise me. Then, as if they were imitating his mother's, his eyes filled with tears. He cried silently. The tears ran down his cheeks and he didn't try to stop them. Or hide them. 'Is my mum dead?' he said. Searched for me through the rain.

I squatted down in front of him. 'Of course she's not. She's fine. Said to say hello from her. She's just a little busy. She'll be busy for a while.' Maybe for weeks – or for years. It all depended. 'I'm going to drive you to Øystese. To your Aunt Sissel. Tomorrow morning. You'll stay with her for a while – until your mother's got things settled.'

It was too hard to explain and I hadn't talked to a child about such serious things for years. And I was afraid he wasn't going to be a child much longer. I was afraid he'd grow up too early, brutally and at once.

I stood up, took his hand and led him along the balcony. Through the lift room, and out on to the balcony of the other wing. Down all the stairs. Out to the front of the building. Out to the car. Into it. I didn't look back. I would have turned into salt.

I sat him beside me, fastened the seat belt around him. Fastened mine. Drove off. Neither of us said a word.

We sat in my kitchen. Darkness had settled down outside in the alley, had pushed the houses aside to fill the city with night, had locked all of us into our four lighted corners, behind our secure windows and to our familiar kitchen tables.

We'd eaten. I'd fried eggs and bacon. He'd had milk and I'd drunk tea. We'd talked about everything except what was on our minds.

He'd told me about his school. His class. His schoolmates. His teachers. And a girl named Lisbeth who wore pigtails and had a dog named Arnold.

I'd told him about when I was a boy after the war and about the city's burnt-out vacant sites that hadn't yet been built on. I'd told him about the shacks we'd put up and the battles we'd fought. With gangs as rough as Joker's but who we'd fought to the finish. I told it all with the calm a certain length of time always lends such memories.

We forget the times we came home with bloody noses, skinned knees and head wounds. What we remember is the one time when there were so many of us that we routed them. Chased them out of their own street and into the park in a rain of rocks, bits of wood, empty tin cans. A rain of everything we could lay our hands on. Or use.

Afterwards we went to the living room. Turned on the TV and saw the end of the evening news and a horse-faced man

| 148 |

who said there'd be rain and thunder the next day. Snow in the mountains.

I asked Roar if he was sleepy.

He nodded.

I straightened up my bed and got ready for a night on the floor. Or on the sofa. Except that the floor was roomier.

I found a new toothbrush. He brushed his teeth, borrowed my soap and facecloth. Then he went to bed.

I turned out the light, stood in the doorway and looked at him. 'Goodnight, Roar.'

'Goodnight.'

I sat up and stared at the flickering TV, a dead aquavit in one hand and nothing in the other. The images on the screen had no content. Meant nothing. Even the clear fluid in the clear glass meant nothing. When people die too soon that's how it is. And that's how you feel about it.

The phone rang at ten. It was Hamre. 'Magistrates' court tomorrow at eleven. We'll ask for three weeks' custody. Ban on mail and visitors. Just wanted to let you know.'

'No mail or visitors? As serious as that?'

'It is.'

'Has she – who's her lawyer?'

'Smith.'

'Fine-Print Smith?'

'That's right. Old Fine-Print. The best there is. So that's something anyway. For her, I mean.' A long dark pause which felt like a vacuum in the telephone system. Then he said: 'How's the boy?'

'Asleep,' I said.

'Well. You're taking him in the morning?'

'That's right.'

'Be in touch when you get back.'

'Relax. I'll be seeing you.'

'Don't doubt it for a minute. Goodnight, Veum.'

'Goodnight.'

I sat there with the phone in one hand and the aquavit in the other. Then I put the phone down, emptied the glass in one gulp and went to bed. On the floor.

27

I woke early. Couldn't go back to sleep. Too many nameless monsters inside me, too many things lurking behind tall, bare, black trees. They wouldn't leave me alone.

I let Roar sleep and sneaked into the kitchen. Abandoned one of my principles and drank coffee on an empty stomach. Brewed up a huge cup, sat and stared into it as into a bottomless well. But there was nothing to read in the well, and there weren't any grounds in the cup. All the grounds were inside me. Behind my eyes. On my tongue. And in my soul. If I had one.

I tried thinking things through. Jonas Andresen was dead. He'd lived his last day and for the first time in thirty-odd years the sun rose on a hemisphere where Jonas Andresen didn't live and breathe. It wouldn't make much difference to the rest of us. It had meant everything to him but he'd gone to the mysterious country, to foggy deep valleys and hidden woods. He'd climbed to those mountain kingdoms waiting for all of us when our days are finally numbered.

He'd died quickly and brutally. I myself had seen him going to his death even though I hadn't seen the exact moment. I'd seen Wenche Andresen running out of her flat after it had happened. And later on I'd seen Solfrid Brede leaving the lift.

And I'd seen Jonas Andresen. Too late. A few minutes and one eternity too late.

He was stabbed with a knife Joker would have used. But

Joker hadn't used it, because Joker was with me when it had been used.

Who had used it?

I saw Wenche Andresen's drawn face again. When she sat on the sofa with her hands clutching the handkerchief I'd given her. I saw her eyes and her mouth. I saw Jakob E. Hamre. I saw the knowledge in his eyes, the certainty around that firm mouth of his. I saw his calm expression.

Who else was there? Solveig Manger? Her husband? Or a stranger whose face was still shadowed, who hadn't yet moved into the light?

It was the police's job to find out. Mine was simpler in a lot of ways. It was to drive Roar to Øystese and myself home again. Drive towards an uncertain future on the way there and to a misspent past on the way back.

Outside, a new day was reluctantly dawning. When time had been created, this day had been coded as a new day in March, as a day of restless clouds racing across the sky with lovely flecks of blue between them. The low-hanging sun draped some dawn-yellow rays over the city, between the clouds, but they quickly disappeared again. Spring was aiming its searchlight at us, but then it drew back to safer places, waiting for better times.

Roar stood in the doorway. Barefooted. In his underwear. 'Varg? Are you awake?'

The road from Bergen to Hardanger is a road most Bergensers can drive with their eyes closed and with plugs in their ears. At least as far as Kvamskogen. But this winter it had snowed up in the mountains and this was the first time I'd driven that way. I'd had better things to do than ski up to Kvamskogen and back down again. I'd rather go fishing. In white water. Or in aquavit.

Around Skuggestranden you drive on one of the latest improvements to what might be called a motorway and a lot of the excitement is gone. Now you can see two hundred metres ahead of you.

Like all little boys, Roar liked being in a car. I watched his tense expression slowly change to eagerness. He became talkative.

'You're a very good driver, Varg.'

'Think so?'

'Have you – have you chased a lot of criminals in your car?'

'Not a lot. Just every Friday. On *Detective Hour*.'

'Tell me.'

'There's not much to tell. It happens so fast you don't remember a thing afterwards. You're just glad to get out of it alive and in one piece.'

'Oh. But …'

There's a café a little before you get to Tysse. It's in the middle of a sharp turn and there are always lorries parked outside. It doesn't look very inviting from the road. But if you go through the place, you end up in a dining room that reminds you of an old-fashioned winter garden. With big windows like the squares on a chessboard and a wonderful peaceful view of the sea glinting between tender foliage if it's summer.

Now naked branches clutched at the picture but it still gave you the feeling of leaving a garish world behind, of escaping from reality and entering a wonderland. No matter what you ate, you sat there and stared through that big window. It gave you a crick in your neck, but you were in a better mood when you slid behind the wheel again. That landscape put peace in your soul, steadied your hands and improved your eyesight.

Roar and I ate shrimp sandwiches with more mayonnaise

than shrimp in them. They were garnished with a limp lettuce leaf and an even limper slice of lemon. But the view was beyond interfering with and you didn't pay a sales tax on it.

I drank another cup of coffee, and he drank his soda through a straw. The straw was red and the soda colourless. The table-cloth was green and the view …

Three lorry drivers were at another table. They had voices like the sounds you hear in a coal mine shaft and fists like bull-dozers. Their faces were as wide and square as the lorries they drove. It was a sign of the kind of work they did, a symptom or an occupational disease even though the Workers Protection Act couldn't cure it.

I couldn't hear what they were talking about. But it didn't matter. I could hear those rumbling voices and that was good enough. They belonged here just as they belonged in all the world's roadside cafés. On all the world's highways. The last dedicated cowboys.

If you meet one of them some dark night in the middle of a curve and your car's smaller than a locomotive and you're too far over to the left, you've had it. You won't be worth more than the mixture of blood and petrol spilling across the road where you and your car were a few seconds earlier. You're not worth that kilometre where you drove over eighty, or that minute you saved so you'd meet your own unexpected death on time. In the middle of a curve. In an instant coffin of twisted metal and dripping oil …

But the view …

Roar sipped his soda through a red plastic straw. I looked at his face. Who did he remind me of? His mother? Father? I tried to visualise them. Wenche Andresen with her eyes closed and her mouth suddenly ready to kiss. And Jonas Andresen with glasses and his moustache suddenly decorated with beer foam, his fingers around a glass. And suddenly dead.

No. He didn't remind me of either of them. He reminded me of himself. Of a little boy wearing a worn-out blue ski jacket and jeans with patches on the knees, of a boy who'd suddenly appeared in my office – when? How many days ago now? Five? Six? And he constantly reminded me of another, younger boy who hadn't appeared in my office for a long, long time.

'Do you think that's pretty?' I said, nodding toward the window.

He looked questioning. 'What is?'

'The view.'

'The view?'

No. He was too young. You don't see the view when you're eight. You have to have been in love for the first time before you begin to see the view.

We finished our drinks and we left.

The roads over Kvamskogen were clear of snow but black with rain. The snow lay up on the mountainsides in a thin, miserable layer. You'd have to go much higher before you could count on clean fresh ski trails.

They were good roads. The days of the legendary washboard roads over Kvamskogen were past. Tourism had reached even this part of the world. Though not without opposition.

We drove quickly past the jam of summer cottages that made the landscape look like a field of stubble and swooped down through Tokagjelet where the tunnel swallowed us up and spat us out as if we were spoiled fish.

Then the land flattened out again, out towards Hardangerfjord and Nordheimsund. And suddenly it was spring.

It was one of those moments that only come once this time

of year. Suddenly it's as if a celestial hand folds the clouds back and lets the sun loose over the landscape. The sun rolls down the mountainsides, picks up traces of last year's green, mixes them with winter's brown and white and dirty grey and throws them at your feet like dice in a back-yard game. It's spring.

It was spring. Sunlight fell like a net over the land, over the nose-diving mountainsides behind us, over the roads that threw themselves at the fjord, over that blue-white fjord down there and over the blue-grey mountain on the other side. Over the red, white and green farmhouses, over a red bus puffing toward us. Over an old woman wearing a heavy grey skirt, a brown cardigan and a black scarf on her head and standing by the side of the road at a milk collection ramp. She looked at us with a time-worn face. It was spring.

And I kept quiet so as not to break the spell, so as to keep the whole picture from shattering into a thousand pieces. And I noticed in the sudden silence that Roar had seen it, too. That he'd also seen the sudden sunlight over that luscious landscape. He'd felt the same change in himself, had felt the sun setting a new weight on the scales of time, felt an old winter ebbing away and a new spring moving like a flood tide down in the fjord, out in the sea, up in the sky. So maybe you didn't have to be in love after all.

The short stretch between Nordheimsund and Øystese lay along a fjord that shone like blue silver and reflected cascades of sunlight, celebrating spring.

So we arrived in Øystese with winter still in our blood but with spring-like hope in our eyes, and summer-like longing in our skins – until winter and death suddenly seized us again. When we remembered why we were there.

28

Roar's aunt and uncle lived in a large cube-shaped house that looked newly refurbished outside and in. It stood high on the mountainside, surrounded by budding fruit trees, with a view of Øystese and of the fjord and the mountains on the other side of town. It must feel strange living in the middle of a postcard.

Roar's aunt came running down to the gate before we were out of the car. She'd been waiting for us. She hugged Roar for a long time. And that made him cry again.

Then she stood up and we shook hands. 'Sissel Baugnes.'

'Veum.'

She was clearly older than her sister. Sharper face. She was around forty and didn't try to hide it. Narrow lips. Long strands of grey in her dark blonde hair. Her eyes were red-rimmed and there were dark shadows in her face. The shadows of a lot of sleepless hours.

She wore a full blue skirt and an eggshell cotton blouse. Her hands were pink and there were freckles on her bare arms.

'It's been a terrible shock – for all of us,' she said and searched my face as if to discover new shocks and more bad news.

It has been,' I said. 'For all of us.'

'I'm sorry. I'm not thinking. You'll have a cup of coffee? Something to eat?'

I thanked her. She looked like the right person to drink coffee with on a day like this.

She settled me on a sofa in a living room that reflected a peaceful, average family life. There were more photographs than books in the little teak bookcase and the TV the corner was old. Black and white. The black radio with its shining FM antenna was newer. It was playing music from a Hamburg station. A hint of South American rhythms mixed with a West German flute arrangement and a choir of angels. The flute for your ears, the honey for your soul. If you didn't have much of an ear for music and your soul wasn't too wicked.

A red-brown cocker spaniel came yipping in and flung itself wildly on Roar who got on his knees and let it lick his face. 'Rover!' he said. 'Hello, Rover!' It had to be called Rover. Any other name would have been impossible in these circumstances.

She came back with freshly made sandwiches on a pewter plate and poured coffee into solid little cups with roses on them.

'The girls are in school,' she said, trying to talk about everyday things.

'How old are they?' I asked.

'Bent's eleven and Anne-Lise's thirteen. Reidar – my husband – is going to try to come home early.'

'What does he do?'

She drew a hand across her forehead and through her hair. 'He's a shop manager down at Samvirkelaget. He used to have his own little business but it got to be too hard. Too much competition. He was never at home. He couldn't spare the time to be at home, and he couldn't afford to hire help. At nights he used to restock the shelves, price the merchandise, do the accounts and update the inventory and orders. It's not that he isn't busy now. He is. But at least it's not as stressful.'

She seemed upset underneath that calm. She wasn't nervous or hysterical but she was tense just the same. Almost irritable.

A thin network of red veins ran across that sharp narrow nose and her lips looked pale and dry. 'I cannot understand it – how the whole …' she said.

Then she looked at Roar. 'Roar, could you take Rover out in the garden and play?'

Roar nodded. Looked at me. 'You're not going yet, Varg?'

'Of course not, Roar. I'm not leaving all that soon.' There it was again. That strange voice. Not mine. Somebody else's.

As soon as Roar had left, she said, 'The police said – they gave us to understand … Is it true that Wenche's suspected of – that she …' She couldn't finish. She stared at me. Incredulous.

'She is.' I leaned forward. 'But I don't believe it. Not for a second. I don't know your sister very well. As a matter of fact, I met her for the first time less than a week ago. But I don't believe she killed her husband.' I swallowed. 'I don't know if the police mentioned me.'

She shook her head.

'I'm a private investigator. It's my job to find out things. Things which aren't as serious as murder cases – but I don't see this as a "case". This is a tragedy which has hurt people I like. And I promise you, Fru Baugnes, I promise you if there's anything that can be found out, anything that can change the police position – if it's there to find, I'll find it. I give you my word …'

She looked distantly at me. 'We just cannot believe it. She – she loved Jonas so, and she was so unhappy – I've never seen anybody unhappier – when it was over and they separated, because of, because of …'

The front door opened and we heard heavy footsteps. A man came in and both Sissel Baugnes and I stood up.

'Veum,' she said. 'This is Reidar, my husband.'

Reidar Baugnes and I shook hands. 'Pleasure,' he said.

He had a wrinkled face and I figured he was in his late forties. A man with a strong profile, dark blue eyes, a narrow mouth and a chin which had never been able to decide if it were a chin or a neck. He wore a grey work apron and there were three ballpoint pens and a yellow pencil in his breast pocket. His voice was thick. As if he had a cold.

'We were just sitting here talking about ...' Sissel Baugnes said.

She brought him a coffee cup from the kitchen.

They seemed happy together. Contented. They were at the halfway point in life and had passed their crossroads. They had just one direction to go in now and they didn't need a compass. Nobody stopped them and asked tough questions. No strangers crossed the road in front of them and made them change course.

I looked at Sissel Baugnes. 'Your childhood home. I'd understood that it was fairly strict.'

Her husband answered. 'Who told you that? Jonas?'

There was a little edge to Sissel Baugnes' voice. 'I know Jonas used to describe it that way. He never was comfortable with us. Too different. He was from the city and we were from the country. He liked describing us as pious, too religious. But that was ... wrong.'

And she said 'wrong' as if it were the strongest word in her vocabulary.

'He was a snob,' her husband said. 'And we could see what was going to happen.'

'We weren't like that,' she said. 'We came from a God-fearing home, but it was a joyful, beautiful Christianity. Not depressing or dark. My father – he's dead now, God rest his soul – but

I've never heard a person laugh better than he could. He was a good person through and through. Kept his good humour and his faith in his Saviour during the last long years of his illness. We didn't mourn him when he died. How could we? He'd gone home. He was safe. It was sadder for us who were left behind – we had to experience the loss …'

'My mother. How I'm going to break this news to her I haven't a clue. If anything'll kill her, this … She and my father never understood Jonas. He never understood them. I'm not saying it was his fault. Or theirs. They came from two different worlds. And now …'

'Now, look what's happened,' Reidar Baugnes said.

She became more emphatic. 'I simply cannot understand it. When two people marry and promise – I can't understand how one can desert the other. I can forgive his coming from another world, but that, that I can't forgive. Or understand.'

Her husband nodded. Agreeing. 'Are you married, Veum?' he said.

'No.' I didn't feel like explaining.

'No. Then you wouldn't understand. But a marriage – an association between two people who love each other, it is – it should be – so sacred, so pure that nothing – nothing! – can come between them and ruin things.'

I ate a sandwich so I wouldn't have to comment. Then I emptied my cup. Stood up. 'I'd better be leaving. I've got to get back to town.'

They stood up. 'We're grateful for what you said just now,' Sissel Baugnes said. 'If we can help in any way, just get in touch with us. We don't have much money, but – some …' She left it hanging in the air where most questions of money hang before they disappear by some miraculous means.

'Promise me just one thing,' I said. 'Take good care of Roar, if …'

They nodded. 'We'll look after him as if he were our own son.'

That made me feel better. I thought he'd be better off with his mother, but if things didn't work out – this wasn't the worst home he could land in.

Reidar Baugnes followed me to the front steps. When his wife had gone in, he said in a low, confiding voice, 'I wouldn't say this in there. But out here, man to man, Veum, I'm a man with normal appetites. And there are plenty of temptations in today's world. Down at the job – there are plenty of young sexy girls. Egging you on. Not what you'd call shy. I could certainly …'

He stared intently as he thought about what he could certainly do – if he had the guts.

'But I've learned to control those appetites, Veum. I could never do that to Sissel. Not in my wildest moments.'

'Of course you couldn't,' I said. 'I understand.'

'That's the right thing, isn't it?' he said. His tone was almost grateful.

I said goodbye and went down to the garden. Roar was playing with the little dog. When I walked along the path, he came running to me and locked his arms around my waist. Looked up at me. 'Are you leaving now?' he said. 'Do you have to?'

I looked down at that young unfinished face. 'Afraid so. Got to. Got to get back to town. You know. You'll be OK here, Roar.'

Will you be seeing my mum?'

'Probably.'

'Tell her – tell her I love her and I'll wait for her – no matter what she ...' He didn't say any more and I'd wonder all the way home how he would have finished that sentence: no matter what she's done?

You can't really hide things from children. They know everything from the time they're born. Somewhere inside themselves.

In their blood. Or hearts.

I leaned down and hugged him tight. Felt that frail little boy's body. His narrow back, his spine like a pearl necklace. His shoulder blades like misshapen wings, his neck like a little tree trunk.

Then I left in a hurry and drove off without looking back. It doesn't pay to look back. You always end up missing people before you've left them.

On the way out of Øystese I thought of Reidar Baugnes' last words and of what Jonas Andresen had said to me two days earlier. Reidar Baugnes had talked about 'appetites' while Jonas Andresen had talked about 'love'. And I asked myself whether they hadn't been talking about the same thing.

And I'd already started missing people. I'd already started missing him.

29

On the way down from Kvamskogen, I turned off on to a gravel road that led to a valley which began as a U but ended in a V. The road twisted upwards. It was passable this early in the year because there'd been so little snow, but I still wouldn't be able to drive very far.

When the road became too slippery, I swung off it, parked and left the car. Walked uphill fast. Filled my throat and lungs with the sharp mountain air.

This wild, beautiful valley would lead me past some abandoned summer pastures up to the mountain's bare top. If I had the time and the energy. The valley would have been green and lush with birches if it were later in the year. Now it was yellow-brown, barren. Covered with patches of snow.

A wild little river tore along the valley floor. Later, the trout would line up to reach the large deep mountain lake the river came from.

I'd spent quite a few hours – not so many maybe, but they'd been good ones – fishing for trout by that river. I'd waited for the kingdom of heaven, the explosive struggle, the prize for patience, while the sun crept up the mountainside and the air got steadily colder and clearer.

Having had a father who'd hated the outdoors and who spent most of his spare time in museums or bent over books on Norse mythology, I was grown up before I hauled in my first trout. And later on I learned to appreciate those rare escapes from the city. I was too much of a city person to stand being away too long from the traffic, the smoky patterns over the rooftops and the dirty caress of exhaust fumes against my skin. But every so often it was good to get away, scrape the city's dust from my hide, spend some hours in clean air by a clean river and wait for a willing trout. And this was a good valley to know about. An hour's drive from the city.

Sometimes night would darken around me before I went home. I'd build a fire by the river. Make coffee in a soot-blackened can, drink it out of an old tin cup. Then I'd sit there in the darkness with the light from the fire and snapping dry twigs the only other living things. I'd listened for other sounds, but the birds had fallen silent. A solitary hedgehog might root around in the bushes and every once in a while there might be the croak of a frog. Otherwise everything was as quiet as the stars overhead and the mountains all around.

I didn't have my fishing gear with me now, and I'd only come here to get away for a couple of hours, to put a little perspective on things, sort my thoughts into their right pigeon-holes, file my impressions. The air was colder than I was dressed for and I wasn't wearing boots. The snow kept me from going further, so I was forced to turn around and walk back to the car.

Anyway, this wasn't a valley for these thoughts. It was too narrow. It didn't free your heart, your brain or your attitude. You didn't break loose. It turned you inward towards a chaos of thoughts, and made you think of a different, more effective kind of release.

When I got back to town, I went straight home. Showered, put on a shirt and tie.

Then I went to Bergen's finest hotel. If you're not wearing a tie they won't serve you in the bar. You can sit in the restaurant and the waiter will bring your drinks. But I liked the bar.

It was still early and the place was half full. Or half empty. Depending on how you see things. I settled on a stool and latched on to a double whisky. I drink whisky in bars. It suits the decor better than aquavit. You can drink aquavit at home, in the mountains, at sea. Anywhere but in bars. In bars you drink whisky or vodka or those fancy drinks you need a dictionary to order. But I'm a simple guy with simple drinking habits and the dictionaries were at home. So I ordered whisky.

There was a woman nearby. That's the way it is in this hotel. There's always a woman nearby. It's about the best place in the city if you want a woman, and you can choose your ages and price ranges.

From the back this woman could have been in her twenties. She was dressed in a black silk blouse and a full black skirt. A wide tight belt. Slim legs. Long loose yellow-blonde hair. Something told you the colour wasn't natural.

When she turned around, you saw she was closer to fifty than twenty. A face without illusions. Exactly the kind of woman I needed tonight.

Our eyes met. I nodded at my glass and then looked questioningly at her. She stood up and walked over to me with swinging hips and thirsty lips. But she wasn't thirsty for me. She ordered a dry martini and it went on my bill.

'Call me Sun,' she said in a voice which sounded like a badly tuned radio.

'Call me Moon,' I said.

Her face was lined but not weather-beaten. A face more at home indoors than out. I doubted she'd know the difference between a trout's head and its tail. She'd probably never drunk coffee from a soot-blackened pot and if she had, it had been a long time ago.

Her eyes were bright and watery from too much gin, but her

lips were wide and generous and used to drinking straight from the bottle. I didn't mind calling her Sun.

'I was thinking of having a bite to eat,' I said.

'I'll keep you company,' she said. 'But I never eat after four. Can't take it.'

We sat at a table on the balcony and looked down at the few guests who strolled through the lobby. The only tourists were the inevitable pair of ruddy-faced Englishmen. Otherwise the clientele consisted of travelling salesmen, businessmen and more-or-less professional participants in seminars.

'I'm only passing through,' she said.

'Pass through every night?' I said.

'On my way from Laksevåg to Sandviken,' she said. 'I've just moved into a new flat.' She watched the smoke from her cigarette curl slowly up to the ceiling high above us.

After what felt like a couple of hours, a surly waiter brought me an over-cooked pepper steak and some mushy vegetables. But the potatoes weren't too bad.

'If you wanted to – we could go to my place. To my new flat,' she said.

'Perhaps we could. I've always been interested in new flats.'

There were deep furrows on either side of her mouth and I could see the pores on her skin.

'The only thing is, the rent's a rip-off.'

'Oh? Well, my wallet's got a loose mouth and my account's on its last legs, so …'

Her flat wasn't exactly in Sandviken unless you called Øvregaten Sandviken, and it didn't look all that new either. But she had an unopened bottle of first-class whisky.

'Somebody forgot and left it here,' she said, bracing herself against the wall.

I didn't feel especially good and she didn't look especially good. A face without illusions.

When she undressed I saw her body had lost its illusions, too. A long time ago. But it was just the kind of body I needed on a night like this.

I wasn't surprised that she kicked me out. I loved her like a middle-aged marathon runner who's run in the rain and come in somewhere between number eighty and number ninety. I loved her like the messenger who barely manages to creep as far as the queen's feet and deliver the word to her before he dies. I loved her like an old circus elephant who's seen too many seasons and too many trips around the ring. I loved her with the warmth of a coal stove which has stood for years in an empty house. And I hid my face between her legs so she wouldn't see me crying.

Afterwards I rolled out of bed on to the floor and inched towards the whisky bottle under the table. Lay on my back and poured the rest of it into me. Then the fog rolled in, and something large and white bent down and tried to hoist me up while it cursed me up one side and down the other.

So it didn't surprise me that she kicked me out. Even before I'd got dressed. I stood at the bottom of the stairway in the dark entrance hall, and struggled for what felt like hours to get myself into my trousers.

Some kids stopped me in the street, shoved me against a wall and took my wallet. I leaned against the wall and watched them take off with the remains of my cash. Couldn't do a thing about it.

But I did make it home. Woke early. Said to myself: the only release that's going to do you any good is finding out the truth.

Then I showered, shaved, put on clean clothes and was in

Officer Jakob E. Hamre's office before nine o'clock. I wasn't at my best. But at least I was there.

30

Hamre's expression was ironic. 'You don't look so good.'

'Who, me? I haven't felt this good in a long time.' Which said more about how I had been feeling lately than it did about how I felt now. And anyway, it was a lie. Whisky the day after tends to leave the ashes of old newspapers in your mouth and you can't seem to get rid of them. I'd already stopped trying.

Hamre sat on the law-abiding side of one of those desks everybody is issued with in offices that have the personality of a deodorant. The walls are always grey-white, the books are always same books, the view's always the same. A beautiful inspiring view of the middle of a bank built in the most forgettable possible style.

I sat on the client's side – along with the ghosts of all the suspects, all the eyewitnesses, all those who had information they thought might matter to an investigation. It wasn't a comfortable chair, but it shouldn't have been. It was the kind of chair you don't want to settle down in and so you get right to the point and you don't waste time chit-chatting.

Hamre handed me a typed statement of what I'd said at the scene of the murder.

'Fill out the personal stuff at the top,' he said. 'Otherwise I hope it's correct.'

I read through it. The letters seemed to bunch oddly into words. My eyes were tired. But it was correct as far as it went.

I filled in the blanks and then signed.

'He had a girlfriend. Did you know that?' Hamre said.

'Umm – who did?' I said.

'The Pope,' he said. 'Who do you think we're talking about?'

'Oh. The Pope. I didn't know he went in for that kind of thing.'

Hamre moved a transparent green rule carefully from the left over to the right. Studied it for a few seconds. Then he moved it back. It was probably his way of counting to twenty.

'Jonas Andresen had a girlfriend. Did you know that?'

I looked at him.

'You knew that,' he said. 'Why didn't you tell us before?'

'I didn't know her name,' I said. 'And anyway, it wasn't easy with Wenche, with Fru Andresen there.'

'How close are you two anyway? Good friends?'

'Who?'

'You and Wenche Andresen.'

'She and I? I've only known her for about a week. We haven't had time to be good friends.'

'But that doesn't necessarily mean you haven't slept with her.'

'No. It doesn't necessarily mean I haven't. But it does mean that I haven't. In this case.'

'All this – you saw her running, you saw Jonas Andresen going to the door, etc., etc.' He nodded at the statement. 'This isn't some kind of friendly favour?' He let the question hang there a while. 'You really saw all this?'

I wasn't in shape for these questions. 'Yes, I saw it, and no, it isn't a friendly favour. If I'd been going to do her a friendly favour, I'd have done her a friendlier favour. I wouldn't have given Joker – Johan Pedersen – an alibi, for example. And I wouldn't have recommended she stand there with the knife in her hand when I showed up.'

'Of course. But you're the only one who says that's what happened. For all we know, her fingerprints were already on the knife before he was stabbed. Yours and hers are the only prints.'

'The only ones?' I let that sink in. It sank all the way down and I could hear it hitting bottom. 'I see.'

'By the way, we've questioned his mistress – and her husband.'

I looked up from the depths. 'You have?'

'We have.'

'And?'

'When did you say it happened? Can you pinpoint the time? Exactly?' he said.

'No, I can't. No. I think it was around four. Not later.'

'Right. And the woman – his mistress – was at work until five past four. Unless she used a helicopter, there's no way she could have got from the middle of town all the way out there in five minutes. Lets her off.'

I breathed more easily. For Solveig Manger's sake. 'And her husband?'

'Even better. He was holding a literature seminar up at the university from three to five that day. Eight witnesses. And he didn't know about the relationship – until we told him. That's what he said anyway.'

Now I breathed harder – still for Solveig Manger's sake. It's not the kind of news you want your partner to hear – and especially not from others.

'We haven't been able to locate any potential enemies. Except for this thing with the woman and not much sense where money was concerned, Jonas Andresen seems to have lived a decent life. He was popular with his colleagues. Business contacts. His only close relative is a sister. Married and living in Stavanger. They see each other once a year. She comes home every Christmas and lays a wreath on their parents' graves. Then she rushes back to Stavanger in time for Christmas ribs and such. So you can see it hasn't been a close relationship. Like so many of them.'

He stopped, found a sheet of paper and slowly read through it. As if he'd forgotten I was there. Then he peered at me over the top of the paper. 'So, in fact, our only suspect is Wenche Andresen. And to put it mildly, she's very much in the picture.'

'What about the autopsy?' I said. Resigned.

'The autopsy …' He found a form in another pile. 'Want it in detail?'

I shook my head. 'My Latin's rusty. Just give me the conclusions.'

'Well,' he said, scanning the paper, 'cause of death is a knife wound in the abdomen. One lung perforated, stomach lacerated, other organs … He hadn't a chance. And then there's the clear mark of a heavy blow to his forehead. On the right temple. Just about here.'

He pointed to himself and I looked for a bump and a bruise but he was clean.

'A blow?'

He nodded. I could see there was more coming. 'We took a peek under the microscope at the jam jar. As a matter of fact, we found some particles of skin on one edge of the bottom of the jar. We haven't yet made the final comparisons with the victim's skin, but …'

He didn't have to say any more. I'd heard enough. More than enough. He had it just about sewn up.

'One more thing,' he said. 'You said something about his

probably having arrived with some money. The proceeds from the life-insurance policy. Is that right?'

'And?'

'He didn't have any money on him when he … Not that that tells us a lot. We've been in touch with the insurance company and they hadn't heard from him. So we're not going to know what he actually had in mind until …'

'Until?'

'Until she talks.'

'And she's sticking to her original story?'

He nodded. 'She's denying everything. But it won't hold water. We've already been able to reconstruct the sequence of events.'

He ticked off the points on his fingers.

'Point one. Jonas Andresen arrives. Either he rings or lets himself in. He had his keys with him.

'Point two. Enter Wenche Andresen. Jam jar in her hand. Or: she comes up from the cellar with the jam jar right after he's either rung or let himself in. When you saw her running it was probably because she saw the door was open. As she herself says. But she didn't find a body. Not then.

'Point three. She either throws the jar at him or bashes him with it. We don't know why. Yet.

'Point four. He tries to defend himself. Or maybe he hits her. Anyway. She grabs the knife and stabs him.

'Point five. She panics and starts running away, but changes her mind and runs back to the flat. Which is when you saw her, Veum.

'Point six. She screams for help. And you know the rest.'

'But', I said, 'she doesn't own a switchblade. A woman like Wenche Andresen doesn't carry a switchblade.'

| 174 |

'Right. She doesn't. There are still some loose ends. But the outlines are there, and the evidence is pretty strong. There's no doubt in my mind, Veum. Wenche Andresen murdered her husband around four o'clock yesterday afternoon.'

'Any way I can talk to her?' I said.

'There's a ban on mail and visitors. Your only chance is to make a deal with Fine-Print Smith. And regardless, you'll have to get the Prosecutor's OK. On the other hand, I'll suggest she go before the magistrate again. Maybe as soon as tomorrow. And since the evidence is already so clear, I won't insist she be held without mail and visitors.'

'Tomorrow may be too late,' I said.

'Too late for what?'

I shrugged. I couldn't answer that one. I had no valid objections, no reasonable rebuttals. The only thing I had was a feeling that Wenche Andresen hadn't killed her husband. But I could be wrong.

I stood up. At that point the phone rang. He said, 'Just a minute.' Then he smiled apologetically and nodded towards the door. 'See you in court,' he said.

I stopped on the threshold. Stood there a minute. But I still hadn't an answer for him. So I closed the door and left.

31

Supreme Court Attorney Paulus Smith's office didn't look as if it had changed since the twenties. The walls were dark brown, the curtains dark green and there was a brown-and-tan checked parquet floor which reminded you of an elegant chessboard.

And Paulus Smith was king on this chessboard while I felt – if not exactly like a pawn – like a knight. One jump forward and two sideways.

The only things which must have changed since the twenties were the secretaries, or one of them, anyway. And the typewriters. The typewriters were electric. The secretaries looked manual.

There were two of them: a high-breasted, grey-haired woman in a light blouse and a full grey skirt which ended just beneath her knees, a style she hadn't changed since the end of the forties, and a younger woman in her late twenties with dark brown hair parted in the middle and huge dark-framed glasses.

Both of them peered at me like caged owls when I entered the office. The elder had both hands in a grey filing cabinet and looked as if she'd been caught in the act. The younger's fingers were poised over the keys of a typewriter, an expectant expression on her face.

The older one spoke first. She raised her hands and looked at them as if she'd just rinsed them in dirty water. 'How can I help you, young man?' she said.

I've always had a soft spot for women who call me that. I always want to call them 'old woman' but I never do. It's not polite. 'I'd like to speak with Paulus Smith.' 'Speak' would be her word.

She closed one eye, looked at me with the other over her rimless, half-moon glasses. 'Do you have an appointment?'

'No. But …' I said.

'It simply isn't possible. The Supreme Court Attorney is a very busy gentleman. You might, however, eventually talk with one of his –'

A youngish man came out of a door further back in the office. He was at that indeterminate age some people in some law offices freeze into from the time they begin as clerks to the time they retire as clerks. They're always about forty whether they're two years old or twenty or sixty. This one was stooped, dressed in a badly fitting grey suit, a white shirt and a tie I wouldn't have worn when I was fourteen.

He went over to the younger secretary, put some papers on the desk beside her, said something, looked absently at me and disappeared into his office.

I listened for his footsteps. They usually have a quiet walk. But not this one. He was one hundred per cent silent. Maybe he wasn't even there. Maybe I was the only one who saw him.

The older secretary said, 'I could see whether Smith Junior will eventually have a few minutes.'

'I need more than a few minutes,' I said. 'And I'm sorry, but Smith Junior isn't good enough. Tell Paulus Smith it's about the murder case he took yesterday – or the day before.'

She suddenly looked as if she could at least think about taking me seriously. She bobbed her head. 'Well. I will see if …'

Then she disappeared behind a heavy oak door and the

younger secretary turned back to her machine as if she were afraid that I might try talking to her. A few seconds later the old girl came back and announced that the Supreme Court Attorney could give me five minutes.

'Let's make it ten,' I said, and went in.

Paulus Smith was in his late fifties. Short and stocky. Broad chest. Short powerful legs you knew could walk fast and far. Tireless. His white hair was brushed back. His face was the healthy brown of someone who spends time outdoors. He could have just come back from two weeks on the Hardanger plateau.

For years he'd been one of the city's leading defence lawyers. He'd earned the nickname the boys in the police had given him: Fine-Print. If there was a paragraph anywhere nobody else had heard of and he could use it to help his client, he'd pull it like a live rabbit from a hat. He'd filed the whole of the law in an internal system that outclassed any computer and it still worked without creaking.

He stood up behind his desk and walked over to me. Grasped my hand and stared up at me. His eyes were blue and young and they glistened in that furrowed brown weather-beaten face.

'Veum,' I said. 'Varg Veum. I –'

His deep voice interrupted me. He was used to interrupting and to being listened to. 'Yes, I've heard of you. I'm Paulus Smith. Wenche Andresen's told me about you and I've heard about you before. I'd like to hear what you have to say. This is quite an interesting case. Please sit down.'

He showed me to a black leather chair and then settled down behind his desk. His must have been a high chair because he looked a lot taller sitting than he did standing. He rested his arms on the dark brown mahogany, folded his powerful hands. They were sunburnt hands with prominent, almost blue-black veins. Covered with blond hairs. But he folded them as gracefully as if they were the pale, well-manicured hands of an effeminate curate.

'Let's get to the point,' he said. 'Do you believe Wenche Andresen murdered her husband?'

'No,' I said.

His eyes were thoughtful. Interested. 'I don't believe it,' I said.

'Why not?'

I opened my mouth but he beat me to it. 'I don't really care how you answer my question. It's a matter of supreme indifference to me whether a client's guilty or not. A guilty client's case can be equally interesting – it's more of a challenge, anyway. An innocent client is a piece of cake. For me, at least.'

He wasn't bragging. He was simply stating a fact. And it was a fact. I began to breathe more easily. I felt that if Wenche Andresen really were innocent and that if the legendary Paulus Smith and the legendary Varg Veum both got together to prove it – then we had to win. And not a Jakob E. Hamre in this world could stop us.

'As I see it, it doesn't look very promising just now. The way to read it is: she must have done it. There's no other reasonable explanation. The results of the autopsy. Statements of the witnesses – yours included. The state of her marriage. Her background. Everything points to her being the murderer.

'My approach will be to explain why she did it. Why she had to do it. If I were to give my opinion based on a superficial knowledge of the facts, I'd have to plead "temporary insanity" at this point.

'Unfaithful husbands. They're never especially popular with the courts or the man in the street. She'll have people on her side. Without that changing the facts, obviously. But I can already guarantee you this right now. Even if she is guilty, she'll get a light sentence. She'll be out again – certainly on parole – in a couple of years.'

'A couple of years can be a very long time. And she didn't do it.'

He leaned forward. 'You keep saying that, Veum. Now I want to know why.'

'Because I feel she didn't. And because –'

'You feel.' He smiled. Condescending. 'Feelings aren't enough, Veum. Not in a courtroom. We need facts. But I understand. You're young and Wenche Andresen – well ... she's a beautiful girl.'

'She is,' I said. 'But that's not it. I just have the feeling there're things we haven't found out yet. A lot of things went on out there. There are a lot of people we ought to talk to. And obviously, we need to talk to the police too.'

'We?' Paulus Smith said.

'I've got to talk to Wenche Andresen,' I said. 'If you put me on the case, if I investigate the facts – as you call them – do the field work, could I talk to Wenche Andresen?'

He made a tent of his fingertips and nodded slowly. 'You could. As my assistant, the ban on mail and visits wouldn't apply. Is that what you want?'

'The only thing I want is to be able to prove she's innocent,' I said.

He nodded curtly. 'I'm responsible for doing everything in my power to see her acquitted,' he said. 'And for some reason or other I believe you, Veum. Don't ask me why. I'm probably getting old. My brain is beginning to leak. It happens when you've been in this profession as long as I have, Veum.

'I've seen a lot of cases, a lot of misery. And what causes it? I'm not one to stir up tempests in society's teapot. I just look inside the pot and study the tempests. But about half my cases have been caused by social relationships. They've involved a class system which turns out winners and losers, even in our welfare state. And the losers always end up in court. The winners paper over their crimes with money. What are three bottles of beer some poor sod steals set against the million a shipowner hides under his chair year after year? Can you answer me that, Veum? You can. But don't. I already know the answer.

'And the other cases? The French have a name for it. They have a name for almost everything involving love. *Crime passionnel.* A crime of passion. Jealousy ending in murder. The man who comes home, finds his wife in bed with another man, grabs the rifle he keeps in the cupboard, and before the lover can put his trousers on, there he lies. He'll never know or do another thing again. Never again.'

His face was darker now. 'Two kinds of cases, Veum. Crimes for profit and crimes of passion.'

He stood up and walked towards me. I stood up too and he looked up like an excited dwarf. 'I've been with the same wife for forty years. It damn well hasn't been a dance among the roses, I can tell you. But at least it's been the same dance with the same partner.'

'And love?' I said.

'Love?' said Paulus Smith. 'Love's for the young who believe their entire life's before them. Love's for dreamers to lap up as they lie in the moonlight. Love's what girls believe in until they're thirteen and what boys confuse with sex. Love? I'm not talking about love. I'm talking about marriage, Veum.'

'Right,' I said.

We stood and looked at one another for a few seconds. Then he squeezed my arm. 'OK, Veum. You're still young enough to lie in the moonlight and lap it up. Get going. Prove Wenche Andresen's innocent. Give me …' He looked at his watch. 'Give me half an hour. Meet me in front of the police station and we'll talk to Wenche Andresen. Agreed?'

'Agreed,' I said. 'And – thanks.'

'Don't thank me,' Paulus Smith said. 'Just doing my job.'

I left him to do his job. Met a younger version of him outside the oak door to his office. Not as broad-chested and with dark blond hair. And not nearly the same healthy colour.

His face was a little swollen, and he didn't look as if he opened an eye before noon. He looked wearily at me from under his heavy eyelids, quickly realised I had nothing to give him and then ignored me completely. I liked Senior a lot better.

The older of the two secretaries was by the filing cabinet again. I winked at her. Said, 'See you later …' And I didn't say 'old woman' this time either. But it was in the air.

She was a real treasure. She'd been there fifty years, and if you should happen to drop by fifty years from now she'll still be there. She was one of the immortals, the changeless.

I wished her a good eternity, but I'd never want to swap places with her. I'd never make it. The Department of Antiquity in a museum, straight down the hall and then turn left.

I told myself that I'd drop by and check on her. In another fifty years. Or something like that.

32

It had begun to rain. A cold late-winter's rain with the promise of snow in it. I bought three local papers and holed up with a cup of coffee in a second-floor café nearby. The previous day's newspapers were on a shelf. And I did something I'd almost forgotten how to do. I read them. Or scanned them.

There wasn't much in yesterday's papers. 'Mysterious death' in one. 'Man found dead' in another, and 'Stabbing drama in high-rise' in the third. The articles were about the same. The police had already taken a person into custody for further questioning.

I turned quickly to today's papers. The case had attracted more attention. There was more background material. The papers had sent their photographers. They'd interviewed some of the residents, people who'd heard 'something'.

In one paper, a man, whose picture and full name had been published, told how he'd been sitting on his sofa watching the news six months ago when another man in another high-rise had suddenly shot a hole through his living-room window with a small-bore rifle.

The article didn't connect this episode to the murder, but the man's picture was in the paper anyway. And in his little world of three rooms and a kitchen he was now a hero.

From the coverage, it looked as if the press wasn't especially interested in this murder. Not since the killer was probably already in custody. The police were still searching for eyewitnesses, and the inquiry was still in full swing, but Officer Jakob E. Hamre of the Criminal Division predicted he'd be finished with the investigation any time now.

I pushed the papers away. Looked around.

Four foreigners sat at a corner table, drinking tea, eating cake and playing cards. They looked as if they lived there. A ruddy-faced woman in a blue hat was at the table by mine. She stared suspiciously at me over the edge of her paper. Unwavering gaze. Piercing eyes.

At another table, a boozed-up eighteen-year-old was chatting up two teenage girls whose dialect told you they came from somewhere in Sogn. Their heads were together, and they were blushing and giggling. Looking around.

I could hear the constant tonal music you hear in all such cafés. The noises of the cash register, the coffee-maker's gurgling, the clinking of coffee cups against saucers, the scrape of knives, forks and spoons against plates. The air was heavy with cigarette smoke and seasoned with the smell of cooking.

Then I spotted him.

He was five or six tables away and didn't seem to see me. He stared off into space the way people do when they've seen something they wish they hadn't.

He held his coffee cup in front of his face as if he were trying to hide behind it. A tall loose-jointed man who looked like a kid. It pleased me to see he was beginning to go grey and that he was as pale now as he had been the whole time I'd known him – or had run into him. But he wasn't my brother-in-law. His name was Lars Wiik. He was a university lecturer and the husband of a woman named Beate. I'd once been married to her. He was Thomas's new father.

I kept on looking at him and he couldn't help but look in

my direction before he left. When he suddenly 'discovered' me, he smiled like a freshly caught fish, stood up and came over.

'Hi,' he said.

'Hi,' I said.

'I had an hour's break. Couldn't correct another paper. Needed a cup of coffee – a newspaper.'

'How's … Thomas?'

'Fine. He's in pre-school now, you know. Starts primary school in the autumn.'

'I know. I still keep in touch. A little bit.'

'Oh, hell! I didn't mean. But … there's no reason to be … I mean, we don't have to go on being resentful. It was all a long time ago.'

'Everything gets to be a long time ago – after a while.' It made me feel better. This would be a long time ago in a few years. The pictures of Jonas Andresen would fade just as all pictures fade after a while.

'I've got to be going. Have to get back by eleven.'

'Right. Say hello to both of them from me.'

'Will do. Take care.' He smiled and went away. A tall, loose-jointed guy who'd turned out to be a better husband and father than I'd been. I lifted my cup in a silent toast to him and followed him out a few minutes later.

Female prisoners aren't held in the Bergen county jail. They keep them in the cellar of the police station on the same floor as the drunks.

I met Paulus Smith outside the station. He was exactly on time.

We waited in the duty room for a female officer to take us to the cells. Smith's was a familiar face and he didn't have to prove who he was. I was with him and that was good enough for them. Anyway, they knew my face, too. This wasn't my first visit and it wouldn't be my last.

She wasn't in a drunk tank, but it looked like one. It was an oblong, narrow room. A little window of reinforced safety glass high up on one wall. A bunk. A sanitary pail in one corner. A washbasin in another corner with a little towel hanging alongside it and sitting on it a bit of soap wrapped in pink paper. Like an idyllic good-morning gift from a grateful lover. A slat-back chair stood beside the basin. There was a little shelf on the wall. You could write on it, or lean on it, or beat your head on it. Depending on your mood.

Wenche Andresen was standing in the corner under the window when we came in. Her hair was dishevelled and her face as pale grey as the walls. In some strange way it was as if her lips and eyes had absorbed their colour.

She'd changed her clothes. Black trousers, a white polo-neck and a grey cardigan. She'd aged several years in the forty hours since I'd last seen her.

She looked at me. At Paulus Smith. At the officer. And didn't say a word until the officer had closed the door behind her with a telling glance at all of us.

Then Wenche looked at me. 'Varg …'

'Hello, Wenche,' I said.

I was standing just inside that heavy steel door and very much aware of the little white-haired man beside me. He wouldn't miss anything.

From the opposite side of the room she said, 'How's …?'

'Roar's fine. He said to tell you he loves you and that you shouldn't be afraid, and he'll be glad when he can see you again.'

'But – you didn't tell him what I – what they say I …'

'Of course not. I drove him to your sister's. They send their best. They believe you. There's nobody who thinks you –'

'Nobody!' She looked reproachfully at Paulus Smith. 'You should hear them. I feel – oh dear God, Varg – I feel as if they're all against me. As if they've already decided I killed Jonas. As if I could have! I loved him.' She shook her head but she didn't cry. She'd cried herself out. 'It's enough to drive you crazy.'

'I – we don't think you … We've come to help you, Wenche. We –'

Paulus Smith broke in. 'Let's look at this realistically, Fru Andresen. I'll tell you right now it doesn't look promising on paper. But Veum thinks that he can – he thinks he'll be able to uncover facts that'll change the picture. Maybe he won't be able to find out just who did murder your husband, but he'll be able to prove it wasn't you. It's up to the police to find the murderer. We – Veum and I – are concerned only with you. Do you understand?'

She nodded.

'But this means you also have to come clean,' he went on. 'It means you have to be absolutely honest, lay all your cards on the table. Tell us the whole truth about what happened the day before yesterday.'

'But I've already told you the truth!' she burst out.

He stared silently at her. Gaze not moving an inch.

She looked down and then at me. 'I have told the truth, Varg.'

'Of course you have,' I said. 'We know that. But the last time was right after it happened. I'd like you to tell us the whole thing again. As you remember it now.'

'Do I have to? Again? Will it ever be over?'

'I'm afraid, no matter where you go, it'll be a long time

before it's over, Wenche,' I said. 'Probably never. But it'll fade into the background. In time. But if we – if I – can help you, then you've got to tell me about it again. Slowly and calmly.'

'Can I sit down?'

I moved the chair. She looked up at us. 'Does anyone have a cigarette?'

I looked at Smith who found a pack in an inside pocket. 'For clients,' he said. 'I don't smoke myself. Smoking's for kids or the terminal.'

He lit her cigarette. 'As I said,' she began, 'I'd come home and was going to make dinner.'

'Sorry to interrupt,' I said. 'I've got to get it all straight. Anybody know you'd come home? Meet anybody you know? Did you speak to anyone?'

She shook her head. 'No.'

'Absolutely nobody?'

'Nobody.'

'Not one soul you've ever known?'

'No. I really can't remember if I saw anybody at all, Varg. I mean, of course I saw somebody. You're always passing some-body on the pavement. But what I mean is – I don't know the people on my floor. So how could I know all the others?'

'No. Well …'

'Shall I go on?' she said.

'Try.'

'Well. When I decided to make the pudding I had to go down to the cellar for a jar of jam. And when I came back –'

'Wait. You said you walked down?'

She nodded.

'And you met no one?'

'Not a soul.'

'And it takes a while to walk down. And longer to walk back up.'

She nodded eagerly. 'Exactly. That's what I mean. I was away – I'm sure I was away for about ten minutes.'

'Did you time it?' Paulus Smith said.

She looked at him. Puzzled. 'No. But I think it must have been that long because I spent some time looking for the jam. There was only the one strawberry left. Otherwise there was only raspberry and redcurrant.'

'Ten minutes,' I said.

'Yes,' she said. 'And that's when it must have happened.'

'That's when. Ten minutes …' I repeated the times as if they were a coded message I still hadn't deciphered.

'And when I came back, I saw the door was ajar and I thought Roar! The gang! And then I ran.'

'You didn't look down towards the front of the building? You didn't see me?'

'You? Were you there then?'

'I was. I thought you realised I was down there talking to Joker when – the whole thing happened. As a matter of fact, I'm on the police's witness list.'

'That's right,' she said tonelessly. 'You said so the other day. Then – so many things happened. And when I came in, Jonas was lying there on the floor bleeding and bleeding.'

'Was he already dead when you …?' I looked hard at her.

She nodded violently. 'Unconscious, anyway. Oh yes. He must have been dead. He couldn't see me. He just stared at the wall. He didn't say anything. Saliva was running out of the corner of his mouth. And the knife was sticking in him like – like I don't know what.' She looked as if she were about to break down.

'And then what did you do?'

'I … Yes. That must have been when I ran out on the balcony and screamed. And then I went back in …'

'And the knife?'

'The knife? I pulled the knife out. I thought it would help. It was …'

I could hear Paulus Smith sigh. But he didn't say anything.

'And the jam jar?' I said.

'The jam jar? I must have dropped it. In the confusion. I really don't remember everything. The shock …'

'Can you remember where you dropped it? On the floor maybe?'

'Yes – I believe so. And then it broke.' She nodded slowly.

'Try to remember. You didn't drop it – it didn't hit his head when you dropped it?'

'His head? Do you mean when he was lying there?' She looked totally confused.

'I suppose you realise these are leading questions, Veum,' Paulus Smith said. 'They'd never be allowed in court.'

'Right,' I said. 'But I've got to know. And I have to try to help her remember.'

'But I can't, Varg!' she said. 'I can't. It's as if – oh dear God! Maybe they're right. All the others. Maybe I killed him. And I just – I just don't remember it.'

She looked so confused and helpless that I wanted to take her in my arms and whisper, 'No, my darling. No. You didn't do it.' But I didn't. I was the interrogator.

'Don't be silly, Wenche,' I said. 'You know as well as I do that you didn't kill him.'

She hunched in the chair with her face towards the wall. Then she turned and stared up at me from under her eyebrows.

Like an insecure child who's been scolded. 'Yes. I know that, Varg,' she almost whispered.

Nobody said anything for a while. We were both looking at her. I could see Smith hadn't taken his eyes off her for a second. Now and then he shook his head as if it were hopeless. Like a surgeon who hasn't the heart to tell a young cancer patient there isn't a chance. That night's coming all too soon.

Then I said, 'Richard Ljosne ...'

She looked up at me again. 'What about him?'

'You were with him last Tuesday morning. What's your relationship with him?'

She turned red. 'My relationship? What are you talking about? He's my boss. No more, no less.'

I studied her. Her eyes looked at my shirt, at the top button, at my neck. But they were like hot-air balloons with too much ballast aboard. They couldn't float up to my eyes.

'You've got to remember that we're here to help you, Wenche,' I said. 'You mustn't get angry if we ask you stupid questions. If we don't ask them, the police probably will. Later on. And I'm not sure *they'll* apologise when they do.'

She swallowed. Nodded. 'I'm sorry ...'

Her voice was barely audible and she had that same childlike expression on her face.

'Why was he at your house that morning?' I said.

She looked away again. 'He's – he's in the navy. And occasionally he does me some favours.'

'Favours?'

'Yes.' She looked at me as if she expected me to catch on. I was just about to when she added, 'It's not that ... You know I'm not ... I don't depend on alcohol. But I like having a little drink or a glass of wine in the evenings. When I'm sitting alone. You know?'

'Right.' I nodded. 'And Commander Richard Ljosne has access to duty-free booze?'

She nodded again. 'That's right. I don't buy a lot, but … And he's very nice about delivering it to my house when I …'

'So that's what he was doing that day? Making a new delivery?'

'Yes. And that was all. Nothing more. And then he drove me to work afterwards. I wasn't feeling very good as a matter of fact. You know that. All that …'

'And what favours do you do him?'

'No favours, Varg. Not the kind you mean anyway. He's my boss. Our offices – we work together. You could say we're good friends. We're together a lot at work, you know? He's nice. We have coffee together. Talk. I don't have any girlfriends. As a matter of fact, Richard's the only friend I've got.'

'But he's never been more than a friend?'

'I'm telling you he hasn't. I've never … We've never …' She hunted for the words.

I interrupted. 'OK. I believe you. We believe you. Is he married?'

'Richard? Yes, But I don't think they're especially happy. I think they stay together for the children's sake.'

'So he's got children?'

'Three. Two boys and a girl. I believe they're teenagers now.'

'Tuesday. When you phoned me at the office and asked me to talk with Jonas …'

'Did you talk to him?'

'I talked with him, yes. But then when you phoned, I asked if I could come by that evening. But you said it wasn't convenient. That you were busy.'

Now she wasn't looking at my shirt. Now she was looking at her defence lawyer Paulus Smith. As if she wanted him to stop me. As if I were hounding her.

'Where did you go that night?' I said.

She looked at me so suddenly it shook me. 'Out!' she said. 'I went out.'

'Alone? Or with …?'

'With Richard. He'd asked me. He'd been promising me a really good dinner for a long time. It was convenient that night. And he took me out, to a restaurant.' As if to excuse herself she said, 'If you only knew how long it's been – since I've eaten in a restaurant. And danced.'

'You danced?'

'Something wrong? We danced. And when the restaurant closed he drove me home. Said goodnight at the door. That's all that happened.'

'And Roar? Who …?'

'One of the girls in the building babysat him.'

I looked at her. Tuesday night. It seemed as if half an eternity had passed since then. Not about sixty hours. And while I'd been sitting at Bryggestuen listening to Jonas Andresen, she'd been dining and dancing with Richard Ljosne.

'Has he ever made advances towards you?'

'Who? Richard? Never. And can't we stop talking about him? I don't see what he's got to do with this. Richard isn't the one who's dead, is he?'

'No,' I said quietly. 'Richard's not the one who's dead.'

I stood and stared down. The floor was grey cement and since this wasn't a real drunk tank, only an imitation, there was a multi-coloured runner on it. A dirty rainbow. But a rainbow just the same. Then I looked at her. She was so tired.

Drawn. She sat there with her shoulders tensed. As if she'd jump out of her chair at any moment. But she had no place to jump to.

'Just one more thing, Wenche,' I said. 'This – Solveig Manger. Have you met her?'

'Yes.' Her voice was cold. 'I've met her. What about her?'

'She was –'

Her voice cracked like the thinnest porcelain. 'I know who she is. *What* she is. She's a whore. Jonas's little whore.'

'Well …'

She looked at me. Challenging. 'She is! She *is* a whore, Varg. Women who steal other women's husbands are whores. No matter what kind of excuses they come up with.'

'I think you're being too harsh, Wenche,' I said. 'But OK. I understand. You're hurt. You –'

'But when I met her she was as sweet as sugar. Always pleasant. Nice. I'll tell you something. She didn't know I knew about her. She didn't realise I knew what she was the first time I saw her. One of these …'

'Richard Ljosne's married but you went out with him. Didn't you?'

'Yes, I did. And so what? I went out with him. But I didn't sleep with him. And that's the difference! You know everything, Varg. Don't you know that?'

'Is *that* the difference?' I said. 'You could have fooled me. And no, I don't know everything.'

'No. You don't. You really know very little about anything, Varg. Very – little – about – anything …' She'd found her tears. It was just that they took a long time surfacing.

She wept and we watched her face turn red and wither like an old apple. She hid behind her hands. She sobbed against her palms, her wrists. She sobbed with her shoulders, back, thighs, her whole body. All of her.

'I think we've talked long enough, Veum,' Paulus Smith said. 'It's time we left Fru Andresen in peace.' He gripped my arm and glared at me. 'Keep this up,' he said in a low voice, 'and she won't be fit to say anything in court.' He paused. Thoughtful. 'But maybe that wouldn't be so bad.'

I nodded. Said to Wenche Andresen, 'I'm sorry. I shouldn't have said that. You're right. I don't know much about anything.'

She raised her huge eyes from her hands and nodded as if she agreed. Or else accepted my apology.

'We're leaving now, Fru Andresen,' Smith said. 'But we'll be seeing you again. Try to take it easy. It's going to work out.'

'Before we go,' I said, 'can I have a few words with Wenche – Fru Andresen – alone?'

Smith looked searchingly at me. 'No games now, Veum. Remember what I said.'

'I'll remember.'

'Well,' he said. 'I'll wait outside.' He knocked on the cell door and the officer let him out. He told her to close the door but that she needn't lock it. She looked suspiciously at me with a refusal on the tip of her tongue but her respect for Smith won out.

I turned toward Wenche Andresen. She stood up, and I felt her tear-stained face against my throat. Thought: now my shirt's going to get wet. And Smith who doesn't miss anything …

'Oh, Varg,' she said. 'Varg.'

I held her away from me. Saw that red, swollen face, the eyes which weren't about to calm down but which flicked from my mouth to my eyes, and back and forth again. 'Just tell me one thing, Wenche,' I said.

'What?'

'I couldn't ask you while Smith was here. But if you want me to help you, you mustn't get angry. And you've got to answer a couple of questions honestly.'

She nodded.

'Do you have any idea of who else might – do you know anybody who'd want to kill Jonas?'

'No, I … No, Varg.'

I'd asked so as to lead up to the other question. The one I had to ask. I took her in my arms. 'Just tell me. You didn't kill him, did you?'

Her eyes turned from black to blue and the pupils raced from large to small, from small to large to small.

'I didn't kill him, Varg. I didn't. I'm telling you the truth. I didn't kill him.'

'OK,' I said. Stroked her cheek. 'That's all. Take care of yourself. We'll talk again soon.' Then I quickly let her go and knocked on the cell door. Gave her one last look and tried to smile encouragingly. But I don't know if I managed it. I didn't feel very encouraging.

Of course I could have kissed her. But I didn't want to. Not there. Not then. I'd save the kisses until she was out of that cell. Until I could hold her and say, 'You're free, Wenche!' And then I'd kiss her. But not before.

Paulus Smith was waiting. 'Well? What did you want to ask her without me there?'

'I asked her point-blank if she'd killed Jonas Andresen.'

'You did, did you? And what did she say?'

'She said no. She said she didn't kill him.'

He exhaled slowly between clenched teeth. Then he said, 'God knows, Veum. God knows.'

'If He does, He does,' I said.

We trudged up to the main entrance. It felt as if we were emerging from the land of the dead.

'Keep me informed as to what you find, Veum,' he said when we were out in front of the station. He'd become formal again.

'I will,' I said.

We said goodbye. The lawyer walked springily back to his offices and his paragraphs while the detective set off on the longest road of them all. The road to the truth.

33

I found an empty telephone booth in the post office and called the Pallas Advertising Agency. Recognised the voice but didn't react. Said, 'Hello. Is Solveig Manger there?'

A little pause. Then: 'No. Fru Manger's ill today. May I give you someone else?'

'What about giving me you?'

A new, longer pause. Then icily: 'May I help you?'

'No, thanks,' I said. 'Not today. Try tomorrow.' And I hung up. Not very funny but I wasn't feeling funny. Not today.

My car was parked up on Tårnplass. It was still raining but not as hard as it had been. The drops were farther apart now. A good slalom skier could make it dry-shouldered over Torgalmenningen if he went at a good dip. It was foggy up on the mountains, and you couldn't see more than a metre or so up beyond Fjellveien.

As I was unlocking the car, a noisy wedding party came down the City Hall's wide steps. The bride in a dark blue dress printed with tiny flowers, the groom in a grey suit. The wedding party wore everything from dark suits to jeans and leather jackets. A man in dark trousers and a grey jacket backed into the street, stood in a puddle of slush and with an Instamatic camera immortalised the happy couple. They held hands, beaming at one another and the world. With roses in their cheeks, and wind and rain in their hair. A new couple on the way to the slaughterhouse.

As I drove off, I thought of all the weddings I'd been a part of. Of all the speeches I'd heard, of all the sloshed, happy wedding guests I'd sat with, of all the happy couples I'd seen.

You rarely think of what's ahead when you celebrate at a wedding. You laugh and drink toasts and you don't think about tears, or loneliness. Or jealousy. The newlyweds are going to waltz through life and marriage as happily as they dance their first dance together. You don't picture them at the lawyer's. Each in his own chair. Looking straight ahead and as little as possible at the other. Or lying in the same bed forty years later, back to back. As far apart as possible. Nothing more to say to one another, nothing more to do with one another. After forty years of long grey days without funny moments. Or Sundays. Oh, yes. New couples constantly on their way to the slaughterhouse …

But now I had to plan my strategy. First I had to find out what happened at the actual time of the murder. First of all I needed to talk to Solfrid Brede. I'd seen her leaving the lift as I was running up the stairs. Only to find Jonas Andresen – and Wenche Andresen standing over him with that knife in her hand.

I parked in front of the high-rise. Looked up at it as a climber looks at a mountain he's done a hundred times before but is going to tackle again.

Gunnar Våge, bent against the rain, trudged by in the distance, his green windbreaker turned up at the collar, a knitted cap pulled down over his forehead. I think he saw me because he slowed down, but then hurried on as if he didn't want to talk. OK, not right now, I thought. But your turn'll come. Just wait. Just you wait, Gunnar.

I walked towards the lifts. There would be too many

buildings and too many stairs. I'd better use the lift when I could.

Got out at the seventh floor and walked out on to the balcony, read the names on all the doors. Wrong balcony. Went back past the lifts to the other balcony. S. Brede was written on the second door I came to.

I looked in her kitchen window. I had no idea if she was at home. She was probably at work. But on the other hand, she didn't look as if she worked. The kitchen window told me nothing. The printed curtains were pulled back. Dark inside. Neat.

I rang. Heard the sound of high heels clicking quickly towards me. Then the door opened and Solfrid Brede looked out.

She wasn't wearing her fur coat. Her body looked twenty years younger than her face. It was a good firm body. Big breasts. She was wearing a beige mohair sweater and a brown tweed skirt.

In the daylight you could see the beige tinge in her brown eyes and the furrows in her face. The bags under her eyes were even more obvious now. She looked as if there'd been more winters than summers in her life. She reminded me of a woman I'd met the other night. Except that Solfrid Brede looked a lot nicer. Friendlier.

'Hello,' I said. 'My name's Veum. I don't know if you remember me.'

She nodded slowly and looked at me questioningly. Neutral.

'I'm helping the defence lawyer in connection with Wednesday's crime. I wonder if I could ask you a few questions,' I said.

'I've already told the police everything I know,' she said. 'But of course …'

She stepped aside and held the door. It was impossible to pass without brushing against her breasts. She smelled of lilies of the valley. Like a teenager.

I knew these flats by now and went straight to the living room. It was a snug warm room. It suited her. Over-furnished with two sofas and a lot of roomy old-fashioned armchairs you could curl up and doze in. A rocking chair in one corner. Rag rugs fanned out on the floor as if a pack of cards had fallen there. Too many rugs for this floor and they partly overlapped. The walls were papered in dark brown with a pattern of lilies and there were plants everywhere. In the windows. Sitting on shelves. Hanging from wall brackets. It was like a botanical garden. I should have brought my machete.

I headed for the nearest armchair. Then I waited.

'May I offer you something?' Solfrid Brede said. 'A liqueur? Beer? Whisky?'

I was about to say no, but on the other hand, it was going to be a long day. I could use a little reinforcement. 'What about a very very weak one?' I said.

She smiled. 'Finally! A man after my own heart. What kind of very very weak one? Whisky? Brandy?'

I remembered the taste of old newspaper ashes. 'Brandy and soda sounds fine.'

She opened a little cabinet-bar on one of the shelves, poured me a very very weak one and several fingers for herself. Then she sat on the sofa and crossed her knees. There was no way her skirt could have been shorter. We lifted our glasses. *Skål!*

'We are on a first-name basis, aren't we?' she said.

'How could we be anything else after being stuck in a lift together?'

'God, yes. That was awful. But … Well. Tell me.'

'No. You tell me. What did the police ask you?'

She looked at me sideways. 'What did they ask?' She hung on to her smile. 'They asked me where I had been that day. When I left the lift. When the murder happened. I said I'd been here. Then they asked if I'd been alone and I told them yes. He was rather sweet. That policeman. Hamre I think it was. Polite. But I couldn't tell them a lot, as a matter of fact.'

I was disappointed. She couldn't add anything new. 'And did you hear anything? Did you see Andresen?'

She shook her head.

'Did you know the Andresens?'

'In this building? It's like living in Laksevåg and maybe knowing people all the way out in Landås. I mean, it would be just as improbable. Of course I've seen them. But they belonged to another – circle.'

'Are there really circles? Here in this building?'

'Why ask?' she said.

'I just wondered. Just trying to get some idea of what kind of place this is.'

'What kind of a place? You could say it's like a refrigerator. The milk on the lowest shelf doesn't talk to the ice cubes, and the cheese doesn't ever speak to the food on the shelf above it. It's a place to live in. A place to bring your friends to, or chase your partners out of. But it's not a place to make new friends. Or meet new partners either, for that matter. I should know. I've had a few. Husbands, I mean.' She smiled wryly.

'All that many?' I asked.

'Depends on what you mean by many.' She counted on her fingers. 'One, two, three, four. And I divorced them all. Never killed one of them. Not a single one. The idea was that each one should be richer than the last. Then your standard of living doesn't go downhill. My last husband loved me so much I never had to work again.'

That explained her face. Say what you like about divorces, they don't make you look younger. Each one marks your face. And places nobody can see.

I smiled. 'Are you so impossible as a wife?'

'No worse than most.' She rolled her glass between long, white, red-tipped fingers. 'I don't believe marriage is something for ever, and wonderful. If you know what I mean. Personally, I think … I don't believe in these new fashions. Living in collectives. That kind of thing. It's hard enough living with one person, never mind a mob. Each one with his own needs and special quirks. Quirks can be charming in the beginning but they lead to a war of nerves after years of togetherness. When the little details stop being the spice in a marriage and start grating on you.

'I mean, an absent-minded guy is a real joy when you first fall in love. But an absent-minded guy's hell in a couple of years. No. I believe in our Western system of two by two, but I can't kid myself that it's good for your whole life. Ten years maximum. That's a reasonably happy marriage. If we forget the few lucky exceptions. But otherwise? It gets to be routine. Boring! It either blows up or else you end up in Dreamland for the rest of your life. And do you find peace when you're dead? No! No, no, no. They bury the two of you together.'

She put down her glass, and lifted her hands so she could examine her fingernails. 'I think I can say I've been honest anyway. When the marriages stopped working, I left the table. I think we should all be like that. It can be hard when you're going through it, but you come out of it with your self-respect. You land on your feet.'

She drank. 'It can be lonely sometimes. Of course. Especially when you're not so young any more. But, on the other hand …'

She looked at me over the edge of her glass. 'There's a lot a mature woman can do for a man, with a man, that a young girl can't even imagine. A teenager has a better-looking body maybe, but she's like a baby with an electric train. She hasn't a clue as to what to do with it. But a mature woman knows. Isn't that right, Veum?'

'That's right,' I said.

'How old are you?' She looked at me curiously.

'What do you think?'

She looked me over. Paused at my chest which is neither broader nor narrower than most people's. Then at my stomach which is about average. Studied my face. 'I'd bet,' she said, 'I'd bet mid-thirties or a well-preserved forty.'

'Thirty-six,' I said.

She smiled and raised her glass to me. 'The prime of life for a man. Old enough to know the ropes but not so old he'll fall through them. And not so young he'll crack up in the doorway.'

She spoke in parables like a walking New Testament. 'I don't know exactly what you have in mind,' I said. 'I'm busy right now, as a matter of fact. I've got a job to do. And I think I'm in love, as a matter of fact.'

She nodded. 'Nothing special in mind. But you look like a nice guy, Veum. If you're ever lonely, call old Solfrid Brede. Don't count on it, but I just might be home. I have to tell you …'

She had to tell me. But first she had to have another drink. And this one had to be stronger. It was a long grey day and she had no special plans. She offered me one but I was still only halfway through the first.

She sat down. 'I've got a friend. I mean, a lover. It's been ten years, as a matter of fact. On and off. He stuck around through two of my marriages and survived both those husbands. He's a nice guy. I like being with him. He's warm. Good in bed. A guy you can talk to without having to wear your mask. But I'd never marry him. Not on your life. Never!'

'Why not?'

She took a sip. 'I don't really know. Maybe it's because he's too good. Maybe I'm afraid this marriage would last a lifetime.' Her eyes darkened. 'And that's exactly what I haven't got the nerve for. It must be … it must be like going on a cruise and not knowing if you'll ever come into port again. And anyway he's married.'

I nodded. Emptied my glass.

'A dividend?'

'No, thanks,' I said. 'I've got to be going.'

'Veum?' Her voice was husky.

'Yes?' I said.

'You do look like a nice guy. Do you think you could come over here and kiss me?'

I looked at her. Even though she was only half a metre away it seemed too far to plod across that desert. I'd never make it.

'Even if you are in love with someone else,' she said. 'A kiss doesn't mean anything. A kiss is just a kiss.'

In spite of four doting husbands and one ideal lover she looked amazingly forlorn sitting there, asking for a kiss. Abandoned.

I went over to her. Leaned one hand on the coffee table and bent down. The scent of lily-of-the-valley was stronger. Those big breasts bobbed like peaceful waves against a summer beach.

I tucked my other hand under her chin and turned her face

to the light. Looked at it. Her husbands had walked on that face with metal reinforcements on their shoes. Her lover had scratched that face with sharp, newly filed nails. Her sons had ignored it for years, had left it in a child's room along with their other discarded worn-out toys.

Men had left their marks on that face and it had coped with them. She'd faced the storm and had spat in its teeth. And now sat alone in a living room too big for her, with a face too sad for her, with a glass two people should share.

I thought of kissing her cheek the way a son kisses his mother. But I kissed her mouth. Long and slowly, the way people kiss who've loved each other for years.

First with your mouth almost closed. Nipping. Then with your lips open, and searching with the tip of your tongue. And then with your mouth wide open and so hard that your jaws meet and you're like two skeletons clutching each other in the grave in one last desperate embrace. And then with your mouth closed again and your lips puckered. Like teenagers saying goodnight somewhere on a stairway in a twilight-blue street in the past or future. Somewhere in a place we take along in all our eternities. The one place in all the memories we all haul around somewhere or other in our luggage.

She clung to me, breathing faster, her arms around my neck. I stopped kissing her and cautiously freed myself. The conductor had blown his whistle for the last time and the train was leaving. Goodbye, my love, goodbye …

I heard my own voice. I was hoarse. 'Some other time, Solfrid,' I said. 'Some other time.'

'Don't do tomorrow what you can do today. Where this is concerned anyway,' she said.

'But I've got a job to do. I've got to find a murderer.'

She stretched out a hand. Then she let it drop. Her gaze went back to her glass and so did her hand. 'All right,' she said. 'I didn't mean … You're very … Don't forget me anyway, Varg. Some other time then.'

I nodded, standing there in the middle of the floor with a sheepish expression on my face. 'Some other time then. Take care,' I said.

'Yes,' she said. 'You, too.'

She held the door and I left without touching her. As if I were some kind of airy spirit. Afterwards, after she'd locked her door and I was walking along the balcony, I thought she'd been right. Never do tomorrow what you can do today. You never know where you'll be tomorrow. Before you know what's happened you could be sprawled in somebody's entrance hall. Bleeding to death.

34

I checked my watch. Almost one-thirty. I wondered how long Richard Ljosne stayed in his office. I really wanted to talk to him now. More than anybody.

I could phone and find out. I went to one of the telephone booths in front of the high-rise and called the naval base. After a short wait Commander Ljosne answered.

'Hello, Ljosne,' I said. 'My name's Veum. We met the other day – out at A …'

'That's right,' he said. 'What can I do for you?'

'It's about what's happened to Wenche,' I said. 'We both know she's innocent …' I held my breath.

'Of course she's innocent,' he said. 'It's stupid to think anything else. Wenche couldn't kill a fly. And that guy – she adored him. If the cops think otherwise they've gone mad.'

'That they have. I happen to be working for her lawyer and we're sure she's innocent. But I need to talk to you, Ljosne. As soon as possible.'

'Listen, Veum. The day we met – you looked like someone who could run a few metres. Can you?'

'I run a little,' I said. 'Once a week or so. Twice when I have time. When I was in Social Services, I ran for one of their teams. As a matter of fact, I was a pretty fair long-distance runner. But that was some years ago. What –'

'Listen. I leave the office at two on Fridays. Go out running. Then I hit the steam room, and I might swim a lap or two. We have a sports centre out here. If you'd join me, we could talk at the same time. I guarantee it'll do you good – and I promise not to leave you behind.'

'But I haven't got any …'

'I'll ask them to send up a pair of shorts and a tracksuit. What size shoes do you wear?'

'Forty-two.'

'You can borrow a pair of mine. I'm in the administration building. I'll call Security and tell them to expect you. Can you get here by two?'

'I can.'

'See you.'

I hung up and checked to see if my muscles had recovered from yesterday's release. This was the best release of them all and I'd forgotten it. That you run yourself clean, and maybe also learn something.

I was almost looking forward to meeting Richard Ljosne. I've always enjoyed running alone. I'm a lone wolf and therefore a long-distance runner.

The dash – that's like coitus interruptus. All too short and you're left hanging. The middle distances take too much from your soul and give too little back to your body. A long hard run through the woods or on a road, alone with yourself, your body and your thoughts, a run which turns all your stiff muscles to butter and bathes you in sweet sweat – then a quick shower, ten minutes in a steam room, and another shower – that's another thing altogether.

I felt myself getting ready as I drove the short distance to the naval base. I parked outside the compound, signed in, and was told how to find the administration building. It was ten to two.

Norway's largest and most important naval base is predictably enough on the ocean in a park-like setting where the sea clings with long narrow fingers to the mainland. The base itself is a mixture of military camp and park. There's plenty of space between the barracks and enough trees for a whole army of spies to hide behind if they can get past the fences and if they're thin enough. Most of the trees are tall, slim silver birches with well-groomed crowns which they decorate with green in summer.

I found Administration and the second floor. Walked down a long military-looking hall with a freshly polished grey-brown door and grey-white walls interrupted by closed doors. I stopped in front of the one which said: Richard Ljosne, Commander. Wenche Andresen, Office Assistant.

I knocked. Richard Ljosne opened the door.

We shook hands. 'No point in being formal, is there?' he said.

'Not as far as I'm concerned,' I said.

He handed me a tracksuit and showed me into his office. We passed through Wenche Andresen's first. It was spartan. A desk, a chair, a counter and shelves filled with files. Ljosne's office was as ascetic but his desk was larger and there were books as well as files on the shelves. A large map of the base hung on one wall. King Olav hung on the other.

Richard Ljosne had already changed. He wore a red tracksuit and a light jacket; a white hand-knitted cap with a red border was pulled down over his wolf-grey hair. He stood, shifting and bobbing while he waited.

I walked into his office and left the door ajar while I changed. I wasn't going to chance anyone saying military secrets had disappeared while I'd been in there. The tracksuit was one size too small and the shorts could have housed a relay team, but the shoes fitted which was the most important thing.

'Well?' Richard Ljosne said expectantly when I came out. 'It's great having company when you're running. We'll take it easy so we can talk at the same time. That's why you're here, isn't it?'

'That was the idea,' I said.

We trotted out of the building and over towards the gate. 'We have a track through the woods just across the road here,' he explained. 'It's just right for an easy run. See that?' He pointed at the Lyderhorn. 'When I really want to work out I run up to the top. An easy jog from here and then a hard stretch up to the top along the ridge and over to Kjøkkelvik and then back along the road. If you can run that non-stop you're in good shape, Veum.' He smiled encouragingly at me the way a coach smiles at a beginner.

But I didn't feel like a beginner. I felt more like an old crock who's started running again to prevent a heart attack. I was already puffing.

The grade up to the gate was steep. Once we passed Security, we crossed the road and ran up a new slope to a gravel road with buildings on the right and dense woods on the left. A car went by. In the distance a young girl on a chestnut horse bounced toward us. It wasn't raining now and the fog was lifting. But the air was still damp and the visibility was still poor. The girl on the horse seemed like a mirage, a dream, a horse deity in an alien forest, a Greek goddess in a meadow.

The road levelled off. 'What do you think about Wenche – and what happened?' I said.

'She didn't kill him.' He was as cool as if running didn't affect him one way or another. 'She adored him. Too much, if you ask me. Even after he left. She couldn't seem to break loose from him. Begin living her own life. If you know what I mean.'

We passed the rider. She looked at us disdainfully. Just as a young woman on a horse would naturally look down at two middle-aged men in red tracksuits running through the woods.

'What,' I gasped, 'what, what was your relationship with Wenche? Know each other well?'

His dark eyes shot a look at me from under those bushy grey-black brows. 'We're good friends,' he said. 'She's a good colleague. Yes. We know each other well.'

The road suddenly swooped and swung to the left. We passed a paddock and a lot of horses. A boy and a girl in jeans and heavy Icelandic Håkonshallen pullovers sat talking on the fence. Then the gravel road ended and we were in a tangled stand of firs and on a rocky path. Farther on we turned left across a marsh and up a narrow muddy trail. Ljosne ran tirelessly.

My legs were getting heavier and it was harder to keep up with him. The sweat was pouring off me but that was good. I could feel the effects of the recent long car trip and last night's abortive release beginning to ooze out through my pores. My body was getting rid of yesterday's and all the other days' wastes and getting set for the days ahead.

'Wenche turned me on the first time I saw her. Something pure and innocent about her. Don't you think so? Almost virginal. Like a little girl. The kind that melts the stony hearts of old pigs like us, right?'

I wasn't entirely enthusiastic over his description of me, so I didn't answer. Just took a deep breath and ran a little faster.

He looked surprised. 'You want to pick up the beat, Veum?' He grinned. 'OK. OK – you asked for it.'

He sort of leaned into the air and as his body bent forward he increased his speed and the length of his strides. And left me standing.

The trail still sloped upward. We were out of the woods now. Heather stretched away on either side, still grey-black in March, and there was withered pale yellow marsh grass and grey rock.

I ran faster so as not to lose him. Thought: he's in better shape than I am but damn it, he's got to be fifteen years older. I swore he wasn't going to lose me. I hung five or six metres behind his broad athletic back. He didn't speed up. I didn't catch up.

Then we were on a gravel road again. It suddenly swooped down and turned to tarmac. A fast downhill run and we were back on the main road. The whole naval base spread out before us. We were a couple of hundred metres from the main gate and now he sped up. Gave me a wolf-grey glance over his shoulder. Egging me on.

I took him up on it and started sprinting. My speed slowly increased and his lead shortened. I could hear my breath and, to my pleasure, his – when I got close enough. Fifty metres from the gate we were neck-and-neck. Like two trotters on the home stretch. 'You're a good runner, Veum,' he panted.

'You, too,' I panted, and watched the spots dancing before my eyes.

We were still neck-and-neck. A little faster now, but neither of us managed to break free. As we passed Security, I jumped a kerb and made a fast surprise inside turn. That gave me a lead of a couple of metres.

I was in the lead now. It was the way it always is when you're ahead: suddenly you're all alone. All your competition's behind you. Everything is. All the races you've ever run, all the life you've already lived, and you're alone in the universe and above the clouds. You're above the clouds and your head's among the stars and you're running. You're running. Your feet move automatically, your body's floating, your breath's stronger and stronger and you're an angel in a heavenly chariot. You sweep everything aside. You are the champion. You have won …

And then everything shut down. In a flash I saw he'd passed me, and he was running even faster for those last hundred metres to the administration building. When I arrived, he was standing there. Bent over and breathing with long heaving drags, but he wasn't so winded he couldn't look up and smile at me. The winner's smile.

I always told myself afterwards that I'd let him win, that I'd wanted him to talk and that winners always talk more than losers. But the truth was a lot simpler. He had more in reserve. He was in better shape. He beat me.

When our breathing got back to normal, he said, 'A great run, Veum. Now let's pick up our clothes and then we'll go over to the sports centre, try the steam bath and then swim a few laps, OK? And we can talk more.'

I was too tired to answer. I simply nodded.

We sat high up near the steam room's ceiling, a fine room with the right kind of heat. Designed for young men in good shape. Our own sweat replaced the shower's dampness in no time.

Ljosne looked unusually solid for somebody around fifty. His skin had a healthy, ruddy colour which could only come from exposure to the Alpine sun at this time of year. The hair growing in a stripe up his belly and into a thick jungle on his chest was the same grey as the hair on his head.

He became critical. 'You're too thin, Veum. Otherwise you're not too bad. You should eat more. Rare steak, whole-grain bread. Goat's cheese. Doesn't matter if you drink beer as long as you run it off. A guy should put some meat on him so he looks as if he's made of muscle and not bone – not like you. As a matter of fact, no woman likes a skinny man. Same as us. We don't go for women you can cut yourself on. There ought to be a little cushion to roll around on. Am I right?'

I wiped the sweat from my eyes. Didn't answer.

'Have you talked to Wenche? Since … ?' he said.

I nodded. 'Just for a short time.'

'Did she talk about me?'

'Not a lot,' I said. Waiting.

'No. She wouldn't. Wenche's the soul of discretion. That's one of the things I liked about her from the beginning. She's one of these women who only open their mouths to drink a cup of coffee. You know those others – you see them in tea-shops and places like that – they sort of bend over their coffee cups and go at it. They talk non-stop – yak, yak, yak – and you wonder if they'll ever empty those cups? Or whether they're part of the get-up? They only shut up when they're sucking in some new titbit. Ears wide open and their eyes out on stalks. Am I right? But not Wenche.'

He rested his elbows on his knees. His back was covered with the same iron-grey hair. Somebody must have named him 'The Wolf'. Somewhere in Richard Ljosne's life there was a group of people who could say: 'They used to call him "The Wolf".'

'How long has she worked here?'

'I chased her for two or three years, Veum. Not – not like you chase other women. That wouldn't have worked. Not with Wenche. She's quiet and she certainly can act modest and reserved. She's not easy pickings. She's not the type you pour a half-bottle of wine into, spin a line to, and before she knows what's happened she ends up naked in your bed with her legs wide open. Not Wenche.'

The sweat was pouring off me. My eyes stung. My body was heavy. Hot. It was like having and not having a fever. If it was a fever, it was a good one. Healing. 'No. Not Wenche,' I said. 'But you went after her anyway?'

'You bet I did. Jesus! I couldn't help it – nobody who sees her can help it. She gets to you. Where you live. Am I right?' For some reason he looked at my crotch instead of my face.

'No,' I said tightly. 'I hadn't noticed.'

'Something told me – and I've known a lot of women, Veum, something told me that this was a plant you had to nurse along, bring along slowly. And when the time finally came, that plant would bloom, open its bud, bloom as it never had. Never before. Not ever. And I ... I slept with her.'

I felt a stab of cold, as if somebody had suddenly twisted an icy knife in my heart. 'Oh?'

'I did. I laid her. Tuesday.' His head was nearly between his thighs now. His neck looked red and creased, and suddenly he looked older. Beads of sweat gleamed in his hair. It looked thinner and matted. There was a bald spot on his crown and the arteries throbbed in his forehead.

'Tuesday?'

He lifted his head and looked at me like a wounded bull. Red-rimmed eyes. 'I followed her around like a dog for two or three years, Veum. I talked to her hour after hour. One cup of coffee after another. I did favours ... for her. Favours I was in a position to do. Got things for her. Gave her extra days off if she needed them. There was the kid ...

| 216 |

'And then Andresen left and I thought, *now*! But she was as stubborn and as stand-offish and as righteous as ever. And then I swore to myself – I'm damned if you're going to go on making a fool of me, Wenche. If there's a woman on this earth I want, I want you. And you're damned well not going to get away with it.

'We used to say – in the mess – you haven't played your cards right if you meet a woman you can't lay. Every woman's got her own code. But all of them have a code. There's always a weak point. But sometimes it's damned hard to find it. But then Tuesday ...'

'Tuesday?'

'Yes. I'd been asking her out to dinner – for a long time. But, well, I'm married, and it had to be a day my wife was out of town. Or something. And she was in Trondheim on Tuesday. Family stuff. So I said to Wenche: how about dinner? And suddenly she said yes.'

'You hadn't been out together before?'

'No, as a matter of fact. So you know how I felt. What's going on, Wenche? I asked myself. What's happened all of a sudden? Have you got over him all of a sudden? And then ...' He shrugged. 'Not to make a long story out of it, we went out for dinner and then I took her home. Went up to her flat. I mean, I waited on the stairway until she'd sent the babysitter home. And then I fucked her like I've never fucked another woman before, Veum!' He slammed his fist into his palm. 'And Jesus!' he said. 'And three days later ...'

Tuesday. While I'd been sitting and talking with Jonas Andresen. But she had said ...

'It wasn't the usual, Veum. It was really great. Not something an old pirate like me thinks he's going to ... I mean, once you've seen what's between one woman's legs, you've seen it all. It's like going ashore in Marseille, getting a dose of syph, and then going home. That's not my idea of a change of pace. But then – all of a sudden – all of a sudden, you screw a woman twenty years younger than you and *she* teaches you! Makes you want to cry. Am I right, Veum?'

I grunted. 'Did she … did she give you any reason to believe that she'd suddenly surrender?'

He looked at me. A crooked smile. Lurking under his nose.

'Surrender? You sound like an old maid schoolteacher, Veum!' He shoved his face next to mine. 'She didn't surrender! She screwed me so it poured. And then she said …' He clenched his teeth. 'And then, afterwards, she said it had never been so good. So I gave her something, too.'

'Trying to make me jealous?' I said. 'Or what?'

He looked in my direction. 'Don't be a poor loser, Veum. Are you jealous? Had your own plans?'

'My relationship with Fru Andresen is professional – totally, entirely professional,' I said.

'Bullshit, Veum!' he said. 'There's no way a relationship with Wenche can be entirely professional. Take it from me. If anybody could make me consider divorce, it would be somebody like Wenche.'

'She doesn't like divorces,' I said.

'Doesn't she? Well. Maybe not. But maybe she was ready to try again. Climb up the ladder, if you know what I mean. I've got to tell you, Veum, I've had hundreds of women but only one wife. I could have divorced, remarried hundreds of times. But what's the point? It's always the same in bed. And then you have kids and obligations. That's what matters – your kids. They're still there when you die. Am I right? They're your footprints on this world. They live after you're dead. They're witnesses to what you've done. What you've been. What you've accomplished.' He straightened up and then slumped. Stared at the floor.

'I care about kids. My kids. I have an "unofficial" one. I was already married and couldn't … But I've always kept track of that boy. Given him everything I could … Everything I could. I mean, he's my kid, too. He's my son too, even if he does have another name. So I've never got divorced because of the kids. What's the point? I've got as much being married as I would as a bachelor. Maybe more. It's easier for them to screw married men. They don't have to worry about marrying. Am I right?'

Two young men came in. They glanced at Ljosne and sat on the lowest ledge. As far away in the corner as they could. Ljosne blinked at them. Heavy eyelids. But it wasn't as if he were looking at them – they were just something on the scene. He was looking a long, long way off.

'And your wife. How does she fit into this?' I said.

He looked at me. Puzzled. 'My wife? She takes me as I am. I take care of her. Give her a little number when she needs it which isn't often, God knows. I mean – there must be a reason why someone like me plays around. Am I right?'

I nodded slowly. 'I suppose so. That's how it usually is.'

He lowered his voice. 'But back to Wenche. She was something else! If she ever gets out of there … I've got to tell you …' He suddenly looked me right in the eye. 'Get her out of there, Veum. Get her out of there for me.'

I stood up. 'Weren't we going swimming?'

'Oh?' He stood up. 'OK. We've been here long enough.'

We changed into our bathing suits. 'Ever meet Jonas Andresen?' I said.

'A couple of times. He picked her up here at the office. We made a little deal. I … got him some bottles.' He winked at me. 'I liked him. But he was a wimp. Twenty metres on the trail and he'd have had it.'

'But he died,' I said.

'But not from running,' he said.

We swam silently. At first. After the sweat-bath it was like diving into tepid air. You hardly knew you were in the water. Then your skin began to prickle and gradually you woke up. In that green, chlorinated water.

He swam up alongside me, passed me, slowed, and waited for me to catch up. 'What we were talking about, Veum. About getting a divorce. I had a friend, a really good friend, for six years. Six long good years. She was married and I was married and we never talked about divorce or marrying each other. I'll say it again. What's the point? When we had it as good as we did? When you're married you've got to deal with the same old shit, the same old problems – the same old face. Around the clock. Morning, noon, night. While we … We used to meet every two weeks or so, sometimes more often, sometimes not so often, but it was great. It was. Until she married and moved away.'

'But anyway you two skimmed off the cream, didn't you? Kept the best for yourselves?' I said.

'Well …'

We swam.

'These favours – this booze – do you make a lot on it?'

'No, not me. I'm just doing people a favour. People I like. As much for – Wenche – as for myself. Obviously.'

'So you like yourself?'

'Of course I do.' He looked as if he were searching for the right answer. 'Yes,' he said.

'But you take money for it.'

'I don't make a profit. I don't do it for the money. Others do. I don't. Money's not my main interest.'

'No. I can see it isn't.'

'Women are my main interest. Am I right?'

'No,' I said. 'Not really.' I swam past him. And he quickly caught up with me.

'You're your main interest,' I said. 'You use women. Use them like mirrors to reflect your gorgeous well-trained body. You use women to tell you you're still a he-man, that you can still … It's the good old system of use it and throw it away. Women don't mean any more to you than milk cartons, Ljosne. You drink the milk and throw away the carton. Don't bother to see where it lands. It could be destroyed. But it could also happen that your milk carton suddenly stands over a body. With a knife in her hand.'

'You think I …?'

'I don't think anything. I'm just saying what I mean. I mean you care about yourself. Full stop. And in a couple of years you're going to have to depend on your recruits to tell you you still have the old pull. Look around you. You've got plenty to get rid of.'

He looked obediently around, a stunned expression on his face. 'You mean … I …' He looked at all the young men around the edge of the pool: young men with young bodies. New packages in all sizes, in tight little swimming trunks. 'You mean I should …'

We reached the end of the pool and I shot out. He was by the ladder.

'That's ridiculous, Veum.' He climbed up. Fists clenched. 'If we were alone, I'd …'

I stared into his eyes. 'Try it, Lard-guts,' I said.

His eyes and hands suddenly fell to his waist. 'You mean I've gained too much weight?'

'No idea,' I said drily. 'I've never seen you before. But thanks for the preview. I'll remember all your good advice. In case I ever get married – again.' I said the last sentence so quietly that I barely heard it myself.

Then I turned away and walked back to the changing room. He didn't follow. I got dressed. Laid the clothes he'd lent me beside his and left the sports centre.

It was a long tough curving climb up the bill to the main gate but I walked fast. Not because I needed the exercise but because I had to walk off something. Get it out of my system.

There's adultery and adultery, I told myself. There's Jonas Andresen's kind and then there's Richard Ljosne's. And a lot of other kinds, too. Of these two, one was acceptable but the other wasn't worth a damn or a spit in the wind. Ljosne's had nothing to do with love. It had to do with gymnastics.

Or it was like a dice game – you try to score ten thousand before anybody else. It doesn't matter who you play with. Or what happens to them afterwards. As long as you aren't involved.

That sort of game could lead to corpses. That sort of game could lead to people lying dead in entrance halls. That sort of game could lead to people lying on their sides, bleeding from deep belly wounds.

I went through Security and got into my car. I pushed the accelerator to the floor and revved the motor. I burned rubber swinging out on to the road. Two inside curves and then …

I've got to talk to you again, Wenche, I said to myself. About Tuesday. About what really happened.

But not right now. Other errands to do first.

I was hungry, but I didn't know how long Gunnar Våge stayed in his office so I drove back up to those four high-rises and parked in the usual spot.

I was going to be a fixture out here. Maybe I should think about getting myself a reserved parking place.

35

I found Gunnar Våge where he'd been the last time. He was alone in the youth club, standing on a stool. He was hanging up a grey paper poster. The message was in red. Described the club's activities for March. All you had to do was sign up.

There was a course in safe mountaineering for those who could afford an Easter holiday. There was a course in how to build your own radio set for those who might be interested in saying Hello, hello and Goodbye, goodbye to a ham operator in Japan. And 'our popular course' in learning how to play the guitar was being continued by popular demand. It was only the fifth year in a row. Most of the musicians had managed to learn the first three stops.

Gunnar Våge fastened the poster with large green-headed pins to the cork bulletin board. A powerful spotlight shone on him and his bald head glistened. He looked at me when I came in and continued with the job. It couldn't take long and he'd finally have to deal with me. So I waited silently.

He turned slowly. He was wearing shabby corduroys that had shrunk in the wash and were riding up on his ankles, a high-necked navy wool sweater with brown leather elbow-patches, and brown shoes. He hadn't shaved in several days or maybe he hadn't scrubbed his face. Whatever. It was pale grey. But it could also be because of late nights, or the time of year, or the bright light. Or maybe he didn't like me and changed his skin colour according to the circumstances. Like a chameleon.

His heavy-lidded eyes were as sorrowful as always, and they didn't look as if they were expecting me to contribute much in the way of gaiety. His expression said he might yawn any minute now.

'Hello, Gunnar Våge,' I said.

'Hello, Varg Veum,' he said. 'Was it something special? There's open house here at the club tonight and I'm a little busy.'

We stood in the centre of that large concrete room. It could be – as it was – an air-raid shelter, but we could have been the last two survivors of the final atomic war, and I had just asked if he'd like to play cards or maybe Parchese – and he'd said no, he was a little busy.

'It's about a knife,' I said.

'A knife?'

I nodded. 'A knife – and a dead man.'

He pursed his lips. Looked aggressive. 'Aha! Sherlock Holmes strikes again. Oh yes. Looking for a scapegoat? You and the cops. Maybe you're going to solve the case for them? Pull the Joker out of the pack?'

He took a breath and I looked expectantly at him. He seemed in the mood for another monologue.

'But it's too amateurish, Veum,' he went on. 'It's too sub-standard. Hundreds of people carry switchblades. Johan's not the only one. And if you think all these recent nothings could lead to murder, then you're wrong, Veum. You've made one hell of a mistake … But anyway, you're being typically stupid, making a bloody fool of yourself …'

He looked as if he were about to leave. 'Do you know what actually went on on Wednesday afternoon, Våge?' I said quickly.

He stayed put. Shrugged. 'No more than what's in the papers. But I can see you're looking for a handy scapegoat and who could be handier than Johan? The notorious teenage crook, the famous criminal, the legendary kidnapper, the cold-blooded rapist: Johan Pedersen! And they call him Joker. It sounds like a bad American gangster film, Veum. Can't you see that?'

'Can't you see you're sounding like a bad American gangster film yourself, Våge?' I said. 'And you damn well haven't got Bogie's charm either. You take the words out of my mouth before I even say them – and they're words I hadn't even thought of.' I moved toward him. Two paces.

'If – ' he said.

I interrupted. 'If you can shut up for two minutes and not fall in love with the sound of your own voice, maybe some other poor slob could get a word in edgewise. OK?'

'Some other poor slob – is that a kind of miniature self-portrait?'

'Whatever. Call it a five-volume novel if you want to. I know Joker didn't kill Jonas Andresen, and I never thought of finger-ing him to the cops. The cops aren't interested in him either, as a matter of fact. They know. I know.'

'You *know*?' His lips moved but I didn't hear anything. For once.

I took advantage of the silence. 'I was talking to him in the car park when the murder was being committed. Clever, don't you think?'

'Clever,' he said, still softly, but with a sarcastic expression. He reminded me of a disappointed satyr, or a surviving Champagne socialist from the sixties. Or an ex-optimist.

'But Jonas Andresen was murdered,' I said. 'With a

switchblade. And that's why I'm here. You told me a lot of things the last time I was here. About life. Things like that. You also told me you keep an impressive collection of switchblades you've confiscated. Here. And I thought – I do think sometimes, Våge – I thought: you don't go out and buy a switchblade the day before you're going to stick it into someone's belly. A switchblade's something you already have, something you're sort of born and brought up with – or it's something you get hold of. But, as I said, it's not something you go out and buy, not if you're thinking of stabbing somebody.

'But it's something you could also consider stealing. And that's the point, Våge. One very simple question – or two. How do you take care of your collection? Carefully? Is it possible somebody could have made a deal with you and got himself a sample of your collection? Have you missed a switchblade lately?'

I held out my hands. 'It's so simple, Ginger. May I have this dance?'

I demonstrated a couple of steps. I can be a comedian when I'm in front of an audience I don't like. And vice versa.

He wasn't buying it. Said through tight lips: 'No. I haven't missed any switchblades lately, Veum. And yes, I take very good care of the collection. And nothing's missing.'

'Where do you keep them? Here?'

'No, Veum,' he said sourly. 'Not here. At home, in a locked drawer.'

'And where do you live?'

'I live here. Didn't you know that? It goes with the job.' looked around. Ironically. I hoped I looked ironic anyway. 'And where do you stash your laundry?'

'On the twelfth floor. Here in the building, Veum. In a

charming little two-room apartment with a view of this whole paradise and other related wonders.'

'Which ones? The so-called market? Hasn't it moved yet?'

Well, as I said, you haven't hit pay-dirt, Veum. And I've got to say bye-bye.'

I had no charms left to use on him. And something still bothered me. I wasn't sure exactly what. But there was something.

'The cops lifted the fingerprints from the knife. I take it you wouldn't mind their taking yours – if I suggest it to them?'

But I couldn't shake him. 'Of course not. With the greatest pleasure. I've never liked the cops, but – what won't a person do for his old friends? Certainly, Fred, I'd love to dance. Love to! But not with you.'

I looked at him. At the bald skull, the thin blond curls around his ears, the dark stubble ... 'Well,' I said, before I turned to leave. 'Thanks.' Then I walked out of the door and down that long damp concrete hail. Past the red arrows. Then I stopped.

Stood there. Once he was younger. And he needn't have been bald. His head could have been covered with tight blond curls. And he'd been too young to have dark stubble on his face. He'd had down on his cheeks then. Or he was better with a razor.

I turned around and walked back. Walked into the club room. He was in his office doorway. He stopped when he saw me but didn't say anything. He almost looked expectant.

I took two steps into the room and stopped. Then I said, 'You knew Wenche Andresen, Våge. You did. Once. Once in a photograph album.'

And I could tell by his face I'd hit the bullseye.

36

He looked as if I'd caught him with his hand in the biscuit tin. I looked more closely and I knew I was right. I was surer of it every second. He had once been in Wenche Andresen's life. He was still in her photograph album. And here he was ... a few hundred metres from where her husband, or ex-husband, had been brutally murdered. Not that there had to be a connection. Needn't be significant. But it was a little suspicious that he hadn't mentioned knowing her.

'So what?' he said. His voice was reedy now and without a trace of sarcasm. 'What difference does it make who I once knew a long time ago?'

'Everything makes a difference when people die. That way. You loved her. Right? Didn't you follow her everywhere she went? Didn't you move here when she did? I've heard of rejected lovers who have moved to a lot worse places than this just to be close to their sweethearts.'

'Piss off, Veum!' he said. 'I dislike you so much that – that ...' He took a few clumsy steps towards me.

'That you'd consider sticking a switchblade into my belly? Is that what you generally do with people you don't like, Våge?'

His face turned red. Hardened. 'Be glad there aren't any witnesses, Veum. Otherwise you'd be eating your words in some damned courtroom. I dislike you because you're always jumping to conclusions. Because you're always accusing people of motives they don't have or never have had ...'

'That sounds like somebody I know,' I said. 'Somebody I've just met.'

'It wasn't that way, Veum. Yes. I knew Wenche – once. We spent the end of a summer together. August. September. That's all. I …' He shrugged. 'I thought maybe there might be more. She – she was different from most other women I'd – had dealings with. Maybe not an intellectual. But more open. Open to new experiences. She was warm, good, and yes – a woman. A woman you could love more than you did other women. But she … It didn't mean all that much to her – I mean, I didn't. So we split up, after … Well. That was that. There never has been more to it. We went our own ways. And when I accidentally ran into her here, found out that she lived here, too – it was totally and completely – '

'What year was this?'

His face was unusually empty of emotion. As if it were a desiccated sponge at the bottom of a blackboard in a locked classroom at the end of a long dry summer holiday. 'It was – it must have been – 1966. No. '67. Eleven years ago. That's an eternity by now, Veum.'

Eleven years ago. He was right. By now it was an eternity. I'd been in Social Work School in Stavanger in August and September of 1967. I'd just met Beate and we went for long walks along Solastranden. And we felt as if we could walk and walk around Jæren if we had to. Hand in hand with a cold wind blowing in from the sea and a blood-red sun at our backs. 1967. An eternity ago. So many eternities ago …

'But you never could forget her,' I said. 'You said she was special. We're like that. We men. We're always falling in love with somebody we go on loving for the rest of our lives. But we do our best not to meet her again. Because by then she's dyed her hair and her breasts have sagged, and she's got a spare tyre. She's older – just as we are. And no dream lasts for ever. All dreams are basically illusions. It's just that some of us have greater problems accepting that reality than others.'

'Well, I accepted that reality, Veum. More to the point – I never had those dreams. Not for long anyway. When I met Wenche again, it was … completely ordinary. Like meeting an old school friend you liked once. Had something in common with once. But not any more. That time's past. So I talked to Wenche just as I'd talk to any old friend. And that's all there was to it.'

'So that's all there was to it? Didn't you meet her often?'

'I didn't meet her, Veum. I ran into her now and then.'

'And her husband?'

'I never met him. I've no idea what he looked like.'

'You realise I can ask Wenche about this?'

'So ask! Ask until your lungs burst, Veum. She can only tell the truth.'

But truth's a dangerous word. You never know when it's going to swell on your tongue and get too big. Gunnar Våge looked as if he knew it because his face looked as if he'd just unexpectedly bitten on something strange and he could taste it.

'Where were you on Wednesday afternoon, Våge?' I said.

'I think the police should ask me that, Veum. It's none of your business,' he said.

'No, maybe not. You'll be hearing from them, Våge. Good luck.' I turned toward the door.

But I knew he'd stop me before I got too far. I saw it in his face, and I knew he was someone who had to get it all off his chest once he'd started.

'If you must know, Veum,' he yelled after me, 'I was home. Alone. On the twelfth floor. But not in Wenche's building. In an adjoining one. It's not an impressive alibi, but I'd like to take a shot at the person who can say he saw me outside my flat that afternoon.'

'Where?' I said.

'Where what?' he said.

'Where would you like to take a shot at him?' I said. 'Between the eyes? Or in the belly?'

He had it coming. He'd said he didn't like me. And I'm someone who wants to be liked. I'm someone who'll beg everybody he meets to like him.

I left Gunnar Våge in the doorway of his office, where he'd be getting ready for tonight's youth club meeting. And I hurried through the hall and up into that healing grey light. World War III hadn't started. The cars were where they had been, and people rushed by. Lights were going on in the high-rises. They looked like glittering ladders to a heaven we'd never reach.

I looked at the Lyderhorn. As usual the old demon lay there and watched. Always ready, always on duty. Maybe I should take Ljosne's advice. Run up and kick the mountain in its beacon and see if it complained.

There's a lot you can do if you've got the time. So many mountains you can climb up. And just as many you can climb down. Because if life had taught me anything, it had taught me you can't ever stay on the summit. You always climb back down. You have to. God knows why. And God knows what you expect to find there on the summit. Because whatever it is, you never do.

37

I was hungry but I hadn't the stomach for a three-course meal in town, so I drove to the nearest hot-dog stand. It's the most unhealthy food you can imagine. Bits of meat and guts mixed with air, and seasoned with cost-accounting and served with mustard, ketchup and onions because it has to taste of something. And if you're thirsty you can buy coloured sugar water or automatically brewed coffee that also tastes and looks dirty.

This hot-dog stand was located in one of the Inferno's voids, beside a pocket of traffic connected to a parking place, and fifty metres away from a petrol station on a stretch of road so wide and so desolate that nobody had wanted to build alongside it.

I parked in the company of ten or twelve shiny new motorcycles in the season's latest colours: red, yellow and dark blue-green. Old-fashioned black motorbikes were out. These weren't very large. They reminded you of overgrown mopeds and seemed suitable transportation for this decade's youngsters.

And the decade's representatives were outside the hot-dog stand, happily divided into the two sexes. Their fists held bottles of cola and their eyes were wary when I got stiffly out of the car and walked towards them.

Somebody said something I didn't catch.

Laughter. In unison.

'Where'd you get that car? The Historical Museum?'

More laughter. Cackles from a coven of witches.

I smiled. They were of a different calibre than Joker's gang.

These kids were merely verbal. Their faces told you so. They were at the age when anybody over twenty's funny, and whenever more than two are gathered together, there's always got to be a wise guy. I'd been one of them once. No motorcycle, but just the same.

And I knew where they went when they got home. They went off by themselves and sat in front of their mirrors and studied their pimples with the same intensity others gave to the problem of the world's resources. Or else they looked dizzily between their legs and wondered what they ought to do with it and whether a buyer might not come along pretty soon.

It's an unhappy merciless age, an age of confusion, one you never quite get over – because all your ages leave their scars in your soul. I've never wanted to be that age again. There have been times I've wished I were seven again, but I've never missed being seventeen.

I walked over to the counter. Two girls in their twenties held the fort behind it. I ordered four hot dogs with ketchup and was optimistic enough to ask for orange juice. Settled for a bottle of soda instead.

'Out on the town, uncle?' suggested one of the group.

I smiled and started on the first hot dog. 'Out to shorten my life by a few hours,' I said. 'Do you know how much fat there is in a hot dog like this?' I asked a boy who didn't look as if he knew what fat was. He smiled foolishly.

The others overheard my question. It was against the rules to talk to anybody over thirty, so they quickly went somewhere else, leaving the hot dogs and the two girls to me.

They stood so close together they looked like Siamese twins. Not out of affection but because the hot-dog stand was so small. They wore indigo smocks decorated with an assortment of grease, ketchup and mustard stains. Both were pretty heavy. Cheaply dyed hair. It wouldn't be long before they looked like Hildur Pedersen.

It didn't look as if we had anything in common, so I hurried through my meal, finished the soda and drove back to the concrete giants. Before I took the plunge, I stood by the car and looked at them.

Four of them – and how many people? Two or three hundred in each high-rise. About a thousand all told. A thousand people stacked up.

In stacks of drawers with names on them and which they pop out of like mechanical dolls. Mechanical dolls who go to sleep, who get up, eat, get into their toy cars, drive to work and drive back at four o'clock. They eat, sleep, read the paper, watch TV and sleep again. Other mechanical dolls sleep, get up, eat, take care of the kids, do the laundry, babysit, cook, eat, sleep, wash the dishes, read the paper, watch TV and sleep. Others too young to have learned what they should do and so do all the wrong things play, cry, check out one another's genitals in the entrances to dark cellars, play football and fight. And eat and sleep.

Some of the mechanical dolls sleep with each other. Most of them once a week, preferably on a Saturday after a bottle of wine and with the lights off. Some sleep with each other once a month and think that's too often. A few sleep with each other every day. But then – suddenly one of the dolls goes off the rails and sleeps with the wrong doll. And then if you stab him with a knife you see blood. And then you ask yourself if they aren't mechanical dolls just the same.

Maybe all of them hide their secrets, like Jonas Andresen. Their dreams. Like Jonas Andresen. But not many of them turn their dreams and their secrets into realities as Jonas Andresen did. Only a very very few of them die because of it.

Four high-rises. Gunnar Våge lived in one of them. Solfrid Brede lived in the middle one, and so did Wenche Andresen – away for the moment. Joker lived with his mother, Hildur Pedersen, in the third tower. And that's where I was headed.

It had begun to get dark. A grey-blue afternoon darkness that would quickly melt into blue-black and then into pure black. Black starless darkness with a thin drift of rain in the air.

The flat door opened before I rang the bell, and Joker looked as surprised as I did when we stood face to face.

I remembered that reedy voice. On Wednesday. When he'd asked what was going on. But his voice wasn't reedy now. 'I warned you, Harry. Remember what I told you?'

'My memory's terrible,' I said. 'Must be my age.'

His eyes narrowed. 'I told you to keep away from my mother. Leave her alone.'

'Relax, Johan,' I said. 'I'm not here to hurt –'

'I'm not Johan,' he said abruptly. 'Not to you, Harry. You belong with – the others.'

'Are you so sure?' I said.

He didn't answer.

'And Gunnar Våge,' I said. 'He belongs with you. He's on the right side. Is that it?'

'He's honest, anyway. Real.'

'But what's the right side, and what's the wrong one?'

'Some people are with us. And then there's people like you. And you're against us.' He was almost formal.

'You remind me of somebody,' I said. 'In a book I must have read once.'

He tried to get by me.

'Just listen a minute,' I said. 'I've got … in a lot of ways I've got the same background as Gunnar Våge. I think I know how you feel. I know you're looking for something to hold on to. But a switchblade isn't enough. You'll just end up cutting yourself. And terrorising little boys isn't anything to build a future on, Johan.'

'I told you not to call me –'

'OK. What? Billy the Kid?'

'I'm only saying – I'm warning you. Leave my mother alone. Or else.'

I could hear Hildur Pedersen's rough voice inside the flat. 'Who are you talking to, Johan?'

He stared hard at me. 'Nobody – Mum.'

'You call me Nobody, I'll call you Special. And we can go on stage. As "Nobody Special". Sounds good.'

No. It didn't sound good. 'Get lost, Veum,' he said.

'Relax, Johan,' I said. 'I want to ask your mother just one question. No more, no less. And nobody's going to stop me.'

He raised a slim pale forefinger and he reminded me more than ever of a priest. 'I'm warning you, Veum. For the last time.'

I shoved the forefinger and its owner aside, walked into the flat and closed the door firmly behind me. He kicked it hard. And then I heard him hurrying along the balcony.

'Johan?' That hoarse voice was coming from the living room.

'Veum,' I said.

She was lying on the sofa. Her multi-coloured hair stuck out in all directions and she was having problems finding me in the dusk. None of the lamps were on but there were a lot of bottles you could make into lamps if you were handy. They were empty. All you had to do was to get started.

She lay on her side, her head on the arm of the sofa, one fat white arm acting as a pillow. When I came in she tried to get an elbow under her and rest her head in her hand. But she couldn't co-ordinate. She smiled sheepishly at me. 'Hello, Veum,' she said. 'Thanks for the last time.' Her speech was slurred.

'Been swimming?' I said.

Her gaze elbowed its way through the forest of bottles. 'Swimming?' she said.

I sat in a chair on the other side of the coffee table. She gestured toward it. 'Help yourself, as they say.' Then she laughed.

'They're empty,' I said.

She looked sad. 'All of them?'

'All of them.'

She smiled. Problem solved. She bent her free hand behind her and dug among the cushions. Came up with an unopened bottle of vodka.

'He who seeketh, findeth,' she said. Her practised fingers opened the bottle and she did a quick taste test before she handed it across the table to me.

I set it down in front of me. It would be a handy hostage if she didn't feel like talking.

'Aren't you thirsty?' She looked disbelieving. As if it were impossible not to be constantly thirsty.

'Not right now,' I said. 'I'm still driving.'

'What the hell do you want?' Her smile was broad. 'I don't think you've stopped by for a little number.' And she waved both hands like an overweight seal waving its flippers. And then she spread her arms in a standing invitation.

'I was wondering,' I said.

'Well?'

'The last time – when you told me about Johan's father, I don't think you were completely honest.'

She looked cross-eyed. 'No?' she said, as if she really didn't remember whether we'd ever discussed the matter.

'No. Not completely. For example, you said Johan's father sent money every month and maybe he did. But you didn't say he visited regularly.'

'Well, I …' It's not easy to lie when you're sprawled on a sofa and you're full of undigested vodka. 'I … I meant – it's none of your business.'

'No. Maybe not. But then again, maybe it is. So he comes here? How often? Once a month?'

She nodded and shrugged at the same time.

'Every other month?'

She nodded. Crookedly.

'And maybe Johan sees him? Because it's Johan he comes to see, isn't it? To see how he is?'

She nodded again.

'But Johan thinks he's just one of your usual – boyfriends? You've let him see his father again and again all these years – but you've never had the guts to tell him that that was his father?'

'No,' she whispered. 'It wasn't –'

'It wasn't his business? His own father wasn't his business?'

'It wasn't his own father – not after he dumped me that way. He – he could have left his wife. He didn't have to dump this on me. It wasn't the way I told you it was the last time you were here, Veum. It wasn't the way I've told it to everybody who's ever asked.'

She managed to sit up. Hands on her knees and that large head bobbing like a toy between her shoulders.

'I'll tell you about it. You're a good guy, so I'll tell you the truth about … It wasn't just a pick-up at the Starlight Ballroom. It was – it was the only real love affair I've ever had. The only one I can still remember. And it's alive. It's the only one that still wakes me up at night because I've been dreaming about him.

'And I loved him, Veum. And he – he never told me he was married. He wasn't wearing a ring when I met him and we … And I believed every word he said right up until – until I got pregnant with Johan. And then he came clean. Told me he was married and that his wife was also pregnant, and that we …

'He said he'd help me, but he couldn't marry me. And I loved him. I loved him so much I couldn't say no. To anything. So I let him buy his freedom, if that's the right word. I let him buy me this flat and the one I lived in before this. I let him pay for raising Johan. Schools. Like that. And I even let him visit. See his son. And he's come here since Johan was six months old.'

'And you two let Johan grow up like this? Without answering the most important question of his life, without giving him the stability a father gives a kid? Or can give.'

'It was – well, he wanted it that way. He didn't want to risk Johan's suddenly showing up at his door when he was older and causing – problems.'

'And you went along with that?'

'I told you! I loved him!' Her voice was wild with feeling. Then it died into a whimper. 'I still love him.'

I didn't say anything. I felt so out of it sitting there in that room as the twilight grew steadily darker. The empty bottles shone a little and, on the other side of the coffee table, a woman weighing one hundred and twenty kilos was confiding her life's best-kept secrets to me.

Her voice was softer now. 'But where he was concerned? It was just fun-and-games. He – when he came to see us those first years, he and I still, he still wanted … I was younger. Better looking. Not so – heavy. But it's been years now since he's so much as kissed me. It's almost like – a normal marriage now. It's been over for him for years. If there ever was anything really there. But it'll never be finished for me until I am. Finished.' She searched for me in the darkness. 'Love's a funny thing, isn't it, Veum? I mean, that it seldom manages to hit the same two people at the same time?'

I nodded. She was right. If these past days had taught me anything at all, it was that. That love's a lousy marksman and seldom hits two bullseyes in a row.

'Too many marriages are garbage,' she said. 'I'm glad I've been spared that anyway. I haven't had to live with half-truths, half a love or half … half everything.'

Another thing I'd learned from all this. People who have got to live alone always have a good excuse or some kind of rationalisation. It's the only way they manage to survive.

I found the thread again. 'And you weren't being entirely honest when you said he was a sailor, were you? Not entirely.'

'No. You're right.'

'He was a naval officer.'

She nodded heavily.

'And his name's Richard Ljosne.'

She scowled. 'How did you find that out, Veum?'

'He told me himself – indirectly. Or else I jumped to some hasty conclusions which turned out to be not so hasty.'

I stood up. So now I knew. Without being entirely sure of what it told me or whether it told me anything. Maybe it was just a coincidence. Maybe when you start nosing around in people's backgrounds, their pasts, you always find a few skeletons in the cupboard. Everybody's got them.

I handed her the bottle. 'Here you are, Fru Pedersen. It's a long time until morning.'

She took the vodka and glared at it. 'Too many long nights, Veum. Too many bottles.'

I nodded. It was an epitaph I could use myself one of these days. 'Take care of yourself. See you.'

'Take care, Veum. Thanks for coming. Always nice to see you. Find your way out?'

'Umm.'

The bottle lay between her thighs like an exhausted lover. I left. There was nothing more we could give one another. I'd asked my questions, she'd answered them. And I moved on. I was a swarm of locusts. I consumed everything I found. I left lives picked clean and nights emptied of their secrets behind me. I was the sun. I left a trail of scorched fields, dying forests and blasted lives behind me. But if the sun kills, it also gives life. Rain always follows a drought, winter always gives way to spring. But drought and winter always come first. The truth always demands first place in the queue. I cautiously left Hildur Pedersen's life behind me.

Nothing more to do now. I was eaten up and burnt out myself.

I walked stiffly to the car park and my car. Put the key in the ignition, let in the clutch, turned the key.

No reaction, just an unwilling grunt.

I tried again, a little more violently. 'Come on!' I growled. Then I leaned my face against the windscreen. I should have caught on. The car wasn't just stone dead. It had been murdered.

The shadows came alive around me. There were a lot of them this time. Not just five.

38

There were too many of them.

For a second I considered locking the car door. But then they'd just break the windows, slash the tyres, bash up the bonnet. Turn the car into a bigger wreck than it already was.

They came closer. Circled around the car. Dark oblong shadows with staring pale faces. Some were armed with steel pipes, bicycle chains and other charming weapons.

I'm not a brave man, just a little rash now and then. I began to sweat. My stomach turned queasy and my legs were weak.

They waited quietly in their circle around the car. The distances to the nearest high-rises seemed greater than those in the Sahara, and those winking lights as far away and as unreachable as the summit of Everest. Except for that lynch mob around my car, the car park was as empty and deserted as the Pacific. I felt as if even the Lyderhorn was leaning forward expectantly. Just like them.

I got out of the car. Fast. There were twelve or thirteen of them and my only chance was to hold them at bay by talking. Find an opening and get out of there as fast as I could and hope to all the gods that it was fast enough.

But Joker had learned. Before I could open my mouth, I heard him say, 'Get him!'

And they got me.

They came on so fast I hardly had time to put up my fists. I could feel fingers, fists, legs, boots and steel pipes hitting my body's tender spots. A bicycle chain cut through my clothes and slashed my underarm. I was thrown, slammed into the car on my way down and was kicked in the chin before I hit the pavement. I felt a knee in my stomach and fists hammering my chest.

I aimed a blow upward, hit something hard. Saw something soft, swore, and was kicked in the groin. Heard ugly singing inside me. Somebody laughed. I could hear them cursing.

I curled up. Covered my head with my elbows, bent my head down as far as I could, and pulled my thighs up over my most vulnerable parts.

My eyes were streaming. I couldn't help it. I was crying as much from fury and humiliation as from pain and fear. Is this it? I thought. So undignified? So unfair?

I passed out. The hard ground relaxed under me, as open and soft as a feather bed. A wonderful warmth spread through my body. A warmth that burned away all the pain, a great numbing warmth.

They'd begun to let up now. A last boot in the small of my back, a contemptuous kick at a helpless leg, a gob of spit in my face. It wasn't just tears wetting my face now. It was something stickier, more viscous.

Suddenly somebody was very very dose. I felt thin hard fists yanking me up. Through a shimmering red veil I could see a face shoved into mine, a pale, cold face. A priest. 'I warned you, Veum. You'll stay away from my mother for keeps now.'

Then he let me go and I sagged to the ground. It didn't hurt. It was soft and warm. The only thing I wanted to do was sleep and sleep …

I heard footsteps going away. They sounded like a herd of buffalo. Then it was quiet. And then the voice was back.

Somewhere above me the sharp toe of a boot, a toe sank into my side.

The voice said, 'And if you think you're the only one who pussyfoots around your whore, you're wrong. People were winning that jackpot long before you showed up!'

A last kick and then a pair of feet going away. The thunderangel flew over a burning meadow.

I raised my head and tried to see him. See whether he was carrying a fiery sword and wearing a halo of flames. But what was the point in raising my head?

I lay on the ground, half aware of the smell of petrol and oil from my car. Looked up into an uneven lunar landscape of rust and hardened dirt. I was in a canopy bed whose canopy was grey, brown and black, a canopy of rotting silk edged with spiders' webs and mouse shit. And there was a strong smell. A smell of death.

I vomited. Slowly and gently. I was on my back. Immobile. And then I could feel it welling up, my mouth filling and running over, my injured lips opening. And then I threw up, as slowly and carefully - as if it were the tenderest, most sensitive kiss.

And then I slept.

39

'Hello?'

I was asleep. I was in heaven. A woman whose hair was neither blonde nor brown nor red carefully bent over me. I felt her breath on my face. Her face was beautiful and she was old enough to have acquired some laugh-lines round her eyes. Her lips …

'Hello?'

Her lips. I tried not to lose the vision of her lips. I hung on to the picture of those lips …

'Hey you! Are you dead or something?'

I opened my eyes. It hurt. It was like opening a rusty cake tin jammed shut two Christmases ago. My field of vision was edged with rust, and the man bending over me was twins. And then triplets. And then twins again.

I firmly closed my eyes.

'Hello?'

Somebody was calling in the darkness. But where was that somebody calling in the forest?

'Hello.' That was my voice and it scared me so much I opened my eyes. The man had stopped being twins, but my voice sounded like a two-voiced men's choir with the castrati on the left. The face bending over me was elderly. About sixty. Only sixty-year-olds these days talk to people who lie dying under old cars. 'Is something wrong?' he asked.

'Hello,' I said.

'Is something wrong?' he repeated. Louder this time.

I could see him clearly now. He had an old man's moustache: white and brown. His mouth was dark and his teeth were brown. His eyes seemed black, his face white. His hair under the hat was grey-white.

He wore a scarf and a dark heavy coat. One hand held a cane. The other hung by his side as if it weren't his.

I tried standing but settled for sitting. The car park whirled around me. I leaned heavily against the car and patiently waited for the universe to settle down again.

'You're bleeding,' he said.

I lifted a hand to my face. It felt as if I were wearing boxing gloves. I felt my face. It was wet. And tender.

'You don't look so good,' the man above me said.

'I never have,' I mumbled.

'I beg your pardon, I didn't hear you.'

I shook my head.

The car park settled down. I tried sliding upwards against the car door. It was working. Slowly. But I was extremely nauseated. I must have been severely concussed. If I still had a brain. I had the feeling it was slowly dripping from my face, on to my hands and then to the ground. From ground thou art come, to ground thou shalt return.

'Was it those youngsters?' he said.

'No, no,' I said. 'I just enjoy lying around in car parks and looking up under my car. Best view in the world.'

He nodded understandingly. 'I can tell you've been beaten up. It's a shame. Want me to call the police? Or a doctor?'

'A doctor? At this hour?' I tried to laugh.

'Does it hurt?' he said anxiously.

'Only when I laugh,' I said.

But it also hurt when I stopped laughing. 'Do you know anything about cars?' I said.

He lit up. 'I had a Graham once. From before the war until 1963. They knew how to make cars back then.'

'Well. This isn't what you'd call a car. More like a piece of junk on wheels, but if you could help me open the bonnet …'

I turned around. That was a mistake. One leg sort of gave way under me, and the car wasn't where it had been. I was aware that I stood and leaned towards the ground for a minute before it spun and gave me a rabbit-punch.

'Hello? Hello!' More than one voice now.

My stomach was in my throat. It contracted. I vomited again.

'I'm going to get help,' a voice said. 'Stay where you are. Don't move.'

'I'll try not to,' I muttered.

The woman with that wonderful hair came back. But she was standing up now and her face was distorted: stretched on one side and shrunken on the other. It hurt to look at her. I opened my eyes.

I lay completely still and breathed slowly. Easy now, I said, just take it easy. And then I tried standing. Very very slowly. Very carefully. Braced myself against the car. It felt like raising a flag-pole with one hand tied behind your back.

But it worked. The ground stayed put under my feet, the car didn't disintegrate behind my back. I gradually eased around to the front. Found the bonnet catch and squeezed it. That drained me.

The bonnet opened with a sullen click. I was dripping with sweat and little black dots exploded before my eyes like startled pheasants taking off.

I took a break. Then I lifted the bonnet and peered with tired sore eyes at that complicated Leyland engine.

They hadn't gone in for real sabotage. I tightened the spark plugs and reconnected the fuel line. Then I stumbled back to the door, opened it and got behind the wheel. Turned on the ignition. The car started like an oldster suddenly in love. It was a little sluggish at first but once it got started, you couldn't stop it.

I let the engine warm up, climbed out, made that endless trip back to the bonnet. Closed it and set out on the long journey back to the driver's seat. I had to make a few stops on the way. Then I got a grip on the steering wheel and stared straight up. I was a little boy who sat there playing cars.

Then I took a deep breath, let out the dutch, turned out of the parking place and aimed at the entrance to the road. Two wheels were against the kerb, the other two in the road. I turned on to the road, found the right-hand drainage ditch and sighted along it.

It worked best when I dosed my left eye and drove between twenty and thirty kilometres an hour. And didn't meet other drivers.

The lights coming toward me were confusing. They spread out in open formation and jumped up and down like a group of disoriented UFOs. And they were brighter than I'd ever remembered.

I had to stop five or six times to throw up along the way. I couldn't leave the car and be sick on the shoulder. I just stayed where I was. But I tried to be discreet. When other cars went by I'd lean out and pretend I was checking the rear wheel, which was in fine shape.

If it had been the rush hour I'd never have made it to Bjørndalssvingen. But I made it all the way. Didn't miss

Puddefjord Bridge and I remembered to get in the right lane after Sentralbadet.

I never found out what happened to the old man who'd once owned a Graham. Maybe he's still looking for help. Which isn't so easy to find these days.

It's been said of Bergen's City Emergency Room that they ought to write *Abandon all hope ye who enter here* in gold letters over the main entrance.

That's an exaggeration. Most people survive. If they show the scars from the visit for the rest of their lives, well, that's how it is. There's no point in complaining if they feel worse when they leave than when they came.

They tell the story of a guy from eastern Norway, who once had to have an ankle set in the Bergen City Emergency Room. When he got back to Oslo and went for a check-up, the doctor took one look at the ankle and asked, 'Bergen City Emergency?' The terrified patient said yes, and the doctor called a bunch of medical students to gather round. They stared at the patient as if he were an extremely rare case. The doctor happily rubbed his hands together and said, 'You have now learned how not to do it.'

Obviously you shouldn't listen to stories like these. Mostly they're untrue. You shouldn't read medical textbooks either. And if you don't have to, you shouldn't go near Bergen's City Emergency Room.

I parked. It was after ten so the main entrance was locked. A sign with an arrow on it directed me to an entrance by the driveway. I followed the arrow, walked up some wide concrete steps and came to a locked door and a door bell. After several misses, my finger found the bell.

Somebody in her late thirties and dressed in white opened the door. You could bet she wasn't married and hadn't ever entertained the idea. She looked as if she wanted to say we don't buy at the door. But she held it open and I wobbled in.

'What's your problem?' she said.

I pointed to my face. Which I felt should tell her something. 'I'm so swollen,' I said. 'Could it be mumps?'

She looked sourly at me. Nodded towards a couple of chairs. 'Sit down,' she said, trotted down a hall and around a corner.

I looked around. Not a doctor in sight. A dark-skinned man hunched in one of the chairs. Black hair fell across his forehead. He was bleeding from an ugly cut over one eyebrow, his left ear looked as if it would fall off any moment and he was holding half of his teeth. His blood dripped in three separate pools on to the floor in front of him: slowly and rhythmically as if the blood were pumping straight from his heart.

I could hear a child crying behind a green curtain. A man in a taxi driver's uniform paced back and forth, glaring at a sign that said he couldn't smoke. He looked as if he might yank it off the wall and use it as a toothpick. He was big enough.

The place smelled of ether or whatever all these places smell of.

There was a washbasin and mirror over in one corner. I walked over and discovered it wasn't a mirror. It was a painting of an extremely ugly person. It wasn't until I raised my hand and felt what used to be my mouth that I understood that I was really looking at myself. It was too much. I ducked quickly out of range, but I filled the basin and tried to wash. When I looked in the mirror again, it looked more like me but not much. Even my mother would have had problems recognising me and old friends would have walked right by me in the street.

My eyes were gummy slits. Mouth two sizes too large and it sloped up towards one eye. My neck looked like one of those freak potatoes people are always taking around to the newspapers. And this morning's beautiful skin had changed into a landscape that would have been a sensation at an agriculture seminar.

I plodded over to the foreigner and sat beside him.

He looked at me with black, mournful, baffled eyes. 'I didn't do anything to them,' he said. 'Why did they beat me up? Because I'm a different colour? Because I come from a different country? I don't understand.'

I tried to answer but the words wouldn't come.

He looked at me. Incredulous. 'But you – you're a Norwegian. And they beat you up. Why?'

'I come from a different part of town.'

He shook his head despairingly, looked at the large white teeth shining in the pale palms of his hands. 'I don't understand it. I don't understand why people beat each other up.'

A doctor came in. One of those young doctors they put on night duty. The kind who always has a snappy answer on his tongue and a soothing misdiagnosis in his back pocket. He stopped in front of us and looked us over. 'Which one of you's going to live longest?' he said.

'He was here first,' I said.

'He's in the wrong place,' he said. 'He's going to the dental clinic. He needs some spare parts.' He motioned to the foreigner. 'Come on, comrade. Let's have a look at those cuts.' And they disappeared behind a green curtain.

The taxi driver stopped pacing and stared at the curtain. 'These fucking Pakis!' he burst out. 'Who the fuck are they to bitch? Move up here, take people's jobs, they get what they deserve.'

I looked up to see whether he was talking to me.

He had a face like a quarry man, but the sledgehammer had smashed him back. Flat broad face. Twenty centimetres between his eyes. Nose as wide as a steam-iron and his mouth sagged to the right from holding a cigarette in the corner. I began to wonder whether I shouldn't go home and go to bed. I could dream up my own nightmares.

'You oughta hear 'em sitting in the back talking that shit. About girls. I don't get the words – can't understand a word they're saying – but I get the music, know what I mean? Once I stopped the cab, turned around and told 'em: I'm telling you, don't go waving your dirty black dicks at Norwegians. You better believe they shut up. Not a sound out of 'em rest of the trip. And I got a ten-kroner tip. What yer say to that?'

I didn't say anything. I sighed.

'And they got so fucking pure in this dump you can't even smoke.'

'Why don't you go outside?' I said cautiously.

'See her face? Ring the bell once too often, she'd rip your stuff off you, take it home and plant it in a flowerpot. Wouldn't think twice. You don't wanna mess with that widow woman.'

The doctor and the foreigner emerged from behind the curtain and the foreigner was sent away to fill out some forms. The doctor turned to me. 'And what trolley did you fall off?'

'Sandvikey,' I said. 'Twenty years ago. It just takes a hell of a long time to get here.'

'You're one of the lucky ones.'

Twenty minutes later he said, 'OK. Here's a prescription. Get it filled and go home and go to bed. Stay quiet two or three days and take it easy a week at least. No sudden movements. No excitement. OK?'

No sudden movements? No excitement? I was in the wrong business. I ought to be working for a florist.

'One more thing,' he said. 'Booze? *Nyet!*'

Before I left I took another look at the mirror to see if the same picture hung there. It did. They'd merely changed the style a little. Added some bandages, and some iodine.

I walked away with my life in my hands. Life's a prescription scribbled by an inexperienced doctor on night duty. He's got handwriting not a living soul can decipher. And the idea is nobody should be able to decipher it. The pharmacist takes a chance. We all do. That's how life is: you survive if the prescription's legible. If you're given the wrong medicine, you get lucky and die.

40

I dreamed. A Polish girl with short dark hair and big black eyes was sitting in my office and making faces. She had to leave in an hour but somehow we both knew we loved one another. Somehow we were soulmates who'd been brought together only to be separated. And I couldn't understand one word she said.

'Do you speak English?' I said and she shook her head and smiled. '*Parlez-vous français?*' No! she smiled. '*Sprechen Sie Deutsch?*' No, no, no. No. She went on smiling and speaking Polish with its clear diphthongs and gutteral sounds.

And then I walked her to a big green tourist bus parked outside the Bristol Hotel. Somehow I'd written her a letter in Norwegian and I gave it to her. I realised she wanted my address and I found a crumpled slip of paper. She had a pencil but the point was broken off, so I scratched my name and address as well as I could on the paper. And we kissed. Her feline tongue entered my mouth, she looked around – and disappeared. Her lips were like a wet leaf falling from a tree in autumn. It touches your face – and is gone.

And when I woke up, I lay there wondering how I could get her letters translated. Wondered whether I knew anybody who knew Polish or whether I could get hold of a dictionary and spell my way through them myself.

I was lying in my shirt and trousers on top of the quilt. I'd taken off my jacket and shoes. Outside the window it was light, but I didn't know what time it was. I didn't remember getting home. I had to think a while before I could remember my name. If anybody had asked me how old I was, I'd have said I was seventeen.

I lay there. I could hear muffled voices overhead, children's voices out in the alley. The never-ending swish of the city's traffic. From somewhere out on the fjord the wail of a ship. A distant jet trailed a veil of sound through the air.

I carefully turned my head towards the window so I could see the rooftops and sky. It was grey-white with a tinge of light brown. Like crêpe paper. My head felt like a rotten orange somebody had stepped on. I lifted my left arm and waved it before my eyes. My arm was leaden, my wristwatch didn't move: the crystal was broken.

I raised my head and looked for the alarm clock. Things splintered and the room listed heavily. I sank back on to the bed and when I opened my eyes again, it was dark. The air was stale. Dim. Somebody was tiptoeing across the floor overhead. He turned off the TV and tiptoed further through life. It was evening in the world and little boys slept. Big boys lay in bed in their shirt and trousers with a head split like a tomato. And a stomach that was uncomfortably hollow.

I carefully sat up. Looked around. The room spun but didn't shatter. I stood up and managed to stay up. Went over to the window and opened it. It banged against the wall. I leaned out cautiously. Cold clean night air washed over me: a mixture of chimney smoke, old exhaust and cold car engines. I rested my elbows on the windowsill and breathed. I breathed, therefore I was. But what time was it? What day?

I left the window open and looked at the clock. Nobody'd wound it. The hands were frozen at two forty-five. I went to the phone. The only number I could think of was Beate's. And her new husband's. I dialled, listened to that distant ringing. It rang five times and then a woman answered. She sounded different. It couldn't be …

'Hello? Beate?'

'Hello. Fru Wiik's out. This is the babysitter.'

'Oh hello. This is Fru Wiik's husband.'

Silence.

'I mean, Fru Wiik's former husband.'

'I see.' She sounded as faraway and as inhuman as a robot.

'Is Thomas – is my son there?'

'He's asleep.'

'Oh. Excuse me, but could you tell me what time it is?'

The time? It's ten-thirty.' I could feel the cold seeping through the line.

'What day is it?'

'What day?' A long pause. 'Saturday.'

Another pause.

'Saturday? Well. Thank you.'

'You're welcome. Goodnight.'

'Goodnight.'

I hung up. 'Happy Saturday, Varg,' I said aloud. 'Happy weekend.'

I went to the kitchen, cut three slices of three-day-old bread, spread them with butter, poured raspberry jam over them, on to the counter and the floor. Drank some milk. It tasted of old cardboard. Swallowed a double dose of the tablets I'd got from the pharmacy the night before. Keep out of reach of children, it said on the bottle. Then I fell into bed and into a dreamless sleep until late on Sunday.

It was a long Sunday. My body hurt, my face looked like a

prop in a bad thriller, and there was no way I could do anything constructive. I tried to keep moving. Back and forth across the living room. Walked for a while with the bottle of aquavit, mostly for company – I didn't dare open it. It was going to be a busy Monday.

The phone rang at one o'clock. It was Beate and she was furious.

'Varg? This is Beate. I'll thank you not to call my babysitter when you're drunk.'

'But I …'

'You really do mess things up for me! What you did when we were married can't be helped, but I don't know how we manage to live in the same town as you! And what do you suppose Thomas thinks of a father who's a ridiculous private investigator? Who doesn't think twice about phoning and bothering the babysitter with his drunken ravings? If it ever happens again, Varg, it's not me you'll be hearing from. It'll be my lawyer.' And she slammed down the phone.

'Hello? Hello?' I said to the dialling tone. Just so I'd have something to say.

I could have called back, tried to explain. But I know her when she's furious. It would have taken too much energy. I was too tired.

I found a tin of meatballs in brown sauce in a kitchen cupboard and a slightly wrinkled green pepper in the refrigerator. Made a kind of stew. I couldn't cope with boiling potatoes and settled for a couple of slices of stale bread. Poured a glass of red wine from a half-full bottle but only drank a sip. It gave me a headache that lasted long into the evening.

The hours withered slowly away. A fresh night took over the city, an old day was gone. I sat in front of the TV which flashed squared blue pictures of cross-country skiers setting world records on a Russian alpine course. I thought about Joker. I thought harder about Joker than I'd thought about another person for a long time.

And I said to myself: next time, Joker. Next time. Next time, I'll cut the cards. And next time, Joker, you won't be so easy to shuffle.

I struggled back to bed about ten and slept like a rock until eleven o'clock on Monday.

Monday's a strange day to wake up to. It's a day to die for some. And that Monday there was a strange feeling of death in the air, as if the dark angel had spread his black wings over the city during the night and had chosen his victim …

I tried to call Paulus Smith but got no further than his secretary. She said he was in court.

'Tell him I called,' I said. 'Tell him I still haven't found anything that could help us. Not yet anyway. Tell him I'm on my way to talk to Wenche Andresen. Some new questions to ask her, OK?'

She said she'd pass on the message, so I thanked her, hung up and walked out into Monday.

41

It was one of those grey days with rain in the air. The sky held its breath as if it waited for the clouds to open and pour with the rain we all knew must fall sometime during the day. It was after twelve and it really was March. The light was brighter and the sun higher behind those clouds. Even though it was a grey day it was not February.

February's a short-legged man somewhere in a forest. He's got frost in his beard, his cap pulled down over his forehead and winter-pale eyes in his strong broad face. March is a woman. A woman who's just woken up in the morning, who turns in bed to avoid the sun and who asks you in a sleepy voice if it's already morning.

Yes, it was morning. It wasn't just the light, it was also the temperature, the shine on the roofs, that cold wind from the north-west with the seeds of mild weather in it, a woman passing you on the pavement and loosening her scarf a little bit so you could see the shadow at the base of her throat …

This time I didn't have to see Wenche Andresen in her cell. I was taken to a little room furnished with a wooden table, some chairs and a guard who sat in a chair by the door and acted as if she heard and saw nothing.

Wenche Andresen walked with short steps, as if she'd already adapted the length of her stride to the limited floor space she now lived in. There was something passive, a sudden apathy in the way she moved.

She smiled thinly at me when she came in and sat in the chair nearest the door. She'd changed in the last seventy-two hours. She'd spent four days and five nights inside four brick walls with a steel door and a square window with matt glass in it.

Days and nights in a cell are longer than those outside. They can feel like years and they leave the marks of years on you. Wenche Andresen looked as if she'd spent six years instead of a hundred hours inside these walls. Her skin was already paler, unhealthier than it had been. The grey shadows under her eyes weren't caused by lack of sleep now but by an invisible fever, the same fever that dimmed those dull eyes with grey frost. She'd already lost the battle. Six years ago.

Her hands lay absurdly weakly on the table. I leaned over and squeezed them to try to bring them to life. But she didn't react. She didn't squeeze back, didn't try to hold on. Her hands lay limp in mine.

'How are you, Wenche?' I said.

No answer. She looked at me and I could see something still glimmering deep in her eyes. 'What – what happened?' she said.

I let go of one of her hands and quickly touched my face. 'You mean this?'

She nodded slowly.

'A little – meeting with Joker and his gang. I've got a date with him later today. Whether he likes it or not.'

'You'd better be – careful,' she said and looked around her. As if to say I'd end up here if I didn't watch myself.

'I've got some more questions, Wenche,' I said.

She looked at me as if she knew I'd go on talking, but there wasn't any hope in her eyes. She wasn't interested in my questions. It made me suddenly wonder what her nights must be like, what kinds of dreams she must be having. They had to be exhausting. She'd changed so much since Friday.

'Richard Ljosne,' I said. 'I've talked to him. We talked about last Tuesday, among other things. The Tuesday night you told me about.'

I held her gaze with mine. But there was no reaction. Nothing.

'He didn't tell me the same story you did,' I continued. 'His description of the evening was different from yours.'

Her look was that of a stuffed animal. A doll. She'd fallen into a Sleeping-Beauty trance. Maybe if I kissed her …

'What really happened when you got home, Wenche?'

After a while she said dully, 'Happened? Did something happen? I told you what happened.'

'You did. But he tells it differently. He says … He says you slept together, Wenche. The two of you. You and he. You slept together, didn't you?'

She drew her lifeless hands from mine and tucked them safely under the table's edge. 'Then he's lying, Varg. And if you believe him, you aren't my friend any more.'

It was the kind of thing she might have screamed, but instead she sounded as if we'd been married for twenty years and she was telling me we'd be having fish dumplings for dinner again.

'I am your friend, Wenche! You know that. And I won't believe him – not if you tell me otherwise. But why – why should he lie?'

She shrugged. 'Men.'

She didn't need to add anything. It was enough. It was a sentence from which there could be no appeal, a sentence which condemned an entire gender to death at dawn. There we'd stand with blindfolded eyes and our dicks in our hands, we who transmitted death and deceit and lies from father to son, from generation to generation.

I wasn't going to ask her again. There wasn't any reason why she should lie. So I moved down the list. 'Gunnar Våge?' I said.

She reacted. Shut her eyes and vigorously shook her head. When she opened them again, her look was sharper. She was coming back to life. 'Oh? What about Gunnar Våge?' she said.

'Why didn't you tell me you knew him?'

She hesitated. 'I don't understand ... I can't see what it's got to – what bearing it could have on – this. I honestly didn't think about him before, before you ...'

'You were together once.'

'We were, but good God, Varg – it was so long ago. I don't go around years later thinking about somebody I was with for a couple of months a long time ago.'

'But he loved you, didn't he?'

'I – I don't know about that,' she said abruptly.

'No,' I said. 'Maybe not. But didn't you think it was funny that he suddenly turned up in your neighbourhood? In the next building?'

'No. Why should I? You meet so many people again – just like that. You go to a party and suddenly you meet somebody you haven't seen for ten years. You go to the cinema and there's a girl you went to school with twenty years ago sitting in the row in front of you.'

'But you met Gunnar Våge and talked to him?'

'Met him? I ran into him several times. In the street. And we exchanged a few words. We hadn't much in common – any more.'

'But at one time ...'

'Gunnar and I? Yes. We had a good time together for two months one summer a long time ago. That was before I met Jonas. Yes. I met Jonas that very same autumn. If I hadn't, who knows? But I did and that was it. I never looked at another man twice after that. It was only Jonas. That's how love is, isn't it?'

'That's what they say,' I said. 'So it was really Jonas who – meeting Jonas caused you to break up with Gunnar Våge? Back then?'

'Yes. Maybe so. But it doesn't mean.'

'What doesn't it mean?'

'You can't believe – you don't think …'

'What can't I believe? What don't I think?'

'Really! It's too ridiculous. It was a hundred years ago, and it's got nothing to do with – it can't have anything to do with this.'

'You don't have to …' I realised I was being too harsh. My voice was too loud. I tried again. 'You don't have to protect anybody else, Wenche. Let Gunnar Våge defend himself if he needs to. His mouth is more than big enough. You're the one we have to clear. Right?'

'Yes, but …' The film of frost covered her eyes again. Her voice lost its colour. Became neutral. 'It's hopeless, Varg. I'll be found guilty. I know it. They're going to lock me up for the rest of my life, and I'll never see Roar again. But maybe it's just as well. I don't care any more. Jonas is dead. And he had cheated on me before that. What's out – what have I got to do – out there?'

I leaned across the table again. 'You've got everything to do out there, Wenche! You're young. Christ! You can start again. Meet a new man. We don't love just one person in our lives.

We love a lot of people – our mothers and daughters, fathers and sons, husbands and wives, lovers. You'll meet somebody new. If not this year, then next year. Maybe not today, but tomorrow. You can't give up now. Understand?'

She was silent.

'After – after Jonas left you and you knew Gunnar Våge was in the neighbourhood, didn't you ever think of – starting up the friendship again? Could you – didn't you ever think you could begin a new relationship with him? He was somebody you knew and had been happy with before.'

'No, Varg. No. Never.' She gulped and then her eyes suddenly filled with tears. There were tears in her voice when she said, 'It's just that …' And her lips silently pronounced a dead man's name.

I let her cry. She wept silently, with her back straight and without raising her hands to her face. Tears streamed from her eyes, ran shining down her cheeks, around her nostrils to her mouth and chin. I watched them as if they were spring's very first ice-free brook, the beginning of a March thaw when the glaciers melt under the young sun and night prepares to celebrate the coming dawn.

And then her tears stopped. I found a clean handkerchief in a pocket, and leaned towards her. Wiped the tear-stains from her face until all that was left were those anxious inflamed circles under her eyes. 'I'll be back, Wenche,' I said. 'Just take it easy. It's going to be OK. I'm sure of it.'

She nodded. Her lips were swollen.

There was a strange feeling in my stomach. I looked slowly from her lips to her eyes. I tried to burn away that film with my gaze, snap the passivity and detachment like a bow string, wake her from her Sleeping-Beauty trance. Without knowing what I was doing, I leaned across the table. I could feel its edge in my stomach, see her face grow larger.

If she'd leaned towards me I'd have kissed her.

But she didn't. She sat like a ramrod across from me, two thousand miles and another love away. So I leaned back again.

'Well. That's that,' I said.

We stood up at the same time. There was nothing more to say.

'Be careful, Varg,' was all she said.

'I will,' was all I said.

The guard stood up too. I watched her take Wenche Andresen away to her cell. Wenche Andresen moved like a patient who's just begun walking again after a long illness. The guard was a sturdy ward nurse leading her patient carefully back to bed.

And me? I was the wind. I blew past people and they hardly knew I'd gone by. I asked new questions and got new questions in return. Love's like that, isn't it? she'd asked.

I believed it. Love's a lonely thing. It's a stone you once found on a beach and carry around in the pocket of a pair of trousers you seldom wear. But it's there, somewhere in the cupboard. And you know it. It'll follow you all your life. From your birth to your death. Love's as blind as a stone, as lonely as an empty beach. And you know it.

I left the police station as light-footed as a locomotive and as happy as somebody who's just identified a body.

42

A cement lid had been screwed tight over the city and it was abnormally dark. The rain would come soon now.

I walked quickly down to Sandkaien and into the building where my office sits when I'm not there. When I went past the cafeteria on the second floor a strong smell of coffee assaulted my nose. But I didn't fall for it and kept going.

I let myself into the office. It smelled of dry radiator air, old dust, abandonment, and it was like a tomb. 'Hello, grave. Here comes the body,' I said.

But nobody answered, not even the echo of my own voice.

I took off my jacket and sat behind the desk. A calendar hung in the middle of the wall. It still showed February, but I knew I wasn't going to stand up, walk over there, tear off the sheet and turn the year ahead to March. Besides, I liked February's picture better. It was a photograph of the harbour with a drift of snow over the roofs and mountains and the kind of sky a six-year-old would have painted: pure and blue.

I swivelled the chair and looked through the window. An angelic hand had splashed a handful of water against the pane. It was pitch-black outside now. The cars of Bryggen had their headlights on as if the drivers had forgotten to turn them off after the Eidsvåg Tunnel.

I could see the grocers down at the market hurriedly stretching tarpaulins across their stands, people scurrying to shelter with their umbrellas on guard.

Then the sky split down the middle. Lightning ripped the darkness. The thunder sounded as if Mount Fløien and Ulriken had collided and now were exploding into thousands of fragments. The thunder rumbled and rolled between the mountains like boulders. An invisible hand dashed a flock of chalk-white gulls against Ask Island and they protested loudly as they vainly tried to brake with their wings. A pigeon with black button eyes landed on the cornice outside my window and hurried into the corner where it stood with its head cocked and waited for the voice of doom to fall silent and the wheat to be separated from the chaff.

And then the rain came.

It was as if the sea itself loomed like a wall over the city. The raindrops were huge, heavy and grey, and they fell in cascades. They burst on the pavements and streets, in seconds turned the tarpaulins in the market into bulging hammocks. They turned the gutters into spring-crazy mountain brooks, sent brown water seething into the drains with the speed of a hurricane.

The streets emptied in minutes. People sheltered against walls, under gateways, in doorways and entrances to the public toilets. The shops filled with people just looking around and in cafeterias four or five strangers sat at each table.

I sat in my office and watched that violent drama. New bolts of lightning struck the city like fountains of fire. New thunder claps rolled over us like water rushing into a basin. A deluge washed the city clean for the forthcoming week and flooded away all traces of the weekend.

It was almost half an hour before it was over. The lightning died away over Fana like distant distress signals from a flashlight with a fading battery. The thunder weakened to a distant rumbling. The rain tapered off and lay like shining silk on the rooftops, the trees on the mountainsides and farther out on Strandkaien. It glistened on the colourful umbrellas of people leaving their hiding places, one by one, with their white upturned faces and eyes like newly lit suns. The storm was over and life could go on.

I flipped through the phone book, found the right number and called Richard Ljosne. When he answered I said, 'Ljosne? This is Veum.'

'Oh? Hello again. Thanks for – the last time.'

I listened to his voice and I could see him. The Wolf. Wolf-grey hair. On guard behind his desk. Steel in his arms and legs.

'I've just been talking to Wenche. She said not to give you her best.'

'What do you mean?' he said.

'She said not to give you her best.'

'No?'

'No. She wasn't exactly pleased by what you told me.'

'That I … But did you tell her …?'

'You lied, didn't you, Ljosne? You didn't sleep with her last Tuesday, did you? You didn't get that far. For once you had to pass, didn't you?'

I listened to the silence. The sky was already getting lighter. It had stopped raining. 'Well? Ljosne?'

'Well, perhaps I didn't,' he said slowly. Reluctant.

'Why did you lie, Ljosne?'

I would have liked to see him but I didn't have time to travel that far just to look at the stupid expression on his face when he said, 'You know – how it is, Veum. Between us men.'

'No. No, I don't know how it is. Tell me about it. You're the one who's seen the world. You're the expert on women.'

'Listen, Veum. You don't have to be a smart-arse. I know I

– I know it was stupid. A person ought to keep his mouth shut now and then.'

'Not just now and then,' I said. 'All the time. But you still haven't told me how it is between us men.'

'Well. Well. No, I didn't sleep with her. That's true. But sometimes you say more than you mean to. Am I right? And I'd already said plenty – about all the other women. And I told you Wenche turned me on. How could I go on to tell you about my biggest rejection? Just like that? I couldn't do it, Veum. I couldn't. I'm too much of a man to admit I was turned down.'

'So she said no?'

'So she said no. Simple and direct. No. I asked if I could come in. And she said no, absolutely not, Richard. And that was that. She said no and I went home and slept with myself instead.'

'And was that so hard to tell me?'

'Damn right it was, Veum.'

'As hard as the other thing?'

'The other thing?' Long pauses between the words.

'About your son. The Man Without a Country. Johan Pedersen. Joker. Your son by a woman named Hildur Pedersen. A son you've kept track of and helped all his life but always at a distance. Why didn't you tell me, Ljosne?'

'I … I … I don't see what this has to do with anything. A man's entitled to some secrets.'

'As long as he's not hiding a murderer.'

'A murderer? That's ridiculous, Veum. You can't mean that Johan had anything to do with …'

'No, Ljosne. I don't mean that. I know he didn't. But we're dealing with a murder and the more secrets, the harder it is to get to the truth. If there is any, other than –'

'Veum.' His voice was hoarse. 'I've got money, Veum. I can pay. If you'll just keep my name out of it. So people won't know about Johan. I can –'

'What's wrong with an illegitimate child these days, Ljosne?'

'It's not that. But people will know and they'll say I let him down. That I made him what he is today.'

'Maybe they'd be right.'

'Listen. I don't know who's paying you for what you're doing. But I doubt it's Wenche. I'll be glad to pay my share of your fee, Veum. So you can help her. If you'll just …'

I stared at the ceiling. This was the moment just before somebody knocked a hole in it and started pouring gold pieces on to my head. People promised me money right and left, but it never made it to my letter box for some reason. Maybe there was something wrong with the delivery.

'My fee *will* be paid, Ljosne. Any more secrets for me before we hang up?'

'No. No, but –'

'So long, Ljosne. See you some time at the old folks' home. Or at a truss sale. Run today, Ljosne, but stay off my roads. OK?'

'I –'

I didn't wait to hear the rest. After I'd hung up I realised he could have got me some bottles of aquavit cheap. But then I realised they wouldn't ever taste good.

I had a very important call to make. The bright patches of sky had grown. Maybe we'd get a glimpse of blue before it faded and got dark.

I called the Pallas Advertising Agency and asked to speak to Solveig Manger. 'One moment please.' The voice was bored.

I waited, looked at my watch. The display worked under the

broken crystal. Already after two. Somewhere behind that grey-white wool blanket the sun had fallen two degrees closer to the horizon. Like the ghost of a distant summer it was sneaking quickly and guiltily across the sky without ever showing itself.

I heard her voice. It sounded anxious as if she hadn't heard much good news recently. 'Hello? This is Solveig Manger.'

'Hello. My name's Veum. Varg Veum. I'm a private investigator, and I –'

She interrupted. 'If this is a joke, then –'

'No, no, Fru Manger. It's no joke. I'm sorry if it sounds like one, but –'

'I'm sorry. I'm a little – sensitive just now. I've never talked to a private investigator before.'

'No. Right. You haven't,' I said. Relieved. 'Not a lot of people have. Until I call them. But I – I'd be exaggerating if I said I knew Jonas well, but we – we got pretty close late one evening before he … And he talked about you in a way that … Well, you might want to know what he said, and maybe you could tell me something about him. As a matter of fact, I'm trying to find out what really happened.'

'Find out what really happened? I thought the police … I … OK, just a minute.' She'd been interrupted and I could hear her saying, 'No, not just now. Could you give me five minutes? OK. Close the door if you don't mind.' And then she was back. 'Hello! You said you wanted to talk to me?'

'I would really like to,' I said. 'If it's not too much trouble. I thought a lot of Jonas, as a matter of fact, even if I didn't know him well. I –'

She interrupted again. 'Let's get one thing straight – Veum. That is your name?'

'It is.'

'My husband knows all about Jonas and me. At least he does now. The police were kind enough to tell him. I suppose they felt they had to.' She sighed so you could have heard her all the way across Vågen. 'So there's no money in case that's what you were thinking. Not to insult you, but –'

Now it was my turn to interrupt. As calmly as I could I said, 'People have the wrong impressions of private detectives, Fru Manger. They see too many American films. They get the idea that we're broad-shouldered, dark-haired studs with a bottle of whisky in one pocket and a sexy blonde in the other. If we're not dirty little grease-balls with egg on our ties who comb our greasy hair over bald spots and make a living blackmailing naughty housewives, the truth is …' I looked around the office.

'The truth is,' I said, 'that we're little grey non-entities who hang out in shabby little offices with a stack of unpaid bills we've let go so long that they don't bother us any more. And we own calendars we haven't the courage to tear February off. And we look like encyclopedia salesmen.' I drew a deep breath. 'When can we meet?'

'Tell me,' she said thoughtfully, 'do you usually talk like this?'

'Only when I'm sober,' I said.

'I don't know if I see the point in –' she said.

'Don't let my nonsense scare you, Fru Manger. I get carried away, and then I'm not responsible. But face to face with a lady under sixty? I'm as lovesick as a thirteen-year-old and as dangerous as a wingless fly.'

'There's a tea-shop in Øvregaten behind the Maria Church,' she said.

'Right. I know where it is.'

We could meet there. About three-thirty?'

'Great. I'll be there.'

'It'll have to be quick. I've got to be home by four-thirty. My husband …' She didn't finish the sentence and I could understand why. Manger's patience was bound to be a little strained.

'No problem,' I said. 'See you then.'

I hung up. 'Good lord,' I said to myself. I'd done it.

I stood up, walked around the desk and over to the calendar and raised my hand. Stood there. 'No, not yet,' I said. 'Not just yet.'

Then I locked up and dawdled the two floors down to the ruination of everything man considers edible. Ate my dinner as slowly and carefully as a condemned man might. But no condemned prisoner could ever have deserved that punishment.

43

The Bergen Electric Ferry Company owns and operates the little ferry which crosses Vågen between Nykirken and Bradbenken. The company's logo – B.E.F. – is painted on the sides of the boat.

We called her *Beffen* when we were kids and made that endless journey across Vågen to practise gymnastics in the Viking Hall.

Later we took *Beffen* to go to dances in that same hall. The ferry stopped running just as the dance was over. And those of us who couldn't find a girl to see home 'somewhere out in Sandviken' because all the girls worth seeing home lived 'somewhere out in Sandviken', or in the opposite direction from where we were headed – we, who didn't have a girl to see home, had to *walk* all the endless way around Vågen.

They've changed *Beffen* since then. The old brown-and-white wooden boat is now fibreglass. Orange-and-white. She rides higher in the water now and her engine sounds different.

For old times' sake, I walked out to Gågaten, bought a paper at a news-stand and then walked down to take *Beffen* across Vågen to Dreggen.

Those years in Nordnes always seem clearer when I travel this way between seasons. It gives me time to think about those days.

I can't remember that the trolley went all the way out to Nordnes. But I do remember my father getting off the bus up in Haugeveien with his conductor's satchel over his shoulder and his cap not exactly four-square on his head. His face was ruddy in the summer and a sort of greyish-red in winter. It was a strong face. Round, with a fullness in his cheeks on either side of his mouth. His mouth was always tense. As if he were just swinging off or on to a trolley that hadn't stopped or started yet.

He'd come down the steps from Haugeveien and I'd come running, calling him. Saying hello. He'd ruffle my hair, look at me with his pale clear eyes and ask if I'd been a good boy. And then he'd go home to his books and newspapers. And a quarter of an hour later my mother'd come up from the alley and call, 'Varg! It's dinnertime!'

I can close my eyes and see her face to this day. Always pale, but a face of gentle contours – like the rest of her. Her mouth belonged to a prettier – or maybe a younger – face than hers. Her eyes were warmer and darker than my father's, and her voice was always welcoming.

I can remember the checked tablecloth. I remember the salted cod one day, haddock in white sauce the next. Fish dumplings one day, fish chowder the next. Potato dumplings and salted meat one day, hash the next. Dessert on Sundays. Jelly with a synthetic taste and warm vanilla sauce. My father at one end of the table, my mother at the other. I sat in the middle, facing the window. The window was the fourth person at the table because time and the seasons were out there: brilliant sunshine, pouring rain, or snow and glittering hoar-frost. Once – and an eternity ago.

They're dead now. And it's been a long time since I sat at a dinner table with as many as three people around it. And there's almost nothing left of the Nordnes I knew.

I boarded *Beffen* and walked aft. Looked back at Nordnes, at the tall ugly brick buildings that edge Vågen now, at that infinite variety of misbegotten architecture that stretches like the Great Wall from the market to Nordnesbakken.

Suddenly it hurt. As if *Beffen* were taking me away from my own promised land, from my childhood. I thought of those I'd left behind. Of the dead I'd escorted to their graves. Of the faces I'd never see again. Of the houses I'd never again run between. Neither as a little boy nor as a grown man. Because all those houses were gone. Not one was still standing.

We chugged towards Mount Fløien and Dreggen, and the parts of Bergen that were still relatively unchanged. Small wooden houses still defended their turf up on the mountainside. Old buildings still stood along Bryggen. And Mount Fløien still surveyed the whole, its contours as they always had been, contours nobody could change. Or could they?

I walked through *Beffen* and on to dry land.

44

She had chosen a little tea-shop. It was as much a baker's as a tea-shop. Too small to sing arias in. It wasn't a place to get personal. I'd have suggested another spot.

The room was divided by a display case full of bread and cakes. In the back, to the right, a refrigerated case held racks of soft drinks. Two little tables, each with two chairs, stood between it and the door. There was another table under the window to the left of the door. That was it.

I picked the table nearest the soft drink's counter. It seemed the most private, if you could call sitting half a metre from the soft drinks and three metres from the door being private.

An elderly grey-haired woman whose face was a network of laugh-lines stood behind the display case. She wore yellow: blouse, skirt and apron. I ordered two rum cakes and a cup of hot chocolate with cream. It was three twenty-five. One of my bad habits: I'm always five minutes early.

She came through the door, the late afternoon light at her back. She didn't have to look for me. I was the only other customer.

As she walked to the table, I saw how small and delicate she was. She held out a pale slim hand and said, 'Hello. Solveig Manger.'

I stood up and said, 'Varg Veum. Hello.'

We shook hands. She apologised for being five minutes late. I said not to worry and she smiled as if she were used to men saying that. Then she went to the counter and ordered coffee and a roll.

She came back, unbuttoned her coat and sat down. She must have had that coat for years: it was weathered green corduroy with full lapels and a wide belt with a dark brown buckle. She was wearing a soft beige blouse printed with little brown and orange autumn flowers. The blouse didn't tell you much about the body under it. There was something romantic and mysterious about her, and you could imagine those soft little breasts and the taut diaphragm and the sweet smooth belly lower down. Her shoulders were narrow but straight and she sat with natural grace.

She was wearing a green corduroy skirt. The small breasts and broad hips made her look a little like an ice-age sculpture. She was no luscious Venus, no voluptuous Diana. But hers was a body you could easily fall in love with. It suddenly made you feel tender and protective.

I felt she shouldn't have to look at my lumpy, ugly, battered face and I ran my hand across its lower half as if I could hide it.

'I've seen you before,' she said. Looking at me searchingly.

I rested my hand on the table. 'Can't we use first names? It'd be so much easier,' I said.

She smiled. Cautious. 'All right. I'm Solveig and you're ... Wait – what was it? Vidar?'

'I almost wish it were.'

'Oh?' Her eyes were such a dark blue they seemed almost black. Her hair hung straight and girlish around her face: not blonde, not brown and not red, but all those colours. I agreed with Jonas. From a distance, it was the first thing you'd notice about her.

'It's Varg,' I said.

She didn't laugh. 'Listen. It's not going to be easy being friends,' she said. 'I just can't believe everything you say, I don't believe you're a private detective. And now you – your name really is …?'

I nodded. 'It really is. My name really is Varg. And I really am a private detective.'

She smiled. 'Well, yes. I do believe you. Now I've seen you.'

She had a lovely face. Not classical. It was too individual. Her mouth was quite small but her lips were neither too full nor too narrow. When she smiled her cheeks curved and there was the hint of a dimple in the corner of her mouth. Her nose was straight and narrow, and she had a determined chin. If it hadn't been for her eyes and hair, she'd have looked like any pretty woman. But her eyes said she was a very nice person and her hair …

I was looking at her hair when she said, 'This is when you ask me what colour my hair is.'

'Am I going to?' I said, smiling at her.

'Everybody does, sooner or later. Usually sooner.'

'And what do you tell them?'

'Sort of in-between. Or else chestnut blonde. Because they never know what to say.'

I liked her. She sat there on the other side of the little table with her back straight and she looked into her coffee cup as she talked. Now and then she'd glance quickly up at me, but her eyes didn't linger on my face. They returned to search the darkness in the cup.

She wasn't a young girl. The fine laugh-lines at her eyes said she was over thirty. And these recent days had marked her. I guessed the dark blue-grey shadows under her eyes hadn't been so obvious a week ago, and she hadn't had those lines of tension at the ends of her eyebrows either. Those lines reminded me of antennae. They either disappear when your grief lessens or else they stay with you the rest of your life until one day – if you're lucky – you too leave a little circle of mourners behind.

'Solveig …' I said.

'Yes?' She looked up at once and I could hear the sudden anxiety in her voice.

'I … A week ago – last Tuesday – Jonas and I were together at Bryggestuen, and he …'

Her eyes glistened. Her mouth trembled. Then she pressed her lips together and quickly brushed her eyes with her right hand. 'I – I'm sorry …' she said.

The woman behind the counter disappeared into a back room. We could hear the scrape of a chair and the loud rustle of a newspaper.

'I don't want to upset you,' I said. 'I really don't. I'll be honest. I asked you to meet me because I want to know more about you and Jonas. Because I want to find out who really killed him. And because I really didn't know him very well. We only met that one time.'

'Just – just last Tuesday?' She looked wonderingly at me.

I nodded. 'Yes.' I was hoarse.

'That was – his last day. I've thought about it. I've tried to remember everything we did that day. Everything we said to each other. But there was nothing special. It was just an ordinary day. One of your usual everyday days. And I didn't know – we didn't know. How can we live, Varg, if we know? Or should we live every day as if it's our last?' She searched my eyes. 'Would you have done things differently?'

'Of course. Of course I would. I think I would.'

'Of course you would. Everybody would. But we don't

know before – before it's too late.' She bit her lips with her small square teeth. 'I loved him.'

Oh God, I thought. 'Listen, Solveig, I … Before you say any more,' I said, 'I want you to know you can trust me and …'

Her hand rested on mine for a few seconds. She squeezed my wrist and then took her hand away. Her voice was soft and warm. 'I know that, Varg. I know your name's Varg and that you're a private detective, and that I can trust you not to repeat anything I say. I can see that in your eyes. As a matter of fact, I've a feeling we could have been friends in other circumstances.'

'Jonas told –' I said.

'Excuse me. I interrupted you,' she said. 'Jonas told …'

'He told me – about you. He said he'd never told anybody else about you. Before. I don't know why he chose me. He was a little drunk, but …'

'There comes a time, Varg, when all secrets have to be told. You go around knowing something nobody else knows, and there isn't anybody you can tell. You want to. You need to. But your mother'd probably be shocked, and your best friend probably wouldn't understand. You know you can't talk about it to anybody. Except to the person who already is the secret.

'But then one day you meet somebody, preferably by chance and – not to insult you – somebody you won't meet again, or not too often. And then, finally, you talk about it. And it's good to talk about it. Because it's a secret love you've been carrying around. And you want to share it with somebody. Share the happiness of that love. Even though it's – not legit.'

She said the last word almost as an afterthought, and there was a wrinkle between her brows. Quite thin, dark brows. Natural colour. A touch of mascara on the lashes. A thin film of pink lipstick on her lips. Otherwise she didn't use make-up as far as I could see.

'Jonas talked about you in a way I've never heard a man talk about a woman before. He – it was almost contagious.' My last word wasn't an afterthought. It came out before I could stop it. 'I mean, I …'

'I've thought … You can imagine what I've been thinking since that morning the police phoned and said …' Her voice sank to a whisper. 'That he was dead.' She coughed and went on. 'I've thought about our time together. About the time we were given. I've never … They were the happiest years of my life, Varg. Absolutely. Others can call it adultery or whatever they like, but I've never been so happy before.

'From those first scary feelings to the – the warmth we shared. And now to this. I remember when I first fell in love with him. There were unsettling little symptoms at first. I tried to suppress them, pull myself together. I told myself: you're happily married, Solveig, happily married! But my God, it was like trying to stop a runaway locomotive. The next thought was obvious: was I so happily married, if I could fall in love with somebody else?' She looked at me questioningly.

'You probably weren't,' I said. 'But can't you love a lot of different people at the same time?'

She nodded slowly. 'Maybe so. But not with the same feeling. And later on – a long time afterwards, as a matter of fact, because it began slowly with Jonas and me – later on when we began seriously being together, we loved each other so much there wasn't room for anybody else. For Jonas and me – it was just the two of us.

'He – he was the one who faced reality. While I hesitated. And that's what I've thought about. I mean, it's one of the things. Maybe I waited too long. Maybe this happened because I waited too long. If I, if we'd done what we talked about, made a break, burnt our bridges – moved to another city – then maybe he'd be alive today. My – love.' She said that last word almost inaudibly. Then she continued.

'Jonas always said … I believe he had quite a good – a good physical relationship anyway – with his wife. He always said that what he felt for me wasn't primarily physical, at least, not before we'd been together. It was something romantic, he always said. But for me … I mean, my romantic feelings for Jonas were strong. I don't mean they weren't. But physically – for me he was … I've never known anything like it. He was …'

She lowered her voice. Clasped her hands together so I could see the shine of her wedding ring. It had got darker, a blue-grey dusk. You could hear the regular rush of traffic. A yellow bus stopped in front of Schøttstuene across the street.

'He was the first,' she said. 'The only one who ever made me feel like a woman. Completely!' She lowered her voice still further. 'We – Reidar, my husband, and I – it isn't so good for us that way.'

Suddenly she blushed as if she'd just now realised she was sitting here telling her most intimate secrets to somebody – a man – she hadn't known half an hour earlier.

We sat in silence for a while. A customer entered. A middle-aged man who bought half a loaf of wholewheat and then left. The waitress sold it to him, then returned to the back room. On the way she glanced at the clock.

'Do you know Reidar – my husband?' Solveig Manger said.

'No,' I said.

She fished a wallet from her handbag. Opened it and took out a picture which she handed across the table. It was a snapshot of a man in high green sea-boots, bleached jeans, a checked flannel shirt, and a blue anorak. He was sitting on a rock by a river somewhere. He had thick blond hair cut quite short and a red beard, but the smile inside the beard belonged to a teacher, to little Miss Goody Two Shoes.

'Reidar,' she said.

I nodded. 'Jonas said – he liked him. Said he was something or other in American literature at the university. A Hemingway specialist. Said he'd faint if he saw a live trout.'

She smiled dully. The problem with Jonas – now and then was that he could be a little categorical. Reidar's no Hemingway, thank God. I'd never have married him if he were. But I think he's seen more live trout in his life than Jonas ever has – had. And he is an outdoor person. That's how we met, as a matter of fact. Up in the mountains. In Jotunheimen. He – we're good friends. We live together. And I once loved him very much. Before I met Jonas. Now? Now I don't know. Maybe I can love him again now Jonas is dead. If he'll have me. It's been a shock for him too. He had no idea …'

'About you – and …?'

'No idea. He came home after the police talked to him. He looked awful. But he didn't say anything. Didn't accuse me. He just looked at me. I … That was the worst, if you see what I mean. He's a decent man. He'd never – he'd never lay a hand on me. But I don't know what'll happen – to us.'

She stared into space as if it didn't matter. As if the rest of her life stretched before her like an endless bus trip. A trip home on the bus through a blue-grey dusk which would never turn to night, never turn to dawn and which would never end.

'Reidar wouldn't ever understand,' she said. 'What Jonas and I had – nobody else could understand it. Only we could.'

'The lovers' privilege?' I said cautiously.

'Maybe so. Maybe it's just an illusion. Maybe it wasn't so special after all. Maybe it was something everyone experiences at one time or other – if they're lucky.'

She emptied her cup. 'It's strange,' she said. 'It's funny how things in life sometimes just seem to happen. Ten years too late. Jonas and I should have met ten years ago. When we were young and free. We were certainly meant for one another. Right from the start. There couldn't have been anybody else. After a while I couldn't imagine life – without Jonas. And he said it was like that for him too. We did something other people will say was wrong but there wasn't anything else we could have done. We loved each other. It was love.'

I emptied my own cup down to the white layer of cream in the bottom.

'Of course we talked about divorce,' she said. 'And he couldn't hold out. Whatever you decide, Solveig, he said, I'm going to cut loose. And he did. But I – I put it off. I thought of the children. How would they react? And I have to admit it – I thought about what people would say. I thought about friends and acquaintances, about relatives. Colleagues. My family. His family. All the people who'd turn their backs on me. On us. And I thought it would take a lot of courage to stand up to all that. I wasn't really sure I had it.

'But lately … Oh Varg, it's so heartbreaking. Lately, in these last few months I finally decided. It's been a long painful process, but I really got to the point where I could choose between duty and love. We're all selfish, aren't we? We want to be happy, make a good life for ourselves. So what should we do?'

Her eyes were completely black now. 'Jonas was ready for a divorce. So was I. Finally. And then this – this terrible thing happens.' She took a deep breath. 'Nothing matters now. It's no use. Jonas is dead. Reidar knows about us. He may leave me. Then I'll be left without either of them. I'll be alone with my memories of some happy adulterous years.'

'I –'

'But what's adultery? Is it what you do when you're with the only person you love? Or is it what you do with the person you're married to and don't love? Whenever Reidar and I slept together – I couldn't help it, I really got angry with myself – I couldn't help thinking about Jonas and how good it was when we ... As a matter of fact, it got so I felt guilty when I was with Reidar. Because I felt I wasn't being faithful to Jonas! Does that make any sense at all?'

'It does,' I said. 'As a matter of fact, Jonas said just about the same thing when he told me about you.'

She shrugged her narrow shoulders despairingly and stared at me. Then she gave me an unusually mournful smile. It was the saddest smile I'd ever seen. It was the smile of a woman who stands by a grave and asks: Was that it? So short? Over so soon? It was the smile of a child who stands on a beach, looks at the sea and asks: Is this the ocean? All this emptiness? And it was an unusually beautiful smile.

She looked at the clock and she looked at me. 'I think I've got to go. Was there anything else you wanted to ask me?'

I tried to think. No good.

'As far as that goes,' she said, 'I haven't let you get a word in. I've talked you to death. Have I – have I helped you?'

'I don't know. I doubt it. Not with finding out ...' I said. 'But you – and Jonas – have taught me something I didn't see clearly before, something I never could have completely understood on my own. Something about love.'

She nodded sadly and gave me a shadow of that mournful smile. 'Well. Then maybe it isn't – pointless.' She tried to sound cheerful. 'Some other time – some other time. You'll have to tell me about you. Shall we go?'

I stood up. She buttoned her coat and we went outside. I carefully closed the door behind us, nodded to the woman who was beginning to clear our table.

We stood outside the tea-shop. A cold spring wind blew her hair away from her face and I saw it: open and vulnerable. 'You forgot to tell – haven't I seen you before somewhere?'

'Last Tuesday,' I said. 'I came to the agency to talk to Jonas. I was waiting in Reception and you walked by.'

'Oh yes. Now I remember. Well.' She held out her hand. 'I'd better say goodbye for now. I'm glad I could talk with you. It – I think it helped. Thank you.'

I held her hand firmly with both of mine. 'Thank you, Solveig,' I said. I could hear the tears in my voice. I memorised every feature of her face. In case I'd never see her again. In case this were the last day – for one of us.

Then it was over. I let go of her hand. She turned and walked toward Sandviken. She looked back and smiled at me over her shoulder. The green corduroy coat fluttered in the choppy wind. I watched until she'd disappeared. She didn't turn around again.

It was strange standing there, staring after her. I couldn't break loose. It was as if one part of me had left the rest on the pavement, as if I'd never be the same again. As if life – and everything else had suddenly taken on a new and disturbing meaning.

A lone raven flew past the Maria Church's medieval double spires. It was as if a scrap of the blue-grey dusk had torn loose and fluttered by. Like a random page from an old newspaper, a random day in an old life.

45

I drove to that development behind the Lyderhorn through what had once been Laksevåg.

It was dark now and you couldn't tell if it were autumn, winter or spring. But I associate Laksevag with spring. We'd ridden our bikes through it when we were kids and it was always spring then. Those were the first long rides on our freshly oiled bikes, the first exciting trips we'd make before summer came and we had other things to do. The roads were still wet after months of sleet, snow and rain. We breathed the cold clear air of a late frost under a sun which hadn't yet risen high enough to do more than cast its golden glow on our bare necks and close-cropped hair. And our fingers froze.

Since then I've always had a feeling of spring or a holiday whenever I've driven through Laksevåg. The post office makes me think of savings account books showing my hoarded holiday money. A café makes me think of those cafés I stopped at somewhere in southern Norway when I was on a bicycle tour. Cafés with their watery meat cakes, their soft drinks and the flies on the table tops and in the windows.

The closer I got to the old arena, the more my face hurt. It was as if there were new life in my old bruises, as if my body refused to visit that place again. Refused a new encounter with the ground, with brutal young fists and boots.

The big shopping centre still looked as if it were ready for take-off. I drove up to the four high-rises and parked in front of the second one. Stayed in the car and looked around. But I couldn't see anything. The shadows were faceless, the darkness empty of shapes. As far as I could tell.

I got out of the car. The air was cold and clear and I had a feeling there'd be frost again tonight. Little puddles would freeze and the elderly would slip and break their hips tomorrow morning. I looked up at Wenche Andresen's flat. Automatically. It was dark. Night had already fallen there.

But that wasn't where I was headed. I walked to the highrise that housed the youth club. This time I didn't follow the red arrows. I read the names on the letter boxes. Gunnar Våge. Twelfth floor.

I walked around the corner to the lift. Somewhere a giant took a deep breath and the lift was hauled up twelve flights.

Gunnar Våge's flat was in the north wing, nearest the lift room. Nobody answered when I rang. I stood for a while by the railing and looked out. Except for the roof itself, I was as high up as you could get. The next logical stairway would be the Lyderhorn. The people below seemed tiny, and my car an abandoned toy. Nobody was near it. Nobody was opening the bonnet and tearing up the wiring. Nobody melted into the shadows around it. I rang Våge's bell again. No answer.

So I took the lift back down and walked to the building where Joker lived. Took the lift this time too. Along with an unsociable man wearing a parka and horn-rimmed glasses. His face could have been that of a man-about-town when there were such things and when parkas belonged to pictures of arctic wastes.

I rang Hildur Pedersen's bell. After the usual wait, she opened the door. She didn't look especially thrilled to see me again. 'I have nothing to say,' she said before I could open my mouth. 'Go away. You've already –'

'I don't want to talk to you,' I said. 'I want to talk to Johan.'

'Why?' she said.

'Let's just say we've got some unfinished business – it's about some boots.'

'Boots?' She studied my face and I saw something like a smile flit across hers. 'Has somebody been using you as a dance floor, Veum?'

'They never went to dancing school, that's for sure,' I said. 'They never asked me to dance. I've never been a wallflower before. And now they've used me to decorate the tarmac.'

'I love listening to you, Veum. But not when I'm standing in a doorway and holding up 120 kilos. And I'm not in the mood to ask you in.'

'As I said. It's Johan I –'

'He's not at home.'

'No?'

'No. He's out. God knows for how long.'

'No idea where I could find him?'

She shrugged so the balcony rocked. 'No idea.'

She started to close the door. All I could see was a pale strip of her face. 'Bye,' she said. Then she was gone and all that was left was the view. But it was the view from a lower altitude and it didn't offer much. I walked slowly down the stairs.

I thought about my meeting with Solveig Manger. I listened to the echo of her voice, saw her hair. Thought of how it would be to lean forward and take in the scent of her hair, the warmth of her skin. Or sit somewhere in the twilight and fish silver from her deep dark eyes. Or just sit and look …

I tried to imagine Jonas Andresen – and her. I tried to imagine them in bed together. She. On her back. Naked with her legs spread and her hair streaming across the pillow. He.

With tousled hair, straggly moustache and his arm across her white breasts.

But it didn't work. The only picture I could see was two people hand in hand, their breaths frosty in a winter-still park somewhere. Under trees like black clawing hands, hands that clutched at a pale grey sky with its promise of snow. The only thing I could see was two people with their arms around one another, their bodies close, on their way from nowhere to nowhere. And then. Suddenly he's gone. And she's walking alone.

But Wenche Andresen … I tried thinking about Wenche Andresen. But that didn't work either. I saw Roar. I could imagine Roar. A sudden anxious thought struck me. As it will a father who's away from home: how's Roar doing in Øystese? Is he OK?

But Wenche Andresen …

Maybe Solveig Manger was the kind of woman you almost never meet but who can suddenly erase all the images of all the women you've ever met, loved, known. Maybe that was what happened to Jonas Andresen too.

Too?

I was down. I walked to the front of the building.

I felt as if I were close to some kind of breakthrough, some kind of solution. As if the talk with Solveig Manger had released something inside me, as if I really knew all the characters in the play for the first time. Jonas and Solveig who'd met ten years too late. Wenche, who vanished somewhere between. Roar, who couldn't decide anything, but for whom things were decided, who was a child and like all children – innocent.

I still wasn't sure what roles the others played in relation to those three adults and a child: Reidar Manger, Richard Ljosne, Gunnar Våge, Solfrid Brede, Hildur Pedersen – and Joker.

Joker. I had an account to settle with Joker. I felt I had to talk to Joker before I talked to anybody else.

I went back to the car and got my flashlight. Then I walked past the last high-rise, crossed over to the woods and went up to the hut where Joker and his gang hung out. Maybe they were all there. Sitting and waiting. Looking forward to another round with Willing Veum. Your handy-dandy punching bag.

Once again I stumbled through the darkness up to that rickety hut. The trees rustled weakly. Somebody started a motor cycle down below me. Then the sound faded. Somewhere a cat howled, tuning its fiddle for the night's courting.

The hut stood silently among the trees. Seemingly deserted. That's how it had looked the last time but Roar had been inside. And when we'd come out, the woods teemed with life. I made a wide circle around the hut. Made a few fast side-trips into the trees. Couldn't see anybody. Then I aimed the flashlight at the trees, tree trunks, bushes. There were footprints in the mud around the hut, but not a soul in sight.

I went over to the wall with its splintered surfaces of second-hand laths and knobby fragments of cement. An iron strap jutted out. As I stood by the doorway the only thing I could hear was the blood hammering in my temples and ear drums. I cautiously pulled the curtain aside with my left hand. Not a sound. I looked around again. Then I shone the flashlight slowly through the doorway and aimed it across the packed-dirt floor and the dirty newspapers.

The light picked up something. A pair of boots. I quickly aimed the beam higher. Joker was sitting there. Waiting for me. With his back against the wall and his legs sprawled. His eyes stared at the doorway as if he'd been waiting a long time.

He sat and sneered at me. With two mouths. The lower

mouth was a gaping, wide-open gash across his throat. It was the ugliest sneer I had ever seen.

46

He had bled. The blood had run from one end of the gash in his throat in a neat trail down his neck and into his blood-stained shirt. It was like the blood running from a vampire's mouth after its deadly bite. But the smile didn't show a vampire's teeth. It was a narrow-lipped, toothless smile. One carved by a knife.

One quick lethal cut, and one had been enough. He'd fallen against the wall and had slid down it. The heel of his boot had caught and rolled up one of the old newspapers as he'd sagged to the floor.

His upper mouth really smiled. A broad grin showed his little rat teeth and turned him into a travelling lay preacher. But he'd held his last prayer meeting, and was on his way to meet the last of all congregations. There'd be no more boats back, no more gangways leading to shore.

I stood there and shivered. And was suddenly aware of the forest at my back. It was as if the trees had tiptoed closer, like the Indians in Disney's *Peter Pan*. I whirled around, spearing the darkness with my flashlight. Nothing. The forest hadn't changed.

But that didn't mean somebody wasn't out there. Somebody could be out there in the darkness, somebody who'd just killed. He could be holding a knife the blood hadn't had time to dry on.

Somebody who uses a knife once doesn't mind using it

again. Especially if this isn't the second time, but the third. Whoever might be standing out there in the darkness and watching me was probably the same person who'd also killed Jonas Andresen.

But Joker – why was Joker dead? Joker had been in the car park with me when Jonas Andresen had been killed. Had Joker seen something after I'd left him? Had he seen somebody running down the stairs on the other side of the building as I was on my way up? Had he seen something and tried a little blackmail? Had he made a date to meet the person he'd seen – and had the date turned deadly?

The questions kept coming as I searched the darkness under the trees, looked down towards the glittering high-rises.

But who was it?

With my back against the door lintel, which felt like a mere splinter against my spine, I shone the flashlight into the hut again. Searched the floor. No knife. Nothing but a body. A youngster who'd never grow up. A body that would be ashes in a week and a soul that had gone to wherever it is souls go.

There wasn't anything more I could do here. I was neither a doctor nor a theologian. I left. Cautious and alert. The darkness enveloped me, the stars overhead blinking like distress signals in a black sea. I walked fast and I stopped abruptly. Listened. Nothing. No footsteps fading into silence behind me, no sounds that suddenly weren't there.

I walked on constantly looking behind me. To the side. I kept to the middle of the path and as far from the trees as I could. Reaching the car park was like returning to civilisation. My fingers were locked around the flashlight and my muscles about to cramp.

There was a phone box on the pavement by some low leafless

bushes. Even a dwarf couldn't have hidden there. I called the police station without looking at the dial and I didn't turn my back on the door. After I'd delivered the evening's happy news, I hung up fast, got out of the phone box and sheltered in its light until the first car arrived. I don't think I moved until I saw Jakob E. Hamre walk towards me with a grim expression on his face.

47

As we led the little police delegation up through the darkness, Hamre said, 'I have a colleague, Veum. Down at the station. His name's Muus. I'm sure you know him.'

I nodded.

'I happened to mention you had something to do with this case. I should say – with the other case. He didn't give you an especially good recommendation. Veum? he said. Keep that guy away from anything to do with the case, Jakob. The fellow's like flypaper, he said. Turn him loose in the dark and you can bet he'll find himself a dead body, he said. He said dead bodies have a thing about you.' He paused dramatically. 'I'm beginning to see what he meant.'

'He doesn't like me,' I said. 'We once met over a body, and I stumbled over his murderer for him. He didn't like me any better after that.'

Hamre stopped and our followers almost ran into us. I heard one of them swear. 'You guys keep going,' Hamre said.

'The hut's straight ahead,' I said.

Hamre and I stood there. Then he turned to me and his voice was acid. 'I'm a policeman, Veum. A detective. My life consists of misery and cruelty, of people who murder one another because of a bottle of beer or a safe with fifty kroner in it – or a useless cheque book. Or because people sleep with people they shouldn't. Or for a million other stupid reasons.

'Three hundred days a year I investigate robberies and other more or less violent crimes. When somebody hands me a body on the three hundred and first, I try to find out who did it. Along with about fifty other slobs who've made a living out of the medal's back side. I don't expect a medal either. Police chiefs and judges and Ministers of Justice get medals. Detectives get ulcers. I don't expect citations or decorations or any other damn thing. I don't expect so much as a pat on the head. But a dead person is something I take very seriously. The dead aren't something you play games with. You don't sit in an office with a view of Vågen and wait for them to fall in your lap.'

'Listen,' I said.

'Shut up, Veum. I give this speech only once, and I don't hand out the transcript afterwards. I don't give a shit how you pay your rent, or for your car, or your booze or your daily bread. I don't give a shit if you sneak around and tail cheating husbands and wives until your eyes fall out of your head. I'm telling you just one thing. Stay the hell away from dead bodies. And I've a good mind to lock you up until this case is dosed.'

'Can you lock up all your suspects, Hamre?' I said.

'I can lock you up. And that would do me.' He suddenly looked tired. 'Listen, Veum. It isn't personal. You're a nice guy. I'd have a beer with you if things were different and if it wouldn't put me on the shit-list down at the station. Just do me a favour, will you? Don't go finding any more bodies. OK?'

'Well.' I shrugged. 'I'll try not to.'

'Do that little thing,' he said. Then he walked quickly up to the hut. I followed him. Slowly.

I waited outside with a young constable whose face looked as if somebody'd walked on it. It was a flat square face like a postage stamp. His mouth was tense, the muscles rippled along his jaw. We had nothing to say to one another.

I tried to think about something else. Something pleasant. What was Solveig Manger doing? Was she relaxing, a book in her lap, legs propped up, staring into space? Was her husband sitting in another chair, a biography of Hemingway in his hand? Was there perhaps a TV on the opposite wall? Were they watching a new and different life unfold by the light of the screen?

They'd never be alone again. There'd always be another person in the room with them. And that person would always be dead.

No, it wasn't pleasant.

Hamre came out of the hut and glared at me. Or through me. 'They're never very pretty,' he said.

Nobody said anything.

The other cops followed him. We stood there. Silent and helpless. It's always like this. Nobody knows what to say. And nobody wants to start doing what's got to be done.

Hamre looked at me. 'You didn't touch anything?' he said flatly. 'It's just the way you found him?'

I nodded. 'Yes. I didn't see – a weapon.'

'Right. And you didn't see anybody on your way here?'

'Not a living soul.'

'Don't be funny, Veum.'

'I wasn't …'

'Yeah, yeah, yeah.' He brushed me off. 'What were you doing here anyway?'

'I wanted to talk to …' I nodded at the hut.

'What about?'

I walked up to him. 'See my face? It's never been pretty, but maybe something's happened to it since you and I last saw each other.'

'You can't miss it. I mean your face.'

'There was no way Joker and his gang could miss it.'

Pause. Two cars stopped on the road and a new search party began combing the woods.

The four cops looked at me. 'So in other words, you two had unfinished business?' Hamre said.

'Yes, but I …'

He interrupted. 'We're not that stupid, Veum,' he said. 'We know you didn't kill him. And we don't think you're that stupid either.'

One of the cops piped up. 'You're famous for never killing anybody, Veum. You just beat their brains out.'

I took a look at him. I'd never seen this one before. I must have made an impression. His face was covered with mustard-coloured freckles, and the hair sticking out from under his cap reminded me of withered grass.

'Didn't catch your name,' I said.

'Isaksen,' he said. 'Peder Isaksen.' His was a voice you'd like to forget. Like the last sentence in a bad novel.

'OK. Calm down, you two. That's enough,' Hamre said. Then he walked over to the newcomers.

I looked at Peder Isaksen. He looked at me. Hard. Just another fan of mine. Welcome to the club. No way I'd ever feel lonely.

'Do you need me?' I said to Hamre's back.

He swung around, his mouth open, and he jammed a finger in my face. 'Don't move, Veum. Don't move so much as a metre. And let's not hear one word out of you.' Then he turned away.

He didn't hear one word out of me. I leaned up against a tree, sucked on a cough drop and tried to look as if I were bored out of my mind.

48

An hour passed. More police came. The activity around the hut was strictly routine. People arrived, ducked through the doorway and looked inside the hut. Then they straightened up, their faces stony. Some of them disappeared inside and came back out after a while. I began imagining what they were doing in there. When I'm bored I have a dirty imagination.

Nobody talked to me. I could have been part of the tree I was leaning against. Once Hamre came out of the hut, looked worriedly past me at all the buildings and said to a colleague, 'That's a hell of a lot of people to check up on.'

As I stood there I tried to imagine what had happened.

Joker could have arranged to meet somebody here at the hut. They'd gone inside, probably to talk. There'd been an argument and one of them had pulled a knife. Either one of them. They'd fought for the knife and Joker had lost.

It was so easy to say. But it was only a theory and it didn't tell me who the other person was. And it didn't tell me if this death had anything to do with Jonas Andresen's.

There was one person I needed to question and I wanted to get to him before Jakob E. Hamre did. But Jakob E. Hamre had told me not to move by so much as a metre. He'd also told me not to talk, so maybe he wouldn't notice my disappearing. Not immediately, anyway. I knew he would sooner or later, and my only defence would be to hand him a murderer.

I stood and watched. It wouldn't be long now before Hantre

turned things over to the technicians and began the investigation itself: the endless, routine rounds of questioning.

The police had already trampled the mud around the hut into a map of chaos. Some of them stood around in small groups and talked, and none of them paid any attention to me.

I stepped a little way away from the tree. Went back to it. Stood by it. There were some junipers growing behind it and if I could just slip between them I'd quickly be invisible in the darkness. I leaned my shoulders against the tree and gradually started easing around it. Hamre came out of the hut. He stood in the doorway. I could see him glance quickly in my direction but I acted as if I hadn't noticed. He motioned to a technician, said something to him, and the two of them disappeared inside the hut.

I disappeared behind the tree. Flitted sideways between the junipers, quickly sneaked ten or fifteen metres down that sparsely covered slope and then moved faster. I held my breath, waiting for somebody to yell. Nobody yelled. I went even faster. Branches hit my face and twigs snapped underfoot but still nobody yelled.

Once on the road I slowed down so I'd look like an ordinary citizen. But as tense and stiff as I was, I knew I hardly looked like somebody out for an evening stroll.

I walked quickly to the high-rise. Got in the lift. Pressed the button for the twelfth floor.

The lift began to move. Like a majestic seagull it slowly soared past the floors: first, second, third. I thought of Wenche Andresen. She'd taken lifts like this one. Fourth, fifth, sixth. Jonas Andresen had taken lifts like this one before all lift doors had closed for him. Seventh, eighth, ninth. I began to think of Solveig Manger and wondered if she'd ever taken a lift like this one. But I never finished the thought.

The lift stopped between the ninth and tenth floors. And the lights went out.

The most frightening thing wasn't that the lift had stopped or that it was as black as pitch in there. What really scared me was that after about a minute the lift rose again. Not evenly and slowly as it had, but jerkily. Somebody was up in the motor room. Somebody was using the emergency hand-crank to run the lift. But it wasn't because of a power failure. Somebody was slowly but surely hauling me upward. Somebody who had already killed.

49

When you're stuck in a lift and the light goes out, it's dark. There's no sky with its pale stars, no moon somewhere below the horizon to cast its shadow of light against the vault of heaven. No distant electric lights, no windows you can run to, no bonfires down in the valley. There's nothing. You're in the middle of blackness, and if you stretch out a hand you discover that the blackness is hard, metallic, and close, close around you.

If you're stuck in a lift with the light on, you have some sense of security. The light shields you in the hollow of its hand. But when you're stuck in a lift and it's dark, there is no security. Then it's as if the lift's shrinking around you, as if it's only a question of time before you're crushed between the heavy steel walls.

What I felt when the lift stopped was pure, naked anxiety. The kind which grabs and shakes your body, the kind with no limits or meaning, no source. No beginning. It takes over your stomach, your guts, it squeezes your heart, your throat. My mouth went dry in seconds and I had trouble breathing. My ears roared. I had to lean against the wall and if I could have seen anything, I would have felt it was spinning. But the darkness was so intense that there wasn't room to feel faint in. Because if you're going to feel faint you've got to have at least one reference point, no matter how unstable it is.

When the lift started moving, the anxiety changed. Became

focused. There's nothing like a nameless infinite fear, but once you know what to be afraid of, then you can brace yourself. Fight back. No matter how bad it is.

And I knew what to be afraid of. I knew somebody was cranking the lift up to him. I knew I had to try to get out of the lift before he cranked it all the way up. Otherwise he'd be standing there waiting for me and he wasn't about to hand me a medal for good conduct.

Suddenly there was a break in the darkness. It was light from the oblong window in the door to the tenth floor going by. It happened so quickly that I couldn't react until it was too late. The lift continued to jerk upward. My only chance was to be ready for the next door. The only time I'd be able to escape was when the lift was exactly level with the door. A few centimetres below, a few centimetres above, and the door wouldn't open.

I walked to the wall where the door should appear and rested my hands against it. Felt the wall sliding downward. Waited for the separation between the wall and door.

There!

The door's lower edge eased down from the ceiling, but the other one must have known what I was up to and he cranked faster when the lift reached the crucial point. The window came into view and I fumbled despairingly for the door handle. Found it, grabbed it and when the lift was level with the door, threw myself to the left and tried to yank the door open.

It moved a little before it slipped back into place. That was that. The lift rose tirelessly. Then I realised that there were twelve floors but that the lift probably went as far as the motor room. That gave me a new chance. The twelfth.

I got set again, but this time I held one hand against the wall and the other ready to grab the door handle.

There!

A new door rolled down the wall. I tensed my muscles, planted the soles of my feet on the floor and against the wall, and stared blindly towards where I knew that oblong of light would appear. It slowly moved downward. And then the lift stopped. Ten centimetres below the door. He'd caught me off-guard. I tried to look through the window but it was too high. Then I was nearly thrown off my feet. The lift shook violently. Then it glided by the door and continued upward. He'd outsmarted me.

I knew there was only one way out of this. Like it or not, I had to meet him.

Now that the lift had passed the door, it stopped. And I stood there in the darkness on the threshold of a cement coffin crammed with machinery. I didn't have to wonder why the lift had stopped. He was catching his breath. It hadn't been easy cranking it up by himself.

But it won't be long now, murderer. Don't give up. Whet your knife, murderer. A new victim's on his way.

As I stood there, I searched for something I could use as a weapon. The only thing I had was the little flashlight. Not very effective, but good to have. Maybe I could manage to blind him with it.

I was sure it was a him. A man. No woman could have cranked the lift up so skilfully. A woman would have invited me in for a cup of coffee or a quiet drink. And it would have been a quiet drink. The last one. A woman would have poisoned it. A woman would have put her arms around me and slit my throat with a stiletto. Or she would have tried appealing to my sympathy and understanding. She wouldn't have invited me to a deadly tango in the darkness on the threshold of a lift. No. It was a man.

And I was pretty sure who the man waiting for me was.

That gave me two trump cards to play. But they were the only ones. The other cards – whether I'd survive, whether I'd be able to ask my questions or whether I could do anything at all in the next hour – were not. And there wasn't a Joker in the pack now. It was between me and him.

The lift moved again.

'Roll out the red carpet,' I said softly. 'Here comes the clown.'

Nobody answered, and the darkness was as total as ever. My eyes still hadn't adjusted. I had only an inkling of the lift's four corners.

The lift jerked several times, as if he were standing there kicking the crank. What would he meet me with?

If he had a gun, I hadn't a chance. He could pepper the whole lift with a sawn-off shotgun in seconds and I'd end up as a couple of kilos of hamburger. And that's how I'd look. Exit Varg Veum: of earth thou art come, to hamburger thou shalt return …

With a little jump the lift stopped in front of the thirteenth door. The thirteenth door on the thirteenth floor. Sounded terminal.

The oblong window was black. I couldn't see anything. I listened to my tense ragged breathing. Not many choices. I could open the door and try to rush into the darkness and to one side before anything happened. The most dangerous moment would be when I opened the door and stood there in plain view with only one free hand. Or I could wait for him. But then I'd be boxed in.

I waited. The endless seconds became one minute. Two minutes … I didn't have the nerve to wait any longer. I gripped the door handle with my left hand. And shoved. Followed the door to the left so that it was a sort of shield. And when I'd opened it all the way, I lowered my head and hurled myself out into the darkness.

50

The darkness consisted of a powerful smell of oil, hard edges and the other one. The smell hit me and I fell over something which must have been the hand-crank. Something hard and painful which caught me just above the knee.

A part of the darkness swung down at me. It felt like a crowbar and it hit my right shoulder with murderous violence. A little higher and it would have split my skull in two.

The other one groaned bitterly when he heard me scuttle away until I bounced off a wall and had to stop. I wanted to howl with pain but clenched my teeth. My shoulder felt as if it had been bitten in two. The arm was numb. I strained and stared at the darkness. Nothing.

I heard the sound of puffing and fast, almost tap-dancing steps. Then something knocked the plaster off the wall just beside my head. The concrete underneath rang like a bell.

He'd bombed twice. But I couldn't bet on his keeping it up. And I didn't want to end up in two, like a sliced grapefruit. I kicked out blindly. Got him but not well enough. I aimed a futile blow with my good left arm, but he'd already tumbled out of range.

I tried moving to the side but the plaster crackled under my feet. I stood still.

We were as quiet as mice in the darkness as we tried to make out one another's contours. My eyes began to water. They hurt. My right hand was coming to life. It was a painful birth. But as the feeling came back, I also discovered I was still holding the flashlight.

I found the switch, held the light in front of me. I wouldn't light it until I was sure where he was. I listened intently. I thought I could hear him breathing on the other side of the room. But I didn't know what lay between us. He was probably familiar with the set-up. He'd been here before. He knew where the lift motor was and that its crank would booby-trap me in the darkness.

I should have had a weapon. The only things I had were a flashlight and myself. And one arm wasn't in good shape even though it was working again. My shoulder hurt, and I began to think my collarbone was broken.

Now I heard him!

I clearly heard him shift his weight and knew he was tensing for a new attack. Then things began to happen. I aimed the flashlight at the sound and he came for me.

The beam hit his face. It was pale, distorted. Ghostly. He rushed at me, twirling the crowbar like a baton. I ducked and butted him in the stomach. My forehead hit his belt buckle and it tore off a strip of skin.

He doubled over but held on to the crowbar. Bashed my shin. I yelled with pain. I went berserk. Or panicked. But I managed to get a hold of his leg, stand up and heave him backwards against the wall. I heard him hit it sideways, lose his grip on the crowbar, fall to the floor and claw the wall like a terrified rat.

Then it was quiet. Almost. I could hear him panting and I could hear my suppressed groans. I felt sick. But he'd lost his crowbar, and maybe I was in better shape than he was. I had to find him. But I'd lost the flashlight. I felt my way to the wall and crept in his direction. Stepped on one of his legs. He twisted aside and kicked. Got me in the knee. I was about to fall and I lost my balance just as he got to his feet. Something hard and knobby hit my face. He'd landed a good one. I thought about falling stars, soaring fireworks, rockets and satellites and pigeons suddenly taking off.

I lay down and slept. I must have passed out for a couple of seconds, and I dreamed he was searching the darkness for his crowbar. I remember thinking: Wake up, mister! You've got to wake up.

And I did. Just in time. Rolled instinctively to one side. He cursed furiously when he smashed the concrete where I'd been lying. And then he stood over me. The crowbar hit my chest and I curled up to protect myself.

He hit me again. Hit my arm. My back. Came too close to my head. I stretched out to my full length and rolled further into the darkness. Hit something hard and metallic. It could have been machinery. Or a door. I could hear him panting and swinging the crowbar. I frantically felt for a handle. If that was a door.

It was. I found the handle, yanked the door open and tumbled out. Expecting to fall head first down a steep concrete stairway. No stairway. A big black opening. Stars. A veil of fresh wet mist smelling of dew. I'd fallen through a doorway on to the flat slippery tar-paper roof. I took two steps forward, but my legs gave way and I fell flat. I could see Gunnar Våge coming towards me. Still holding the crowbar. His skull gleamed, his curly fringe was tousled, his face was like a clenched fist which would never relax again. He didn't remind me of the idealistic youth leader I'd met before. The only thing he reminded me of was death. The worst death of all. My own.

Everything stopped for a few seconds. I looked around. The roof was flat except for the lift shed and some ventilators. A fifty-centimetre-high concrete wall edged the entire roof. It was high enough so you couldn't roll over the edge and down to the ground below. But it wasn't so high that you couldn't stumble over it or be shoved.

Gunnar Våge was showing the effects of the fight. He walked stiffly towards me and he gripped the crowbar as if it were the only thing he owned in the world. It was. And right now it was also the most important thing in the world. That crowbar could be the extra point that decided between him and me, between the first and second division, between life and death.

I struggled to my knees and managed to stand up. Shook my head. 'I don't get it,' I groaned. 'I don't get it. What are you trying to do? What's the idea?'

'No idea. Action.' He sneered at me. 'You touch zero, the point where everything's dead. Where nothing around you moves. Then there's only one thing left to do – and that's act.'

'And the idealist becomes a fascist – just like that?' I was lisping.

He didn't answer. Almost like a karate fighter, he took two steps forward, planted his feet, gripped the crowbar with both hands and swung.

I could still move, but that deadly crowbar hit my right shoulder once more. And it felt as if my shoulder had been torn off again, as if my whole body would split in two. It felt like a stroke. I had just one chance of surviving. Use my dirtiest tricks.

I ducked and kicked at his belly. Blindly struck at the hand which held the crowbar. I hit the side of his wrist. His arm swung up, his hand opened in pain, and the crowbar arced up into the air, bounced against the wall and silently disappeared into the darkness. If anybody was walking his dog down there he could come home with a skewered sausage. Or a flag-pole in his head.

He punched me in the ear. I heard a brass band playing a march backwards. And then we clinched. In the drifting mist with the stars and the Lyderhorn the only spectators, we danced a strange duet. Like two old pugs, the oldest boxers in the retirement home's back yard. We pounded one another's backs with exhausted fists, tried for half-nelsons, tried to gouge out one another's eyes with blunt fingers. One two cha cha cha. One two cha cha cha.

We broke away from one another like two disappointed lovers. We swung at the empty air and staggered backward. I fell down. He staggered toward me. I lay there. He kicked dully at me.

His eyes were glassy and empty, carved from dirty marble and painted with enamel. There was something feverish about him. Manic. Obsessed. The corner of his mouth was bleeding, he had a bad abrasion on his forehead, one arm hung limp at his side. He was breathing heavily, and he looked more and more like a ghost. But I knew I didn't look much better myself. And I was down while he still could stand up. Two old sparring partners on Christmas Eve. Just before the knock-out!

'But why, Våge, why?' I gasped.

'Why what?'

'Why did you kill them?'

He flamed with rage. 'That little worm? He tried to black-mail me!'

Then his voice sank almost to a whisper. 'He asked me to meet him up there. Said he knew about Wenche and me. Had seen me – visit her. Said he knew why I'd killed – her husband. He – that little jerk he threatened me. I told him, OK. I'll meet you up there. But I'm coming alone, and I don't have any money with me. He wanted money, you know.' He stared at me almost pleadingly.

The mist was about to turn to rain.

'So I met him. He wanted money but I didn't have any. And I wasn't about to pay him one red penny. He – he pulled a knife on me. Threatened me. I'm the one – I was the one who helped him, defended him. Protected him. I really wanted to help him, Veum. And he pulled a knife on me.

We fought for it. He – lost. I mean – that wasn't the idea, but it turned heavy. Happened so fast. Suddenly he was lying there. Dead. Then I knew what had happened.' He lifted his face to the rain. 'It was self-defence.'

I spat out the words as if they were cracked apple seeds. 'Self-defence? So it was self-defence when you also killed Jonas Andresen?'

'Jonas Andresen?' He stared at me.

'Jonas Andresen! Man, don't you read the papers? Don't you know the names of the people you kill?'

'Haven't you caught on yet? I loved her! I've loved her for eleven years, Veum. After those two months in 1967 there wasn't anybody else. Do you think I'd want anything bad to happen to her? You think I could – I could hurt her? You don't know anything about love, Veum. Not if you think that. What you call love are graffiti on a wall, pictures in a book. What I wanted was to run my hand through her hair. Kiss her. Make love to her. I could never kill anybody she loved. And she was crazy about him. That's what was so hopeless. She was as crazy about him as I was about her.'

'So you figured if you – got rid of him, then …'

He walked over and planted his foot in my face. I took it like the obliging soul I am. The back of my head slammed against the roof and my face felt like newly laid asphalt when careless boys suddenly step in it. I bit my tongue and tasted a mouthful of warm thick blood.

'Hell no!' he snarled. 'I didn't kill him.' He raised his head and howled like a wolf at an invisible moon. 'All of you hear this? I did not kill Jonas Andresen!'

He bent down and grabbed my jacket. Hauled me up with his last bit of strength and smashed me in the face. I hung in his fists. He fell forward and dragged me down with him. We lay about a metre from the wall.

He got to his knees and began dragging me towards the edge. 'But by all the gods,' I heard him mumble, 'I'm going to kill Varg Veum if it's the last thing I do.'

I tried kidding. 'That it will be,' I said.

Clenched my teeth and stood up. Now I was the one standing and he was on his knees. He looked up at me with eyes which were both pleading and full of hatred. 'Eleven years, Veum,' he whined. 'Eleven years of nothing. No love, no happiness. Just hate and suspicion. And terrible terrible boredom. And then a dream. I tracked her here. Took this job to be near her. Just to be where she was. Let life sail by on the horizon like an America-bound ship. But I had to be the rowing boat slowly reaching the coast where she lived. Do you understand?'

'I don't understand a thing,' I said.

It was raining harder. We were soaked. The rain washed the blood off us. We were a couple of dishevelled exhausted kids at the end of a dangerous game on the brink of a long drop.

He lunged, got a grip on my neck and forced me toward

the edge. I gave ground, felt the depths behind me, the pull of the vacuum. So I rabbit-punched him as hard as I could. He sagged against me and I fell backwards.

The edge of the wall dug into my spine. For a couple of seconds I swayed over and back ... Then I scrambled panic-stricken back on to the roof.

He stood up. Rose up like the phoenix from the ashes. I knocked him down. He was glassy-eyed.

He got up. Stood there shaking his head. But he'd been about to throw me overboard. So I knocked him down again.

And then I called it quits.

Fresh blood trickled from his mouth as I dragged him towards the doorway and the security of the lift shed. He was babbling as I towed him. 'I didn't kill Jonas Andresen, Veum ... I didn't kill him ...' Tears ran from his eyes and mixed with the blood and rain.

When I hauled him over the threshold he howled as if we were crossing the threshold to Hades: 'You'll burn in hell for this, Veum! You'll burn!'

'Tell it to the police,' I heard myself say. 'They're hell's doormen.'

51

Jakob E. Hamre was pretty quiet in the car on the way back to Bergen. He turned once and looked at me. 'Do you know what we'd have done to you if you hadn't had Våge with you?' he said abruptly.

I didn't ask. And he didn't tell me. He was saving it.

When we got to the station Hamre spoke to one of the other officers. 'Get hold of Paulus Smith. Ask him to come as soon as possible.' Then he spoke to me. 'You wait here until Smith arrives. We're going to visit your friend. You'd best come too. Otherwise you won't sleep tonight. Right?'

Without waiting for an answer, he disappeared into the lift. I stood in the hall. Not having a Christmas tree, they'd planted a uniformed constable in one corner. He stood and stared fixedly into space and waited for somebody to start arranging presents around his feet. He had about nine months' wait.

Outside, people with blank faces drove around in cars with the headlights on or sat in rows in oblong yellow buses and stared through the shining windowpanes the way strangers' faces look at you out of photograph albums.

Paulus Smith arrived by cab twenty minutes later. He came towards me, a pleased expression on his face, took my hand in both of his and said, 'A brilliant job, Veum. I hear you've found us a murderer.'

'He found me,' I said. 'And I'm afraid he also found himself another victim first.'

'What?' he said. Shaken.

I told him what had happened while we waited for Jakob E. Hamre to reappear. The more I talked, the more disturbed Smith looked. I'd just about finished my story when the lift door opened and Hamre stepped out.

'Good evening, Smith,' he said formally. 'She's in the visiting room. They're waiting for us.'

We walked silently to the cellar, down that stairway which separates the sheep from the goats. There were five of us in that bare little room. Two women and three men.

Wenche Andresen sat alone on the long side of the table, Paulus Smith and Jakob E. Hamre on the short. I sat at the corner between them. The constable perched on a chair by the door. A tape recorder waited in front of Hamre.

Wenche Andresen seemed even tenser now than she had ever been; her face was more drawn, the feverish shine in her eyes seemed even brighter. She folded her hands on the table. You could see the muscles twitching and how she tried to relax them. She finally twined them together as if they were two exhausted wrestlers.

Paulus Smith looked as if he'd been interrupted in the middle of a cocktail party. His skin glowed under its tan and there was a twinkle in his eyes as if he hadn't recovered from the last good story he'd heard. His chalk-white hair gave him a look of purity, nobility and infallibility. Perfect for a lawyer.

Jakob E. Hamre reminded me of a cabinet minister, of a man holding all the cards and ready to take part in a TV debate which would spellbind thousands of people across the country. Self-confident. Safe.

The constable looked like a rejected chapter in a bad novel. Her hair was bound tight at her neck and she had a face that shouldn't have been so bare. She looked straight ahead of her through the whole seance and didn't blink once.

I didn't look especially good myself. When I'd shaken hands with Wenche Andresen she'd said, 'Every time I see you, somebody's done something to your face, Varg.' And she had looked at me searchingly, as if to reassure herself that it really was me underneath it all.

After everyone had sat down, there was a tense silence around the table. It was expectant, strained. As if we all waited for someone to break the silence with a scream or stand up suddenly and turn cartwheels or do something equally unexpected and crazy. But nobody did anything but wait for Jakob E. Hamre to start things off.

Little by little we all looked at him. Paulus Smith with pleased anticipation, Wenche Andresen with tension and anxiety, I with a feeling of dull misery.

Then Jakob E. Hamre stretched out his slim, long-fingered hand and started the tape recorder. In a low monotone he recorded the place, the date, the time, and who was present. Then he paused. Looked directly at Wenche Andresen. 'We have just arrested Gunnar Våge,' he said.

We all watched her. We saw that short sentence sink in, and reflect in her eyes. Which became enormous. Her mouth became a circle. Then there was a long drawn-out gasp. She anxiously searched our faces, one after the other, as if she were looking for some kind of explanation, comfort. One or the other. But we were three men and we didn't respond. We merely watched the tears silently begin as she took in what Hamre had told her.

'Gunnar?' she said.

There was a pause.

'Did he …'

'He killed Johan Pedersen,' Hamre said.

She looked at him. Baffled. 'Who?'

'Joker,' I said. 'This evening.'

She shook her head. 'He killed Joker – this evening? But – but Jonas? Why should he …? I can't see that –'

Hamre interrupted. 'How well did you know Gunnar Våge, Fru Andresen?' His voice was firm but pleasant. He was as polite as usual, but you could see a trace of impatience, a little restlessness under that smooth surface.

'I –' she began. Then she bit her lip and blushed. She looked as guilty as we all do when we blush.

I stared at her, but she wouldn't look at me.

'I've known him a long time,' she said reluctantly.

'For how long?'

'We were together – I think it must have been in – in 1967. Just for a month or so before I met Jonas …' Her mouth pronounced his name as if she wanted to hang on to it, keep it for ever.

'And later on?' Hamre said.

'Later on?' She wet her lips with the tip of her tongue. 'We – I met him again, out there. I met him in the street one day. Around noon. He spoke to me. Don't you recognise me, Wenche? he said. And I had to take a good look at him. He was bald, but I recognised him. Obviously.' She stopped and stared at her intertwined fingers.

'And then?' Hamre said.

She looked up at him. They might as well have been alone in the room. Paulus Smith, the constable and I had become part of a stage set. We were the audience at the drama she and Hamre starred in. Their glances met, clashed, sprang apart.

'You resumed the relationship?' Hamre said.

'We *resumed* the relationship,' she said. Sarcastically. 'You make it sound like a business deal or something. Yes. We *resumed* the relationship, but not right away. It took a while. He said … he said he'd been looking for me, that he'd moved out there, got a job just so he could be near me. Maybe meet me again. It – it made an impression on me.'

'I can see how it would.'

'Oh you can, can you? For a long time, I'd been aware it was over between Jonas and me. And I needed tenderness. Love. I loved Jonas. I still do. I'll love him until I die, even though he's already dead. The thing between Gunnar and me – that was different. I mean, it was pretty much one-sided. Like the relationship between Jonas and me. But this time the one-sidedness wasn't on my side, I mean.'

'So you started a relationship with him?'

She nodded silently. Swallowed. Her eyes flickered.

My head was throbbing. A real headache was on the way. Paulus Smith looked bleakly at her. She looked at Hamre.

'When did it happen?' Hamre said. 'Was it before or after you and Jonas Andresen separated?'

She sobbed painfully. 'Before! But it didn't mean anything. It wasn't adultery. It wasn't that way. It was finished between Jonas and me. I felt it. With every fibre of my being. As if all the love inside me had turned to ice. It was locked up in the darkest places inside me. Do you know what I mean? It wasn't long before Jonas – left. But it happened before he did!'

'Is it possible that's why your husband left you?'

'Who? Jonas? Never! He had his – her. Solveig what's-her-name. I don't think he ever had a clue about Gunnar and me. He would have shown it. And anyway, he would have said something about it when he left. No. Nobody knew but Gunnar and me. We were as careful as we could be. It wasn't very often.

'We only got together when we were absolutely sure. Either at his place – mostly there – or at mine. But it was safer at his place. We were happiest there.'

'Were you happy together?'

That baffled look again. 'Happy? As happy as two disappointed people can be. It was good to be able to show real tenderness again – to be shown it. Have it. Good to be able to share something with somebody else, even if it was a secret, something dirty. Something – ordinary.

'You've got to understand. I come from a very strict background where things like this are involved. Adultery's a deadly sin. Unforgivable. No matter what the circumstances. Jonas's adultery didn't make mine any better. Didn't excuse it. Do you understand?'

'Did you two ever talk about … ?' He stopped. Rephrased the question. 'Fru Andresen, can you tell me why Gunnar Våge would murder your husband? Was he jealous?'

She shook her head. Puzzled. 'We were almost divorced already. There wasn't any reason why he'd be jealous. It was already over between Jonas and me.'

'No feelings involved then? Not on your side?'

She didn't answer. We watched her search for the words. She opened her mouth several times but no sound came out.

'You realise that the evidence still points to your having killed your husband? In spite of what happened tonight,' Hamre said.

Paulus Smith broke in. 'Listen, Hamre. Slow down, man. You can't mean that …' He looked at me for help. When I didn't say anything, he continued. 'Gunnar Våge killed that boy this evening. And as far as I understand, he's already confessed it.'

'Not officially,' Hamre said.

'No, but nevertheless,' Smith said. 'The motive's dear enough. The boy had something on him. He knew Våge murdered Jonas Andresen. He was with Veum when it happened, and he could have seen something Veum didn't ...'

'Could that be possible?' Hamre said sourly.

'It's ninety-nine per cent certain he saw Gunnar Våge stab Jonas Andresen and then run down the stairway opposite to the one Veum ran up. When Våge realised today how much the boy really knew, there was only one thing he could do. If he wanted to cover his tracks. It's as simple as that, Hamre. As simple as that.'

I leaned across the table and looked at Wenche Andresen. 'You lied to me about Gunnar Våge, Wenche,' I said.

The others were quiet. Wenche Andresen slowly turned and looked at me with those same big dark blue eyes I'd first gazed into less than two weeks ago. I looked at that mouth I'd kissed and had hoped to kiss again. Remembered how softly, how sweetly she'd offered it to me when I kissed her that first and only time.

'You lied to me,' I said. 'Everything else was the truth. I've been able to check out the rest of it, more or less. You told me the truth about Richard Ljosne. He had to admit he lied when I confronted him with what you'd said. But when I asked you about Gunnar Våge, you lied. Why, Wenche? Why?'

She turned from me to Hamre as if his duty were to defend her from me. 'I can't understand why Gunnar would – why he'd kill Jonas,' she said.

'No,' I said. 'You can't understand why. We can't understand why either. But maybe it's not so strange. Because Gunnar Våge didn't kill Jonas. You did.'

She spun around and looked at me, her face scarlet.

'Listen, Veum,' Paulus Smith said. 'Listen, this is …'

Jakob E. Hamre leaned across the table and looked intently at her.

'You did it,' I said. 'And it's been you all along. We just haven't seen it. I just haven't seen it. But I get it now. And that's why you lied.'

'Why?' she said.

'You lied so nobody'd know you'd had anything to do with Gunnar Våge. Let alone that you'd been at his place. Let alone that you could have gone through his things and found the knife you killed Jonas with.'

'He gave it to me. Gunnar gave me …'

'And why was that? Did you two plan …?'

'You don't get it, Varg. I don't think you understand anything. Yes, I got the knife from Gunnar, but it wasn't because I planned – we planned to … It was so I could defend myself if – if Joker and his gang didn't leave me alone. In case they kept on bothering us … I kept it in the top drawer of the chest in the foyer … in case they tried to break in or something …'

'But nobody tried to break in. Jonas showed up. And you killed him.'

'It was crazy,' she said. 'Crazy. It never should have happened, but …'

Hamre's low-key calm voice interrupted. 'Tell us about it, Fru Andresen. Calmly now. Tell us what happened.'

She looked at him almost gratefully. I realised I was tied in knots. And I felt infinitely lonely. As lonely as you could get. I looked at those intertwined fingers of hers again. That was how lovers hold hands when they moon over one another. But she wasn't mooning over anybody, and the only person she twined fingers with was herself. Maybe she only loved herself, when you got right down to it.

'I came back from the cellar,' she said, 'and he'd already let himself in. Suddenly it got to me. You don't live here any more, Jonas, I said, you've no right to let yourself in now. He looked embarrassed. And then he began to apologise. Said he'd been so broke he'd been late with the payments. And on and on.

'I don't know what happened. But suddenly I saw red. It was as if all the hurt and hopelessness suddenly flooded over me. And things went black. And I thought how he'd wrecked the whole thing. With his adultery. He made me cheat. He made me commit a deadly sin.

'I threw the jar of jam at him and it hit him on the forehead. He's always had a quick temper, and he slapped me. Right in the face, so I fell against the chest of drawers and banged my hip. It really hurt.

'I opened the drawer and found the knife and I – I hit back. I stabbed him. It – it just seemed to sink into him, and I … He leaned forward. I don't know if he even saw the knife. He looked so confused.

'What have you done, Wenche? he said. But I couldn't stand the way he looked at me, so I pulled the knife out and stabbed him again and again. And again. He started towards me, and then – he fell.'

She stared darkly into space. 'He lay there. I walked by him. Went to the door. Went outside. I remember screaming for help. I don't know what happened after that. I think I fainted. I remember how frozen I was when you – Varg was first, and then …' Her voice trailed into silence.

We knew the rest.

'It happens so fast,' she said. 'Ending a life. One, two, three: just like that. Gunnar's and mine too.'

'And Roar's,' I said.

'And Roar's,' she said tiredly. As if he were a distant relative she'd once known long, long ago.

We sat there. After a while, Hamre turned off the tape recorder. It was dead quiet in the room.

Then Smith stood up. Heavily. 'You did a great job for the defence, Veum,' he said. Leaden sarcasm.

Hamre and I stood up at the same time. We looked down at Wenche Andresen. 'Can I have a few minutes alone with her?' I said. Hamre looked at me. Deadpan. 'You can't do any more damage than you already have.' Then he nodded and left the room with Smith. The constable still sat by the door but I didn't count her. She was part of the scenery.

I went to Wenche Andresen, leaned over the table, bracing myself on my fists. She looked up at me with the same eyes, the same mouth. But I'd never kiss her. I knew that now. I'd never kiss her again.

'I'm sorry, Wenche,' I said. 'But I had to say it. I had to. I believed you the whole time. I was sure you were innocent, that you didn't do it. But when I finally realised you lied to me, I had to say it. I hope you understand.'

She nodded silently.

'I really liked meeting you. You and Roar. Those evenings – I … It's been a long time since I've felt so good. If things had been different, who knows? Maybe we could have – found each other. Maybe we could have meant something to one another.'

She looked at me.

'But it's too late now, Wenche. Much too late.'

'I'm sorry, Varg,' she said. 'I didn't mean it to be this way.'

I studied her face for what I hoped was the last time: eyes, lips, the drawn skin, the anguished expression …

And I thought about Roar. About the father she'd already deprived him of. And about the mother she was about to deprive him of. What would happen to him? To her? To me? I wondered where we'd all be in five years. In ten. There were too many questions and only one life to answer them in. Just one life – and it's over so quickly. You go around with it in your hand one minute. Somebody's taken it away from you the next, and you're lying on the pavement.

I straightened up. Heard myself saying, 'I make a date with you. Put it down: at six o'clock in the evening, a thousand years from now …'

'What are you talking about?'

I shrugged. 'Just something I once read.

Then I turned and quickly left the room. Didn't look back. Hamre was waiting. 'Smith's already left. I don't think he could have stood the sight of you again this evening,' he said. 'I can understand how he feels.'

I looked at him and this time there was no escaping his irritation. 'What do you really think you've accomplished in all this?' he said.

'There are accomplishments and accomplishments,' I said.

'The same murderer is still in custody. Nothing new there. It's still the same solution I gave you last Friday. The only new development is that between then and now, a guy's killed a kid.'

'Maybe it is exactly the same solution,' I said helplessly. 'But there are always a lot of sides to the truth. I've talked to a lot of people since Friday so maybe the reality isn't exactly what it used to be. Not when you get right down to it.'

'Sometimes I think the only thing you're good at is playing with words, Veum.' Hamre sounded tired. 'It's the only thing you don't always screw up anyway. I happen to care about the facts. And they tell me an ordinary guy's turned into a murderer and a live kid's turned into a dead body since all this started last Friday. The guy could have gone on living his not very successful or exciting life, and I'll admit the kid's future didn't look very bright. But each of them had a life ahead of him, Veum. There were two chances there that something might have come along some day. You've deprived them of those two chances once and for all. Do you get the point? Do you know what I'm saying?'

I knew what he was saying.

Silently, we walked up the stairs and I went home.

52

I was at the police station the next day. I was questioned once more about what had happened the previous evening. Then I signed the statement and left without anybody cheering or throwing confetti.

I took my time walking down to the office. Then up the stairs. Through the door with its pane of pebbled glass. Over to the desk. I wrote my initials in the film of dust so everybody'd know it was my office even though I wasn't always there.

I sat down. My head was empty and my heart was like stone. I could see Håkonshallen across the rooftops. Beyond it were the outlines of a mothballed oil-drilling platform out in Skuteviken. Each of them was a cenotaph marking an era with a span of about seven hundred years. I felt seven hundred years old myself now and then.

I looked in my notebook for a number I'd written down several days ago. When I found it I looked at it as if it were some kind of magic formula. Or a key to the future.

I dialled the number. Got through to the switchboard. 'Is Solveig Manger there?' I said.